PRAISE FOR BROOKE LEA FOSTER'S NOVELS

Our Last Vineyard Summer

"A quiet powerhouse of a novel—deeply atmospheric, emotionally resonant and steeped in the history and heartbreak of generational womanhood."

—*Woman's World*

"A perfect blend of secrets, misdeeds, and unexpected love . . . a gripping, timely story that will captivate readers from start to finish."

—Amy Poeppel, author of *The Sweet Spot*

"[This] has all my favorite book ingredients—intriguing mother-daughter dynamics, a vivid Martha's Vineyard setting, a gripping dual timeline and, best of all, a family secret bombshell that I never saw coming."

—Martha Hall Kelly, *New York Times* bestselling author of *Lilac Girls*

"Evocative and rich . . . captures the enduring and complicated love between mothers and daughters."

—Jo Piazza, internationally bestselling author of *The Sicilian Inheritance*

"An engrossing and poignant look at family in all its complicated depth. It had me gripped from the first page."

—Annabel Monaghan, *USA Today* bestselling author of *Nora Goes Off Script*

"A radiant, sun-flushed summer novel packed with beaches, secrets, and sisters. Foster has imbued this brilliant, feminist beach read with skill and heart and optimism. This is historical fiction at its very best, as relevant as this morning's news, as enjoyable as a summer day at the beach."

—Nancy Thayer, *New York Times* bestselling author

All the Summers in Between

"Intense and beautifully written . . . A delicious taste of glamour and intrigue."

—Rhys Bowen, *New York Times* bestselling author of *The Venice Sketchbook*

"A mesmerizing story of the complexities of female friendship and the yearning of women to live full lives. . . . You won't be able to turn away."

—Beatriz Williams, *New York Times* bestselling coauthor of *The Lost Summers of Newport*

"This one had me racing to turn the pages . . . Pick it up . . . and cancel your plans for the rest of the week!"

—Katie Couric Media

On Gin Lane

"At once a page-turner that kept me reading into the night, and a reminder of the importance of carving out a place for ourselves, whether it is by creating art or finding where we belong."

—Janet Skeslien Charles, *New York Times* bestselling author of *The Paris Library*

"The glitzy late '50s Hamptons sparkles like a coupe of champagne in this tantalizing novel from the talented Brooke Lea Foster. . . . A delightfully complex tale of deceit, social maneuvering, and self-determination that will have you cheering for the gutsy main character as she fights for the right to control her own fate."

—Kristin Harmel, *New York Times* bestselling author of *The Forest of Vanishing Stars*

"We can smell the ocean, we are poolside for Bellinis and luncheons, and on the courts for daily tennis matches. But behind the aesthetically pleasing atmosphere, there are cracks and lies in the facade. . . . What other lies, misleading untruths, and fraud are behind all the glamour? It's a perfect summer read for the pool or beach."

—*Chick Lit Central*

Summer Darlings

"I was immediately seduced by *Summer Darlings*. Foster cleverly conceals her characters' deceits and betrayal beneath a stunning, sun-spangled surface, and Martha's Vineyard is portrayed with glamorous period detail. This is one terrific summer read."

—Elin Hilderbrand, #1 *New York Times* bestselling author of *The Hotel Nantucket*

"Innocent intrigue segues into a love triangle—and goes out with a blackmail-backstabbing bang."

—*People*

"Beautifully written and richly detailed—it pulled me in from the very first page. Heddy is an unforgettable heroine, and I'll be recommending this book to everyone I know."

—Sarah Pekkanen, #1 *New York Times* bestselling author of *You Are Not Alone*

"I was swept away by *Summer Darlings* and its fiercely unforgettable heroine, Heddy Winsome. This perfect summer read blends it all: intrigue, romance, a gilded atmosphere, and gorgeous writing."

—*Entertainment Weekly*

"The enchanting beaches, dazzling parties, and elusive social circles of Brooke Lea Foster's 1962 Martha's Vineyard carry secrets and twists that keep us breathless. A delicious read filled with an acute sense of place and unexpected discoveries about class, status, and ambition."

—Marjan Kamali, bestselling author of *The Lion Women of Tehran*

"*Summer Darlings* has all the ingredients of a delightfully fizzy beach cocktail . . . If you like your summer escapism with a nostalgic splash of *Mad Men*–era glamour, you'll love this surprisingly twisty debut."

—Karen Dukess, author of *The Last Book Party*

ALSO BY BROOKE LEA FOSTER

Summer Darlings
On Gin Lane
All the Summers in Between

Our Last Vineyard Summer

BROOKE LEA FOSTER

G

GALLERY BOOKS

New York Antwerp/Amsterdam London
Toronto Sydney/Melbourne New Delhi

G

Gallery Books
An Imprint of Simon & Schuster, LLC
1230 Avenue of the Americas
New York, NY 10020

This book is a work of fiction. Any references to historical events, real people, or real places are used fictitiously. Other names, characters, places, and events are products of the author's imagination, and any resemblance to actual events or places or persons, living or dead, is entirely coincidental.

First Gallery Books trade paperback edition July 2026

GALLERY BOOKS and colophon are registered trademarks of Simon & Schuster, LLC

Interior design by Jaime Putorti

Manufactured in the United States of America

10 9 8 7 6 5 4 3 2 1

Library of Congress Cataloging-in-Publication Data is available.

ISBN 978-1-6680-3440-8
ISBN 978-1-6680-3441-5 (pbk)
ISBN 978-1-6680-3442-2 (ebook)

Interior map illustration by Sarah Schlick

To my parents, who taught me to love the sea

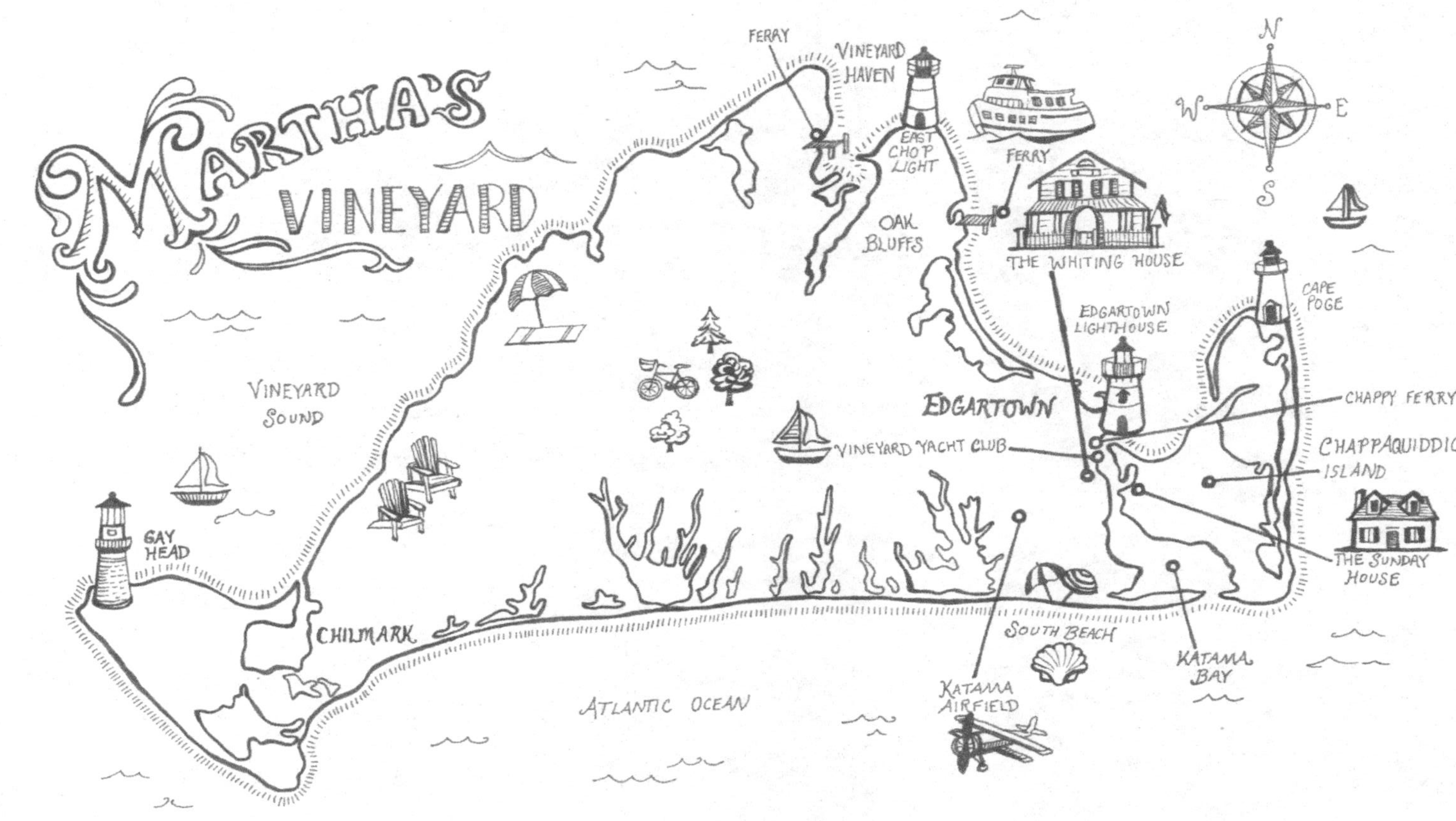

MARTHA'S
VINEYARD
VINEYARD SOUND
GAY HEAD
CHILMARK
ATLANTIC OCEAN
FERRY
VINEYARD HAVEN
EAST CHOP LIGHT
OAK BLUFFS
FERRY
THE WHITING HOUSE
EDGARTOWN LIGHTHOUSE
EDGARTOWN
VINEYARD YACHT CLUB
CAPE POGE
CHAPPY FERRY
CHAPPAQUIDDICK ISLAND
THE SUNDAY HOUSE
SOUTH BEACH
KATAMA BAY
KATAMA AIRFIELD
N
S
E
W

CHAPTER ONE

Betsy

Morningside Heights, Manhattan
June 1978

The city in summer was something you escaped, or at least that's what her mother had always told her. That June, though, there had been so many perfect sunny days, such an endless whirl of dreamy dates and good night kisses, that entire weeks began to blend. Her neck sticky with heat, Betsy impulsively stepped into the cool spray of an opened fire hydrant near her off-campus apartment, watching a few children splashing in the water. She had just finished an early shift at the diner near Columbia, hurrying home so she wouldn't miss the possibility of his call, when she decided that she didn't care if her pink-aproned uniform or brown ponytail grew damp. She'd been so anxious about seeing him, so excited for what he might propose between them, that even the water dappling across her bare arms felt like possibility. If he didn't call tonight after class, she'd see him tomorrow, and then tomorrow would be the first day of the rest of her life.

Climbing the three flights to her studio in the dim stairwell, Betsy opened the door to her unmade bed, a tornado of shoes at the center since she'd had to hunt for her tennis shoes that morning. She swept her eyes to the hot plate where she cooked, the rickety kitchen table, and the shower wedged in a corner by the shabby desk where some other graduate student struggling in this impossible university had sat for hours too. When her father had visited during her sophomore year, he'd winked at Betsy's mother and said, "Why do small spaces always seem so full of dreams?" Her mother had been putting fresh sheets on Betsy's dorm bed: "Because you cooked up a plan to be a United States senator while sleeping in an orphanage janitor closet."

Betsy smiled, remembering how proud her father had looked when she graduated from Barnard, carrying his suit jacket over his shoulder. How he'd pressed a letter into her hands telling her he admired her perseverance in her Latin classes, the way that she'd studied twice as hard to keep up with her classmates. What her father didn't know was that Betsy had only worked as hard as she did in the hopes that he would notice. Her mother too. But Virgie Whiting didn't only advocate for perfect grades; she wanted Betsy to be a leader. *Organize a march to get Columbia College to admit women, Betts! Write an editorial for the newspaper!* It *was* hard to believe that in 1978 the Ivy League university still didn't allow women to enroll in their undergraduate programs, but many women liked having a separate college in Barnard, even if her mother saw a single-sex education as hypocrisy. Lucky for Betsy, Columbia admitted women for graduate studies. "Those crusty old men on the board are afraid that young women will distract their virtuous male students with their pretty faces," Betsy's mother had told her when Betsy had gotten into the graduate psychology program last April. "As if women aren't there to sharpen their brilliant minds too. Well, you'll show them, won't you, Betts?"

Sometimes she heard her mother's voice at the oddest of times, like when she crossed the quad and lifted her shoulders back to stand straighter. Or she'd be reminded of her after passing a Barnard classmate wearing a T-shirt quoting her mother's iconic words delivered after the historic women's march down Fifth Avenue: "The decade is hers too." It was an odd conundrum to want to be everything your mother expected, and nothing at all. Betsy had worked hard this past year to distance herself from her mother and two older sisters, and she'd started to believe that she was happier without their nagging. Going home had started to feel like a battlefield, with someone in the family typically annoyed with someone else. She and her sisters would spend the entire visit tiptoeing around tensions, going to the movies and out for dinner, while whatever simmered below the surface remained. Her family was broken, and without her father, they weren't even a real family anymore. Betsy didn't know how to put them back together again. Instead, she bowed out of plans and avoided their phone calls.

Besides, she had Andy now. *Her boyfriend*, she reassured herself.

Betsy took a cool shower, ate cold pasta, and lay in her underwear on the crisp sheet she'd arranged on her dormitory-style couch. She clicked on the television, adjusted the rabbit ears to get less static, and waited for the cheery opening song of *The Love Boat*. Halfway through the show, the phone rang. Finally. Andy was calling. She dove for the handpiece, already anticipating his voice.

"Betsy, honey." Her heart deflated. It was the great Virgie Whiting, hero of the feminist movement, the voice of her generation—and to Betsy, just Mom. Her mother launched into a series of questions about the heat. At least she wasn't talking through one of her latest cover stories for *Ms.* magazine.

Betsy said a pleasant hello. "Yes, I'm melting, Mom. It's awful but I'm fine." She braided her fine brown hair to get it off her neck as her mother started going on about drinking juice to retain energy, then jumped to the possibility of blackouts, like last summer when the lights went out in Manhattan for twenty-four hours and all hell broke loose. Then came her mother's lingering fears about the serial killer who had been caught. "It's like the city goes crazy in summer."

Betsy hated when her mother's anxiety unraveled like this.

"Stop worrying. I'm safe and sound in my apartment." Betsy couldn't hear what Captain Stubing was saying on the television, so she leaned closer to the small speaker, momentarily tuning her mother out.

"Did you hear me, Betts? I don't think I can do this summer alone." Her mother's voice sounded unsteady, like her voice box was crackling with its own kind of fever. "Please come to the island. Dad is everywhere, and I just think—I think having you here would help."

Betsy turned down the volume dial. When Betsy's father died last year, her mother hadn't cried at the funeral. Her voice hadn't trembled when she'd insisted on delivering the eulogy at his wake. But Betsy had heard it a moment ago, the way her mother's words slipped into shakiness.

"Mom?"

Her mother coughed—she was an elegant smoker, her head tilted back, her lips releasing pretty threads of smoke—then cleared her throat. "The Senate asked me to go through Dad's papers, and it's been harder than I expected. Anyway, you can't possibly stay in Manhattan all summer. It's a certain kind of hell."

"I love the city in summer," Betsy lied. "You can finally eat outside at the cafés."

Her mother sniffed. "Yes, with a rat running over your foot." Somehow her mother could lace a simple sentence with a dozen years' worth of guilt trips.

"That's an exaggeration, Mom." What Betsy didn't say is that she needed to sign her summer lease for July and August this week, but she'd been putting it off on account of Andy. Dr. Andy Pines, the man she was going to follow to New Hampshire and hopefully marry. When he left for his new job at Dartmouth in two weeks' time, she planned to be with him, but she needed to be certain before she gave up her Manhattan studio.

Betsy pictured her mother calling from the small white cottage in Martha's Vineyard with its white picket fence and arbor with roses growing in tangles. It was her family's *only* house. When she was growing up, Betsy's parents had rented a series of New York apartments and later, Kalorama rowhouses in Washington, where they'd lived when her father was in the Senate, each of them plagued with some problem, whether it be a roof leak or rodents. Money had never flowed through the coffers like it did for many of the other elected officials that they knew, so they'd relied on the Vineyard house to anchor them as a family. Betsy had always loved the way the sun spread across the wide-plank pine floors each morning, how she'd sail most of the day at the local yacht club and return home to do cartwheels on the lawn overlooking Edgartown Harbor. She still kept a few old sundresses hanging in her closet and two changes of clothes and bathing suits in the dresser so she could show up at any point and enjoy the island, although it was rare to get there for more than a week these days.

"I've been working with a professor on a research project," Betsy fibbed, knowing this would placate her mother. Anything that proved she was working toward a shining goal got her attention. "It's not that easy to pick up and leave, Mom." Betsy sucked on a piece of ice from her glass of soda.

"If it's about money, I can send some Western Union." Her mother waited for her to say something, a lull on the line. Betsy's eyes drifted back to the television. *Why isn't Andy calling me?* She would see him tomorrow morning when they spoke about her thesis paper, sure, but they had bigger things to talk about. She was hoping he'd stop by tonight and ask her to dinner. Pull a small velvet box out of his pocket and get down on one knee.

Betsy spit the ice back in the glass, then fanned herself with a newspaper. She was about to say she couldn't come, that her research was too darn important.

"It's a bit of an emergency, honey."

A flash of heat, her head spinning. The same reaction Betsy had when Louisa called her last summer with the news of their father's plane careening from the sky. She was suddenly walking down the hall in the dark, feeling for the light switch, afraid what she might find when she turned it on. "Mom? Is Louisa okay? Is Aggie?"

An inhale, a big exhale. She was definitely smoking. "Oh, it's not your sisters, Betsy. It's the house. Dad, he . . . left us in a bad way. Louisa and Aggie are coming home too. I need the help, but Louisa can't stay very long, and Aggie has the kids."

The implication that her sisters had more important things to do annoyed Betsy. "I have a job too. I can't just leave."

"You're off for the summer, and you never even mentioned the research project until five minutes ago."

It wasn't that Betsy didn't love Martha's Vineyard. It was that she couldn't stand the thought of being trapped in the house with her family again, her mother and her sisters bossing her around. And yet, she had to go. You didn't say no to someone you loved.

"I suppose I can ask Dr. Pines if I can have time off from the clinical study." She would still have to work things out with Andy. Maybe she would meet him in New Hampshire instead.

Her mother sighed. "Betsy, we're going to have to sell the house."

Betsy had always imagined bringing her own kids to the Vineyard. She'd planned to show it to Andy this summer. "But Mom, it's all we have left of Daddy, of our childhoods," she heard herself stammering. The television grew staticky, and Betsy stared at the fuzzy screen as her mother said she'd explain everything when she arrived.

When she hung up, Betsy immediately dialed her sister Aggie, in Boston, to see what she knew, but there was no answer.

Andy's office was in the heart of the Columbia University campus on the fourth floor of the beaux arts Schermerhorn Hall, with its facade of Indiana limestone and a quote carved over the elaborate entrance: "Speak to the earth and it shall teach thee." The inscription had intimidated Betsy when she first stepped into the building for classes last September, but she barely noticed it anymore; hurrying through the doors now made her a bit numb to the grandeur. She'd spent most of her time in her graduate classes avoiding raising her hand—whenever she spoke up, her male classmates, who outnumbered female students five to one, found some way to belittle her arguments.

Betsy knocked on the frosted glass cutout in the pine door, ajar just enough that she could see a couple of cardboard boxes beside the professor's office chair.

"Come in," Andy said. His hands were folded on the metal desk, the desktop clear of the stacks of thick textbooks and medical journals she was accustomed to seeing. He didn't rise to close the door, and he didn't unthread his fingers and embrace her either—those fingers that had caressed her in places so private it made her blush.

"Thank you, Dr. Pines." It was what she called him on campus, to keep their relationship a proper secret. "I have so much to tell you. My mother called and I need to go . . ."

His expression remained impassive—there was no wide smile, no playful eyes—and he motioned for her to sit down as he shuffled a few folders around. He was young, only thirty-two to her twenty-three, but he appeared older now, more formal. She swallowed her nerves and lowered herself onto the chair, watching as he pulled out her thesis paper; there was the neatly typed title page, the shadow of a blot of Wite-Out where she'd needed to correct the date.

"Let's get down to it, shall we? I'm afraid your paper didn't quite make a solid enough argument, and I had to give you a score you may be disappointed with."

He tossed the paper on the desk, a large red F flashing in what felt like neon lights in the right-hand corner. She felt a ringing in her ears.

"I—I don't understand," she said, working hard to get him to look at her, really look at her, and exchange the intimacy she'd felt with him when their bodies were twisted in the sheets just last week. "An F means I don't pass. If I don't do well in your class, I'll have to retake it and then I won't be able to graduate on time next year."

He darted his eyes down to the desktop. "I'm afraid we'll need a complete revision. Professor Warner agreed after reading it. He'll step in as your advisor next fall."

"You're passing me off? Does that mean I have to retake the class?"

She'd worked hard on the premise of her thesis, "Self-Esteem: Sex Stereotyping or a Girls' Way?," a topic that had come up at her parents' dinner table. Were girls taught to believe they were less than men or were they conditioned to be so? Betsy had sorted through whatever research she could find, which admittedly had been slim, but she'd pulled in Freud's theory of fathers and daughters and a few others. To silence any critics, she approached the topic from a position of science, keeping her emotions out of her arguments entirely.

His voice was gentle, and she imagined him kissing up her neck, how they'd connected in the first place after talking about theories of attachment. "The premise was faulty. You didn't express any unique thought, and there was just not enough evidence to support your ideas. I did warn you of this."

"But you saw my annotations? The research on the topic isn't robust, I agree, but it's why I thought I could use this paper to apply for a grant. Maybe run my own case study."

"Perhaps. If you can find something new to say. But academics don't repeat research, they synthesize it." Odd, because she'd talked to Andy about her thesis many times, and he'd always thought the topic unique. "Ms. Whiting, your belief outweighs fact-based science, and you're taking leaps that cannot be supported in the field of psychology, at least not yet. Research shows that women don't even develop a true identity until they settle on a husband."

"You believe that?" Betsy bit at her chapped lip, pointing to her sources page. "Anyway, that's been refuted. Very clearly in Naomi Weisstein, 1968."

"The concept isn't widely accepted."

Betsy hadn't been looking for a boyfriend. She'd been sitting in class that January, doodling, marveling at how normal everyone seemed while the loss of her father still pressed down on her heart. The professor had been late, and when he rushed into the room, he'd apologized kindly. Betsy had looked up at his tweed blazer and chiseled cheeks, the way the young man kept running a single hand through his hair when he spoke. "I'm Dr. Pines," he'd said, smiling at her. This made Betsy sit up straighter in her seat, feeling for the long strand of wooden beads at her neck.

She sat up straight now too. Her mind left the paper and whatever Andy was droning on about. It was as though he wanted her to get so upset that she'd storm out of his office and never speak to him again.

"Your interest in counseling is a strength of yours, Ms. Whiting, but completing your degree will be a struggle if you cannot separate emotion from science."

Betsy chewed at her fingernail, still trying to understand what her lacking paper meant for their relationship. "Why wouldn't you have guided me to a better topic or sources?"

Andy folded his arms against his skinny chest—he was wiry, like her older sister Aggie—and he leaned back in his seat, taking a studious position that indicated he thought he was about to say something insightful. "I suppose we were busy having other conversations."

"I would say so." She pressed the soft of her palm against his bare wrist. "I don't care about some stupid thesis. I just don't want to lose you."

"You shouldn't be so, so . . . frivolous." He met her gaze, then slipped a nervous glance toward the hallway, voices approaching from somewhere in the stairwell, snatching back his hand. Rising, he closed the door, his leather loafers screeching against the waxed floor as he returned to his desk.

"Dartmouth is a tenure-track position, Betsy, and I want to start fresh. You and I won't work in the long term. You must know that."

"I am not frivolous. I'm . . ." Happy. She had been happy with him.

The office smelled like a musty mélange of dust and yellowed paper, sharpened pencils, and typewriter ink. It made her queasy. "But I could come with you to New Hampshire. I could rewrite my thesis at the Dartmouth library."

God, she sounded desperate. Is this what her mother meant years ago when she'd called Betsy her neediest child?

He shook his head at her. "Roberta and I are going to give it another shot," he said.

"You said she was selfish and unreachable." He'd also said the divorce would be finalized any day now; a lie, clearly.

"People change." Andy lowered his brows, then pulled Betsy up to stand so they were facing one another. His unshaven face, clean-lined and freckled, was inches from hers, and he kissed her forehead with tenderness. "I'm sorry, Betsy. You're a great kid, and I really enjoyed this." He pushed a lock of hair out of her eyes, and it took all her might not to latch her arms around his neck and hold on. "Professor Warner said to stop by after this and keep in touch with him this summer. We want you to succeed here."

She felt her knees buckle. They were in love. He'd said as much three weeks ago, before he got the offer at Dartmouth. He'd held her hand at the jazz club bar and said, "I can't imagine life without you." At the time, she'd thought that meant they'd be together forever. It was the logical next step after months of serious dating. Now it was clear that he was already imagining their lives apart.

I will not cry, she told herself, snatching her paper off his desk and tucking it under her arm. "I gave legitimate sources, and I used the proper research channels. Maybe it's *your beliefs* that are limiting *your understanding* of my topic. Maybe it's the subject matter that made *you* uncomfortable."

It was her mother's stock approach, call a man out for being sexist and he'd stammer and fumble, and while he decided to shut down or fight back, you figured out your next move. It would be impossible to make it to the elevator without tears.

"Good luck with Roberta. And your career."

"Thank you, Ms. Whiting, and you as well."

She slammed the office door in his face.

CHAPTER TWO

Betsy

Edgartown, Massachusetts

Betsy lugged her enormous suitcase and knapsack of textbooks out of the taxicab and onto crowded Main Street in Edgartown, thinking that the air was positively chilly for June. Summer was always a slow start on this tiny island off the coast of Cape Cod, but by July, the temperatures would soar, the frigid waters growing tepid. Then there would be beauty all around, showing itself in different colors of hydrangeas, a shoreline that drew a jagged line to blue, soft sand lining the endless ocean.

"Two dollars, miss." The cabbie's front teeth overlapped at the center. "Are you going to see your family?"

"My mother." Betsy felt inside her macrame tote for cash; the bag was jammed with two romance novels she'd purchased on a whim in the Amtrak station, even if she knew she should save her money. Already this trip was costing her a fortune. Tourists stepped around Betsy's luggage, a row of pretty shops lining the sidewalks, some selling pastel-colored sundresses and others stocking *Jaws* T-shirts, since the movie had catapulted Martha's Vineyard to celebrity status since its release three summers before. "But I'd rather be spending the summer alone."

"Don't be smart now. Everyone needs their people—it's like a good dose of medicine." He reached for her five-dollar bill, handing her back her change.

"You obviously haven't met my mother." Betsy smirked. "Or my sisters."

There was the sickly-sweet smell of fudge, tourists in thin cashmere sweaters browsing the shops, their doors open to the fresh air. Betsy traipsed along the sidewalk with the rest of the ponytailed summer crowd, walking down the one-way street to her parents' summer house. *Here comes Betsy*, she heard a voice in her head, *crawling back home with her tail between her legs.*

She'd given her landlady notice earlier that day, sliding a typed letter under the old woman's door after Betsy had stuffed every belonging worth keeping into her suitcase. She'd brought the textbooks so she could rework her final paper, even though she'd convinced herself during the journey to New England that there was no point in returning to grad school come fall. The only thing that had kept her going these last few months was Andy. Maybe she wasn't cut out for psychology after all. She was tired of her male classmates accusing her of being too emotional when they discussed a clinical case, tired of them leaving her out of study groups and talking in those obnoxious scholarly voices when they attempted to one-up each other in class.

A few minutes' walk from Main Street, Betsy could see her family's familiar white clapboard cottage on South Water Street, its historic green shutters standing proud with a flag flapping off the small front porch. Her father wouldn't be in the house, only his things would be, and she didn't want to be here without him. Last May, after he died, no one bothered to travel to the Vineyard, the summer months overtaken with the funeral and memorials and checking in on their grief-stricken mother in her Georgetown apartment. She paused in front of the house's white picket gate, a memory of her and her sisters holding a lemonade stand on the sidewalk. She could see Louisa blowing bubbles, her and Aggie chasing after them while running their fingertips along the fence slats. How Betsy would always call after Aggie and Louisa to wait up, how she'd always felt like she couldn't keep pace. It hadn't occurred to Betsy how much she missed the island until now.

Betsy let herself in, stepping into the sunny living room, the house smelling of her mother's jasmine perfume. She was relieved to see that the cottage and its rooms were identical to how they'd left them. The room was a time capsule. How many books had Betsy read on the well-worn navy couch with throw pillows emblazoned with goldfinches? The large model sailboat she and her father had built a decade before remained on display on the mantel, the opposite wall covered in framed photographs of her and her sisters with their arms pretzeled around each other at various stages of their childhood. They were on the beach, on the porch, on *Senatorial*, in a backyard dressed up with ribbons in their hair. There was Betsy at four, Aggie at eight, and Louisa at nine, and so on, until Louisa turned fifteen and the pictures stopped. Almost like the family had ceased to exist after 1965.

"Mom?" Betsy's voice drifted through the empty living room, past the faded wallpapered dining room where her mother had insisted on squeezing in a mahogany table for eight many years ago.

"In here."

Betsy stopped short in the doorway to the kitchen. There was no sign of her mother, only her eldest sister, Louisa, standing at the faux-brick counter with her shoulder-length light hair in a headband, her signature braided belt cinching the waist of a white shirtdress. She was barefoot, and still, she carried herself like a woman shopping for fine jewels at Tiffany's. Discerning, doubting. "Hi," she said.

"Oh, hi." Betsy darted her eyes to the white metal cabinets and the old fridge her mother refused to part with. She'd been preparing for the strangeness of seeing Louisa, poised to act as though nothing ever happened between them, in order to keep the peace for her mother, but a bitterness rose up in Betsy's throat. "I didn't know law firms gave vacations."

"Only to those that work the hardest." Louisa didn't miss a beat, even as she sliced the lemons. She stopped, her knife splaying to one side, and she briefly met Betsy's eye. "I have a week or so. How have you been?"

Betsy looked away, trying to decide what to say to someone you hadn't spoken to in a year. Louisa had written her a letter in April, but Betsy hadn't bothered to read it. "Fine. You?"

"Fine."

The black-and-white wall clock ticked, its cat shape and bulging eyes comical. She and Louisa had always squabbled, even with five years between them, while kindhearted and generous Aggie, a year younger than Louisa, played the role of mediator. Their father always said she and Louisa had clashing temperaments: Louisa's fiery nature was easily irritated by Betsy's easygoing one. Her mother saw it differently, though, once telling Betsy that she'd never be happy unless she found a way to stop competing with her eldest sister. After a year of psychology classes, Betsy had a different theory: Louisa was annoying.

Louisa squeezed the lemons into a pitcher. "I can't believe you actually came."

"What is that supposed to mean?"

The smallest of smiles curled Louisa's thin upper lip. "You're just always so *busy*."

"Shut up. I am busy."

Opening the cabinet, Betsy pulled down a glass, turned on the tap and drank down a glass of water. Why did Louisa's hair always have to look so perfect, shiny like a summer day and with layers that fell softly around her angular face? Betsy was proud of her own bangs though, a bold decision that she'd decided made her look like the actress Jane Birkin. Betsy even owned a striped tank she'd seen Birkin wear, and she often let her hair blow about her face loose and carefree like the actress. "Are we really selling the house?"

Louisa sighed. "It appears that way, but Mom hasn't said much yet. I got here last night. Aggie's outside with the babies."

On the second night of her father's wake last May, Louisa had accused Betsy of trying to pick up a boyfriend. It had infuriated Betsy. She and Aggie had been circulating as they were expected to, merely being polite, and Betsy couldn't get out of a conversation with a handsome young Senate aide about her father's outsized influence on his career. Her mind had blurred at what he was saying, but when he departed, Louisa had cornered Betsy in a spray of funeral flowers. "I picked the coffin, the headstone, organized the catering, and now I have to babysit Mom too. The least you could do is take a turn holding her arm like I have all night, instead of trying to find a boyfriend." Louisa had wrapped her black blazer around her loose black dress.

"You never think I'm doing the right thing." Betsy snatched her arm from Louisa's grip.

"Well, it's not enough, Daddy's girl." Louisa had stormed off, giving her the cold shoulder for the rest of the funeral, and Betsy had given her the cold shoulder since, an anger festering and growing into something bigger than the fight.

"Where is Mom?" Betsy managed.

"She's up in the study, working on some article, like always."

The previous year sat between the sisters like a wall too tall to climb. "At least she's writing again," Betsy said.

Louisa nodded. She stirred the sugar and water into the lemonade pitcher, resolution knitted in her eyebrows. "Anyway, we're here now, so we might as well be cordial."

"Isn't that convenient?" Betsy wouldn't let her off that easy. She wanted an apology. What her sister had done had hurt her so deeply at a time when her heart had been bruised; it had felt, and still felt, unforgivable.

"Fine, have it your way." Louisa added ice to the pitcher, stirring once more. "But no comments about the five pounds I put on. I already feel like a hippo."

Louisa had been top of her class at Barnard, then attended Harvard Law, where she'd earned an editor job on the Law Review and had her pick of gentlemen admirers. Why would she mention her figure?

"To me, you look like nothing but an overworked constitutional lawyer," Betsy said. She switched on the small transistor radio in the window, the chorus of "Stayin' Alive" lightening the moment.

Her sister smiled at her goofy dance moves. "I'll take it as some version of a compliment."

Aggie and the kids barreled toward the back door from the yard, and Betsy was grateful for the interruption in the uncomfortable reunion with Louisa. Her middle sister glided inside with her pale blue eyes softening, her long, blond curls clipped to one side with a barrette. The baby, Mikey, hoisted on her hip; little Tabitha toddling behind. "Betsy! I'm so glad you're here. When Mom told me about the house, I was worried how you'd take the news. Are you okay?"

"Why were you worried about *me*?" Betsy hugged Aggie, then bent down and scooped her niece into her arms, kissing her soft pillowy cheeks. Everyone was always worried about Betsy.

"Because you used to count down the days before we left for the island every summer. I'm upset about the house, too, but you always loved it here most."

"I guess. I mean, it was Mom that made us come here."

Aggie nodded like she didn't agree, then stuffed a binky in the baby's mouth. "Okayyy. Well, you loved it, too, right? To think that it's our final summer. It's so depressing."

Louisa poured each of them a glass of lemonade. "I feel like we've barely finished mourning Dad, and now we're going to mourn this house?"

Betsy always thought her older sisters were like two different versions of the same person, her mother even nicknaming Louisa "Mopsy" and Aggie "Flopsy" after the bunnies in *Peter Rabbit*, since they were always up to something. The names had always made Betsy long for a similarly rhyming name like "Bopsy," just so she'd feel closer to them.

Betsy threw Tabby into the air; her toddler smiles easy to earn. She was a dead ringer for her father, Dr. Henry Talbot, a surgeon at Mass General in Boston. Aggie had met him running the Boston Marathon four years before, a whirlwind romance that ended with a wedding one year later and two kids in three years' time. "I still don't get why she needs all three of us here at once. Couldn't we have come in shifts?"

"A show of solidarity. You know Mom." Louisa sat down at the kitchen banquette, her dainty hands folded on the tabletop as the windowed room revealed the comings and goings of the three-car Chappy ferry on the other side of the glass. "What I want to know is just how bad her finances are. I didn't think it possible that Dad could muck things up from the grave."

The baby began to cry, and Aggie handed him off for a moment to warm a bottle in a metal pot on the stove. "Do you think it's something in the will that's changed?"

Betsy wished she'd painted her toenails and wore a nicer skirt, now that she saw how pretty her sisters looked. "Mom probably mismanaged her accounts. She's always holding those feminist lunches at the Hay-Adams."

Louisa rolled her eyes. "Mom charges for those lunches, Betsy. She doesn't *treat* everyone."

Betsy's stomach growled, and she reached for a loaf of Wonder Bread and a jar of crunchy peanut butter, spreading a spoonful on a slice. "Okay, so what did Dad do?"

It annoyed Betsy that she was looking at Louisa and waiting for an answer, that she and Aggie were so accustomed to letting Louisa interpret the world around them, just like they did as young girls.

Feeling their expectant looks, Louisa shrugged. Betsy noticed delicate fine lines near her eyes.

Said Louisa: "Well, we all know Dad had secrets."

Betsy headed upstairs, her suitcase bumping against the settling steps. It was a relief to finally be alone. At the top of the landing, with its familiar warping in the wood from a bad leak during the 1938 hurricane, Betsy paused at the closed door of her mother's study. Listening to the keys of an electric typewriter noisily hitting paper on the other side, Betsy felt ten years old again. A whir of impatience, the same desire to turn the knob and interrupt her mother, swing open the door and announce herself with dramatic flair. But house rules were house rules. If the door was closed, Betsy and her sisters could only open the door if there was an emergency. Otherwise, her mother would come out for twenty minutes at noon and then return to her office until four o'clock every day. It was nearly the latter now.

Betsy fell onto one of the beds in her old yellow room, the paint faded and dull now, thinking she might as well unpack. She propped herself up on one elbow so she could take in the busy harbor below. The distant voices of boaters carried through the open window, along with the rhythmic lap of the water. From here, she could see the white Edgartown lighthouse with its black tip. She followed the water line to the small island of Chappaquiddick, looking for a run-down house in the distance with a towering oak tree on the front lawn. *There it is.* She smiled. The house once belonged to her oldest friend, James Sunday. She wondered if he ever visited the island anymore. They'd lost touch when they were teenagers, mostly because Betsy's father had never liked the boy.

She could hear Louisa climbing the stairs in the hall, her steps quick and light from years of ballet, and only then did Betsy realize that her sister's belongings were in Betsy's old bedroom. It made sense—Aggie would get the large front bedroom with the kids, so Louisa and Betsy would need to share. Betsy sat up on the larger bed when Louisa entered, her sister nodding to the smaller twin-sized daybed against the wall, making clear she expected Betsy to sleep on it, which was ridiculous. Of the three sisters, Louisa was the most petite, five foot four with long, slender limbs, while Aggie was the tallest at nearly five ten. She'd always carried herself with a swanlike elegance thanks to her towering frame.

Louisa straightened the lace doily on the nightstand. "Of course, we can sleep in the big bed together, but you better not kick me."

"How about we wedge a pillow between us, so we don't accidentally touch in the middle of the night?" This made her sister laugh, and Betsy felt a pang of satisfaction, even if she had zero interest in talking to Louisa. "It's fine."

Betsy rose to stand and pressed her hand on the springy twin with the thin coverlet; everyone knew it was the worst bed in the house, reserved for Aunt Lacey or a friend visiting from college. Now it was Betsy's. For the entire summer. Betsy unzipped her suitcase and opened a dresser drawer, arranging folded denim shorts inside.

When she was half Louisa's size, Louisa would read to her and Aggie, sitting on the edge of her bed and licking her fingertip like a librarian as she turned the pages of *The Berenstain Bears*. They'd played school in here, pulling chairs up to the bed to form makeshift desks. In later years, when her parents had big arguments about her father's work, which happened weekly, Louisa would pull her sisters in here and translate what was going on. One time, she'd hugged Betsy to her chest, Betsy suddenly aglow. Louisa could fill up all the holes inside her when she was affectionate. She'd said, "Don't be sad, Betsy. This is the part when Daddy apologizes for sneaking cigarettes, and next, he'll tell Mom he can't live without her, and she'll crumble, they'll sip a glass of port and go to bed giggling."

"Betsy, is that you?" Her mother hurried into the sunny bedroom in a burst, her coke-bottle reading glasses pushed atop the cascade of pretty, loose waves framing her face; everyone in Betsy's family had gotten her mother's light hair and ocean-colored eyes except Betsy, who took after her father's darker features. Looking at her mother now, Betsy thought her a dead ringer for Dyan Cannon in that new movie *Heaven Can Wait*.

Her mother squeezed her so tight, Betsy felt like she couldn't breathe.

"Hi, Mom. I got in an hour ago."

She cupped a hand on Betsy's cheek, smiling. "Oh, honey, you look so wonderful. Graduate school has been good to you."

Betsy wished she could show her mother the earrings Andy had given her; instead, she'd left them on the nightstand in her old apartment. "Well, I don't know about that." She pictured herself in class, feeling intimidated to raise her hand in a classroom full of male counterparts. Betsy had been so certain that psychology was her passion when she applied for the graduate program: It was widely joked that people with the biggest problems were drawn to psychology since it gave them a chance to study themselves. As much as she loved listening to people and wanted to help make changes in people's lives, she did often feel her mind wandering to her family, the good and the bad. But her classes felt distant from the job of an analyst. One professor had sat Betsy down in her first semester and inquired whether she'd be a better fit in the education program since she seemed well-suited for school counseling. But Betsy didn't want to work in a school. Sometimes she wished she could rent an office, call herself a therapist, and start seeing patients—without ever having to return to get the degree.

Her mother held Betsy's hands and swung them about. "I'm done working for the day, girls. I was thinking I'll make spaghetti and clams, and we'll play Scrabble on the porch."

"You're a crowd pleaser, Mom," Louisa said, a genuine smile forming. She had gone into the bathroom to change into her bathing suit, slipping a floral sundress over it. "But first, let's go for a swim at the beach."

"Oh, Betsy." Her mother squeezed her hand. "It's so good to see you, honey. You've been so far away."

"I'm only in New York, Mom." She knew what her mother was saying though, that she'd been distant in general. Now, standing here in her summer bedroom, her mother was making it so hard for Betsy to hide her emotions. All at once, Betsy felt the pain of the breakup slam against her chest. She bit the insides of her cheeks.

"Well, I'm happy you're home."

"Me too," Betsy managed, a waver in her voice.

Because this sweet little house by the sea was home. Now that she'd given up her apartment, Betsy had nowhere else to go. She didn't even have a plan for her future. The inside of her cheek suddenly tasted of metallic, and still, Betsy smiled at her mother broadly when she said she needed to change too. For the swim.

"Don't be long," her mother said, tapping her back twice. "It's been so long since I've had all three of you here. I want us to get reacquainted and tell each other everything."

Betsy had to give her mother credit for trying. She wanted them to engage in one of the most important (and challenging) aspects of patient therapy: acknowledge what you might be holding back.

CHAPTER THREE

Virgie

Vineyard Haven Ferry, Martha's Vineyard
July 1965

Virgie couldn't believe they'd made it to the ferry dock. Following the instructions of two cranky attendants, she'd crept her butter-yellow Ford station wagon onto the *Islander*, the beloved boat that had been transporting her family to the island for a generation. Even with an ache in her lower back from driving, Virgie had to admit that the ferry's gleaming white facade and the futuristic way it invited you to drive onto the ferry and drive off going in the same direction still filled her with promise. Here was this twenty-three-mile island (a mere nine miles in width) floating in Vineyard Sound that had drawn her since childhood, instilling in her everything she believed about her family: that this island was their anchor, these shores a place to reconnect, relax, and run amok with the tides. In thirty minutes, they would dock in Vineyard Haven, and she'd drive her long, lumbering car into an early summer evening, the busy streets of the sweet little village bustling with tourists. By tomorrow, Virgie wouldn't even remember the nine-hour (and rather awful) drive from Washington.

All of it will be worth it when you wake up in your summer bedroom with the breeze ruffling the curtains, Virgie reminded herself. She imagined the anger Charlie would feel when he arrived home from the Senate and discovered an empty house and foil-wrapped plate of chicken à la King. She knew he would be beside himself, and yet she'd been beside herself too. That Virgie wanted to leave early for the Vineyard had been an ongoing argument; his irritation at the popularity of her newspaper column Dear Virgie had been the wedge. A big fat slice of the tartest key lime pie sitting right between them, and both refusing a bite.

"I need to get out of this car." Louisa used her fifteen-year-old might to push open the door, straightening the pleats of her shorts around her new curves as she stood; her blond hair was cut with glamorous short bangs and a wavy chin-length bob that matched her shapely eyebrows. "Aggie has been farting since we passed Providence."

"Have not," hollered Aggie, kicking at her sister in her enormous bare feet through the open door. She sat up and clasped shut her rubber-soled sandals. "I'm sorry, Louisa, if you're smelling your own breath."

Lovely, Virgie thought. *We've been reduced to animals in a pen.*

At some point on the drive, Betsy had crawled onto the floor—she'd been annoying the older ones the entire drive by begging them to play cat's cradle with her beloved elastics. To get her away, Aggie had encouraged Betsy onto the foot mats, so she could stretch out her legs across two seats while Louisa, in her short shorts, squished against the door and buried her nose in a Patricia Highsmith novel.

Betsy popped her head out the back window. "Wait! I'm coming." Virgie's youngest daughter, always in a red-and-white polka-dot headband, tripped in her rush to get out of the car. Much to Virgie's dismay, her ten-year-old had insisted on wearing her scuffed black-and-white saddle shoes, refusing the pale pink sandals she'd bought her for summer. Motherhood could be maddening in ways big and small.

Waving a five-dollar bill out the window, Virgie called after her girls. "Louisa, take your sisters to get chowder."

"Why do I always have to take care of them?" Louisa snapped back, becoming aware then that there were other vacationers staring, her pimpled cheeks turning the color of watermelon.

"It's one time, not every time." Virgie grimaced.

Virgie's own mother had never driven alone—she wouldn't dare to drive, even in their New York suburb, instead waiting on her husband to shuttle her about. Her mother wore smocking necklines and was nothing like Virgie, who could cook a soufflé, paint peeling trim, hammer a nail into the wall, *and* write a newspaper column. Virgie's was an adulthood formed in opposition to her mother's propriety. Even choosing Charlie had been a form of resistance.

Louisa groaned, snatching the money and storming off, Betsy right at her heels and Agatha—with those long awkward legs, bony at the knee and muscular in the thigh—following closely behind like a hunched giraffe.

Virgie hated to admit that she wished Charlie were here. Then again, he probably would have just turned up the Yankees game on the radio and expected Virgie to break up any arguments between the girls anyway. If she pulled her small notepad out of her purse to scribble down an idea for the column, he'd frown; but what he didn't understand was that writing the column had been a lifeline when it was offered to her last year. She'd been drowning in boredom while the girls were at school each day, and the column gave her a new kind of purpose. Angling the rearview mirror to see her reflection, Virgie grimaced, using her fingers to comb her wind-blown hair and tie a sheer black headscarf around her crown. *Better*, she thought. Then she pulled out her compact and reapplied a thick round of peach lipstick. The last thing she needed was to run into someone from Washington who reported back to Charlie that his wife looked as though she were falling apart.

Because she wasn't falling apart. Virgie had come to the island on her own to give her daughters a real summer and to give herself time to figure out why she and Charlie were bickering so much. "Honestly, the drive was nothing," she would tell Charlie on the phone later that night. "I don't know why you're making such a big deal out of it."

Virgie found her girls spooning creamy soup and salty crackers into their mouths on the upper deck where crowds of visitors crammed into the limited shade. Dropping her raffia drawstring purse in her lap, Virgie sat between Betsy and Louisa, smiling at them when they acknowledged her. It had been a stressful ride, with Betsy crying when they got stuck in traffic on the George Washington Bridge, and Aggie complaining endlessly about not going to Birch Lark.

"Shut up," Louisa had snapped as one highway exit blurred into the next, after Aggie complained she'd never try archery. "Birch Lark isn't all that great. My friend says the food is mush and the cabins have bugs."

At that, Aggie had heaved her back into the seat. "Well at least I could play basketball there."

"Not if Daddy can help it," Betsy had snickered.

The plan all along was that they'd visit the island as a family in August when the Senate was in recess; in the meantime, since it was an election year, Virgie would attend campaign events with Charlie in New York in June and July, while the girls were shipped off to Birch Lark Camp for Girls. Yet, when it came time for them to leave, Virgie didn't want her girls attending some snobby sleepaway camp with the children of diplomats and government royalty. She wanted them on the Vineyard, running barefoot and swimming and having the same kind of summer she'd always had. Plus, there was the matter of getting Louisa away from Brandon Millerton. She'd found out only last week that Brandon would be at the Birch Lark boys camp, just a mile down the road. Her daughter didn't need any more trouble.

The horn of the steamship blared, announcing the boat's departure. Virgie looked at Louisa. It gave her the curious sense that she was looking in the mirror: They had the same golden hair, the same straight nose and light freckles. They were fair to a fault, both in skin tone and in life. "We're off to the island." Louisa grinned, craning her neck to see over the railing as they left the mainland.

The velvet quality of the sea swept away the stress she'd had pinned between her shoulders, and Virgie decided she'd call Charlie tonight and apologize for leaving without saying goodbye. She couldn't think of a single time she hadn't gone along with his plans, down to the timing of their second child. But she knew he wouldn't stay mad forever. Once he heard the light in her voice, he would see that the island was exactly what she'd needed.

The ferry slowed as they approached Vineyard Haven, Virgie's eyes crinkling at the sight of familiar houses lining the cliffs. How far she'd traveled this year, and how reassuring it was to return to this comforting place. Last month, she'd been part of a delegation of political wives who were sent to England to lunch with the queen. They'd nibbled chicken and mushroom pie in a formal room at Buckingham Palace, and the young queen had given a speech about a woman's responsibility as a voter, a mother, and citizen. "Always ask questions, even as women," the queen had said, the diamonds in her crown sparking a million little gasps in Virgie's mind. It had made her question everything she knew. Small things, like: Why did she wash her face every night and apply cold cream—was there actual proof this did anything? And bigger things, like: Why did she smile politely at people at cocktail parties who said offensive things rather than respond curtly?

The ferry bumped into the pilings of the dock, and then came an announcement on the crackly speaker welcoming passengers to Martha's Vineyard. She and the girls gathered their things and moved with other vacationers toward the painted-steel stairwell leading down to the car park. Virgie watched the back of her daughters' heads as they walked down the steps, each one a couple of inches shorter than the other. A line of growing women who would one day watch their own daughters descend into the dim, cavernous belly of the ferry, driving out minutes later into blinding sunshine.

CHAPTER FOUR

There were cobwebs in the corners of the living room she hadn't seen the night before, and before Virgie could even think of attempting breakfast, she found herself going about the house with an upside-down broom and brushing them off the ceiling. The lace curtains in the living room had yellowed, and she fetched a stepladder from the root cellar, accessed through a pair of metal doors outside, so she could remove the drapes for washing. Then she opened all the windows despite the early morning chill, determined to free them from the stale air. By afternoon she'd have the wood floors gleaming, the fridge wiped clean, and the cupboards stocked.

There was that low-level vibration in her hands again, almost like the muscles of her fingers were trembling on the inside. But when she stared at her hand, she could hold it perfectly still. Nerves, her doctor had told her. A flare-up that had started on the highway yesterday all because she dreaded the phone call with Charlie. She had phoned him last night after she and the girls put clean sheets on the beds and everyone turned in for the night, but there had been no answer at their small Kalorama rowhouse.

The last nuclear fight they'd had was last August. They'd left the Chilmark estate of Senator Prescott of Massachusetts. He'd had a party to celebrate his fiftieth birthday. She and Charlie were cutting through the back roads by the illuminated Ferris wheel of the Agricultural Fair when Charlie asked why she'd spent so much time talking to Wiley Prescott, the senator's younger brother, who happened to be a bit of a playboy. The truth was that she'd noted Charlie's continual checking in on her from afar, and she'd tried to get out of the conversation, but it *had* been an interesting chat. Wiley had said the women reporters at his family's Boston newspaper were the best of his staff, and when she mentioned that she had always wanted to be a writer, he encouraged her to contact an editor at a paper in New York, which was how her Dear Virgie column had come about.

Last week, after reading her latest column, Charlie had marched into the kitchen where she was pan-frying salmon and yelled: "Do you even think of me when you write these things?"

Do you even think of me when I smell the perfume of another woman on your collar? Virgie hadn't said that about his latest dalliance—suspected, never confirmed—although she'd wanted to. Instead, she'd flipped the fish in the pan. "I simply did the math, Charlie. If a woman cooks six nights a week from the age of twenty-five until the average age of seventy years, she will have cooked fourteen thousand dinners. I'm not even counting breakfast or lunch." Of course, Virgie had also suggested in her article that the burden on women *might be* unjust; that while men wanted to imagine their wives prancing about the kitchen like gazelles, they often thought of cooking as a dreaded chore.

While running a dust cloth along the living room bookshelves, Virgie wondered when exactly things had gotten so fiery between them, but it was hard to say. Certainly not when the girls were little or before he won his first election. In those first few summers on the island, after they inherited the summer house from her aunt and uncle in 1951, Charlie was a first-term congressman from New York without any committee obligations. They'd begin each weekend with scrambled eggs and a walk on the beach while passing Louisa and Aggie from one pair of arms to the other. At night, they'd listen to the radio by lamplight near the open windows and snuggle on the navy-blue couches. It was her father's brother who bought the house in 1935, but he and his wife, Celia, never had children, so each summer they adopted Virgie as their own. By the 1940s, the island changed immensely when the air force used the Vineyard's landing strip to practice dropping air bombs, and when the war ended, some men stayed. By the '50s, summer tourists had discovered the island, thanks to a reliably traveling ferry; in Edgartown, there was a fruit stand, a barber, a hat store, and a few pool halls, and life everywhere was altogether simpler.

"I'm starving, Mom," Betsy muttered as she came downstairs.

Her youngest child was an early riser, and Virgie smiled at the sleep crease across her daughter's cheek. "I'll look through the cupboards in a few minutes."

The thud of the newspaper slapped against the front door; the work of their reliable paper boy, a local kid named James who lived across the harbor. Betsy ran to the window to knock and wave at the scrawny child on his rusted bike, and he waved back, a sweet smile brightening his face. The boy's arrival was as predictable as everything else on the island, a neighborhood built upon tradition and community. Virgie gazed out at the view of glistening Edgartown Harbor, the small ferry to Chappaquiddick arriving on the small island opposite them. She went about opening the cabinets, finding a bottle of canola oil and an unopened box of pancake mix she'd been smart enough to put in the refrigerator before they'd left; there was no syrup, but this would do. She plugged in the Frigidaire, the refrigerant gurgling back to life in the ice box.

A mouse skittered across the baseboard, disappearing behind the stove. Virgie screamed and jumped about like her feet were on fire. It was something no one told you about summer houses: you never knew what kind of critters you'd find when you unlocked the house for the season. In the middle of the third pancake, Aggie and Louisa yawned their way into the kitchen, hair scarves still tied about their heads from sleep.

"What is she doing?" Louisa said, disgusted at the sight of Betsy lying on her stomach on the wood.

"Probably licking the floor," Aggie sighed.

"She's catching a mouse, and it's more than I can say about you two sleeping beauties. I need help in the house today."

"We have a mouse?" Aggie lifted her feet up onto the seat of the wooden chair.

Louisa rubbed the sleep out of her eyes. "We always have mice at the beginning of summer, and in July will come the ants. Isn't summer grand?"

Virgie ignored them, putting three plates out on the table and delivering each of her daughters a couple of pancakes, pouring herself tea after from the singing kettle.

"No butter?" Aggie opened the fridge.

"No syrup either. We'll go to Cronig's this morning, and everyone can pick what they want to eat for breakfast this week." It seemed like a good idea, Virgie thought. Then she wouldn't have to deal with their complaints that she was making the wrong thing.

The doorbell rang, which made Betsy yell for everyone to shush: "The mouse is never going to come out if we're all talking."

"No one cares about some dumb little mouse," Louisa said.

Virgie inhaled. "Louisa, go answer the door."

"But I'm in my pajamas."

"We're all in our pajamas. It's probably the milkman."

Virgie turned off the griddle. There was talking at the front, a man's voice, and Louisa bounded into the kitchen. "It's the Edgartown Police. He wants to talk to you."

"Me?" Virgie rinsed the mixing bowl, running a sponge along the sides. Turning off the faucet, she wrapped her robe tighter around her waist. Police made her nervous; she'd once been pulled over by an officer in Washington for making an illegal left turn, and he'd leaned into the car and reached for a lock of her hair, caressing it between his fingers.

"Good morning, Chief," Virgie said, approaching the front door.

He held his brimmed hat at his waist, nodding. "Ma'am." His car was parked on the street, the lights flashing as though he'd pulled someone over in a traffic stop. "I got a call from your husband this morning."

Charlie had called the police? "Oh?" she said. "Whatever for?"

The police chief was younger than she imagined, maybe about her age. "He said you took his children here? That you left without his permission."

They weren't *his* children; the girls were *their* children, and last she checked, she was the only one who cared a hood's wink about them, too. "I assure you, Chief Watters, that this is my summer house, and my husband knew I was bringing the children. I wrote him a note and left it on the kitchen counter myself."

He leaned against the doorjamb. "You're telling me he knew you were coming, but he's telling me he didn't. Which is it?"

"You know, Officer," she took on the voice of a woman who put her husband first. She was that woman, so she wasn't even faking it. "Charlie is a United States senator, and he's often under a lot of pressure. Sometimes he's up all night before a big vote. It's quite possible he's a bit delirious."

"He sounded quite rested," the officer said.

Jerk, she thought, watching as the milk truck pulled behind the cop car. "You see, Charlie has several campaign events this month, but I wanted the girls to swim and sail. To get out of that overheated swamp. Have you ever been to the Capitol in summer?"

"I haven't."

"Well, it's dreadful. The air is so thick you can barely breathe. Anyway, please, let me call my husband and figure this out."

The officer's broad chest filled. "Listen, I don't want to get involved in a domestic dispute—"

"There is no domestic dispute," she cut him off, smiling, then stepped out onto the stoop to clear out some old leaves. "I can assure you that I did not kidnap my own children."

His car lights were flashing. Every neighbor on the block would be asking her what had happened. "Let me give you a piece of advice, ma'am." The officer backed down a step. "A good woman speaks her mind without knocking her house down. Do you know what I mean by that?"

It pained her to nod; what did he know of what women needed? "I think I do, yes."

"Good," he said, turning back to his squad car. "Now go call your husband."

CHAPTER FIVE

Virgie felt a biting sensation in the corners of her eyes. This argument was between her and Charlie, and yet there were three young women staring up at her, the smell of the cooling griddle turning the air pungent. She opened a window. "The chief was asking for a donation for some fundraiser. Now let's everyone go upstairs and get dressed."

Louisa had the kind of round, curious eyes that felt like they could see right into your head. "Are you sure you're okay, Mom?"

"Yes, of course," Virgie said, clearing the water glasses into the sink. "Don't give it another minute of thought." Louisa nodded tacitly, disappearing upstairs.

Moving outside to the back patio, Virgie collapsed into one of five picnic table chairs, watching a large yacht make its way into the harbor: a boat finding its way back home. She wished she could vent to a friend, but she and her best friend Melody had lost touch over a decade ago. Virgie didn't feel like she could reveal her innermost feelings to her Washington friends. Everything was fodder for gossip. Even after all these years, she knew how Melody would counsel her: proceed cautiously. Things could get much worse between her and Charlie if she wasn't careful; she needed to back down. Padding inside, Virgie picked up the wall phone in the kitchen and asked the switchboard to connect her to the Whiting residence in Washington. Charlie was sending her a message, showing her the kind of control that a husband could have over his wife.

It took a few minutes for the switchboard to travel 475 miles south to Washington, but then there was Charlie's voice on the line, distant and crackling. "Hello," he said. Charlie always took his calls in the sitting room in the tufted leather telephone chair, a small American flag pinned on his lapel.

She steadied her voice. "Hello, dear. It was a bit theatrical calling the Edgartown police."

"I'm sorry. I had too much to drink last night and it scared me that I didn't actually know where you were."

"Charlie. I left you a letter on the front table. I even called after we arrived. We've been bickering over this for weeks. You knew full well where we were."

He cleared his throat. "This is humiliating, you leaving me like this. You realize that you can't just do whatever you want."

"And who is going to stop me?" She smacked her hand over her mouth, tasting salt as she pressed her flattened palm against her lips. Of course, she'd thought of saying something like this a million times to her husband, to every man she knew in Washington who spoke as if they knew better than her. But she'd never been this brazen, this direct.

"Oh, Virginia. You can't leave me alone for the entire summer."

She snorted. "You leave me all the time, Charlie. I can't just wait around for you."

A clicking sound came through the telephone as the lines crossed, and for a moment, she heard the muted voices of two women talking about an upcoming violin concert.

"Virginia?" he said gently, as though he wasn't sure she was still there. "I don't know what's gotten into you. These columns of yours. I called the editor of the paper."

There were dried pancake drips on the stove. She soaked a sponge, the cold water stinging her fingertips. "You called my editor?"

"I asked him to cancel Dear Virgie, at the very least put it on hold, since its publication was causing all kinds of marital strife."

She reached for a Brillo, scrubbing the burners. "Is this a joke?"

Charlie blew his nose into a tissue; he suffered from hay fever every summer. "Listen. They agreed to take a pause." Her hands moved faster then, her fingers growing raw. "You can maybe go back to it, Virgie, but I need you to stop writing these controversial stories for the next few months. It might affect voters."

She picked up the griddle to lower it in the sink, forgetting the handle was hot. Her hand stung underneath it and she cursed. "This is your third bid for the Senate. Our voters *know* us, Charlie."

"That last bit of advice about the dinners, it got way too much attention."

She threw the Brillo pad at the wall, grease splattering on the tin tiles behind the stove. "It got attention because it tapped into a real emotion felt by every single married woman in New York."

Charlie talked over her. "Even Senator Holliday complained that you're stirring the pot. A man can occasionally grill, Virgie, but it's part of the agreement a woman makes in a marriage. That she'll cook."

"And here is the problem entirely," she said, sighing with frustration. She picked Betsy's red-and-white polka-dot headband off the floor, setting it on the counter. "As for my other columns, they're simply asking why we still do things the way our parents did. Dr. Spock, for example, believes fathers need to be involved in their children's lives, so I repeated his advice. It's not an earth-shattering idea that a father attend a parent-teacher conference." That had been one of her most widely read columns.

"Oh, dear Jesus," he said. "We need to move beyond this. I see all of your points, my love, I do, but I need you back at my side these next few months. I can't run for office with a wife throwing fireworks into the sky over my head."

Virgie unwrapped her robe, a patch of heat forming up her neck. She grabbed a glass of water and guzzled it down as Charlie kept on about how maybe they could discuss her revisiting the column after November's election, maybe next spring. When she closed her eyes, all she could see were her girls. How she was raising three young women in a world where a husband could call a newspaper and demand his wife's column be canceled. How one of her girls might one day be a woman standing in this very kitchen feeling a sense of loss over something she wasn't sure she ever had: equity. Charlie didn't care two hoots about the fact that their girls wouldn't begin on the same starting line as their male peers. He cared only how they presented to the public, if their hair was coiffed, their dresses tailored to perfection—everything that reinforced his image as the great American senator from New York.

"Don't call me for a while, Charlie." Virgie was pretending to be brave, but her hands were trembling so much she struggled to seal the pancake mix. She'd loved Charlie since she was twenty. How had they gotten to a place where she resented him so much that she wanted to erase him with Wite-Out secretary paint? Marriage could unravel like a thread in fabric, unspooling so quickly you couldn't figure out what it used to look like at all.

"Virgie. Come home to me. You know I don't sleep good without you here."

She slammed down the phone, lifting the handpiece and slamming it down again. She didn't notice how much noise she'd made until Louisa's voice carried out beside her; her white knitted socks pulled up to her knees. "Is everything okay?"

Virgie flinched. She wouldn't cry. She would show her daughters only strength. One day they might be in as much pain as she was now, and she wanted them to know how to bear it. Virgie forced herself to stand straighter, turning to wipe down the counters she'd already shined.

"I'm sorry you had to hear that, darling. Daddy and I are just having a little disagreement."

Louisa took the rag from her mother, wiping the kitchen table. "He doesn't want you to write anymore?"

It wasn't something you could tick off on a grocery list, and Virgie seethed at the fact that Charlie thought it was. "No one can stop a writer from writing, honey. No one can stop anyone from doing anything at all."

But it wasn't true, was it? This decision wasn't hers to make.

A part of Virgie wanted to ring Mrs. Betsy Talbot Blackwell at *Mademoiselle*, but she was too proud for that kind of phone call. What would she even say? That she wanted to write for her again, nearly twenty years later, since her husband had canceled the one thing that brought Virgie personal satisfaction, other than mothering her three girls. She and the editor-in-chief had kept in loose touch since Virgie was a guest editor at the magazine in 1947 when she was twenty. She'd worked twelve-hour days then, and Blackwell had favored her among the eleven other college editors for her work ethic and unique voice, which Blackwell said evoked a modern perspective.

"It's not only how you write that gets a reader, but the worldview you share with them," Blackwell typed on *Mademoiselle* stationery last year in response to a letter Virgie had sent to share news of the Dear Virgie column. "Do you remember the 'About Town' story where you spent an evening with Ernest Hemingway at the Grand Central Oyster Bar, showing his chauvinism without uttering one judgment of him? Use that same clever eye, and you will succeed."

Virgie and Charlie began dating a few months before she started at *Mademoiselle*. She was sitting on the steps of the campus library at Columbia eating a cream cheese and jelly sandwich in the sunshine when she'd noticed a gentleman with a soft pomade wave in his hair sitting nearby. He smiled at her, waved a friendly hello, and she waved back, then darted her eyes away, focusing on a point in the distance. She sensed him edging closer a few inches at a time, and once he was beside her, she said, "Hello," noting that his cheekbones were chiseled but his suspenders goofy and unfashionable. He was holding a legal notepad, his writings filling an entire page, and he set it down, introducing himself.

"I'm Charlie Whiting, a graduate student at the Divinity school."

"Nice to meet you, Charlie Whiting. I'm Virgie. I go to Barnard."

A divinity student? She liked the thoughtful nature that implied. He was cheery and curious and more than handsome, wanting to know at once: What was she studying? Did she like her classes? Where was she from, and what kind of music did she listen to? Every time she answered, he seemed delighted by what she said. She giggled with nerves—mostly because she could imagine moving through the world on his arm.

"What kind of music do I like? I dunno, jazz."

He'd blinked twice, then grinned. "I play alto sax in a jazz band at Sonny's on 125th. Will you come see us Friday night?"

She brought a gaggle of girlfriends with her into the smoky underground club with its red velvet curtains and small stage, Virgie feeling incredibly grown-up sneaking in underaged with her patent leather heels and bright red lipstick. When Charlie finished the two sets, they left hand in hand, him giving her his wool trench coat as they walked the city on foot for hours, talking about their favorite spots on campus and what they wanted to do with their lives, ending up at an overlook to watch the George Washington Bridge at dawn. He said he wanted to run for office someday; she wanted to write. That's when he'd lifted a lock of wavy hair off her face and said, "I've never met anyone like you." He kissed her softly, then passionately, and Virgie grew so lost in his adoration that she wasn't sure she'd ever find her way home.

She supposed that was the moment he became her home, parking herself square in his heart and he in hers.

Two years passed. By then, Charlie's interests shifted entirely to politics and he was an upstart in the New York mayor's office. They'd meet after work at Tate's on Second, a cheap watering hole where they'd munch on peanuts and watch the city whiz by, longing someday to take charge of the blur. Charlie talked about the mayor's mistakes; Virgie, full-time at the magazine since graduation, outlined her dreams for climbing the masthead. When Virgie thought of herself in those years, she saw her pinned blond hair and column of pearls, her square-shouldered jacket and skirt below the knee, everything about her riding the wave of possibility, everyone jubilant that the war years were over, and life had returned to something special.

Her first real assignment for the magazine had been a story about the uptick in designers launching sophisticated trouser lines. She'd titled it: "A Wardrobe Staple Women Actually Want to Wear," which Blackwell told her was "clever." She wrote about a suffragette named Tilly Fowler and a story about the mysterious disappearance of a finance tycoon's wife in Newport. Virgie had just finished writing the Hemingway piece when she discovered she was pregnant with Louisa. She'd told Charlie the news in a booth at Tate's, sipping water, her stomach a swirl of nausea and nerves.

Charlie loosened his necktie and stared into her eyes, his irises narrowed and stunned. "We don't have to have it," she muttered.

"Virgie!" He squeezed her hand. "This is perfect. It's the most perfect thing to ever happen."

He got down on one knee on the sticky floor of the bar, fishing a small velvet box out of his suit pocket, flashing her the same dazzling smile she remembered from the day they met. "I've been carrying this around for the last few weeks, unable to ask your father permission because I was afraid he'd say no because I have nothing to give you. Not even a set of in-laws. But now . . ." His eyes glistened. He could get emotional, but she'd never seen him cry. He held up a small ring with a single ruby, and she imagined her mother frowning at the petite stone. "Will you marry me?"

Virgie had placed his hand gently on her belly. "I won't just marry you, Charlie Whiting. I will give you a family."

He slid the ring on her finger. "And neither of us will ever be lonely again." With this marriage, she would put all his missing pieces back together for good.

"Yes," she said with a cry-laugh, since she knew she'd never be forced to clear an empty glass of gin from her mother's nightstand either. The past would become the past.

"You can continue to work," Mrs. Blackwell reassured Virgie after she shared her good news, and Virgie had reported to the office, even as her belly grew, and men gave her dirty looks as she stepped into the Condé Nast elevators looking like she had a camping tent clipped around her. Charlie wanted her home, too, particularly after a cramping scare in her sixth month, but she didn't give in until a month before her due date.

Even as Virgie had gotten the baby blues—perfectly normal, the nurses had told her—and she'd walked around the city like a zombie, Charlie had announced he wanted to run for office. Her last article for the magazine was written in despair a year after Louisa's birth, as she tried to eke out the words while struggling to get out of bed on some mornings. "How I Survived My Motherly Blue" turned out to be a groundbreaking piece. She'd quoted multiple nurses in the magazine, supporting the idea that the emotions surrounding childbirth were tumultuous, and gave women ideas for how to tame the depression. *Soak myrtle in the bath. Walk as much as possible.*

"What are these men scared of?" Virgie railed to Charlie back then, baby Louisa cradled in her arms. "That women aren't going to have babies anymore? My article was to help people."

"Your writing is so vivid, Virgie," Charlie had said. "Your article scared the hell out of me. I didn't even know a woman could feel that low."

The final time that Mrs. Blackwell tried to lure Virgie back to the magazine as a staff writer was over lunch at Barnaby's. She'd given her the name of a wonderful day care that was near the office and encouraged her to drop off Louisa and her second baby, Aggie, with her tuft of blond peach fuzz, in the morning; a wonderful team of elderly Irish women would care for the children like their own.

"I'll think about it," Virgie had said, and she had, but then Charlie had entered the race for congressman of the first district. From that point on, everything about their lives revolved around his campaigns. How frustrated he'd been as a young congressman four years later when they'd accidentally gotten pregnant with their third, Betsy, the year he ran in a special election for the empty Senate seat. But it turned out that having a pregnant wife on the campaign trail (and then a new baby girl) only helped cement his image as a clean-cut family man who was bringing morals and progressive change to the great state of New York. He won the Senate seat handily in 1955, and he'd won again in 1959. Now he was up for election once more, and rather than helping his chances, Virgie was being told she was ruining them.

For the next couple of days on the island, Virgie tried to get accustomed to the new normal, a summer devoted to raising the girls on her own, avoiding Charlie, and not making too much of a fuss about her canceled column, even if she felt resentment building like the rising tide. She tried to find joy in subversive moments, like looking at Betsy right now. The bottoms of her feet were black, and Virgie wished Charlie could see how out of place her hair was, how she had a smear of dirt up her cheek from playing. She'd been constructing a fort in a corner of the yard with her friend James, the paperboy who called for her that morning after he finished his route. Every ounce of pretension—of little girls playing in pretty sunrooms in party dresses—had been left behind in Washington. Her girls had a week before sailing camp started, and Virgie sat on the Adirondack chair in the grass watching the kids play.

Last night she'd woken at exactly 3:08 a.m. for her nightly tossing and turning. She gazed at the inky water, the moon casting a spotlight across the surface of the sea. If Charlie was going to go as low as he had, what did that mean for their marriage? Did he even love her anymore? Not only that, how could you claim to love someone if you weren't concerned about hurting them? Virgie couldn't exactly call her editor and say it was a terrible misunderstanding and ask for her column back; men sided with men. Maybe she should continue to write it, collecting a stack of back columns to submit after the election.

Or she could accept defeat and move on.

"Spray us with the hose, Mommy." Betsy jumped over an inflated beach ball, her bangs arranged haphazardly behind her headband (she'd trimmed them herself in the mirror last week), with James following, the two of them belly laughing as they tried to evade Virgie, who got up to run after them. She pointed the hose directly at the two kids, laughing as she sprayed.

Suddenly, Virgie wanted to go to the ocean. She needed to see the light feathering the waves, and she rallied Betsy and James to pack up the beach stuff. Wiping her grass-wet feet on the mat at the back door, Virgie clambered up the staircase to Louisa's bedroom, finding her eldest daughter sitting up in her twin bed in a jumper and knee socks. A Beatles record played on the turntable as her daughter seemingly gazed at the walls, a pen and notebook at her side. It was a mystery sometimes what her eldest daughter did all day in her bedroom.

"It's like a cave in here." Virgie pulled the thick drapes open, sunlight pouring into the bedroom. She had little patience for dark teenage moods. "Get your bathing suit on, honey. We're going to Katama."

"Mom, I'm in the middle of something," Louisa said, jumping up and lifting the needle on her turntable. "You can't just start making demands on me."

"Actually, honey, I can make demands on you." Virgie opened the top drawer of her daughter's white wicker dresser, lifting out her favorite striped bathing suit and tossing it to Louisa. "C'mon, scoot."

"I'm old enough to stay here alone." Louisa tapped her pen against her hairless thigh, clean and smooth since she'd started using Wisk hair removal cream a few years before. How much younger Louisa had seemed then. Even last summer, the girls had lined up shells on their bedroom windowsills as a form of decoration, and they were still there: clamshells, oysters, slipper shells.

"I know you're old enough, and I leave you alone all the time, but right now, we're going to the beach."

Louisa threw her pen at the blanket. "Well, don't expect me to swim. I'm not putting my suit on."

After calling her name through the house, Virgie discovered Aggie on the front porch in a white wicker chair, her legs draped over the peeling arm, a sketchbook balanced in her lap. She'd drawn in detail a basketball court, a full roster of players symbolized by small circles, with arrows arranging them in various plays. It was lovely if it didn't portend a conversation Virgie was tired of having.

"Can you go get your bathing suit on? We're headed to Katama." Of all the Whiting women, Aggie was the one you'd look to if you needed saving from a rip current; her muscles pulled at the water with the strength of an Olympian.

Aggie shaded the free throw line. "I just don't get why I can't play, Mom."

"Oh, Agatha, I'm not sure how much clearer we can be. Your father said no, I said no, and our answers aren't going to change." Virgie should have known that forbidding her daughter from joining the private Bethesda–Chevy Chase women's basketball team would only deepen Aggie's desire to play. The idea had felt like a Dear Virgie column, and before everything with Charlie unraveled, she'd planned to propose the idea to her editor: Virgie would pen a fake letter from a mother feeling frustrated that her daughter was insisting on playing a sport that was rough and physical, and then Virgie would respond with step-by-step advice on how to disengage from a power struggle with your daughter. First: rather than emphasizing what she can't do, find something else for her to focus on.

But alas, Virgie would never see that column in print. She'd no longer run to the front door for Sunday's edition of the paper, smelling the newsprint before she saw her byline, opening to the Styles page, where she'd find a small square photo of herself running beside the Dear Virgie logo. She had been so angry with Charlie in these last few days that Virgie hadn't had a moment to grieve the column. Now it hit her square in the chest, the weight of it like a ferry boat plowing right over her. *All to protect his campaign.*

Virgie still had to pack the thermos with ice water; she hoped Louisa was gathering the towels. The day felt like it was slipping away from her, or maybe it was that her life was slipping away. "Why is it so hard to get us to the beach?" she hollered at Aggie, louder than she'd intended. "It's eighty-five degrees out and your cheeks look as red as strawberries. The ocean will cool you down."

All last winter, Aggie had begged her parents to let her try out for the team—she'd sat in Charlie's study in their Kalorama house on numerous evenings, Charlie smoking a cigar, while Aggie tried to make the case that basketball was no different from any other sport. This was a league for girls—it's not as though she was joining a men's team. "A woman's body isn't made for that kind of strain," Charlie argued. "Your arms don't even have the strength to get the ball up in the net."

"Oh, Charlie. I'm sure she could make a basket. I'm more worried the boys will tease her at school for playing a man's sport."

Her husband swiveled his chair, placing his stockinged feet on the desk. "And what if another player slams into her and she falls on the court and gets hurt?"

"I agree with Daddy," Virgie said, nodding and leaving the study to make clear the conversation was over.

The mailman walked a letter up the steps of their front porch, making small talk about the island's fireworks that night in Oak Bluffs.

"I'm going to find a way to play," Aggie said when the mailman left, like it was a fact that Virgie would just have to accept. Her daughters made these kinds of declarations all the time. Virgie had learned to tune them out. Was it possible that she could simply tune out Charlie as well?

Thirty minutes later, they all piled into the car. The little ones, James and Betsy, squeezed into the front seat and took apart Oreo Cremes. There was a parking spot near the first entrance to the beach and Virgie pulled into it. In the blazing heat, they set up near a large driftwood log.

"See you later." Virgie smiled at the girls. She peeled off her sundress and raced to the water, diving in. When she surfaced, Aggie and Betsy were right behind her, laughing and swimming nearby; on the beach, Louisa rubbed tanning oil onto her fair skin while a couple of teenage boys shyly approached. A zap of fear coursed through Virgie. It was as though her fifteen-year-old wore a sign on her chest that flashed the words: *Come get me into trouble.* She noticed James in the shallows, kicking at the water.

"Why won't he come in?" Virgie called to Betsy, who was floating up and over each gushing wave as it rolled in. Aggie began swimming laps.

"He says he can't swim in the ocean, only the sound."

"An islander who can't swim?" Virgie stared at the boys near Louisa, who had convinced her to play catch with a beach ball. She joined them near the dunes in her shorts, a tightening creating a viselike sensation in Virgie's throat. This is how it started with Brandon Millerton. A few innocent flirtations that turned her daughter into a . . .

She exhaled, wishing she could wrap her daughter in shrink-wrap and ship her to an all-girls school.

"I'll get James," Virgie said, swimming toward the skinny child; his shorts were too big and sloppily stitched in the waistband. Her youngest had met the boy back when he'd been enrolled in the local sailing school's scholarship program, and they'd become fast friends even though he was one year older. Virgie had a soft spot for him too. Something about James had always reminded her of Charlie, how it didn't seem like anyone fed him, how no one was ever accounting for his whereabouts.

He was like a piece of tape always looking to get stuck to something.

The sun blanketed her as she emerged from the sea, calling to the boy, "I'll teach you to swim, young man."

He shielded his light eyes, curious to her since his skin was bronze like a penny. On either side of his back were two knobby shoulder bones. "But . . . the waves."

She beckoned him. "It's wise to respect the ocean, but you shouldn't let fear stop you from doing the things you want to do. I'm terribly afraid of heights, but I've taken elevators up the tallest skyscrapers just to see the view."

His eyes filled with wonder. "Have you been to the top of the Empire State Building?"

"I have." She smiled, nudging him toward the sea. "Do you want to hold my hand?" James reached for it, and she wrapped her fingers around his.

Even if she didn't know what to do about Charlie or her column, she knew how to help this boy. She wondered then if avoidance was the key to a happy life; if she should simply pretend that the column meant nothing to her and return to her status quo as a senator's wife, the mother of three beautiful, smart girls. Still, something niggled at her, a sense that Charlie had struck her like a match, igniting an angriness that had been tamped down inside her.

As the first wave crashed toward them, Virgie lifted James up over her head, feeling his abdomen tense in her grasp. But then they were out in the deeper part of the ocean, treading water, Betsy showing James how to go over a wave or dive headfirst into it.

You can't let fear stop you from doing what you want to do. It was Charlie who taught her that. Charlie who had every right to discount himself as a serious contender for the U.S. Senate when they'd walked onto stages holding Louisa's tiny hand and Aggie in her arms, Virgie's belly rounded to a ball, and closer to election day, Betsy in a pram. But she'd seen him time and again, how he could convince people he was worth listening to, how he never let the fear of losing stop him from trying, like that time in Buffalo when he'd entered a rally with six people in attendance, but he'd given the same rousing speech he'd give if there had been six hundred. Well, her column had shown her that people liked what Virgie had to say too; that maybe Charlie wasn't the only one worth listening to.

But she was fearful. She was fearful of the way Louisa was tossing her head back and laughing at something one of the teenage boys had just said.

"Right here, James. Dive with me. NOW."

When all three resurfaced—Virgie, Betsy, and the boy—they splashed each other. It was a good lesson. You had to be braver than anyone believed you to be.

But Virgie wasn't brave enough to leave Charlie, not over some selfish need to feel like she was some big important writer. That was silly of her. Charlie needed her, he'd always needed her, and she couldn't let him down simply because she adored writing a column for housewives. Then again, she couldn't ignore what he'd done to her, and she wouldn't pretend it didn't bother her. Of course it was going to bother her.

Virgie tuned in to the roar of the ocean, the roar building inside her—and she moved away from the children and pulled herself under the surf, screaming with her mouth closed until her lungs were out of air. Bursting to the surface, tasting the salt on her lips, she thought of the myriad bouquets of flowers she would arrange and place in every room without worrying about disturbing Charlie's hay fever. She thought of Charlie grimacing at a house full of kids when the girls and their friends shuffled in after school; how she was always keeping everything quiet and tidy and poised for him to comfortably slip back into a picture-perfect family life; but how those hours were never a true reflection of what she thought a happy household *should* look like: chaotic, loud, joyful. How he hated eating spaghetti, but without him, they could eat it every night. How she didn't have to put on a pretty dress and apply mascara every morning, how she didn't have to pretend to be engrossed in everything he was saying—because sometimes she was so bored to tears that she'd sip her crisp glass of chardonnay at the dining table and think of sentences forming paragraphs, paragraphs forming ideas for articles that would rearrange themselves in her mind. More than cooking spaghetti and making bouquets though, Virgie could see that there was another way to quell the bitterness pooling inside her. She would finally do all the things he didn't want her to do. Bigger things. Things she couldn't even think of right now, treading water in the deep. He would regret his decision to take away her column; she would stick it right back to him and stop considering his opinion since he'd so openly stopped considering hers.

The solution wasn't to ignore what he'd done. The solution was to punish him for it.

CHAPTER SIX

Betsy

Edgartown
1978

Carole King played on the turntable, the smell of garlic and lemon wafting through the screen windows. Virgie spooned spaghetti and clams into mismatched bowls, while Louisa carried each serving out to the patio, where Betsy finished setting the wrought-iron table with a pitcher of water and napkins. Sometimes Aggie was so preoccupied with mothering that she barely noticed what they were doing, like now, as she held the baby in one arm while trying to tie a daisy-patterned bib around Tabby's neck. The toddler used her tiny fingers to separate strands of plain pasta.

After making sure everyone had what they needed, Virgie took her seat, passing around Kraft shaker cheese. She arranged a yellow legal pad beside her plate, and while each sister slurped, moaning in delight at the nostalgic flavors, they listened to their mother chatter on about what they needed to do to sell the house. Her hand trembled as she scribbled names beside the tasks, and it was then that Betsy could see that her mother projected a brave face, but this wasn't going to be a simple matter of packing up and moving.

"We need to clear the shelves of all the dishes and random coffee mugs and simplify the cupboards." Her mother sopped up the broth with a piece of garlic bread. "Then we'll get rid of anything expired in the pantry, so no one knows how filthy we live." They all pretended to laugh, knowing their mother was such a stickler with expiration dates on food, it bordered on compulsive. Virgie put her head in her hand, her fingers pinching the smooth triangle below her collarbone, the skin splotchy and red. "Oh yes, and I have to go through Dad's files, too, for the Senate Library."

"I'll do it, Mom," Louisa said, pressing her hand on top of her mother's, and it was like a tightness in her mother's fingers visibly loosened. Betsy thought: *What a suck-up!*

"Thank you, honey. I appreciate that."

Betsy shot Aggie a pinched look to see if she thought the conversation strange—their mother giving them a to-do list without details of when the house was going on the market.

"Mom, you still haven't told us what happened. Why do we have to sell the house?" Aggie plucked a rogue piece of spaghetti off Tabby's frilly dress.

Louisa lowered her fork. "You did say you would tell us at dinner."

Virgie's face had that distant look, as if she were taking in their image like a deep breath. "I'll never forget how good you girls are being to me. I love you all so much."

"I love you, too, Mom," Aggie said.

"Me too," said Betsy, and they all looked to Louisa, who smiled warmly.

"Ditto." That Louisa was here for the week and not rushing back to the firm meant something to Betsy, and she was certain it meant something to their mother too. "So, what is it? Why are we selling?"

Her mother peeled off her denim shirt, hanging it on her chair, her beaded earrings swaying as she moved. She struggled to get comfortable. "Well, I think it had always bothered Daddy that we never bought a house of our own, which is why his white lie didn't bother me. He liked to think he bought me this house, in a way. When my uncle died, we paid the back taxes on the house and took it over."

Louisa folded her arms against her chest, peevish in tone. "So it's perfectly normal for a man to reinvent the details of his life to woo voters, is that what you're saying?"

"Don't be smart." Virgie passed her eldest the garlic bread. "Sometimes stretching the truth makes for a better story."

Aggie motioned for her mother to get on with it. At the dock, the American flag flapped off *Senatorial*.

"After the funeral, the lawyers told me Dad had taken a loan with Chemical Bank against the house, which was news to me." Virgie pursed her lips, looking irritated. "I thought I could manage the payments, it's not like I don't have an income. But then I started receiving loan payment notifications from a private firm in England, and what the lawyers discovered is that your father took out an off-the-books loan from someone across the pond, then got the Chemical Bank loan. He effectively owed $150,000, and he hadn't paid back anything."

Betsy pushed away her dinner plate. "But there must be some money left. Enough to keep them from taking the house away."

"Or the lenders can wait." The sight of Louisa chewing at her fingernail meant things were bad; her sister had done the same at their father's funeral.

None of them moved.

"The lenders have been waiting on me since Dad died. It's been a year, and they've made clear they want their money. They can force the sale of the house, and they are."

"There must be some other way." Betsy didn't like seeing her mother so willing to give up. "You can't just walk away from this place."

Aggie stood and placed the baby in a bouncy seat. She moved behind her mother's chair, reaching down and lacing her arms around her mother's neck. "She wouldn't be telling us this if she hadn't tried finding a solution already."

Her mother raised her arms up to hug Aggie back. "I've tried, girls."

The buoy bell chimed. Betsy could hear the quiet lap of the water against the dock. She gazed at the lawn where she'd played tag and trapped fireflies in plastic cups on summer nights. Was she the only one who couldn't imagine leaving this place behind?

"Let's get the house on the market by the end of July," her mother said, pulling her date book closer and counting the weeks. "That gives us about a month."

Aggie had returned to her seat, pulling Tabby on her lap now that the baby was happily gurgling and sucking on his tiny fist. "I thought you said we could stay through Labor Day. Henry was coming for a week in August. Remember?"

Betsy was equally surprised; she'd let go of her apartment in the city. "I quit my research job for this, Mom."

Her mother pushed a long chunk of her wavy hair behind her ear. When had their mother taken off her wedding ring? "I'm going to call a Realtor, and we'll hash it out. We'll insist we close in September."

They couldn't help but groan, knowing that they would have to disappear into the recesses of the house every time a potential buyer walked through. No novels on the coffee table. No dishes in the sink. People standing in your house while you overhear them talking about where they'd put their sofa.

It brought back those low feelings Betsy would get when her family moved from one rental house to another. Her mother loved inhabiting a new house, seeing the possibilities in every room, whereas Betsy had trouble saying goodbye to the place they were leaving behind. She'd run her hands along the barren walls, feeling how heavy the uneven plaster rippled with memory. She swore she could feel the house breathing under her palms, that it was telling her not to worry, a piece of her would remain preserved inside for good. That she could always return.

But she never did. You weren't supposed to go backward. Her mother had taught her as much. You needed to look ahead.

After five days on the island, the tender ache Betsy had felt for Andy when she arrived had been replaced with a longing for her father. She saw him everywhere she looked, whether it was in the hammock in the yard, where he'd often lay and read presidential biographies, or in the brilliant blue sky, which reminded her of the two of them sailing on *Senatorial* on clear, windy days. Walking down the sidewalk, she imagined herself on her father's broad shoulders in her early years, and then later, how he'd taken her arm when they headed to a fundraiser at the yacht club as she balanced in her first pair of wedge heels. The thoughts had come to her in the oddest of times, while stirring pancake batter or rising on her heels to smell a rosebush, and they'd come even though her mother had kept a busy schedule of activities to occupy Betsy and her sisters those first few days. Her mother had even skipped her writing schedule these last two days and shuttled them to various windswept beaches for shell combing or swimming.

It had left the sisters with a wormy feeling, knowing they had so much to do for the house sale but no one was doing it, while also offering the reassuring sense that they were on vacation. Betsy knew she couldn't be the only one who saw the irony: If given the choice, they probably wouldn't have chosen to be together this way, and yet it hadn't been as terrible as she thought it would be, even if she and Louisa still spoke to one another in clipped tones that made clear they were annoyed with each other. It was all compounded by the reality that Louisa was supposed to leave that weekend to return to work in Washington on Monday. No one felt ready for her to go.

Their mother had gone to bed early that Friday night, warm humid air falling over them like a blanket, and the sisters had gathered in the Adirondack chairs on the lawn around ten. Aggie sipped a gin and tonic, both of her kids asleep inside. "Is anyone else worried about Mom? I get the feeling that she's a glass with hairline cracks."

Louisa nodded. "Press hard enough and she'll shatter."

Betsy's mother *had* been acting strange, like some kind of extra positive cheerleader. Earlier, she'd talked about Aggie's new middle-part haircut like it made her a more powerful presence, which was odd because it was *just hair*. After that, her mother had carried on about how she'd never slept so well with her girls all home. Then: "Your father wouldn't believe how much the beach improved in town; the sand is the widest I've ever seen it."

Her psychology professors had a word for this nonstop talking and energy: manic.

A light went on in the house next door, and Betsy watched the neighbor close the curtains. "We should probably start packing up the house. Even if you get another week, Louisa, I know the firm isn't going to let you stay *that long*."

"It's true. I'm already pushing it," Louisa agreed. "But I feel like Mom is lonely, like she needed this time with us. But sure, let's start tomorrow."

"She's lonely? I thought this was Mom's thing, learning to stand on your own two feet." Betsy realized how insensitive she sounded and softened her tone. "It must be so hard though, for her to be here without Dad."

"It's hard to be here without Dad," Aggie said. "For all of us."

Louisa emitted a despairing sigh. "They got together so young. She was twenty. How do you live your life with someone that long, and then suddenly, they're gone."

"Well, you keep loving them for as long as you're on this earth," Betsy said, a pang hitting her in the center of her chest. She would love her father long after she needed to look at a photograph to remember the details of his face.

Louisa fiddled with her popped collar. "Betsy, why do you always talk about Dad like he was perfect? He wasn't, you know."

"No one is perfect, Lou," Betsy said. Not even her sister, but she didn't say that. There was no use in being mean.

The buoy bell chimed again in the breeze, the rhythmic sound slowing the conversation. A boat passed in the dark harbor, the small cabin lights illuminating the night like stars. She felt sorry for her mother. She never really thought it possible that her mother could feel that alone, not when she had inspired women to march in protests, not when she was a must-get lunch attendee in Washington political circles. But even a woman like that could feel no love at all when it didn't come from the people she cared about. The last couple weeks had taught Betsy that.

Aggie crossed her legs at the knee. "You know what, girls? Even if things are a little off here, even if we need to let go of the house, I needed this vacation. My life has become an endless string of chopping fruit and chasing Tabby while getting dinner on the table before Henry gets home. I think it's good we're all back together. We needed sister time."

The statement made Betsy shift in her seat, sensing that the conversation was veering into dangerous territory, the notion that Betsy and Louisa *needed* to be forced together for their own good. "At some point in your life, you will stop being the peacemaker in this family, Ag."

Aggie delivered an awkward half laugh in Betsy's direction. "If I don't do it, who will?"

Louisa raised her unpainted fingernails. "I *am* a lawyer."

"But you're half the trouble." Betsy smiled, even if she felt peevish at the truth behind her statement. She remembered then how her mother sometimes sat with Louisa at the kitchen table in her latter teenage years and begged her to talk to her father, how she had told Louisa that she'd be filled with regret someday that she didn't make peace with him. "He calls me moody," Louisa had complained, to which her mother had responded, "He doesn't know how to reach you. You won't let him in."

Louisa ignored Betsy's comment, instead pivoting toward Aggie. "Are you the peacemaker in your marriage too? With Henry?"

Aggie's mirrored locket glowed on her neck. "Sometimes. I always give in first when it comes to an argument, and I always think it's rather convenient for him." Something about the way Aggie said it made her sound like she'd lost a running race. She put her empty glass on the arm of the chair, leaning forward in her chair, frowning. "Can't the two of you just talk? Like really talk?"

Betsy trained her eyes on *Senatorial*, how the mast bobbed from side to side in the breeze. She and Louisa had been civil these last few days, even if they didn't say much at night when they climbed into their respective beds in their shared bedroom. Louisa would read legal magazines, Betsy with her nose in *People* while she fantasized about Andy calling the Vineyard house and announcing he'd made a mistake.

Aggie jostled Louisa in a playful way. "Come on, Lou. You've talked to Supreme Court justices. You can certainly talk to Betsy."

Louisa cleared her throat, but she didn't say anything. It would have been a good time for Betsy to admit how stupid Louisa had made her feel at her father's funeral. How depressed she'd grown afterward, and how low she'd felt having lost her father and her sister in a single week. How she wished that Louisa had just asked Betsy for her help if she'd needed it, rather than snap at her. Betsy could have listed everything she had done right that day, like refilled the plates and napkins when they'd run low, tipped the catering staff, created the collage with the photos of her father with his wife and girls that stood on the easel near the coffin.

Instead, Betsy said, "I hated that we had to bury an empty casket."

Aggie sighed and sunk back into her seat. "It wasn't empty. It had some of his remains, and his photos, and the stuff we put inside."

"No, Betsy's right. It's weird that Dad wasn't in there. Sometimes I think he survived the crash and someone is secretly taking care of him, and he'll show up one day and find us."

"Louisa, that's so impractical of you. They gave us his remains. He was on that plane."

"I know, but I would like to see him one more time."

"To say you're sorry?"

Louisa steeled her voice. "He doesn't deserve an apology."

Betsy never fully understood why Louisa always made her father out to be a villain. "Maybe he did deserve one." Maybe Betsy deserved one from Louisa.

Louisa made a biting face. "If I could, I'd tell him that he had everything he ever wanted. Everything he'd always worked for. So why did he have to go and screw it all up?"

CHAPTER SEVEN

Her mother gathered Betsy and her sisters in the study on Saturday, just after Aggie put the baby down for a nap. The room smelled of patchouli incense and musty pages, thanks to piles of magazines and dog-eared newspapers, stacks of neatly typed articles paper clipped on her mother's large mahogany desk. The heart of the room was a single oversized picture window overlooking the harbor, and on opposite walls, two bookshelves with a mix of nonfiction and fiction titles. Books were scattered elsewhere, too, piled on the end tables, the radiator, stacked on the floor, making it impossible to ever find the one you wanted. While Betsy's father took over the space during the Senate recess in August, it had always been her mother's room. In the acknowledgments section of her most recent book, her mother had even thanked the study, saying she did some of her best work here from Memorial to Labor Day since her mind opened while looking out at the water.

Betsy perched in her mother's swivel chair, allowing herself to imagine what it would be like to be as respected as her mother. Spinning in the chair, Betsy tracked the framed *Ms.* magazine covers hanging on the walls, her mother's name emblazoned alongside the headlined stories she'd penned: Why the FBI is Spying on the Women's Movement; Job Advice if You're "Just a Housewife"; Why the Pill is a Basic Human Right.

"Wait until you see this." Her mother opened the small closet and lifted a cardboard box from the shelf. Then she carried out a cumbersome metal projector and set it up on the wooden desktop, plugging it in and aiming it toward a portion of blank wall behind it. "I found all these old home movies that Dad took when you girls were little. He loved to follow you around, but I forgot about them until last week."

Her mother threaded the canister of film through the antique projector. "Honestly, I'm surprised this thing still works. Can someone close the curtains?" She flicked the metal switch of the projector, and the machine rattled on, a whir of the film looping as Betsy and Aggie swept the navy drapes closed. An image flashed on the wall. A grainy picture of Louisa's cherubic face came into focus, the camera adjusting to sharpen her features. Louisa was about nine, a freckled nose, a complete towhead, a sweetness in her playful expression as she swept her eyes up to the camera, smiling. She was reading to a stuffed bear on the back lawn, the harbor painting a lively scene behind her. There was no sound, but then she began speaking to someone off camera, and the gritty video panned to Aggie, an eight-year-old string bean, doing cartwheels in the grass.

"Oh my gosh," Aggie said. "Look at us. Louisa, you're a dead ringer for Hayley Mills."

"You don't remember how much attention she got for that face?" Betsy had learned to smile politely when strangers remarked how pretty Louisa was; they all did. "The two of you looked like twins. I forgot about that."

"Yes, but I was the much taller version." Aggie had spent a lifetime slouching because of her height until she'd met her husband, who towered over her. "I can't believe Dad took these. I feel like he was always so busy."

"Just keep watching," her mother said without taking her eyes off the screen. "Betsy, you're only four in this one."

The picture shook as her father turned around and walked over to the patio, closer to the front door. He stopped at the picnic table, bent down, and into the frame came Betsy's large brown eyes. The entire room erupted in a swoon.

"Betsy! You're like a little fawn," said Aggie.

Something shifted inside Betsy then. She felt like she could cry at her own innocence, holding *Goodnight Moon*, her stuffed animals at her feet. "It's Bluebell!" Betsy pointed at her old lovey, a blue jay with long eyelashes and a striped sleeping cap. She loved her sisters so openly back then. She loved her sisters now, too, but something had changed between them. At some point, Betsy had worked to keep parts of herself private from them. She didn't want them to know her like they did in this home movie, and when she thought of her family now, there was always a piece of her that felt hardened. Almost like she had to don armor to visit home. She supposed it started in college, but maybe it was before then.

Her mother pinned her eyes to the screen. "You're pretending to read, Betts. You always had to do whatever Louisa was doing."

Her cheeks burned. The art of imitation. That's what Betsy was good at. She thought of Andy telling her she hadn't come up with one original thought in her thesis. The peanut butter she had at breakfast burned up her throat.

"Girls, I know I've told you that Daddy always said you girls made us a family. But I don't think you know how much he beat himself up for not being home enough once he became a senator. He loved to call me during the day and inquire how everyone was doing. 'Tell me one thing about the girls,' he'd say."

Her mother picked up a second canister of film. Suddenly, there were the three little girls in the Vineyard house's living room once more, Louisa and Aggie holding hands and singing, when the glee was disrupted by Betsy plowing into them headfirst, then falling in a heap of giggles. It happened again and again, and no matter how many times Betsy rammed into her sisters, the camera returned to Louisa's young face, her parted hair held back on each side with clips shaped like cherries. Her great big, charming smile.

They hooted, pointed at the screen, and Betsy thought, *The eldest child really is the prize in a family.*

On the wall came another movie, a giant image of Betsy and her mother in the driveway of the summer house. Betsy was on her pink bicycle with the pink banana seat, her hair in long brown pigtails. Her mother, dressed in a stylish belted housedress, beckoned her to pedal. Betsy tried and fell repeatedly until there was a glorious twenty seconds when she balanced and rode straight toward her mother, who jumped up and down cheering.

Betsy turned to her mother, feeling her face go white. "But Mom, Dad taught me to ride my bike. I remember. In DC. On the grounds of the National Cathedral."

Her mother switched off the projector, all of them waking up from some kind of dream when she opened the shades, daylight pouring in. "No, honey, it was me. You learned how to ride on the Vineyard. You don't remember?" Her mother scrunched her nose, disappointed. "It's one of my favorite memories of you because I'd never seen you so determined. Your sisters could do it and you declared you would too."

It was silly to make a big deal of it, but Betsy felt herself sagging anyway. There were certain narratives she'd told herself over the years about her parents; she'd been forced to identify them as part of her graduate course this past semester. The first was that her father was busy in the Senate but always made time for Betsy. The second was that her mother had been busy changing the world, and she'd had no time for Betsy at all.

"What are we going to do with all these videos when we leave the house?" Betsy said, wishing she hadn't sounded so short. She turned to look out the window.

Her mother seemed confused by the question. "We'll take them to Washington with us."

"But what about the gilded mirror in my bedroom? The sailboat Daddy and I built on the mantel?" Betsy held up a small bud vase with nothing inside. "Are we going to throw it all out? It won't fit in your apartment."

"I think stuff just accumulated over the years, Betts, and we can pare it down." Louisa gave her a look that said, *cool it*. "We'll save what matters."

"Matters to who? You or me?" Betsy said. She imagined herself carrying armfuls of their belongings into an imaginary car, preserving whatever she could. It was just stuff, and yet this stuff, this house, it meant something to her.

"We have time to figure it out, honey," her mother said, rolling a piece of paper into her typewriter.

Betsy glanced at the blank wall where the movies had projected. *Had her mother really been the one to teach her to ride a bike?* It didn't add up. Then again, the video they'd seen was taken before her mother was the Virgie Whiting that was asked to speak at feminist rallies, who went on television to provoke viewers, who wrote op-eds to stir up support for national women's groups. It was long before her mother was expected to be the voice of her generation. Before she'd driven a wedge in their family so deep that she and her sisters were forced to take a side.

Because the way that Virgie Whiting saw it, you were either with her—or you were against her. Seeing how innocent everyone seemed back then, Betsy wondered: What had her mother done to their family?

That night, after her mother went upstairs to read in bed, Betsy was restless. She announced she was going to pack up the extra set of china in the dining room hutch, so the glass cabinets didn't look so cluttered. Her sisters brought in the newspaper, and they put on a Motown radio station, taking turns pulling dishes and wrapping them in newsprint, stacking them neatly on the table while Louisa caught them up on the famed Bakke case arguments about the constitutionality of universities establishing quotas for Black students. Louisa was adamant that there needed to be protections in place to support minority students.

"You sound just like Dad." Aggie rolled a crystal flute in newsprint.

"Don't you think he's in all of us?" Louisa said, like the thought of it annoyed her. "The good and the bad."

Betsy reached hard for a china plate. "I talked to him the Sunday before he died. We kept up our eight o'clock calls straight through college."

"He called me that night too—I didn't pick up because I had a friend over," Louisa said, a hint of regret in her tone. "What did you talk about?"

Betsy had written down as much of the conversation as she could remember when she'd learned her father's plane had crashed. "The most important bit was him convincing me that I should only go to graduate school if I saw practical use in it, no matter what Mommy said. If I wasn't certain what to study, I should wait until I was, and then attend. He also said he'd just had the best key lime pie of his life at the Willard."

Aggie liked this, wiggling her toes while smiling. "At least he finally found the elusive best key lime."

She and her sisters had to have talked about this final conversation once before, at the funeral maybe, but she wasn't sure now. "He also mentioned that he was looking forward to coming to the Vineyard house and winding down with Mommy."

Louisa seemed surprised. "That's a first. I always got the feeling he thought the Vineyard slowed him down."

"Yes, me too," Betsy said, nodding. "But maybe he realized how happy Mommy was here—and he liked this carefree version of her best."

"Well, it took him long enough," Louisa said, like it was a thought worth analyzing. "So he preferred Mommy when she was at the beach laying like a vegetable in the sun versus Mommy when she was leading a march in Washington? Sounds about right."

Betsy smirked. "It's not quite like that. She was writing cover stories here, Lou."

The baby howled in the upstairs bedroom, and Aggie slammed the newspaper on the table.

"This child, he's going to kill me." The baby still woke up once or twice a night, waking the entire house with him. "Let me get him."

"How about we go out on *Senatorial*?" Betsy neatened their finished stacks of plates, deciding she'd go to the supermarket to get boxes after work. "I need to talk to you both about something, and I don't want Mom to hear."

"Right now?" Louisa yawned. "I'm ready for bed."

Betsy switched off the dining room light. "Yes, now." She pulled three blankets out of the closet to bring on *Senatorial* in case it got chilly.

The sisters used a flashlight to see in the dark as they made their way down the grass and the wood slats of the dock. The boat creaked as they stepped on board, and they arranged themselves into an L pattern in the bow on the leather benches, the seams torn in spots from years of use. Betsy held the flashlight up under her chin, impersonating Jack Nicholson in *The Shining*, as Aggie tried not to laugh as she adjusted Mikey in her arms.

"If you're going to drag me out here, you better have something good to say." The baby always needed to be touching Aggie, either pressed against her chest or cradled in her lap, to settle. Sometimes Betsy imagined him at eight years old, a child demanding his mother spoon him in his bed.

Louisa grabbed the flashlight and stuck it under her own chin. "Bloody Mary. Bloody Mary." Her prim features morphed goblin-like, and Betsy couldn't help but crack up.

"I think you should do that when you argue a case before the justices," Betsy teased.

Louisa turned off the flashlight, the sisters settling into the dark. "They barely show any emotion when you approach them on the bench. It's like they were born with a furrow in their brow." Betsy asked what they were really like, and Louisa declared Justice Marshall the most intimidating. "You can see his brain clicking into place as the argument unfolds." Louisa held herself like a serious intellectual, impersonating his gravelly voice. "I'm praying that there's a woman justice in my lifetime."

"Mom says it's going to happen when Justice Stewart retires. They're already floating names." Aggie rarely paid attention to politics, but she loved stories of women who persevered. Betsy always thought it was because she'd worked so hard to prove she could play basketball, how she'd been determined to prove that her menstruating body was tough enough to withstand athletics to their doubting father.

Sitting cross-legged, Betsy leaned her elbows against her folded knees. "Okay, so I wanted to talk to you both about, you know, stopping Mom from selling the house."

Aggie glanced over at Louisa to gauge her reaction, but Louisa was in listening mode, her gaze fixed on the ticking stripes of the blanket. "It's a lost cause, Betts," Aggie said. "I don't think there is another option."

Louisa chewed her cuticle. "Do you have some brilliant plan to pay off the debts or something?"

Betsy didn't have a plan; she had a pipe dream. "I don't have an idea specifically, no, but surely there's something we could do? Mom must have some money coming in."

"Do we even know how much is in her bank account?" Aggie asked.

Louisa shrugged. "It can't be much. She's not a staff writer."

Betsy tried again. "Louisa, I know you make a lot of money, and I have some savings from the diner and I'm going to get a job this week. Aggie, maybe you and Henry can help too."

Louisa crossed her legs. "I don't make as much as you might think. I take home half of what my male colleagues are paid."

"That's disgusting." Aggie scooched down on the white canvas cushion, stretching her legs across the wooden flooring of the sailboat. Mikey laid his head flat on her chest.

"Sometimes it's even less than half. I saw a study during my research." Betsy cringed, thinking that Andy probably would have paid her less than her male counterparts if she'd worked as his research assistant.

The sailboat rocked gently with the breeze, the American flag flapping off the back.

"Well, it's unconfirmed, of course." Louisa lowered her hand to her lap. "But my salary couldn't buy the houses my male colleagues are purchasing. Anyway, Betsy, you have a point. Maybe we shouldn't just roll over and play dead here."

Betsy felt the corners of her mouth turn up. *For once, she had a point.*

"Oh, goodness. It's only a house," Aggie said. Mikey began to fuss, and her sister asked Betsy if she could hold him a minute. As she rubbed noses with the baby, Betsy had the strangest sensation: a heaviness in her breasts, a glowing in her chest that felt something like heartbreak. No, longing. She wanted a baby someday.

Betsy felt emotion bubbling up from way down deep. "You wouldn't be upset to let the house go?"

Aggie took the baby back, then kissed the side of Mikey's small cheek. "No, I'm just making the point that maybe it would be good for Mom to sell. Maybe coming to the house is too hard with Dad gone, and in addition to paying off whatever debt Dad incurred, it would give Mom a chance to start fresh."

Betsy watched the baby resettle, sprawling out on his mother's belly, lowering his head gently on her chest. She felt weepy watching him, longing for the child's warmth and the assuring way he looked at her. "Easy for you to say, Ag, you have your own family. You have your own house."

"Oh, honey." Aggie softly patted the baby's back. "You're going to have your own house someday too. This place won't even matter anymore."

"Maybe not, but Jesus, Aggie." Louisa tapped her foot, an impatient woman in line. "Why aren't you more attached to this place?"

"I dunno, I just find it so hard to be here. If we sold the house, then we wouldn't be forced to come here every summer without Dad."

Betsy felt a swelling in her heart. "Dad wouldn't have wanted us to give up this easily, Aggie. He would have told us to fight, and if Mom wasn't grieving right now, she would tell us to fight too."

Louisa smirked. "So you do have some fight in you, Betsy!"

Betsy wasn't sure if it was a compliment or an insult. Before she could decide, Aggie said, "I just don't want us to get our hopes up. If it's going to hurt, I want it to hurt all at once."

The sentiment weighed on them a minute until Betsy could see what the conversation was *really* about: Aggie's belief that discarding the house would somehow alleviate the pain of missing her father. But it wouldn't. The loss of Charlie Whiting would follow them forever. Betsy moved closer to her wiry and muscular sister so their sides were touching, and she looked into Aggie's sad eyes, noting that she could no longer find Aggie's competitive spirit from her years playing basketball. "Okay, I'm sorry, but what if talk of saving the house upsets Mom?" Aggie said.

"We can't tell Mom, at least not yet." Betsy glanced at Louisa to see what she thought.

"I agree," Louisa said. "Not until we have a concrete plan. Okay, Betsy, you start. What is your big idea?"

Betsy pulled her knees to her chest on the boat cushion, the light in the kitchen casting a pretty glow on the house. "What if we asked her friend Wiley to buy this place? That man has more money than a Rockefeller, and we can rent it back from him." She didn't even know if people did that, but she planned to go ask Wiley for her old summer job back at the yacht club tomorrow.

Aggie and Louisa shot down the idea, the baby rousing at the spike of volume in their voices. "Mom would *never* ask Wiley for help. He would have something over her, control of her things, and she would hate that."

"Okay." Betsy realized her mistake. "He's just such a generous person."

"But he would own the house, Betsy. We wouldn't."

Aggie ran her lips on the top of the baby's fuzzy head. "What if Henry and I purchased the house as a summer place? I honestly don't have any idea if we can afford it, but I could ask him. He'd only come on weekends, and then you and Mom could come visit. It would pretty much be ours."

"Only it wouldn't be." Louisa pinched her lips together.

"Hmm," Betsy said, cooing at the baby in her sister's arms. "But you know Mom would feel like she was imposing and never come, which defeats the point."

"Here's what I'm thinking." Louisa took out her headband and repositioned it. The wind was getting to her. "We'll go to the bank and take out a loan."

"They'll give us a loan?" Betsy didn't even have a credit card.

"Of course they'll give us a loan," Louisa said. "We're three responsible residents of the island." She pondered her own words a moment. "I'm going to cancel my ferry tomorrow and try calling my boss. Mom needs me here another week."

Betsy appreciated her sister's commitment, but it was also shocking that Louisa was willing to put her mother before her job. "They'll give you that much time off?"

Louisa nibbled her nail. "Not happily, but I'll say it's an emergency. Anyway, it's a holiday week with July fourth on Tuesday."

They returned to their scheming. "Okay. If you can get Mom out of the house, I can look through whatever financial records there are," Betsy said. "Maybe I can find a ledger and see what kind of savings they have, maybe some stocks."

Aggie sat up, cradling the baby's head. "Okay, that leaves me to talk to Mom about the house. Maybe she's looking for a clean break. She tells me stuff she doesn't tell you both."

Louisa blanched. "You can't be serious."

"It's like having kids put me in a club," Aggie said with tenderness. "You know what she told me? That she could have done more with us if she'd only had two kids, rather than three. I was like: 'Why do you want to erase one of us?' She huffed away, like I was missing her point."

Betsy didn't want to think too hard about the comment. Instead, she motioned around the boat, gulping in a breath. "I'll go down to the harbor and see what *Senatorial* might fetch too."

They shared a moment of silence. Charlie Whiting had loved this boat with its shiny wood and patched-up sail. So did Betsy. The idea of selling it brought forth a complicated wave of emotions. When she looked at its thirty-foot mast, its glossy teak trim, she saw a series of scenes with her father—her dad tying the rigging, Betsy handing him the sail lines, the white billow of a beautiful shiny sail, their faces turning upward with a grin. It was on this boat that a unique and close friendship had developed between her and her father.

Louisa restated the obvious. "Yes, we will need to sell *Senatorial*."

"We could auction off some of Dad's belongings too," Aggie said hopefully. "We could call Sotheby's."

Betsy eyed her warily. "Anything anyone would want to buy of Dad's, we would want to keep."

"Well, we can't hold on to everything, Betsy!" Aggie whispered her exasperation.

Betsy held her hands up in defense. "Okay. But I still think it's a terrible idea."

"We'll revisit the auction, if we need to," Louisa said, her statement the tiebreaker in the stalemate.

CHAPTER EIGHT

The Vineyard Yacht Club sat at the edge of town, a pretty clubhouse perched in front of a busy swatch of harbor. After working at the diner the past year, Betsy didn't want to serve anyone grilled cheese or hamburgers again, so she walked past the restaurant to the small beach where the sailing club kept their fleet. A row of white Opti sailboats were lined up on the pebbly sand, and she asked a baby-faced instructor in navy shorts and collared shirt if he knew where she could find Wiley Prescott. He pointed to a small white shed halfway down the beach, the double doors wide-open. "Thank you," she said, kicking off her cork-soled flip-flops and leaving them near the entrance to the beach.

She found Wiley fixing a sail that had tangled in the rigging. "Hi." Betsy waved, then adjusted her high ponytail. It took him a minute to register it was her. Then the man grinned, his face looking older than she remembered.

"Welcome home, kiddo." Wiley stepped over the rigging to give her a quick hug. "Your mother mentioned you were here."

She let the salt air fill her lungs and felt the tension in her shoulders relax; she was genuinely happy to be at the sailing school. She'd left a piece of her heart here when she stopped teaching after high school. "I always forget how beautiful this place is when I'm living my life in the real world."

"It never disappoints, and it never changes either. That's part of the island's appeal." Wiley delivered a knowing raise of his eyebrows. "What can I help you with, Betts?"

Betsy rubbed ChapStick on her lips. "Any chance you need another instructor this summer? I'm in desperate need of a job."

Wiley tore off a piece of tape, nodding along as she explained her predicament. He wasn't your typical millionaire. Six foot two and lanky like a teenager, even in his fifties, Wiley had always carried himself like a big kid. He'd bought the yacht club from an island family when Betsy was a kid, and he'd renovated the simple captain's house into a more refined, windowed version, which now housed the sailing school for kids *and* happy hours for their parents. He'd even made it more of a social club, adding on a nautical-themed dining room replete with a piano player and steamed lobsters so families could eat while overlooking the fancy boats in Edgartown Harbor. To the disappointment of his members, who were eager to network and chat with the newspaperman who owned a string of papers around the country, he rarely made an appearance. You could most often find Wiley volunteering at regattas or tinkering with the Optis, sometimes puttering around in a motorboat to help the instructors round up kids who lost their way in the wind, or lack thereof. He was beloved by locals due to his expansion of the scholarship program; Betsy's childhood friend James had received a grant to sail, as did a dozen other island children.

"Of course I'll hire you." He smoothed the repair tape. "I need an experienced sailor, and you were always one of our best." Not only would she teach kids to sail every morning and afternoon, he said, but she'd manage the junior instructors too. She'd make two hundred fifty dollars a week, and he asked her to stay through Labor Day, since the college kids often left before. "Can you start right after the Fourth?"

"Yes!" She pretended to worship him with her hands. "Thank you so much. I need out of my house right now."

"And why? Your mother is the loveliest woman I know." Wiley asked her to help him fold the repaired sailcloth, and she followed him outside to the sand.

"Living with her and my sisters is a bit much. I need a little space."

Over the last decade, Wiley and her mother had become close friends, much to Betsy's father's dismay. Her father hated Wiley's left-leaning newspaper and its editorials, which sometimes clashed with his more centrist ideas, and he often complained that Wiley was so rich he didn't know what to do with himself other than pick apart well-meaning political campaigns. Nothing her father said made her and her sisters dislike Wiley though—just like all the other kids at the yacht club, Betsy had always adored him.

"You promise you'll only assign me the good kids, right?"

Wiley stacked the sail onto a pile of other folded ones in the corner of the shed. "I will do no such thing. You and James drove our instructors bonkers." Wiley waved at someone behind Betsy. "Well, look who it is."

She glanced to the side, assuming he was speaking of one of the kids, but this person was taller, older. Betsy pivoted to say hello, her mouth agape when she realized who it was. Nothing but three feet of sand between them. Her eye lingered, cataloging. It was James Sunday, and he looked the same if you didn't count how tousled and wispy his hair was now. The same boyish face, his brows thick but never bushy, the same golden skin tone and bashful smile.

Her cheeks blazed. She hadn't expected to see James since they lost touch years ago, theirs a distance formed less by brutal heartbreak and more of a petering out. It had always bothered her that he had seemed to move on before she had. "Hi," she managed.

"Hi." His eyes grew curious. "I didn't know you were on the island." At that, he glanced at Wiley, who held up his hands like he was innocent.

"My mom needed me to come home." Betsy was talking with her hands now, too, thanks to a nervous tic of hers. "I'm going to teach sailing again. Right here. With Wiley."

Betsy could see everything in James that she had seen at sixteen. The boy with the halo over his head, a heart full of empathy, and long curling eyelashes.

"You look exactly the same," he said, taking a step back. He motioned to her shorts, his cheek registering a faint twitch while his voice sounded light. "I see you're still making your own cutoffs."

That he knew her that well made her want to hug him. She smiled. "I could make better jeans than Gloria Vanderbilt." Her mind raced for things to say. "All I need is a good pair of shears. What are you doing on the island? I didn't think you lived here anymore."

She'd heard through the grapevine that James had moved to California a few years back after his mother died. A lump formed in her throat, a flash of shame spreading down to her fingertips. Why hadn't she sent him a condolence card? She had been too eager to please her father, who'd always disapproved of her relationship with James, but she should have sent James a note anyway. When her father died, they'd received thousands of letters from well-wishers, and reading them had been critical to Betsy's grieving.

"Yes, well, the house is in between renters. I figured there's nothing like an East Coast summer," he said. James wore Nike sneakers and a soft gray T-shirt with BERKELEY printed on the pocket. His cheeks had lost the extra pinch of fat, and he looked chiseled now, like the guy who sang "Born to Run." Bruce Springsteen! James resembled Springsteen, and he stood before her now like he no longer carried the whole world on his back.

"I can't believe you really left." She let her voice cool from its earlier high pitch, looking about for Wiley, but he'd gone down the beach to one of the pint-sized sailboats carrying a can of paint. "I thought you'd always be an islander."

"So did your father." He shifted his weight onto his other canvas sneaker. The accusation silenced Betsy, and with her eye on a passing seagull, she thought about ending the conversation there. Then he continued. "The Realtors are telling me I can get a better price renting with the success of *Jaws* and all, so I'm fixing it up."

"That's what I've heard, real estate prices have skyrocketed." Why were they talking about houses? The last time they were together they were sneaking out of them. "When will you put it up for rent?"

"Labor Day. I figured I'd spend the summer here." He was holding a tub of cement and a couple of boxes of plain white tile, and when he realized she was looking at him, he said, "I'm finally fixing that bathroom floor in my mother's house. I just came by to help Wiley with something."

"You've gotten handy, then?" When she was thirteen, she'd sliced her foot open on the chipped tiles in James's bathroom, her mother angry with her for going to his house when she'd told her not to. Betsy had needed three stitches, and she'd been punished on the night they'd had plans to go to the Agricultural Fair. Her mother made her write a two-paragraph essay to earn her freedom, titled: "Older Boys Are Trouble Because . . ."

God, her mother was infuriating sometimes.

"Pretty handy, yes." James briefly cupped the back of his neck. His hands were bigger now, and she imagined how fast he could pull up rigging on a boat these days. She'd only known him as a boy, then a teenager. He asked her how Columbia was, and Betsy lied, saying she loved her degree program. How did he know she was at Columbia? Wiley, maybe. She asked him what he was doing these days.

"Teaching history at Berkeley," he said, and at this moment, his eyes shone, like he'd been waiting his entire life to tell her this. Or anyone, maybe. "I'm writing on the side."

He'd wanted to be a writer even back then. He'd always adored her mother, and Betsy had hated when he'd ask what she was working on.

What teenage boy cared? Betsy would privately seethe when he went out of his way to read her mother's articles in *Vogue*.

A couple of kids dressed in Vineyard Yacht Club T-shirts ran by them, offering a natural break in their conversation, and Betsy moved to say goodbye. "It's really nice seeing you," she said, uncomfortable admitting as much. Why hadn't she written him a letter to say hello, to apologize? They had been such good friends. Later, they had been in love.

"Nice seeing you too. I'm going to help Wiley . . ." Now James was fumbling with his words. He'd started to walk away, then turned back. "Are you here with your sisters?"

"Tortured as always," Betsy said, feeling guilty when it slipped out. All James had ever wanted was a sibling; he told her one night at South Beach, their bodies pressed together on a lifeguard stand. "Do you have any summer guests?"

How uncomfortable it would be to run into him in Edgartown, a young woman hanging on his arm! But then again, she would be happy for him if he had someone. Maybe she'd feel less guilty about how things had ended for them.

"Just me and my dog, Peanut Butter." He tipped his head at her, "You're the lucky one with the big old family."

"Do you want them?" She smiled, and he smiled back, an image resurfacing in her mind of James wedging himself between her and Aggie on the couch during episodes of *My Three Sons*, how much he loved when all the kids sat in a heap. How sometimes after Betsy's mother sent him home, he'd sneak through the back door and she and James would stay up playing Monopoly while whispering in the living room.

James had defined her summers as much as the island had.

Betsy didn't tell Louisa, Aggie, or her mother that she ran into James. Instead, as soon as she stepped in the front door that Monday, she was thrust into the whirlwind drama at the center of their own lives. The latest contest involved who could make the best grilled cheese for lunch, her mother and Tabby sitting at the kitchen table and acting as judges. She set down a stack of empty boxes she'd picked up from the grocer.

"I worked at a diner for a year," Betsy warned them, donning a floral apron from a hook in the kitchen. "I know trade secrets."

Louisa flipped the first set of sandwiches, burning the edges to black and demanding a second chance, while Aggie, who was up second, was able to master a bread that was a respectable golden brown. But when she cut the sandwich open, the cheese hadn't melted.

"Watch and learn." Betsy squeezed Tabby's small cheek, taking her place at the old-fashioned stove. As she slathered mayonnaise on the white bread and melted butter in the pan, her sisters scoffed that anyone would eat mayo on a grilled cheese. "Everyone who has eaten at a diner has eaten mayo on the bread," Betsy said, turning down the heat in the pan and flipping her grilled cheese. As she waited for the inside to melt, she decided: She would write James a condolence letter, even if it was a few years late. She wouldn't be able to face him if she didn't.

"Voila!" Betsy slid two perfectly golden grilled cheese sandwiches onto her mother's and Tabby's plates, leaning across the table to cut both into quarters. Their eyes lit up when they bit into them, Aggie holding up Betsy's arm like a champion and declaring her the winner. "I make the best banana pancakes and buttery French toast too," Betsy sang out, which made Louisa pretend to be a bad sport. This made Tabby giggle. They "performed" for Tabitha all the time, casting aside their problems in the spirit of making a three-year-old smile, and sometimes the sisters got so silly they fell into their own laughter. While finishing up a few more grilled cheese sandwiches for Aggie and Louisa, Betsy told them about her new job.

"Congratulations, but let's talk about breakfast," her mother said, licking her fingers and rising to toss her paper plate. "You'll be getting up for your sailing gig anyway, and clearly, there's talent."

"All in favor?" Louisa said, counting four hands including her own. Betsy laughed.

"Okay!"

"Excellent. My first request is banana pancakes." Louisa took the first bite of her grilled cheese, ecstatic at its ooey gooey insides.

Betsy smiled. "Aren't you leaving tomorrow?"

Louisa finished chewing, swallowed. "I begged for some extra time, since I haven't used any vacation days."

"It's great news," her mother said, smiling at Betsy. "Is anyone interested in the beach? If these are Betsy's last few days of freedom, let's go to State."

"Sure," Betsy said. But her mind was elsewhere, back in time. James sitting at the kitchen table eating lunch with them. James puttering across the harbor in his small boat to get his swimsuit. James piling in the car with them and going to the beach. Now that Betsy was an adult, she wondered if James's mother ever disliked the amount of time he spent with the Whiting family. If he'd ever fought with her about letting him eat another meal here. A part of Betsy wished she could call James right now and invite him along, toss him in the back seat with her and Aggie and pass around a beach ball.

That night, Betsy took a piece of stationery into bed with her, staring out across the water to where she'd always been able to see James Sunday's house, the crabgrass lawn visible even from here. When they were kids, she'd stare at the dot of movement on the lawn, knowing it was him playing with his pogo stick. She picked up her pen.

Dear James,

My professors always said that when someone dies, patients always want to talk, even years later. I know you're not my patient but my friend, and maybe not even a friend anymore with all the years that have gone by. But I want to say that when I lost my father, I realized how hard it must have been for you to lose your mother. I'm incredibly sorry for your loss, but I'm sorrier that I didn't write.

Your summer friend,

Betsy

With a hint of pink in the sky, Betsy untied the ropes and hopped on board *Senatorial* to start the motor and find the wind. Right as she turned the wheel to pull the sailboat away from the dock, Betsy heard her name. She rose from the leather-style captain's seat. She'd been home nearly a week and a half, and this was the first time she was taking the boat out. They'd watch the fireworks from the lawn later.

"What is it?" Betsy yelled back, spotting Aggie coming down the dock slats in her sweat shorts. The sailboat rocked in another boat's wake while Aggie breathlessly rearranged her elastic headband from her position at the dock. "Mom offered to stay with the kids. Can I come with?"

Betsy glanced back at the house, noticing for the first time that the awning over the patio had discolored so much in the sun that the stripes were barely visible. "Yes, come." Betsy shielded her eyes. "I'm only going to round the point, but it will be beautiful."

The boat puttered away from the dock, and Aggie fell into the seat beside her, within her a bouncing energy that reminded Betsy of a golden retriever. Letting out the jib, waiting for the sail to pull taut and catch the wind, Betsy killed the motor. The lap of the water, the world turning in on itself. That's how sailing could feel, like truth and beauty all at once.

"I always loved watching the house get smaller, didn't you?" Aggie said, the boat gliding deeper into the harbor. "Like we could do anything once we got out of range."

The houses were bigger now than when she was a child. New money from Boston and Washington had trickled in, everyone coming to claim their piece of the reedy green shores, the summer people morphing into something unrecognizable, something fancier and well-oiled. Families with deep tans and color-coordinated outfits. Young fathers who parked big, shiny sailboats at the dock like a Kennedy-esque accessory, sometimes never even moving them. Even the grass at the golf course seemed lusher. Over the last few years, restaurants had opened one by one, each with a sixteen-dollar steamed lobster on the menu. Some of the locals, who had always bemoaned the price of housing, couldn't even afford to buy a house here at all.

Aggie must have spotted James's house at the far end of the harbor, her mind also turning back in time, because she stared at it, saying, "How is James?"

Betsy steered the boat toward his house. "Fine. He's teaching at Berkeley."

"I never really understood why Dad disliked him so much." Aggie's face glowed in the pink of the setting sun. "He was just a kid."

There was a light on in James's living room, and Betsy wondered if he was reading. As a kid, he could spend an entire day buried in a book. One summer when they were about fifteen, he'd begged her to read his favorite novel, *David Copperfield* by Dickens. When she finished, the two of them snuggled up in a lounge chair under a blanket to discuss their favorite lines. Why did she still remember his: *I hope that real love and truth are stronger in the end than any evil or misfortune in the world.* It had struck her even then how much he'd wanted to be loved. How much she wanted to be the one to love him.

"I asked Dad about James when we were out on the boat. I didn't get why he wouldn't let me go to a movie with him for his sixteenth birthday. He didn't answer at first, it was one of those windy days where you had to really pay attention to what the boat was doing, but finally, he said, 'There are some people, Betsy, whose problems are bigger than you'll ever need to understand. The Sundays are one of them.'"

"That's ridiculous. James was so different from his mother," Aggie said.

"Of course he was. But I think Dad believed James wouldn't leave the island, and he thought it would hold me back. I mean, his mother was in bad shape."

A gust of wind shifted the boom, both sisters ducking their heads. Once the wind was tight against the sail, Betsy relaxed again, the boat gliding along the sea. Aggie pointed her toes out, then flexed her feet, stretching with a yawn. "I always felt sorry for James, hanging around our house all the time like he had nowhere else to go."

Betsy elbowed her. "Maybe he just liked me, Ag. Could that be it?"

"Of course he liked you, but I'm talking about when you were little."

"When I was little, I thought his mother was so sad, but after a year studying psychology, I can tell you she was clinically depressed and an alcoholic. She needed help," Betsy said.

The lighthouse was in view now, and Betsy perked up at the sight of the inlet curving through the marsh at low tide, the tall grasses shining in the sunlight, the familiar natural world the anchor she could moor to.

"Ready?" Betsy asked Aggie, who nodded. She tacked, the sails shifting in the opposite direction. They ducked once more. As the sailboat drew closer to the old Sunday property, Betsy could see that the back of his family's small cottage had been freshly painted. There was a screened-in porch with a table positioned inside. The large oak tree stood at one end of the yard.

"I feel like I haven't slept in months," Aggie said. "I swear if Mikey came first, I may not have had another."

Betsy turned the wheel away from her old friend's house. "Henry wouldn't have let you have just one. He wanted a girl too."

"Well, he got them. He got everything he wanted, didn't he?"

Betsy studied her sister's face. "What's wrong, Aggie?"

Aggie fiddled with the hem of her skirt. "Oh, it's complicated. You'll see when you have a baby someday. Marriage just creates this uneven playing field. I couldn't even think about running another marathon—even with me feeding the baby bottled formula. I can barely find time or energy. I play tennis, sure, but my body can't do what it used to. Mom says I should just start training again, but it's not like she offers to watch the kids so I can get out."

"If Mom could hear you right now, she'd say stop building roadblocks for yourself. Get a sitter. Mom would say, 'Aggie—'"

"'You're only stopping yourself.' I know," Aggie sighed, knowing that their mother somehow pulled off whatever she wanted, and she always had.

Apparently, Betsy getting a job marked the end of everyone's "vacation," because at eight thirty Wednesday morning, she was cooking banana pancakes for everyone on the griddle. Aggie and the kids waited on their servings, while Louisa worked on her first stack and announced the banana slices "perfectly caramelized." Diner secret, Betsy said: use two pats of butter, not one. Virgie was upstairs getting dressed, so Betsy left her a plate of pancakes on the kitchen table while she went on the front porch with her breakfast. A woman in a purple skirt suit gingerly took the bricked steps.

"Hi, dear," she said, speaking as a nanny would to a young child. "Your mother is expecting me, from Edgartown Realty." When Betsy still seemed confused, the woman, who had the buoyant hair of someone who still set her hair in hot rollers every night, stuck her hand out as a form of introduction.

"You can call me Sally." She grinned, handing Betsy a business card. "Oh, look at that. My lilac suit is the color of the wisteria growing right up your gutter." She scrunched her round nose in a cutesy way. "It must be a sign."

Betsy smiled politely, her body growing hot with that panicky feeling she had whenever she was worried; involving a Realtor in selling the house was inevitable. "Come with me, we'll find Mom."

She led the woman inside, stepping over wooden blocks Tabby had left in the hallway, and they followed voices to the kitchen. Her mother and sisters were watching Tabby on the floor shaping Play-Doh, her mother's face obscured by her coffee mug. She was dressed like she was going to the bank, in slacks and a sleeveless sweater and loafers on her feet.

"Welcome, Sally," her mother said, offering Betsy a weak smile. "I was just telling the girls that Sally had a last-minute opening. Sally, I take it you met my youngest daughter?" Virgie turned to the woman, who was holding a leather portfolio and nodding, saying something banal like *she's lovely*. "These are my other two: Louisa, my lawyer, and Aggie, my athlete and mother to these adorable grandchildren."

Betsy wished her mother had introduced her as something other than "the youngest."

"I have a grandchild myself," Sally said, scrunching her nose the same way she had on the porch. "Our house was too quiet before my grandson was born."

"I know what you mean," Virgie said, smiling at the wallet photos of the baby boy that the Realtor removed from her billfold. Virgie fawned over him, then padded to the table, setting her coffee down, the mug emblazoned with the symbol for female. "Would you like a cup?"

Sally shook her heart-shaped face, a fake pout in her lips while she clicked her pen. "I do wish I was coming under better circumstances, my dears. I want you to take comfort in the fact that I'll be on the island if you or your sisters ever want to buy a house of your own."

"How generous of you," Betsy said. The Realtor knew full well that the adult children couldn't afford a house on the island, or they wouldn't be letting this one go. Aggie shot her a withering look while they waited for Sally to arrange her folders, pulling a few loose pages from her binder.

"Yes, well, you'd be surprised at how often these things happen. A parent sells a summer house and the adult child rings me before Labor

Day and says they want a home here. Once the Vineyard is in your blood, finality can be, well, final."

The woman studied the contract she'd removed, placing it in front of Betsy's mother.

"I'm going to get ready for work," Betsy said as the agent began to explain what was in the pages, her mother picking up a pen and half-heartedly nodding along. Apparently, her mother and Sally knew each other from a decade ago, something about a woman's club on the island. Trudging upstairs, Betsy brushed her teeth and rebraided her long hair, then pinched her cheeks to combat the sickly pallor overtaking her face. She glanced outside, feeling nostalgic already for the view of the harbor. Minutes from now, it would fill up with small sailors steering their petite sailboats, Betsy teaching them how to jibe and tack. There was just enough wind to get them moving, but not enough to frighten anyone new to the sport.

She forced herself to smile in the gilded mirror over her dresser, applying a coating of glossy lipstick to bring color to her face. The Realtor was right. Selling the house felt so *final*. Running into James at the yacht club had socked her with a gut punch, reminding her of how pivotal her time in the house was in her younger years.

It's just a house. She felt a wet blot hit her wrist, then another, and she wiped her nose with her hand. It was embarrassing blubbering on like this. They were going to get a loan. They wouldn't have to sell.

Because the house wasn't just a house. It was all she and her sisters had left of their childhood, of all those memories they'd made when they were young.

CHAPTER NINE

Virgie

Edgartown
1965

Virgie had never cared for sailing, and she rarely socialized at the Vineyard Yacht Club unless Charlie was in town. Throwing an informal dinner party, inviting a cross-section of local couples and Washington types, and tossing conversation starters out for the table to tackle was her sweet spot. Most of the time she was busy flitting from guest to guest, refilling cocktails and making a few minutes of casual chatter before racing back into the kitchen to check the roast. Maybe she would have an untraditional dinner party and invite several women on the island for dressy cocktails rather than the usual slate of couples. Make her chicken à la King, serve wine in long-stemmed glasses, and talk about how much the island has changed.

Virgie heard the voices of the children walking up from the docks near the spot where they beached their dinghies. As she made small talk with some of the other mothers, she hunted the group for her girls.

"Virgie? Is that you?" An American flag flapped off the yacht club entrance.

She turned to find Wiley Prescott, the newspaperman who had put her in touch with her New York editor last summer.

"Wiley! How lovely to see you." She took in all six feet of his khaki canvas jumpsuit, which made him look slightly ridiculous, like he was a professional airman. "Is that an aviator suit?"

He tugged at the front of his shirt pocket; air goggles stuffed inside. "Yes, I've been offering lessons out at the airfield. Everyone wants to learn how to be a flyer these days."

"The result of growing up on war stories, I suppose." *If he's teaching at the tiny airfield, it's likely he's* purchased *it too*, Virgie thought; he and his brother were quietly buying up so much of the island. "Are you teaching at the yacht club as well? The girls were so excited to start today, except Louisa, who is working at the bookshop." She was babbling. "Are you here for the week?"

"I'm here for the summer. I'm a kid in that respect." Wiley ran his hand up the back of his closely shorn hair, his nose his most dominant feature. "I heard you quit the column?"

Wow, news travels fast, she thought. Her cheeks turned the color of the cherries she bought at the market that morning. "Sorry," he said. "Industry gossip."

She lowered her eyes to the ground, feeling like a bird with a broken wing; she hadn't quit. She'd been forced to quit. There was a very big difference.

"Charlie felt like it was interfering," she said, hoping that she hid her bitterness well enough. "I'll start it back up after the election is over." Now that the column was popular, they could certainly assign it to another writer. She shifted in her striped espadrilles.

"Well, if I were you, I would ask Charlie why his wife giving *practical* advice to suburban housewives is so dangerous."

She bristled. Virgie didn't just give advice. She encouraged women to be better versions of themselves. A friend said reading Virgie's advice was like hearing the ultimate truth; her answers had started to get whispered at the beginning of PTA meetings. "I don't think Charlie's opinions are your business, thank you very much."

He put his hands up like someone was trying to shoot, disarming her with his smile. "Sorry, sorry. I shouldn't traipse through another man's house."

Out of the corner of her eye, Virgie could see Betsy running with James, who was dragging a rain jacket on the ground behind him. "So you're giving flying lessons? Could someone with a fear of heights learn to fly?"

Wiley took a moment to realize that she was the person interested. "For certain. Flying has a way of changing your perspective on just about everything. You might like it." Virgie didn't think he was flirting, and yet she was aware that someone might mistake it as such and she took a step to one side, putting distance between them.

"Can I bring my girls?" she said. Charlie would *hate* if she and his daughters went up in Wiley's plane. Betsy affectionately rammed into her, and Virgie wrapped her arms around her little girl.

"Hi, kiddos." Wiley playfully punched at James's shoulder, then did the same to Betsy. "Of course the girls can come. Just let me know the day."

"Are you that free? Don't you have a paper to run?" Virgie knew the answer. When you had family money like his, there were plenty of other people you could pay to keep the paper humming.

He grinned, patting his chest pocket for the silver pen and small spiral steno pad that he kept tucked inside. "They dread my return in the fall since I'll carry in lists of ideas about how to improve everything from the employee files to front page headlines. But that's summer for you. It's all about the fresh start."

Maybe this summer could be her fresh start.

He waved goodbye, and Virgie waved back. She wouldn't give Charlie a chance to forbid her from flying lessons—she wasn't even certain of the cost—because she wouldn't tell him until after the fact. Watching Wiley go, she considered the differences in the two men: how Wiley was tall and lean and without Charlie's film-star smile that made people wonder who he was. Still, Wiley had a way of talking that suggested he'd remain calm no matter what, even if the plane was nose to the ground.

They began to walk home, Betsy peppering Virgie with stories of high winds and big waves. "Oh, Mom. We have to feed James. His mom forgot to pack him lunch."

The boy kicked at a stone. "I'm not hungry."

"I gave him half my sandwich," Betsy said, which made Virgie squeeze her daughter's shoulder. She was kind to a fault, and when she loved someone, she loved them fiercely.

Aggie, trailing behind, caught up to them with a Black girl in tow. "Can I ride bikes to Junie's house this afternoon?"

Virgie studied Junie, a tall, lanky girl with short braids in her hair. "Hello, Mrs. Whiting," the child said. "My mother is home from the laundry and said I could bring a friend over."

Virgie felt wary of her daughter taking a thirty-minute bike ride to the next town, since they'd be riding along main roads. But Aggie was fourteen now, and she promised to be extra cautious. "Sure, dear. Sounds wonderful. Go get your bike but be home by dusk."

Sometimes mothers had to have faith in the unknown.

That Saturday, they spent the day at the beach to give James another chance to practice swimming and the girls a languorous day in the sunshine. By three, the group walked damp towels and the cooler back to the car. Her daughters rolled down the windows of the steamy station wagon, a satisfied-looking James in the front seat beside Betsy. Falling into the front seat with a satisfied laugh, Virgie started the ignition of the car and pulled out of the parking spot, the girls singing along to the radio, "Sh-Boom" by the Crew Cuts, a jolly sense of summer overtaking all of them: *Life can be a dream, sweetheart.*

As her foot pressed on the gas, a flash caught the corner of Virgie's eye. There was some kind of fast movement, like a bird flying right beside her window. On instinct, she slammed her foot on the brake, Betsy and James knocking their heads hard against the dashboard.

There was the scream of a child.

Now the girl was lying on the ground next to a bicycle, and Virgie, pupils dilating, didn't remember putting the car in park or getting out of the front seat. Only that she was suddenly on her knees on the pavement, scanning the child for broken bones, bloody cuts. She looked for the rise and fall of the child's chest.

The girl opened her eyes, stunned, rubbing her elbow, her face contorting like she might cry.

Virgie reached for her tenderly. "I'm so sorry. Are you okay?"

The child looked okay, shaken up maybe, but without serious injury. "I tried to get out of the way." The girl had been riding in a bathing suit and bare feet; it was a miracle she hadn't scraped her legs worse or hit her head.

"So my car didn't hit you?"

The child shook her head. "No, I don't know. I fell."

Virgie collapsed against the station wagon, tilting her head back to meet the metal door. "Let me take you home. We can put your bike in the back."

Louisa and the girls had crowded next to them, watching, and Louisa had raised the child's bike up to stand.

"My mommy is right down the way," the child said, taking her bike and pointing it in the opposite direction. "We're here from Nantucket. We live there."

Everyone held their breath as they watched her pedal away. Count to five. Breathe in, breathe out. At some point, Betsy had taken her hand, their palms pressing together.

Virgie had seen the oddest thing in that girl.

Charlie always said you could see someone's entire life in their eyes. At the dinner table, he liked to repeat a story about a woman in the Catskills he met while touring the Beech-Nut factory. He said he knew this woman without knowing her a single day, since her eyes were an icy-blue mirror into the heartache she'd had as a war widow providing for three boys. When he'd asked her what she'd needed most, she didn't say money or food or a new house. "I need my kids to have an education," she'd said, her mouth in a frown, "so they don't have to do the work I'm doing now. I don't want them to know what a broken down back feels like." (Of course, Charlie very publicly sent this woman a check for one hundred dollars to go toward her son's vocational school tuition. Photo on the front page of the *Herald*.)

Still, whenever Virgie listened to Charlie repeat this story—at one point, he'd used it on the floor of the Senate in a speech about offering grants to lower income college students—she would question if it was true: Could you really see someone's entire life in their face? She had with Charlie early on. Hidden behind the bright and openhearted surfaces of Charlie's dark brown eyes was a deep well of sadness, a longing to be loved that could overtake him at times. His worst critics mistook it as ego; but with Charlie, he was so desperate to be liked that winning an election felt like winning an entirely new family, rather than the nonexistent one he'd grown up with.

But that child, that slender girl on her bike, she'd given Virgie the queerest sensation. She had a story in her eyes that Virgie couldn't pinpoint.

Virgie started the car and drove off, a seagull flying over them, the bird following them the entire way home. Her girls returning to their inane banter in the car.

It was in the middle of the night that Virgie opened her eyes in the dark, aware of why the strange child seemed familiar to her.

Melody. Her old friend Melody. The spacing of her delicate eyes, her reddish-blond ringlets, the mole on the side of her cheek. The girl was the spitting image of her, except for her complexion; bronze where Melody was fair.

Was it possible that after all these years, her friend had visited the island and hadn't called Virgie? Was it possible that her friend had a daughter Virgie knew nothing about?

On Monday, Louisa returned from work in a mood. She slammed the back door of the kitchen, mumbling a hello to Virgie, who was preparing dinner. Virgie had done the math on how many times she'd been greeted with cranky children through the years; thousands. But she tried to remain calm and not take it personally. She'd read once that the best thing a mother can do for a child is to create a haven for them at home. It was why she hung around the kitchen to catch them on their way in and out; meal prep was only part of it.

"How did it go with Mr. Pendleton?" Virgie asked.

"That guy smells of chicken noodle in a can." Louisa crossed her bare arms over her patchwork sundress. "But otherwise, fine. At least I got to sit and read a Louisa May Alcott novel."

Virgie stopped dicing the garlic for her legendary spaghetti and clams. "Did you help anyone find a book?"

"I restock shelves, Mom. I don't set people up on dates with literary heroines."

This made Virgie laugh.

"I don't get why I have to work anyway." Louisa put her bare feet up on the sofa, talking audibly from the living room. "All my friends are off to France for the summer or shipping off to horseback riding camps upstate."

"Well, we don't have that kind of money." Virgie pulled a can of chopped clams from the pantry. "Dad and I want you to work for your own good. You're going to earn your first paycheck this week!"

Louisa raised an eyebrow, running the bottoms of her feet along the armrest. "When is Dad coming, anyway?"

Virgie had no idea when he was coming. They'd spoken once since their argument, and Virgie had been like a petulant child, offering one-word answers to most of his questions. "He'll get here in August, probably." She put the water up to boil. "Why?"

"Because it's better without him, that's why."

A few months ago, Virgie had found her eldest daughter crying in her bedroom. The debate club had won the regional championships, thanks to Louisa, who argued the winning position. She'd gone out to celebrate with friends and come home sullen and depressed. Virgie assumed she'd had a falling-out with a friend, until Louisa lifted her wet face off her patchwork quilt: "I hate Daddy. I'll hate him my entire life."

Virgie had pressed her for more, but Louisa would only say that her father was selfish and hateful.

"Is it because he didn't come to your debate?" Virgie had rubbed circles on her daughter's back. The reality of Charlie's busy schedule was that he sometimes put constituents before his wife and girls. Louisa didn't answer.

That night, she and Charlie had gone for a walk to Dupont Circle, strolling past the replica of the Spanish Steps near their house. When Virgie shared what Louisa had told her, Charlie had stopped, taking his wife's hands. "You of all people should know that she's a hormonal girl with oversized opinions," he said. "Everything hurts girls at this age, but I couldn't leave the Senate today. I had a bill that I had to vote on. Should I abstain because my daughter is on the debate team? She must understand that, Virgie."

And it was true. The world didn't stop because Louisa demanded it to, and the faster she learned that the better. Virgie had told Louisa as much the following morning at breakfast, which had caused her to storm out of the house, screaming in a high pitch: "Ask him for the truth, Mom."

Since then, Virgie had tried to smooth things out between her daughter and husband, using family dinners to nudge Charlie into inquiring about Louisa's debate results or race time in track. But Louisa remained stubborn and silent, her anger hardening.

* * *

With the smell of the garlic and lemon on the stove, Virgie could see Betsy and James through the kitchen windows motoring his aluminum rowboat across the harbor. It wasn't right to feed a child dinner without asking his mother, and Pamela wasn't picking up the phone, so Virgie had sent them on a mission home on his boat. The water of Edgartown Harbor was calm and protected, and the crossing would take only fifteen minutes each way. Virgie remembered the sense of expansiveness she'd felt the first time her parents had let her walk home from a friend's house alone in the dark at the same age.

Louisa came to stand at the window, popping pretzels into her mouth. "That boat looks like it's going to sink."

"Oh goodness, Louisa. It's a little boy's boat. An entire childhood could be made happy with a rickety boat like that."

"My entire childhood would have been made happy without you forcing me into those stiff sailor suits every summer. Why does Betsy get to run around in shorts with holes in them?"

Her daughter dropped back onto the couch and began reading *Little Women* for the millionth time; outside, there was the unmistakable click of a kickstand. Aggie parked her bike and raced up the patio steps, coming in the back door. She offered to make the salad, and as she washed her hands, she said, "Do you know that in France girls play basketball in tournaments, that people come and watch the games?"

Her daughter reached for the head of romaine lettuce, while Virgie pressed her forehead against the kitchen cabinets. These girls were relentless.

CHAPTER TEN

It wasn't typical for Virgie to pay such close attention to another person's child, but when she walked Aggie and Betsy to sailing the following morning, she noticed James wasn't carrying a bagged lunch. She pulled the boy aside, just before the children ran off down the small beach to the teenage instructors. "Honey, do you have anything for lunch today?"

He dug into his shorts pocket and pulled out a mashed-looking peanut butter sandwich. He held it up for her to see, pride shining in his face. "I do."

"Wonderful." Virgie found the apple and piece of penny candy she'd packed in her purse, just in case, and she handed it to him. "Here's a little something more, in case you're still hungry."

Wearing the only dress she ever agreed to wear, a faded striped sundress with ties at the shoulder, Betsy waited for James a few paces away. When he caught up to her, they sprinted to their counselors. He had been spending nearly every day at their house, and while the boy was kind and he occupied her youngest daughter, Virgie had started to wonder about his mother and father.

On instinct, Virgie grabbed her car keys, and minutes later, she pulled the station wagon onto the small Chappy ferry. She paid the tender fifty cents for the two-minute crossing and, standing with her back to the driver's-side door in her navy linen shift dress, Virgie took in the horizon as the boat traveled across the waterway. From this vantage point, she could see her bedroom window, and she wondered what her life would have looked like if she hadn't met Charlie. She certainly would have married another man within the year, possibly someone she didn't love but who was well liked by her parents. No, Charlie had been the right fit; the two of them daydreaming from the start that they would make a fabulous political couple, the two of them bonded in the belief that whether you were a woman, a Negro, an orphan, or a war veteran, you deserved the right to an education. Nothing about their lives should surprise her, not the Washington political circles they ran in or the expectations he had for her. What she hadn't expected was that she would ever wish she was the one sitting behind that big mahogany desk at the Russell Senate Office Building. It was 1965, and women were talking about starting an organization for women that would mimic what the NAACP did for colored people. So why was it so hard for Virgie to make the same demands in her personal life?

The boat bumped against the wood pilings; the ferry moored to the dock. Virgie drove her station wagon past the Chappaquiddick Beach Club and along the curving roadway of the bucolic island, turning down a dirt driveway where a small sign nailed to a tree announced "Sunday." Her car dipped into a muddy pothole, the springs of the tires squeaking as the car bounced along the road. Virgie couldn't imagine driving here in winter when snow would make it even harder to pass. She parked in front of a small white Cape Cod with peeling paint, a single propane tank near the front door where there was also a rotted stack of firewood.

Virgie knocked on the front door, holding a tin of biscuits she picked up in town the day before. The volume of the television fell silent, and a young-looking woman with an older version of James's apple-shaped face opened the door. She had a bandage taped to one side of her forehead. "Hi," she said in a timid voice. She couldn't have been older than thirty. "May I help you?"

Virgie stood straighter. "Hello, my name is Virgie Whiting, and I'm Betsy's mother. Our children have become friends."

"I'm Pamela Sunday." The woman wore an aproned housedress, and while she didn't move to shake Virgie's hand, she did open the door wider. "Would you like to come in?"

They faced one another inside the cramped entryway, and Virgie waited for the woman to beckon her deeper inside. When she didn't, Virgie strode to the kitchen and set the biscuits down on the counter. "They're from the market in town. I hope you like scones."

The woman closed the door and yawned. With watery eyes, she smiled. "Would you like tea?"

"I would love that."

As the woman moved about the kitchen, searching for teacups and matching saucers, Virgie took in the house. There was plastic on the golden velour couch. The room smelled of Pine-Sol and Pledge. There wasn't a dish in the sink or an empty glass on a table. How nice it would be to live in a house so free of clutter; her daughters left their stuff in every room—a juice glass on the kitchen counter, discarded socks on the living room floor.

Virgie walked to the living room picture window to look outside. From here, she could see the row of houses that lined the harbor across the way, including her own, which was dwarfed by large formal colonials on either side. She turned to Pamela and smiled, thinking the woman looked like Lucille Ball with blond hair. "Do you know that the children flash the back door lights to say good night in the evenings?"

Pamela nodded. "It's so nice that they've become close." The water was ready, and Pamela poured the tea into a simple teacup with a chip in its rim. They sat at the kitchen table. Pamela pointed outside to an oak tree, large strong limbs twisting out with greenery. "They asked me to borrow two scarves to tie around their heads to play pirates the other day. They're big kids but still little, right?"

"With two older ones, Betsy feels so innocent in comparison."

Pamela wrung her hands together and Virgie realized she was nervous. She didn't know what to do next. Perhaps she shouldn't have dropped in on her without calling first. "Well, I'm sorry to bother you, but I just felt as though it would be nice to get to know you a little better, since our children are spending so much time. Do you work, dear?"

Virgie was only several years older, but the woman seemed in need of a mother herself.

"I'm a secretary at the elementary school." Pamela cleared her throat. "Sometimes I pick up shifts at the yacht club as a waitress in summer, but they haven't needed me."

"Oh, I don't think I've seen you. What does your husband do?"

"He's not with us." On one wall in the kitchen was a single framed photograph, Pamela in a white tailored suit standing beside a darker-skinned gentleman in a gray wool suit with a matching cap; James had a caramel complexion and light eyes like his mother, and Virgie had assumed he was white, though his father, while not Black, didn't look Italian or Greek.

When she saw Virgie staring, Pamela frowned. "He immigrated as a teenager from South America, Brazil."

Virgie pretended she was only trying to figure out where the photo was taken, saying as much. "What happened to him?"

"There was an unexpected storm, and no one really knows what happened, but he left early that morning on his trawler, as he always did when he was working. The boat was never found." The woman's teacup trembled as she set it down, its bottom chattering against the saucer.

"Isn't that something awful? I'm very sorry."

The woman touched the bandage on her forehead, pressing down its edges, her eyes so light they looked faded. "I do my best, but I suppose it's just not enough sometimes. My husband's family is from Wisconsin, and they come to visit once a year, but otherwise, it's us. This is the house I grew up in, but my parents are gone."

Virgie avoided the crack in the teacup as she sipped the Earl Grey. She changed the cross of her legs. It was awkward asking about a person's cupboards, but if they were bare, Virgie could help. "I noticed James is hungry sometimes, that he doesn't . . ." Virgie swept her eye toward the closed refrigerator, the sink without dishes from breakfast. "I can drop off groceries once a week, a few slices of turkey and bread."

The woman's soft eyes glared. "We don't need handouts."

"Of course not." Virgie wished there was some way to let her know it was only kindness she was offering. An idea came to her. She wasn't sure she should propose it, and her voice came out slow and unsteady. "I could use some help with cooking at my house. It wouldn't pay a lot, about ten dollars for three nights a week, but it would include leftovers to take home. James has been eating with us most nights anyhow, and sometimes my girls peck like birds."

Pamela's shoulders pushed back, and she elongated her spine in her seat, meeting Virgie's eye directly. "Which nights?"

"Mondays, Wednesdays, and Fridays." Virgie figured that would help the woman string together enough food for the week. It would also give her somewhere to go. Sometimes a person simply needed a little space from her everyday life. Then Virgie could put the issue of James out of her mind. In aiding his mother, she would aid him. "You could begin this Friday?"

If Charlie complained that they suddenly had a part-time cook, let him. If you're so against the idea, she'd say, you come to the island and cook in her place. This made her smile inwardly. Imagine telling a husband such a thing and meaning it.

* * *

Virgie was in her silk pajamas reading in bed when the telephone rang. She picked the handpiece off her nightstand, knowing it was Charlie. They'd spoken only once since their disagreement, clipped pleasantries about the children, but she couldn't avoid him forever.

"What do you do once the girls go to bed?" he said. His voice was quiet and needy, like he'd already sipped a gin and tonic, which always brought out his insecurities.

"I read," she said, putting her book down. "*The Thorn Birds*. You?"

"I'm signing off on a few fundraising events. I was hoping you could organize a Ladies Tea on the island in August." She fell silent, unwilling to agree that easily. His voice turned cloying. "I know you're mad at me, Virgie, and I hate myself for what I asked you to do." He paused. She could hear his thoughts churning. "But I'm struggling here. I miss talking to you before I turn off the light every night, and knowing you're this mad at me, I can't even focus on the Senate floor."

She missed him, too, and still, she felt her mouth fall open; is that what he thought would win her over? The feeling of being missed? "In other words, if I'm not going to come home to you, you like knowing that I'm busy at work planning a fundraising event."

"Maybe it's the wrong answer, but yes?"

"Okay, dear," she'd managed through gritted teeth, cradling the phone in her neck. "I'll organize a Ladies Tea." These events were most frustrating since Charlie dictated the discussions at them, even if Virgie made the guest list and invites, hired the caterers, and spent half a day prettying herself up for the society ladies. "Also, you should know that I'm taking flying lessons this week with Wiley at the Katama Airfield. We all are."

At that, she'd dropped the phone, accidentally hanging up, and when he called back, questioning her sanity, she'd said, "I'm sorry, honey, but I already gave up my column. How could you ask me to give up flying too?"

He emitted a long, deep sigh. She imagined them lying together in bed, facing one another and Charlie caressing her back, whispering in the dark so the girls couldn't hear. "Virgie, do you remember the day we met? At the library steps? I was dying to talk to you. Have you ever wondered why?"

She rose to face the open window, staring at the moonlight illuminating the harbor. "Why, Charlie? Because I was the only one crazy enough to smile back?"

He laughed with sincerity. "No, it was because you had a curiosity about everything around you, and you had this open expression. I'd seen you before, striding across campus, and I envied the way you moved through the world like you belonged. Like the world was made for you to live in." She liked when he described her like this. Virgie noodled her finger in the dial, waiting for him to make his point. "But now, it's like you don't want to belong. It's beginning to feel as though you want to be contrarian."

She cut him off; he could be so shortsighted. "Coming to the Vineyard without you doesn't make me a contrarian. It's summer! Now good night, dear. I'll call you after we fly."

"If the weather is bad, please don't go." Charlie paused. "Can I call you tomorrow night?"

"I don't know. That column, it meant something to me." She hovered her finger over the plastic button, ready to hang up.

"I know, I'm sorry, but . . . I love you, Virgie."

Now it was her turn to sigh. "I love you too, Charlie. Good night."

Virgie yanked open the curtains that Saturday, the sun pouring through the windows, and clapped her hands together. "Wake up, girls."

She'd been up since six, dressed and ready in Bermuda shorts and a flowy blouse, her hair tied up into a French twist, so it wouldn't blow into her eyes. "I have a surprise for all of you, and it involves the friendly skies."

It had been nearly impossible to keep the flying lessons a secret, but she mostly had, even as Pamela reported to the Whiting residence last night to prepare her first supper. She'd rather sloppily slathered chicken legs in barbecue sauce and baked them in the oven, then followed a recipe for potato salad, which turned out to be too salty, but still, it had been nice having another adult around. While the woman washed the plates and glasses from dinner, Virgie caught up on laundry. The evening was warm and still without darkness, and James and Betsy played tag alongside the occasional firefly. Every several minutes, the boy came into the kitchen, the room alight with the glow of an orangey-pink sunset. "Are you all right?" he'd ask his mother, to which Pamela would pat his back and wave him along.

"Come on, girls!" Virgie pulled the blankets off Louisa, exposing bare feet and calves jutting out from a pink cotton nightgown.

Louisa smacked a pillow over her head. "I'm sleeping, and I have to work today!"

What a waste of time sleep could be! There was so much life to be lived, and today was a prime example. "Louisa, you don't work until two in the afternoon, and it's only seven in the morning. Do you know what we're doing today? We're going up in an airplane. We are flying a real-life plane!"

Aggie had climbed out of bed moments before and stood brushing her teeth while leaning against the doorjamb, her expression unenthused. "A plane. What plane?"

"It's an old war biplane." Virgie couldn't believe everyone wasn't squealing. "Agatha, you must be thrilled. This is up your alley."

Aggie ran to the bathroom to spit, then waltzed back. "Where are we flying to?"

"Up and over the water, maybe a circle around the island."

Aggie clasped her hands together in prayer. "Oh, Mommy! Maybe we can fly home to Washington, and I can see my friends?" she pleaded like she was asking to see a movie.

Virgie didn't want to kill the mood, so she tried to appease her. "Well, not on your first day, but maybe you can work up to that."

Betsy scampered in, her wild hair making clear she'd jumped out of bed. "I'm going to go up in an airplane. But how? I don't know how to fly."

Virgie found herself laughing, lifting her young daughter in an embrace. "Wiley is teaching us. Today is our first lesson."

"Wiley?" The word rolled off Louisa's tongue like sour lemon.

"Yes, he's giving us a great price to try it out, so let's be grateful."

"You could get locked up for taking kids in an airplane, but okay. I'll try it." Louisa sifted through her clothes without looking up.

"Yes! I knew you girls would be excited." Virgie gave her eldest daughter a hug that went unreturned. She wondered if Louisa would ever look at her like she did when she was young, like Virgie was the only person in the world that mattered. Or if Louisa would ever willingly spend time with her again, rather than begrudgingly doing so. "Wiley said to bring a sweatshirt. It might be cold up there."

They drove the farm roads to the airfield, a grassy expanse adjacent to the powdery sands of South Beach. Wiley, waving as they pulled into the dirt lot, leaned over the cockpit of a black shiny plane with two white stripes on the wings. He hopped down the steps. "Hi, everyone. Welcome," he said, pulling off his leather gloves. He put his hands on his hips, the sun turning his center part golden. "Hello, Virgie."

She pressed the front pleats of her shorts flat. "Hi. We're so excited, a little nervous too." Heat flushed up her neck as she sensed Louisa's eyes pinned to her. Virgie didn't know what to do with her hands. Finally, she rested them on Betsy's shoulders.

The Katama Airfield wasn't so much an airport as a small shed to get out of the sun, and beside that, a row of a half dozen other small private planes.

Betsy raised her hand. "Wiley, isn't this the plane that does circles over the ocean sometimes?"

"Yes, but I won't do anything like that with you." He fastened the top button on his gray air suit. "Our ride will be nice and smooth. We'll see a bit of the island too."

Aggie stopped biting her nails. "You can do rolls with me in the plane."

"Your father may kill me." He folded his arms over the pocket on his chest. "No, today we're going to stick to the basics, and if you seem confident enough, I'll let you steer."

The girls followed him to the plane, and he showed them where they'd be sitting, pointing out the functionality of each circular dial. He held up a small bag of ginger chews, in case they felt airsick, and asked who had sunglasses. When Louisa was the only one to raise her hand, he said he had a pair of air goggles in the hangar they could borrow. "It's so bright up there it's easy to be blinded." He dashed off to the small metal structure, then jogged back and handed Virgie the goggles.

Louisa and Betsy closed in on Virgie, and in a loud whisper, Betsy said: "What if we all die?"

Virgie didn't hide her response, interrupting Wiley's laughter and pulling her daughter's skinny frame against her: "Well, the bright side is: Only one of us can die at a time. A plane can only crash once, right?"

"No one is going to die." Wiley banged on the body of the plane. "This girl is as reliable as they come." He asked who was going to go first, and all three daughters pointed to Virgie.

"How do you know the plane is a girl?" Betsy wrinkled her nose. "James told me boats are always named after girls, too, but how do you know?"

Glancing at Virgie with a grin, he turned his attention to Betsy, as though her question was the most important one in the world. It was something Charlie would do, and she thought then how a journalist and a politician weren't all that different: both were always trying to get people to do what they wanted. "Well, women are a comfort to us, whether we're pilots or sailors," he said. "Women find a way to protect the people they love. If the plane is a girl, she'll keep you safe, just like she does everyone else in her life."

Pulling the air goggles over her head, Virgie chortled. "I'm not sure I buy that, Wiley. I always thought those names were about control. If a boat is a woman, you can tell it what to do, where to go, how slow or fast it can move. Same with airplanes."

Wiley squinted at her. "Virgie Whiting, when will you see that the world is not against you? The world is yours for the taking. Wait until we're racing like birds through the clouds."

At that visual, Virgie's pulse skittered. She was taking herself a thousand feet in the air where anything could happen, but she couldn't back out. Her girls needed to see that a woman could take risks. A woman could have courage. Courage to stand up to her husband about something she believed in, or maybe just the courage to disobey. If the world said women shouldn't be pilots, then she would prove to her girls that they could be. Right here, right now.

Her knees buckled under her weight as she climbed up to the cockpit.

Louisa crept up behind her, lingering on the ladder while Wiley fiddled with those mysterious dials. She leaned close to Virgie so no one else could hear. "Are you and Dad getting a divorce?"

The question brought Virgie careening back to earth, her daughter's fierce eyes reminding her how easy it was to muck up a marriage.

"No, we're not getting a divorce. Why on earth would you say that?"

Louisa's eyes were glassy.

"Oh, sweetie, no. I love your father. I've only ever loved your father. Wiley is only a friend. He's your father's friend too."

"Not really."

The way her daughter looked at her now, full of accusation and fear, made Virgie fiddle with a dial on the instrument panel.

"But going up in this plane, Dad's going to be upset. It's like you're *trying* to upset him."

Once when Louisa was nine, she'd asked Virgie why she'd been sad lately. Virgie wondered how Louisa could have intuited her mood—even now it was as though Louisa could sense Virgie's topsy-turvy emotions. She cupped the smooth of her daughter's cheek. "This isn't about Dad. This is about you and it's about me. It's about showing you girls that life can be exactly what you want it to be."

The plane bounced with Wiley's weight as he got out of the back seat to look over the side of the plane, then dropped back into it. The pilot always sits in the back to keep the plane balanced, Wiley had told them.

Her daughter looked at her like she had snakes coming out of her head. Louisa stepped off the plane, backing away as the propellers kicked up, the smell of gasoline and cut grass finding her nose. Virgie hollered over the engines: "Dad wants you to get out of your comfort zone. Your lives are too easy. You need challenges. We're going to write goals."

"What?" Louisa pointed to her ear.

It became clear to Virgie. Her daughters should be using this summer to make bigger plans too. Charlie wanted them to get a lofty degree, yes, but how far did he want them to go? How far did he believe they could go? "We're going to write goals!"

Wiley turned to glance at her, holding up his hand in a thumbs-up motion, as the plane jounced while taxiing on the uneven ground to the freshly mowed tarmac. In the distance, she saw her girls sitting on top of the picnic table, watching with a combination of anxiety and awe. Louisa pulled her knees to her chest, while Aggie cheered like she was clapping at Yankee Stadium. Betsy too.

The plane took off down the grassy runway, and Virgie closed her eyes for a moment in the front, whispering a prayer: *Please, God, bring me back to my girls*. Faster, faster still, until the bumps of the ground disappeared entirely as they rose into the sky. The feeling made Virgie think of her first date with Charlie, when they'd ridden the Cyclone at Coney Island, and he'd been more scared than she was. As soon as she'd met him nearly two decades ago, she'd known that her entire life would be in service to him. Not only would she be his wife and confidante and lover, but she would support him in every aspect of his political rise. Being an elected official was all he wanted, a distraction to the reality of his past, the ultimate form of reinvention. She'd wanted to save him from his loneliness, and saving him had given her purpose in their early years. When this plane landed in twenty minutes, he would still be the one she would want to call first. She'd tell him how small the island looked from a thousand feet in the air, how when you passed through a cloud, the air turned cold and wet all at once.

The plane banked over the ocean, and Virgie grinned under her leather air helmet. The exhilaration of being up in the air brought back more memories with Charlie, that summer when he ran his first congressional election. Back then she'd accompany him to factories and apartment buildings and spout off ideas about workers' rights. She'd pass out campaign postcards with Charlie's name on them on city street corners, and when someone asked if she'd met the candidate, she'd smile and say: "I married him." Years later, when she was pregnant with Aggie, holding a pint-sized Louisa by the hand, they'd gone door-to-door with Charlie in a poor neighborhood in Queens, and she'd thought it one of the most meaningful experiences of her life. The way silver-haired women in aprons and missing teeth would invite them in for a lemonade, or the way mothers with dark circles under their eyes would share their dreams for their own daughters. These women would tell them of their struggles—younger women who needed childcare help to work, divorced women without enough money to pay for food, elderly women with no one to care for them. How she and Charlie would take those stories and go home and lie in bed and talk about what type of legislation could help a person like that. Was it expanding the reach of government welfare or raising minimum wage from $1.25 to $2? Maybe there needed to be access to preschool, regardless of a person's income.

The plane turned back toward Edgartown, and Wiley yelled for Virgie to hold the throttle; she gripped it, her heart pounding as she looked down, trying to find her house. She saw Pamela Sunday's instead, the rusted-out Buick visible even from up here. Just yesterday she had seen James and Betsy reading *Where the Red Fern Grows* together in the hammock, and she'd thought how lucky Betsy was to have a friend like him. How she and Charlie had been best friends before they were lovers, and how she hoped each one of her daughters experienced that kind of deep and enduring love. The love that came with disappointment when a person changed on you, the joy that emerged when they evolved alongside you.

Wiley lifted his hand and pointed down to the lush, flat landscape as they cruised over the harbor, the sailboats looking like toys. A happy yelp escaped her as she spotted the rooftop of their summer cottage, the small widow's peak off her and Charlie's bedroom. Years ago, they would sit out there when the babies were asleep, and one night, during the summer just before his first Senate election, when they were both bouncing with nerves and excitement, Virgie had taken his hand and said to him, "I'll always love you, Charlie, but you must promise me that you will put your women constituents first. That you will help us pass a childcare tax break or some kind of equal pay or both."

"Of course I will. This is our campaign. I'm merely the face."

Wiley told her to let go of the throttle, and she released her clammy hands. She could see the landing strip, and Wiley started to lower the plane over the farm field. In the distance, she could see her daughters, specks on the horizon growing larger with every second. The thing no one ever told you about having children is just how scared you'd feel all the time about hurting them. She worried she was pushing them too much or not enough, and she knew the world they'd enter was like a hungry wolf ready to pounce and eat them up. Louisa would enter her junior year in the fall and then soon enough she'd be off to college, which made this one of Virgie's last summers with her girls all together. There was an urgency inside her. If she didn't teach them everything she knew about male bosses and male egos and men who made promises they wouldn't keep, they'd go out into the world without direction, without knowing the dangers that lurked in seemingly benign places.

The plane was nearly to the ground when an unpleasant sensation bubbled to the surface. That *New York Herald* headline from a few years back: WHY WOMEN LOVE SENATOR WHITING. Only, the article wasn't about the legislation he'd been proposing. It was about a woman he'd been caught in a tryst with, which he denied vehemently, and how his good looks had won him many female admirers. How even New York women voted for him, in part, because of that unforgettable smile and neat row of white teeth! The article had sent Virgie into a fury. It was insulting to Charlie as a candidate, and it was incredibly insulting to women. As if women voters only cared for a candidate who charmed them rather than won them over with their ideas and proposals. She could have *screamed*, and she did—at Charlie.

He'd apologized. He always apologized. Another memory then: she and Charlie having cocktails at Katharine Graham's elegant Georgetown home, the newspaperman's wife pulling Virgie aside and saying, "He has the kind of charisma that can get a man in trouble. I know something about that, and if you ever need to talk . . ."

Virgie was expected to turn the other way, smile, and move on. It's what women did! That was when she began to carry her resentment like a handbag.

And yet, this life! Together, she and Charlie had built an incredible one filled with interesting people and heady conversations and three beautiful girls that challenged her every single day. It was somehow perfect and imperfect all at once, and if she hadn't met Charlie, she wouldn't have any of it.

The plane bumped against the landing strip, the grass rumbling under the plane's wheels, a wheelbarrow racing through a mowed grassy meadow.

The propellers slowed their spin as Wiley steered the plane to the end of the runway. After squeaking to a stop, Virgie peeled off her goggles and tossed her head back against the leather headrest. She'd done it. She'd gone up in this single-engine two-seater and she'd flown away—but she'd come back. She'd always come back to her girls.

Virgie lowered herself down in the footholds and jumped into the warm grass. Betsy and Aggie ran up to her, both wrapping their spaghetti arms around her waist. They ran hand in hand toward Louisa, who remained at the picnic table, acting cool. Virgie perched beside her, waiting for Louisa to say something. Didn't Louisa realize that Virgie had feelings? That she needed to feel loved, just as Louisa needed to feel it?

"Girls, you're never going to forget the feeling of going up in the air. There's a weightlessness to it, and yet the weight of life closes in, and you see what really matters. Truly, this may be the first moment of the rest of your lives."

Using the back of her Jesus sandal, Louisa pushed off the picnic table. "We've been on commercial jets, Mom." She signaled to Wiley that she was ready.

"Not an open airplane, not a plane where you could stick your arm out of the cockpit and rest the other on a yoke."

Reaching for Louisa's frail shoulder, Virgie attempted to give her a squeeze, but her daughter ducked away. Virgie followed her to the plane. "Looking down on the island, Lou, I realized how infinitely big life can be, if we want it to be. Sometimes our small little lives don't seem to add up to anything, but what I realized flying up there is that it does matter. Every one of our actions on earth matters."

Virgie thought of how she was helping Pamela and James, and how happy Betsy made him. She thought of Louisa working at the bookstore, and how important it was that she was working, and Aggie's new friend, a Negro whose skin color didn't separate the two girls, even if headlines separated white and Black children each day. That was what she'd decided up in that plane: that the most important thing she could do in this lifetime was to accept people as they are. Maybe these were small symbols of change, but she wanted to believe they mattered.

Before climbing up to the seat in front of Wiley, Louisa turned and said, "You sound like the lady with the signs at the Seventy-Second Street subway stop, Mom."

"Well, maybe she has something important to say."

Don't be afraid to ask for love. Virgie had seen the woman holding the sign just before she left New York around Christmas; it had inspired Virgie to open her change purse and toss two quarters into the woman's paint can labeled TIPS.

As the plane set off into the sky, Virgie wished she and Louisa were closer. She wished she was closer to all her girls, and she wondered what other women did to develop a deeper relationship with their daughters. There were women she knew who forced their daughters to engage in activities they enjoyed—shopping, lunching, tennis. Other mothers won over their girls by being a passive but supportive presence in the home, tidying the sheets in the closet while casually sweeping into their bedroom to talk. Some mothers wanted their girls to be just like them; others hoped they were nothing alike. Virgie and her girls were always coming and going, sharing meals, playing Scrabble, reading—and yet, sometimes each one of them felt like a puzzle she was perpetually trying to unlock. They were exhausting. Maybe Virgie wasn't the type to bake Christmas cookies, and she wasn't trying to learn piano so she could help Betsy practice. But she would continue to make lunches and wash the breakfast dishes and drill them about their lives, all while battering herself for what she didn't do right or what she didn't say.

An idea for an article came to Virgie then. An essay called FLYING LESSONS, the subhead: WHAT I WANT MY DAUGHTERS TO KNOW ABOUT BEING A WOMAN.

Charlie wanted her to forget her column. Fine, she'd forget it. It was already gone.

The essay couldn't offend Charlie. It was nothing but a mother giving her daughters advice. A different kind of romance. The premise as benign as they come, and for Virgie, this wasn't about ambition or making a name for herself. It was simply about speaking her truth.

CHAPTER ELEVEN

James was sitting on the front steps reading a library book when they pulled into the driveway. From afar, his limbs looked longer than Virgie realized, and the contours of his face were beginning to chisel, a boy on his march to puberty. He jogged down to the driveway in shorts and sneakers, a tiny hole forming in the canvas near his big toe.

"Aren't you supposed to be at the regatta?" Virgie turned off the idling car and got out with a wide grin, still on a high from the flight. She'd thought he was racing that morning.

The boy's hair was slicked back with gel, and he sucked in a breath like he had something important to say. For a moment, Virgie thought he might profess his love for her young daughter. "I was up late," he said. His eyes tracked Betsy as she emerged from the car, clutching her stomach. "Can you play?"

She groaned, running to the back door. "I might yak."

Virgie slammed the trunk. "We went flying in Wiley's plane, and the movement didn't agree with her." There were plumlike circles under his eyes. "Why were you up late?"

The boy bent down to the ground, using his hands to trap a cricket. "Got him!" James's expression lit up—he was stuck at that confusing age where he had enough muscle to do twenty push-ups, but all he wanted was to play with his plastic soldier figurines. He opened his cupped hands to give Virgie a peek at the creature. "People think they're so hard to catch, but I know how to make them feel safe."

"You watch everyone around you, don't you? You know how to make your mother feel safe too."

He didn't take his attention off the cricket, and Virgie was set to give up on him saying anything more when he said quietly, "Sometimes she drinks from a bottle."

Virgie crouched beside him, intuiting that he was sharing something important. "What kind of bottle?"

He licked his dry lips, keeping his gaze trained on the insect cupped in his hands. "I dunno. The red stuff usually makes her cry; the brown stuff just makes her mean."

Pamela's house had seemed so immaculate. There hadn't even been a bar cart. Then again, Virgie's mother had hidden her bottles with the cleaning products under the kitchen sink. It dawned on her then why James had continuously checked up on his mother in the kitchen when she'd come over to cook dinner for the first time.

"Why don't you come inside for a while, dear. I'm sure Betsy will be ready to go watch the regatta after she recovers from this morning. Sound good?"

The child lowered his hands to the grass. It took the cricket only a few hops to jump from sight, and James stood, pushing his hands in his pockets. He followed Virgie up the house steps. "Do you know crickets have incredible vision?" he said. "They can see all different directions at the same time."

"Just like you," she said. "You have seen so much." A tender bruise palpated her chest, the memory of her own mother sitting outside on the patio of their house in broad daylight, a cigarette in one hand and a glass of water in the other.

Only years later did Virgie realize that it wasn't water at all.

On the couch, Betsy had her color-drained cheeks pressed up against the back cushions while James worked on a puzzle. She'd refused to leave the house since her stomach was still queasy with airsickness, and if she wasn't going to the regatta, Aggie declared she wasn't going either. James followed suit, calling his mother to explain but finding no answer.

"What do ginger chews taste like?" James tried to fit a puzzle piece into the unfinished map of the continental United States. Betsy adjusted her headband. "Dirty socks," she said, and they fell into a pile of laughter. Virgie left the two of them behind on the sofa and called her older girls into the kitchen. They made clear their displeasure with well-timed huffs, the teenagers settling into the banquette, the sun streaming through the windows behind them.

"What are you going to torture us with now?" Aggie flicked a toast crumb across the table.

"Well, there's something I want you to do with me." Maybe this was how she'd be closer to her girls, by teaching them just how much harder they would have to work in life. Handing both of her daughters a stenographer notebook and a sharpened pencil, she started on the speech she'd been gathering in her head. How humans were put on this earth to reach their potential, but how could her girls reach their potential unless they knew what to reach for. Women without plans faltered; women with plans went places.

Louisa crossed her long, slender legs. "Mom, can't we just play Scrabble or something?"

The house was a mess; a stack of fresh laundry was folded on the coffee table, breakfast dishes and juice glasses from the morning in the sink. "Would you rather clean the house?" Virgie ran her finger along the baseboard of the kitchen, holding it up to show them the dust. "There's plenty else to do, if you'd rather."

"Nope, not me." Aggie threaded her hair up into a high ponytail, readying for the challenge. "I have lots of potential I'd rather discuss."

"Good. Let's jot down our goals. Remember, life goals can be anything." Here she emphasized her next words, a bit of sarcasm in her voice: "Goal one. Be kinder to my sisters. Goal two. Give my mother a break sometimes."

"Keep killing the mood, Mom." Louisa straightened her arms overhead, yawning.

Had the kitchen always needed a paint job? There were cracks in the wall, narrow hairlines where the plaster had settled under the weight of the house. "You need this the most," Virgie gently scolded Louisa. "Start jotting."

Louisa drew spirals in the notebook. "I'm thinking!"

This was an exercise that had come out of the essay she would write her girls, the one she planned to give to Wiley for consideration. She'd penned the beginning. *Just because my firstborn was a girl didn't mean I didn't have dreams for her. While a boy can come into this world and his mother can cradle him, believing he can be anything he wants, mothers of daughters begin the journey with more trepidation. Because at some point, our daughter may ask us to do something, and we'll have to break her heart by saying, "No. Girls can't do that." As my eldest daughter approaches the ripe age of sixteen this year, a time when she wants to hear nothing from me, I find myself wanting to tell her everything.*

The ideas came quickly then, like they'd been welled up inside her and only now did they have a reason to come out.

1. Don't believe the classified ad pages. Just because a job is listed on the men's side of the ad pages doesn't mean you can't apply for it. Women can do any job listed, even

welding and plumbing. You only must ask a man to train you.

2. You will be measured by a different yardstick. A professor in college told me once that unless I was going to do 110 percent of the work of a political science major, I should major in home economics. He's right. Don't let them believe you won't work harder than the smartest boy.

3. Education first. Always. If a man loves you, he will wait for you to finish.

4. If a boyfriend is awful to you or someone mistreats you at work, the police may not protect you, but your mother will. Know that you can always go home.

5. Fight for what you believe in, even when everyone around you doesn't agree with what you're saying.

There was so much more she wanted to say but she lowered her pencil when she saw Louisa get up to pour herself orange juice.

"Okay, I'm ready, Mom." Louisa had been the least excited to go up in the plane, but when she'd descended, she'd run into Virgie's arms with the corners of her eyes glistening.

"I will never say that an airplane doesn't have a spirit," Louisa had said, trading her cool teenage remove for an open heart. Virgie didn't let go of her daughter's embrace until Louisa did.

"I've been so upset," her daughter had said, standing in her white knee socks and sneakers in the airfield, her expression pleading with her mother to understand. "I've been so disappointed and ashamed about everything with Brandon, having to visit the clinic and getting rid of, you know. But I'm more than Brandon Millerton. Someday I will be someone else entirely, and I don't care if he thinks I'm disgusting or not."

"You're not disgusting. You're human, and he took advantage of you, coming on that strong." If Virgie could erase the Brandon Millerton situation entirely from her daughter's memory, she would. She hated that Louisa would carry everything about that procedure for the rest of her life: the smell of the sterile office, the whir of the suction, how she'd curled into a ball in her bed when they got home and refused to leave for a week, eating only chicken and rice soup.

Angling the yellow pad off the kitchen table, Virgie read Louisa's words, hoping to glimpse the ambition of Athena, the determination of Demeter, in her teen daughter.

"'One: become a wife. Two: have a baby. Three: speak my truth.'"

Virgie lowered the notepad, sagging against the table. "I'm intrigued by number three, 'speak my truth.' It's something your generation will do better than mine." She crossed out Louisa's first two answers with big black Xs. "You just flew an airplane, like gosh-darn Amelia Earhart, and all you can think about is being a proper wife?"

Louisa tipped her chin with pride. "What is wrong with that? You're a wife and mother."

"Don't you think I know that?"

Louisa squinted at her. "Are we so terrible?"

Virgie frowned. "No, that is why I'm doing this. You're everything to me."

It was maddening the way children listened to the wrong things and never the right ones, Virgie thought. How it could make her heart feel like it was shrinking to the size of a pea. Ripping a fresh piece of paper out of the notepad, Virgie slid the blank lined sheet in front of her eldest daughter, still sitting at the table. She emitted a long, low sigh.

"Think bigger." Virgie handed her back the pencil.

Opposite Louisa, Aggie erased whatever she had written, her cheeks flushed. They could hear the squeals of young children playing Wiffle ball two doors down, the whiz of the plastic ball.

Louisa pushed the notebook away. "I don't know what the right answer is!"

Virgie snatched the pencil and numbered the first three lines, hoping it would trigger an idea in her almost-sixteen-year-old. "The right answer is what's inside you. When you lay in bed at night, what do you think will make you happiest? Think of one thing."

Louisa wrung her hands. "Making you and Daddy happy."

This felt like waiting in line at Cronig's on a summer Saturday. "Not us. YOU. Do you know that you girls live in a country where the dean of a prominent medical school was recently asked if they have a quota for the number of women admitted to the school, and the dean said, 'Yes, we do. We admit as few women as we can.' It's not funny, and he thought it was, and it was presented in a national newspaper as such. You need goals, girls, so that you can look that bozo in the face someday and say: you can't stop me."

Aggie blew the eraser shavings off the pad. "But if they won't let women into med school, he can stop me. Right?"

"NO," Virgie yelled. She called Betsy and James into the kitchen, and her youngest trudged in holding her stomach, still looking pale.

"Do I have to?" Betsy complained.

"Yes," Virgie said. "Take a seat." Betsy and James slid into the banquette.

Louisa shrugged. "I don't want to be a doctor. I can't even look at a cut on my own finger, and I'm not a good writer like you." Then she brightened, and Louisa picked up her pencil and wrote, *Get straight A's.*

Virgie put a check-plus next to *A's*, then she said, "Yes, yes, but think bigger. You too, Aggie. Getting good grades is essential. You're right. Think harder though. You live in a world where men tell us that we cannot buy a couch on credit because we're women. In some states, women who don't change their name after marriage can lose their driver's licenses. Their driver's license! So tell me. What will make you happy? What would make all women happy?"

Louisa posed it like a question. "Having people take us seriously?"

Holding a hand up to her ear, Virgie said, "Can you repeat that?"

It might have been frustration that made Louisa yell, but she yelled, "Having people take us seriously."

"Now both of you say it," Virgie instructed, an electricity spreading through her, and as they did, the sisters smiled out of embarrassment.

"Ding, ding. Congratulations. You got the right answer, and if people take you seriously, what do you want to be?"

Louisa raised her hand like they were in school. "A lawyer? I like to argue my points."

A crisp nod. "You're on the debate team at school. That makes perfect sense."

Virgie watched her daughter smile at her pencil marks. *1 was to get straight A's. 2 become a lawyer.* "But what about this summer? You need a goal for summer," Virgie said.

"That's easy," Louisa said. "I want to take more flying lessons."

A smile spread on Virgie's face. She wanted to get back up on that airplane too.

Shifting her attention to Aggie, Virgie said a quick prayer that her middle daughter had thought beyond the conventions of "wife and mother." Aggie had been erasing and rewriting her answers since the discussion had started, and Virgie tapped her pencil on the paper as she read them. Her middle daughter often surprised her, and she had now too:

1. train for the NYC marathon
2. golf with Daddy
3. convince parents to let me join the Bethesda–Chevy Chase Women's Basketball Team

"I really like the first one," Virgie said, thinking back to those days when Agatha would set up obstacle courses in the living room and make her sisters compete for the best times. "We should come up with a running plan. I know a gentleman who ran a marathon. Do you want me to call him and ask about training?"

"Nope. I want you to convince Daddy to let me play basketball. I have a book about it from the library."

"Oh, Aggie. Stop. I already told you, you'll be the laughingstock of the boys at school."

In a notebook Betsy doodled a small bunny munching on a carrot. Now that her mother crouched beside her, Betsy tried to hide it. "I'm too little for this."

Louisa and Aggie laughed, and Virgie began to braid Betsy's long, knotty hair. "Ten? Absolutely not."

James held up his piece of paper. "My goal is to find my father."

The Wiffle ball careened into their yard, a grade-school-aged boy running across the lawn to retrieve it. "Oh, honey, your father was lost at sea years ago."

Betsy added whiskers to her bunny. "James thinks his father might be stuck on Nomans, and he might be right."

"What's Nomans?" Louisa shook her head like it was the stupidest thing she'd ever heard. Aggie asked what happened to his father as if she was asking about the weather, and as the boy explained it, Virgie fetched a package of Oreo Cremes. She gave each child three.

James licked his lips. "Anyway, Nomans is the tiny island off Chilmark. They did war exercises there, and my father fished in the waters off it. What if he's been living as a castaway?"

"I've always wondered if you could swim out there," Aggie said.

"We should form a search party and go out to find him," said Betsy, making it sound like an installment of *The Hardy Boys*.

"No, no," Virgie said, waving off the idea. "Let's not mistake false hope with ambition. Now back to the question at hand." But Betsy and James had already slinked off to the sofa, whispering more about Nomans Island.

CHAPTER TWELVE

Betsy

1978

Betsy had always loved teaching at the yacht club, and it was funny how easy it was during that third week visiting the island to slip into her old summer routine. After a morning meeting with campers to discuss the wind and where they would sail, she helped the kids attach sails to the small boats, dragging the Optis or 420s or Sunfishes off the beach and into the harbor. By ten, she had the children in life vests sailing. Today she was accompanying a pair of precocious nine-year-old twins whose parents left the boys with a nanny during the week. The boys had limited interest in how to operate the boat, the one named Seth often pinching her calf, only to claim it was his brother.

"Boys, stop fooling around." Betsy pushed her sunglasses on top of her head so they could see she meant business. "Sailing is about the coolest thing you can do in summer—someday you might take a girl out on a boat."

"Bleh." Petey pretended to vomit into his hands. "I'd rather be playing kickball."

"My dad says girls can't sail and he doesn't know why we have a girl teacher." Seth waited for her reaction, a flash of mischief in his eyes, but Betsy was unruffled. She handed the boy the tiller, encouraging him to steer.

"Well, your dad has never seen a powerful girl like me go sailing," she said. Betsy showed the boy how to pull tight against the wind, then how to avoid getting hit in the head with the boom. Working with kids had always suited Betsy's personality, but when she'd mentioned an interest in teaching middle school to her mother, she'd blown her off. "Women are always being told they'd be a great teacher or social worker. Get a job at a newspaper and they'll put you on wedding announcements. Well, ignore that person. You can do what you want! You can be a scientist!"

The refrain had made Betsy and her sisters fall into belly laughter when Virgie had said it, and in their teenage years, any time one of them felt a shred of self-doubt, the other would yell out: "But you can be a scientist!"

The irony was that when Betsy was in graduate school and her professor had encouraged her to switch to school counseling, she'd realized that her mother was right. Women were encouraged into more nurturing fields. It had made her push harder in her program, and she decided she would be a clinical psychologist working in private practice. She even knew what she wanted her specialty to be: women. Housewives and career girls, and all the women in between. She wanted to help women find the balance they craved, to help them find confidence to stand up to their abusive employers, to stop letting people in their lives relegate them to the second row. One of her professors had told the class that a psychologist's biggest interests were often dictated by their biggest hang-ups; a man with mommy issues would probably most often tune in to the parental tensions of his clients. It had made Betsy wonder if she was interested in helping women only because her mother had, the only difference being that Betsy would work with one woman at a time. A smaller life, sure, but that was okay with her.

Many of my clients spend their entire lives trying to avoid becoming like their parents, only to realize that chasing their affections doesn't make them feel whole. It was a different professor who told the class this, and thinking of it now, Betsy thought maybe it was true.

Maybe her psychology classes hadn't been all bad.

It was warm on the water now, and Betsy unzipped her windbreaker, stuffing it in her dry bag. All at once the boys got into some kind of scuffle about steering, and Betsy scolded them once more. "Boys, boys! Sailors need to pay attention to everything. One time when I was out on one of these very boats as a kid, something scary happened."

Now she had their attention, and she told the story like it was an episode of *The Swiss Family Robinson*. She told them about how she and her friend James had snuck away from morning lessons to attempt a sail to faraway Nomans Island, where he believed his missing father was stranded. The sun was strong, luring them out of the harbor, but then the wind picked up in the wrong direction and they got their boat stranded in a cove. "We'd been forced to drag the boat ashore and walk the beach for help," Betsy told the children. "If we'd tuned in to the wind, we would have felt the threat coming." Their boat was grounded since they'd broken the rules and left the safety of the harbor, she said. "Our parents made us volunteer to fix up the yacht club as punishment."

But the punishment had also been fun since they'd been stuck together all day, hammering shingles onto the sailing shed on the beach, mopping the kitchen floors in the yacht club, organizing files in Wiley's office, and snooping around his desk. That was the day she'd discovered that Wiley kept a photo of him and Betsy's mother in his desk drawer, her mother dressed up in a long iridescent dress and Wiley's arm around the small of her back. When she told her mother about the picture, admitting she thought it odd, her mother had hugged her. "Aw, Betts. You keep pictures of your friends in your drawers, too, don't you?" She *had* kept a photo of her and James in her nightstand drawer beginning in fourth grade, the two of them in his dinghy while mugging for Betsy's mother's 35mm camera. Later, in her teen years, she'd tucked a second Polaroid of them in her diary, the two of them lying on a beach blanket on his lawn while reading Walt Whitman.

After the last camper was picked up on Wednesday, Betsy made her way home through town. She walked into a house smelling of potato salad, with Aggie and Louisa looking deflated on the navy couches. Louisa shook her head. "The Realtor said we need to clean out everything, and it's a bigger job than we thought," she said. "The house is going on the market in two and a half weeks." Cabinets and closets, most of their personal belongings had to get put into boxes and stored in the attic.

A different thought niggled at Betsy as she listened. Why wasn't Louisa returning to Washington as planned? She'd announced last night that her boss had encouraged her to take as much time away as she needed, which had sent Aggie and Betsy to whisper on the patio when Louisa went to shower. Neither of them believed a law firm would allow an employee, let alone a woman employee, to take off that much time. "Something is up," Aggie had said, and Betsy had agreed.

Betsy slumped into a living room armchair. "We've already packed a good bit. Isn't that enough?"

"People need to imagine that the house is theirs," Aggie said, the sarcasm evident in her voice. Upstairs, Betsy could hear the furious click-clack of the typewriter in the study.

Betsy sighed. "Well, we might as well start on dinner."

They spent a few straight days packing up old records, figurines, and dishes, each one of them volunteering to take on a section of the house and Betsy working between shifts at sailing. By Saturday, they needed a break. The theaters were still packed with the release of *Jaws 2*, but it was getting terrible reviews and the Whiting sisters had decided they didn't want to spoil the first one in seeing the second. Instead, the plan for this Saturday night was to go to Oak Bluffs to hear a folk singer performing at Ocean Park, a lush green space facing the sea.

After her second week teaching, Betsy had been looking forward to a day at the beach with her own thoughts. Her mother and Aggie had decided to take the kids window shopping in busy Vineyard Haven, while Louisa announced that she was meeting a friend for lunch. Betsy hadn't been bickering with her eldest sister as much, thanks to their shared desire to save the beach house. A meeting at the bank was set for next week. This morning, Aggie had even pulled her aside after breakfast.

"Things are really thawing out between you and Louisa," she'd whispered as soon as Louisa left the kitchen to get dressed.

"Well, I'm still pissed at her," Betsy said, drying the last dish and putting it into the cabinet they'd pared down to include six bowls, six dinner plates, six saucers, and six salad plates. "But she's being nicer than usual. Do you think she wants something?"

Aggie pushed the baby's swing with her bare foot, Mikey blowing strawberries. "Sisterly love?"

Betsy emitted a high-pitched scoff. "You know as well as I do that Louisa doesn't want my love. She wants my admiration."

"Well, maybe she wants both," Aggie said. She looked like she'd been awake for hours, in her pale pink striped knee-length skirt and matching sweater-shirt, blue eyeshadow and liner already applied.

After everyone in the house had left, Betsy packed a beach bag with a fluffy towel and suntan lotion, a small cooler with a Tab. Then she spread jam on a ham sandwich. Just yesterday she'd noticed the wild blueberries growing along the garage, popping one of the ripest plump versions into her mouth. Later she'd pick the fruit and make her own jam to spread inside a crepe at one of their next breakfasts.

Betsy went to fetch her bike from the garage, tossing her bag into the basket, but then she realized she'd forgotten her sunglasses. It was a minor miracle she hadn't lost them yet. She was always losing something. Betsy raced up the crooked steps and grabbed the glasses off her dresser.

She glanced inside the wide-open door to her mother's study. It was the first time she'd been in the house without her mother since she and her sisters hatched their plan the other night. Betsy crept inside the room, the floors creaking underfoot. She felt like she was trespassing, the smell of her mother's jasmine perfume permanently etched into the air. Crouching down in front of her large wooden desk, Betsy pulled out the drawers, one by one, running her fingers along the depths to see what her mother stowed inside: more books, letters, binders without anything notable inside. In the bottom drawer were files, one devoted to "Book Ideas," another for "Article Ideas." A hanging folder labeled MAGAZINE ARTICLES had a collection of clipped glossy pages, while EDITORIALS contained the yellowed edges of aging newsprint.

She rifled through the center drawer, finding pencils and erasers, black flare-tip pens, and a checkbook. Flipping through the mostly empty ledger, she thought of how her father had always complained that her mother didn't record her expenditures. It was partly why Betsy kept a meticulous checkbook, down to the cent, even if lately she'd been stowing cash in her top drawer; her father had sat with her and her sisters myriad times to teach them to add and subtract on the thin gray lines, pleased when Betsy's math was correct.

Betsy moved to the opposite side of the desk, opening more drawers. There weren't any folders, just a stack of typed pages with a paperweight on top. The paperweight was a rock from Fuller Street Beach that Louisa had painted with a rainbow when she was seven or eight. Curious, Betsy lifted the stone off the crisp sheets, realizing by the title "Charlie and Me" and the paper clip holding the pages that she was holding her mother's latest writing project.

A screen door slammed, and she froze, listening with the intensity of a watchdog and reassuring herself that if it was her mother, she could say that she had only been looking for paper and pen. Once

Betsy heard voices coming from next door and not downstairs, she relaxed into the chair. Resting the pages on her lap, she flipped through.

> *Charlie wasn't always the man people thought he was. His complicated past haunted him, making him distant and unforgiving at times, even to his girls. On many occasions he left me feeling uncertain of which husband would come home: the man who would do anything for me and his daughters, or the man who resented us for not being able to chase away his demons for good. I often told him: "You need to stop hiding your pain. A seamless campaign does not create a seamless heart."*

Betsy turned fast to the next page, then the next.

> *He could be impulsive at times, and he expected me to jump at his every need. One morning I woke up in our Washington bedroom and watched him dress in a suit, knotting his tie. "I have a meeting with Kennedy," he told me. "I want you to come." I yawned, barely awake.*
>
> *"But Charlie," I said, "what will I do with the girls?"*
>
> *"Kennedy is bringing his wife, and I think he wants you there, or maybe she does." Charlie put his hands on his hips and pouted. "Believe it or not, you're the draw these days."*
>
> *That was our life at times, a mad scramble to make a meeting, to get a law passed, to get people on our side.*

There were other vignettes, all of them snapshots that told stories of her mother and father's years in Washington. The stories didn't seem to be in any sort of order date-wise. Was this a diary or just her mother's way of recording memories? The information was much too private, and it made her father seem like a shadowy villain in a comic book. What did her mother mean when she said, *I didn't know what husband was going to come home*? There were certainly dark times in her childhood. Betsy could remember the winter her father stayed in his room for weeks. Her mother tended to him in bed, even though he didn't look sickly, telling Betsy and her sisters that he wasn't feeling like himself, until one day he returned to the Hill.

Sometime later, Louisa had shown her and Aggie their father's pill bottle, telling them he suffered from sadness.

Her father had been prone to mood swings, too, she could acknowledge that, but that was who he was. Just because he sometimes arrived home from the Senate in a tirade, stomping about the house and yelling at the girls to pick up their toys, didn't make him a bad person, at least not to Betsy. He was stressed. He was under pressure. But he wasn't *mean*. With someone as brilliant as Charlie Whiting, Betsy's mother said, the good came with the bad.

She returned the pages to the drawer, setting the paperweight in place and sliding it closed.

First, her mother announced the sale of the house, and now, she had a secret writing project. These last few weeks, she and her sisters had been worried that their mother was lonely and sad, but maybe she wasn't lonely. Maybe she was filled with guilt that she was about to turn their family inside out like a soiled shirt, holding it up for all to see.

The buoy bell chimed with the choppy waves. Betsy opened a bag of potato chips, even if it was early morning, and ate them by the handful while standing at the kitchen counter. Then she broke them into pieces over an omelet just like she'd seen Carlos do at the diner; it was one of the most popular items on the breakfast menu and perfect for Sunday morning. When Aggie trudged in wearing a pair of lime-green baby-doll pajamas, Betsy was lost in thought. "Morning," Aggie said, settling Tabby into her booster seat with Mikey cradled in her arms. "Are those potato chips?"

Betsy grabbed another handful of Lay's. "Take a bite. I promise, it's good." Last night's wine pulsed in her temples. After they got home from music on the lawn, they had played Scrabble on the porch, wrapping themselves in blankets. It was a tradition her mother and sisters had in summer: Shower off the sand and salt water from the beach, eat dinner, and then pull out the family's favorite board game and set it up outside under the stars. Theirs was the serious kind of Scrabble board that spun so every player could see the words in the correct orientation, and they'd played until midnight, since Louisa had demanded a rematch after she was pummeled in the first game. She'd won the second, everyone laughing when she'd taken the top with the word "fiz," an unusual but legal spelling of "fizz" on a triple word, earning forty-five points. Betsy didn't bring up what she'd inadvertently discovered in her mother's study, but she'd been tense, guzzling multiple glasses of wine, sticking her tongue out at Louisa when she asked her if that was her third glass.

She'd woken in a contemplative mood, and as Aggie warmed Mikey a bottle, Betsy sat at the table with her bag of chips. "Do you ever think it strange that the world seems to change every day, but you get back to the island and time stands still? The house looks like it did when I was five. Sometimes I feel like a little kid standing here cooking breakfast."

Aggie turned off the stove and pulled the bottle out of the hot water. "You don't remember the house when you were five, do you?"

"I remember Louisa stealing my Tiny Tears doll and holding her head under water in the bathtub to see what would happen."

At that moment, Louisa walked into the kitchen. "What did I do now?" Her sister snickered when Betsy repeated the story. "You acted as though I was trying to kill that doll, and I actually got punished." Louisa slid into the banquette, sniffing the omelet, then taking a tiny bite and moaning.

Betsy needed to make her mother one. She folded over the eggs in the pan, lost in thought, frustrated when some pieces of the omelet stuck. Finding those pages in her mother's drawers had given her an overwhelming desire to protect this house, like preserving it was the only way to preserve her family. They had always felt like a family on this island, more than they ever felt like one in Washington, where cameras followed and time with her parents grew scarce. She tried to remember what it had felt like to be a kid here, bare feet and climbing trees, riding bikes until dark and throwing fishing lines into the harbor alongside James.

"Can you believe another family will be living here by fall? We'll never see the elm tree on the front lawn turn yellow again."

"I'm just afraid one of those slick financiers from Boston will tear this place down," Aggie said, holding the bottle to Mikey's lips.

"Mommy wouldn't be able to bear it." Louisa said it as their mother walked in the kitchen in a silk robe and moccasins, her hair pulled back into a chignon.

"Why do you all look so glum?" she said with a chuckle.

"We're just going to miss the house," Aggie said, careful not to sound like she was casting blame.

Her mother's face remained impassive. She kissed her grandchildren, then carried her omelet outside to the patio, while saying, "Oh girls, people sell houses all the time and move on. We're going to be okay."

Betsy flicked on the transistor radio, looking at her mother through the glass doors. "Mom is faking all that positivity. She has to be."

"Of course she is," Louisa whisper-yelled back. "Why do you think she went out there? She can't bear to hear us talking like this."

A Rolling Stones song came on: "Ruby Tuesday." Betsy's eyes traveled around the kitchen's scuffed white metal cabinets. "What is the first thing you would do if you could buy this house?"

Louisa finished her last bite, then cleared her plate in the sink. "Rent it for summer income. It would pay for itself."

Flying a fork through the air like an airplane, Aggie tried to coax Tabby into eating the omelet. "I would paint the rooms in bright colors. I love those pretty marigold-color bedrooms I keep seeing in magazines." Aggie pouted at her daughter's tightly closed lips.

"Yes, same," Betsy said. She had so many ideas: put a powder room on the first floor, repaint the chipping exterior a fresh coat of white. "I would start simple, like rearrange the living room. Imagine if you could sit on the couch and see the water."

Aggie gave up, sprinkling potato chips in front of the toddler. "Then why don't you do it? It would be so easy to change things up, and Mom won't care. We need to pack anyway."

Her father was the one who disliked when furniture was rearranged; after a tumultuous childhood, he appreciated consistency. The sisters left the dishes in the sink and traveled into the front room to the navy-blue couch with white piping. After concocting a plan, they moved the two overstuffed chairs to the opposite side of the room. Then the sisters lifted the heavy couch, inching forward little by little, and repositioned its back under the windows facing the street.

Betsy flounced down on the sofa's familiar pillows. From here, she could look through the kitchen's large picture window and see the harbor, and Chappaquiddick beyond. "Wow. An entirely fresh perspective," she said.

"It makes the room feel cozier," Louisa said, casting her gaze about. She dragged the coffee table to its new spot in front of the couch. "Actually, the room feels brighter too. It would be fun if this place was ours, not Mom's, and we took turns staying here."

Aggie put the baby on the floor. "I have a friend who does that. They agree on a calendar at the beginning of summer. She gets two weeks in the house each season, and there are two weeks when anyone can visit."

"Yes, but is Mom getting only two weeks?" Betsy said, and the sisters acknowledged it wouldn't work; this was their mother's house. She squinted, staring out to the back lawn. "Can't you imagine Daddy right now walking barefoot in the grass in those striped bathing trunks he loved, how he was always holding a yellow legal pad and making notes?"

Louisa smirked. "You talk about him like he was some kind of god."

"Wasn't he? He was certainly an important figure in American history. How many people can say that about their dads?"

Louisa sank into the couch, putting her bare feet up on the table. "I guess."

"Is anyone else nervous for our meeting with the bank? Getting a loan would change everything." Aggie tickled the baby's tummy; the child laughed.

"I'm hopeful, but . . ." Louisa got up to straighten a painting that was leaning to one side. "I read an article recently that unmarried women are rarely taken seriously by bankers."

Aggie grinned. "Well, then I'll do all the talking."

Their mother padded in, her glasses pushed onto her head, remarking with shock. She played with the position of one of the overstuffed chairs opposite the couch and sat. "Do you know this is how my aunt and uncle had this room set up? But when we took over the house, Daddy and I wanted to put our own spin. Now the only problem is where to fit the television."

Betsy snuggled into the couch pillows. "The only problem is that we're going to leave behind this view forever."

Her mother pulled her robe tighter. "Oh Betts, the house isn't everything. In the end, it's just four walls and a roof." Betsy went to open her mouth to mention the secret writing project she'd found of her mother's, then thought better of it. It would result in a fight, and she'd given up on fighting with her mother and sisters. If she was upset, she went silent and pulled away, and that was what she would do today.

They spent the rest of the afternoon working in the house with a series of James Taylor records blasting through the speakers, Betsy burrowing herself in the packing of tchotchkes in the dining room. That night, they all suffered through a terrible movie about a disco owner whose son burns down his club, Betsy's mind wandering the whole time. Restless, she went outside to clip flowers, putting a small vase of blush roses on her nightstand, then making one for Louisa since they shared a room. There was no point in returning downstairs, so she flipped through the latest issue of *Vanity Fair*, wishing that the metal springs of her twin bed didn't rattle every time she adjusted her position. Soon Louisa came to bed, too, and she sat across from Betsy, looking like a princess propped up with six pillows on the cushiony mattress, writing a letter on a piece of cream stationery.

"Who are you writing to?" Betsy asked, as if she didn't really care. The sound of the pen hit hard against the page as her sister wrote furiously, and when she didn't answer, Betsy said, "Michael Evans?"

Louisa lowered her pen. "What do you know of Michael Evans?"

"I saw his address on the envelope on your nightstand."

She went back to writing, not saying another word. Betsy switched off her light, and ten minutes later, Louisa did the same. Betsy reached for the box of saltine crackers she'd left on her nightstand to snack on. Every few minutes, Betsy turned from one side, then the other, hearing her sister struggling with a similar inability to get comfortable. Louisa thrust one leg out of the quilt and pushed up on her elbows.

"Are you eating in bed?"

"Just a cracker," Betsy said. She sucked at the saltine to soften it, so she could swallow the last bits. Her sister slumped back into her pillows, the moonlight streaking across the ceiling. "I don't really understand how someone as important as you was given time off from work. You're always saying what a critical legal member of the team you are."

"As critical as they'll let any woman be." Her sister rolled onto her side, sighing. "I just told Mom the same thing. Clarkson and Hobart's vacation policy is quite generous, and other than a day for Daddy's funeral and a day when I had the flu, I haven't taken time off in three years. I'm the first one to arrive in the morning and the last one to leave. They know I'm a hard worker. Why are you so concerned?"

Betsy leaned onto the small ledge of the windowsill, watching the darkened lighthouse in the distance, the flash of its tip. The salt air smelled of low tide, its pungent scent reminding her of digging through the mudflats for clams with James and her sisters. "I noticed the diamonds in your ears. Were they a gift?"

"You can be so nosy."

"Were they?" Details of her sister's love life was a fascination that began early and carried on still. "You wouldn't buy yourself something like that. I know you."

She heard Louisa sit up in bed, the creak of the wicker headboard at her back, the slide of the sheets as she drew her legs into her chest. "Don't tell Mom, but I've met someone."

"Why is it a secret? Mom would be happy for you." Betsy preferred this side of Louisa, the one that opened like a flower at the most unpredictable moments rather than the tight fist she often was.

"Mom told me not to bother with marriage until I make partner." In the dark, Louisa pressed her crossed hands over her heart. "Hence the complication. He's a senior partner at another firm, and I'm still an associate. And yes, his name is Michael Evans." Betsy could hear her sister's smile at the sound of his name. Maybe this was what Aggie and Louisa had done as teenagers, whispered in the dark, while Betsy had been stuck alone in her bedroom, forced to go to sleep two hours before them.

"Why is that a problem?" Betsy imagined Andy's suede loafers, how he wore those adorable, dotted bow ties.

"The problem is that if my colleagues find out, no one will take me seriously. I'll just be Michael's girl. Constitutional lawyers run tight in DC, and if I marry him, then what? A husband-and-wife team billing hours at opposing firms? A woman partner having a baby. It won't happen, and who will get canned first? Me or him?" Louisa kicked her blankets down to the bottom of the bed.

"You?" Betsy was about to say that she shouldn't accept that, that she could fight the way Mom told them to.

"Do you know how many times a week I nod along with my male counterparts even if I disagree with what they're saying? 'I'm so thankful you let me join the team fighting the Ford Motor discrimination case, sir.' 'Oh, and double thank-you for taking the opening argument I wrote and passing it off as your own in the meeting last week.'"

Betsy frowned. She had always imagined Louisa sitting behind an imposing desk, a series of male colleagues coming into her office for legal advice, then facing the court and declaring something unjust. "Then why do you even do it?"

"Because Mom said it would be this way, but I should shoulder on and it will get better," Louisa said. "And I do, every day, but sometimes I just want to scream."

Silence sat between them for a few minutes, Betsy feeling some relief that her sister's perfect life wasn't all that perfect. "What's he like? Michael Evans."

He was incredibly smart, the only man in law that Louisa thought might be smarter than she was. He held doors open for Louisa. He frowned whenever he heard of one of her male colleagues asking her to get coffee. She and Michael always went to the same spot: a blues club in a rough part of town that had the best chicken wings in the city. They'd been dating three months.

"Have you, you know?"

Louisa threw a pillow across the room, and it landed on her head. "Betsy!" Louisa hopped out of bed and opened her makeup case, pulling a round plastic shell out of her purse. "Thank you for reminding me."

Well, there was the answer.

In the darkness, Betsy tried to fall asleep once more. She turned over onto her back, wondering if James had received her belated condolence letter. A part of her had fantasized that it would erase any awkwardness between them, that he'd walk down to the yacht club and thank her for it, but he hadn't returned to help Wiley. How strange that it wasn't that long ago that she used to daydream about marrying James on the deck of the yacht club, the other sailing instructors and her sisters as members of the wedding party—a sixteen-year-old's fantasy that included a tiered cake with a fondant sailboat on top. But the one time she admitted to James that she wanted to stay with him on the island someday—move into a house on the beach, snuggle up under the harvest moon and bake pumpkin bread—he'd smiled at her as if he knew the stars were aligned entirely different. "You can't stay here, Betsy. Your father wouldn't allow it."

Betsy felt her arms and legs grow heavy with sleep, her mind falling into the soft, cushiony pillow under her head, when she heard Louisa's voice puncture the stillness in the room.

"I'm sorry for accusing you of not doing enough at Dad's funeral."

Betsy tensed awake, her nose suddenly aware of the salt air drifting through the cracked window. The ricochet of laughter from people on a distant boat.

"Oh," Betsy said.

"I tried to call you and apologize, but you wouldn't take my calls, so . . . I kind of gave up."

Betsy was afraid to breathe and reveal the shudder in her chest, so she stared at her sister's still dark form in the bed, her body lying on her side, her head pressed to the pillow.

"Mom didn't want to make any decisions after Dad died, and I was falling apart inside too. I was so overwhelmed. I cracked. You happened to be the first person I saw, and it was verbal vomit." Louisa paused, and in the dark, Betsy could just make out Louisa rubbing her face with her palms. "Anyway, it was wrong and I'm sorry. I regretted it that night, but it took me a few weeks to call you. Then you wouldn't . . ."

Betsy pulled one of the throw pillows to her center, steadying her thoughts. She'd been so hurt after the funeral that she'd gone home and cried herself to sleep in her bed, her roommate pulling a blanket over her and setting a teacup of Earl Grey on her nightstand. She'd vowed that she would never trust Louisa again. Tension with her family had unfurled even more after that, with Aggie taking Louisa's side, calling Betsy every few weeks and encouraging her to talk to their elder sister.

To forgive. Instead, Betsy had stored all her built-up resentment inside herself, providing her with a false sense of control. She liked that she would decide when and if the argument ended, not Louisa.

But coming home this summer had chipped away at her hardened shell. Things weren't perfect between them, but they were getting better. Maybe she had been emotionally spent, too, after the funeral and taken Louisa's actions much too personally. Seeing red, it had been hard to acknowledge that Louisa had taken on the bulk of the planning. She'd even welcomed guests to the ceremony with a smile as if it was a lovely occasion that had gathered them, not her father's death.

"It's okay," Betsy managed to say. She never really understood why Louisa and her father were on such bad terms, other than he didn't come to her debate in high school. Betsy had wondered if there was more, something her sister hadn't told her, but the one time she'd asked, Louisa had told her to mind her business. "That day was . . . a lot. For all of us."

The corners of her eyes burned like she hadn't slept in a hundred years. Betsy wasn't sure if she was ready to say sorry back. The conversation had caught her off guard, and she wanted more time to figure out what specifically she should apologize for. The buoy bell continued to ring, a low quiet song that had served as the soundtrack to Betsy's thoughts for as long as she could remember.

"Okay, well, good night," Louisa said.

"'Night." Betsy closed her eyes, inhaling the smell of the sea, feeling like a steady boat anchored in placid waters. Betsy wondered if Louisa ever pictured her as a little girl the way Betsy remembered Aggie and Louisa when they were young. If she ever thought about how Betsy would climb into bed with her after a bad dream. If she remembered that Betsy had saved her allowance to buy her the Joni Mitchell album she'd wanted for her eighteenth birthday.

She wondered if Louisa knew that Betsy would get so angry at her mostly because she always felt like she was disappointing her.

CHAPTER THIRTEEN

The next few days passed in a blur of summer. Long beach days, invigorating bike rides. The sweet smell of honeysuckle. Juicy red tomatoes sliced and sprinkled with salt. Reprimanding unruly kids. Running her hand over the sea when it was still and glassy. Crisp cocktails on the porch. Naps on the lawn. The bluest sky of the year. A scatter of shells collected at Lighthouse Beach. Homemade blueberry jam spread on fluffy pancakes. The first ears of summer corn. A game of Horse with Aggie. The baby with his enormous eyes watching them from the stroller. Tender lobster dipped in melted butter. Sunsets over *Senatorial.* Tabby's tiny hand in hers. Soft summer tablecloths and pale pink water glasses. Hydrangeas arranged in pitchers.

There were boxes too. Stacks of simple cardboard boxes they'd collected from behind local stores and stowed in the garage to use for the packing. Betsy parked her bike inside the garage after work that afternoon and grabbed a Campbell's soup box the size of a typewriter, carrying it inside through the back door. She tried to spend an hour or two each weekday helping her sisters organize the house so the weekends could be more fun, but they had started to do a little every day anyway. Later in the week, she and her sisters finally had that meeting at the bank in Vineyard Haven to talk about a personal loan, but for now, Betsy looked forward to tackling the coat closet.

Betsy dropped the paper bag with the cleaning supplies her mother had asked her to pick up on the kitchen counter. She followed her sisters' voices to the narrow stairwell, and then up the crooked steps to her mother's study. Inside, Louisa and Aggie were nestled around their mother, who was sitting at her desk and flipping through a photo album. On the navy Oriental rug, Tabby colored in a Wonder Woman coloring book while the baby slept in his bouncy seat.

"What are you guys doing?" Betsy said. Aggie waved her in with a dreamy expression.

"You have to see these pictures of Mom and Dad's wedding." As children, the girls used to pull the same quilted white photo album off the shelf in their mother's study, smudging the sticky laminated pages with their small fingers. Betsy could lose herself in those albums when she was knobby kneed with braces, trying to imagine how she would ever morph into something as lovely as her mother. Sometimes she and her sisters had pretended to get married after putting down the album, Louisa acting as the priest, while Aggie was the bride in her Easter dress and Betsy the groom in her father's bow tie. At the end of the ceremony, they'd make their Barbie and Ken dolls kiss.

Betsy stood behind her mother, taking in the smooth bright faces of her parents in 1948. She pointed to a square black-and-white picture with teeny, scalloped edges. "That dress! So sensible, Mom!" Her mother's tailored white skirt and jacket were paired with a glamorous mid-length veil that she'd glued to a headband layered in statuesque flower petals. She wore nylons and crisp white pumps, a corsage of dahlias pinned to her lapel.

"The war was over by then, and some of my fellow brides had these long silk dresses that were so beautiful since you could finally get real fabrics again, but your father and I didn't want that kind of wedding.

We wanted a quick ceremony at the courthouse, and then a very big party."

Louisa leaned toward the page. "Was it legal to be married this young?"

"I was twenty-three!" her mother laughed. "We *were* young though, and several years later, we had a huge thirtieth birthday party as a combined anniversary and birthday thing. Dad was in the Senate then, and it doubled as a fundraiser for voting rights. For good publicity, of course, but he serenaded me in front of everyone, singing 'My Girl' into the microphone in the most tone-deaf voice. Louisa, you must remember that?"

Louisa shrugged like she didn't care for the memory. "Didn't Dad call me up onstage?"

"Yes," Virgie said with a smile, "and you helped him sing a few bars. People went wild."

"'I've got sunshine on a cloudy day . . .'" Louisa sang in the quiet room, turning the page of the photo album. Her sister always sang along to the radio like she was Ella Fitzgerald reincarnated. It was a bit much.

Each photograph had a thin gold line creating a frame around it, the pictures set up to look antique. Or maybe it was the venue, since they'd had their reception at the Harold Pratt House, an old beaux arts mansion in Manhattan that housed the Council of Foreign Relations. One of her mother's closest friends at the time, Melody Fleming, got them a deal on the lavish, wood-paneled space. In one photo, her father grinned alongside her mother at a long banquet table. He wore his finest suit, the same gabardine pairing he wore during his most important meetings in his job as the mayor's chief of staff. His thick crown of brown curls was slicked flat with pomade. He held up a glass and looked to be mid-sentence, her mother squeezing his arm. A toast.

"Look at how confident Dad looks with his hand on your back," Louisa said. "He was a salesman even then."

Betsy swatted at Louisa's obnoxious comment. "He's not selling something. He's just enjoying his wedding day. Mom was his one great romance."

"Your father *was* charming from the start," her mother said, chuckling and pointing to a picture of an older man with a receding hairline, a large mole on his cheek. "Oh, goodness. Look at your grandpa in this photo. He's probably only a little older than me now. How strange, to catch up with your parents in age."

"You look better now than Grandpa did back then though," Louisa said. She went to stand by the window.

Aggie picked up the album to look closer, then lowered it down. "Dad's expression in this one is so practiced though, even before he ran for office. Do you think he knew back then that he would become a senator?"

"This was probably his first campaign speech." Her mother pressed the pictures' edges flat where the corners had lifted with age. "Everyone clapped when he finished, some dabbed at their eyes. Your father was a natural. He spent a lot of time imagining that he was a senator, practicing talking into the mirror. He liked to think that if you believed something enough, it would happen, and he was right."

Aggie picked up Tabby and showed her a picture of her own grandfather. Then she kissed her cheek and set her back down on the ground. "What was Dad saying in the speech?"

From the window, Louisa moaned. "I can't think of a single interesting wedding speech, and I've been to about a dozen weddings this year."

Her mother gazed at a distant point in the room like she was watching a movie. "He told them about the orphanage, how lonely he'd been growing up there as a teenager, and how he used to lay in his bunk bed and stare at a photo of himself as a child with his parents and dream about creating his own family someday. He told the crowd that when he met me, he met the love of his life, and better than that, he'd found himself a family, which of course, won him the heart of every aunt and cousin I had, whether distant or close."

Similar notes had made their way into many of her father's stump speeches. Betsy knew one of the lines by heart: "Just like you, I realized early on that hard work, grit, and determination would get me to where I was destined to go, and hard work, grit, and determination will help me get this country where it needs to go. But we need to do it together."

His stock line on the campaign trail, whether he was in a factory town upstate or the hallowed halls of the Plaza. *We need to do it together.*

Her mother turned the page to another one of Betsy's favorite pictures. An eight-by-ten black-and-white photo of her mother and her maid of honor, Melody, with her pretty Irish complexion and dark green flowing dress, laughing together about something her mother couldn't remember. "Whatever happened to your friend Melody?"

"I don't know," her mother said. "We just lost touch sometime before you were born. I ran into her once on the Cape, and we promised to keep in touch. She even gave me an address in Boston." Her mother sighed. "But we were just too busy."

"That's disappointing," Aggie said, sitting beside Tabby and coloring with her. "I'm sure Dad didn't make it easy to stay in touch with people."

Her mother closed the photo album and handed it to Betsy, who dutifully stacked it back on the shelf. "Yes, well, his work certainly shaped much of our lives." Pulling off her reading glasses, she set them down on a stack of freshly typed pages.

"Your work shaped our lives too, Mom," Louisa said, as some sort of consolation. Her mother nodded and opened her mouth to say something, then didn't say anything at all. Louisa moved toward the doorway. "Well, I'm going to keep packing."

"I'll be right there," Betsy said. She spoke like a teacher insistent that a student wait to begin a test. "And don't start without me like some martyr and then yell at me because I didn't help."

Louisa made a face, then paused as Aggie asked, "Can I ask you something personal, Mom?" Louisa lingered in the doorway as she tucked her ruffly blouse into her bright blue shorts, looking like Sandy from *Grease*.

"Sure. You know I'm an open book," her mother said.

"Did you ever regret marrying Dad? Did you ever wonder if you would have been happier with someone else?"

Betsy flopped down on the tufted leather sofa against the windows, a series of thin quilts spread across the seat to cover the cracks in the leather. Louisa came back into the room and sat beside her, all of them listening to the distant voices of boaters drifting through the window in the silence that followed.

Her mother leaned back in her chair, pressing her bare feet against the desk drawer. "I want to say no, because I never loved anyone but Charlie." She twirled a pencil in her fingers like a baton. "And yet, I have to say yes, sometimes. Your father was a complicated man. He had so much unfinished inside him. I always saw him as a type of Humpty-Dumpty; he'd glued all his pieces back together so seamlessly, and yet I could see the cracks. He could feel them."

Betsy pressed against the sofa back, feeling like she had to say something in case her father's spirit was sitting on the edge of the windowsill listening. "But he was good to us."

Louisa laughed in that condescending way she always did when she found her sisters intolerable. "Oh, Betsy. Being the youngest certainly shielded you from the worst of it, didn't it?"

"Even though things were complicated with Mom and him, he *was* good to us," Betsy said. Something about the way her sister said *the worst of it* left a swishing sensation in her middle. "Just because you didn't get along with him doesn't mean he was a bad person."

Virgie came to sit beside Betsy, placing a warm hand on her bony knee. "Charlie was a good person, one of the best, but he was layered. Just like we're all layered."

"Is that what you would call it?" Louisa's eyes bore into her mother like a spear. Then she spun out of the room. "This conversation is getting depressing. I'm going downstairs."

"Okay," her mother said, nodding.

The pounding of her feet vibrated the cottage as Louisa trudged down the steps.

"I know Dad could be hard at times, and I remember that he would get inexplicably sad," Betsy found herself saying by way of explanation, "but what about when he would take us on the campaign trail and invite us out to talk to the crowd and tell everyone how proud he was of us?"

"Louisa and I despised that." Aggie crossed her legs and leaned down in a twisted-up stretch. "It's like we were his show horses."

"Or when he'd play tag with us on the beach? Or show up at my college with show tickets? Or how we'd go out on *Senatorial*?" Betsy tried.

Aggie swept her eyes around the room. "He took you out on *Senatorial*, Betsy. We hated that boat. I'm realizing this with men. They all have something that consumes them more than their wives."

"And what consumes Henry?" Her mother returned to her desk, glancing over her glasses at Aggie.

"His patients," Aggie sighed. "The practice. The hospital. They always come first."

Her mother took a fresh piece of paper and rolled it into the typewriter. This was their cue: it was time for her to work. Betsy imagined the pages sitting in her bottom drawer, the terrible things her mother had been writing about her father. "You must admit, Mom. Dad made everything feel special."

"Oh, honey," her mother said. "He really did, and he worked hard not to disappoint you, any of us really. You put him on a pedestal, and he loved that. He wanted you to keep him there."

Betsy didn't like how her mother had turned around her words, making her father sound insincere. "I'm so confused. Did I grow up with an entirely different man than Louisa and Aggie?"

Aggie began packing her daughter's crayons, gathering the coloring books into her arms. "It's hard to see some of the bad when you're the favorite."

Betsy pinched her own thigh, hard. "I was never the favorite. The true favorite in this family is the person not in this room."

Her mother pressed her eyes closed, then opened them. "I need to write, girls, and just so you know, there is never a constant favorite in a family. My favorite child changes every day, depending on how you're treating me."

"Well, most of the days of the week you had the same favorite. It was Louisa, and it still is." Betsy felt a lump in her throat. She'd never said those words aloud, not even when she was a teenager. Now the feelings were real, something that would need to be wrangled with.

Aggie encouraged Tabby to toddle toward the door. "I don't know, Betts. I think I was Mom's favorite."

Her mother exchanged a knowing look with her middle daughter, a lowered eyebrow and an expression that read *She has no idea what she's saying.*

But it was true. Everything in their family had always revolved around the tender care of Louisa. It was Louisa's school day that her mother focused on when the girls got home from Sidwell Friends. When Louisa was given a solo in the winter concert in junior year, her mother bragged about it to anyone who would listen. The morning that they dropped Louisa off at college at Barnard, her mother had sat on the steps of the campus library and cried.

Instead, it was Charlie who had taken Betsy to college, just the two of them driving up the New Jersey Turnpike together from Washington. It was her father who bragged to his friends at the yacht club about how well Betsy could tack a sailboat in the wind. Sometimes her father would wake up on Sunday mornings in winter in Washington and take Betsy out for scrambled eggs. Things with her mother had always felt strained in comparison, like her mother was too tired to pay her much mind because she was busy and the older two had beaten her down. While Betsy knew her mother loved her, in the same way you know that the sun will be highest in the sky at noon, there had been a hierarchy in the way she and her sisters were treated, with Louisa reigning queen in her mother's heart, and the rest of them fumbling to remain relevant.

Things had been feeling okay, maybe even good, these last few weeks. Betsy had received an apology from Louisa. She was feeling close to Aggie again. She loved her job at the yacht club. But she could feel a vibration, a negative sound pushing some long-held belief out of the broken recesses of her heart, and as much as Betsy didn't want to say anything to stir up emotions right now, the words were already leaving her mouth.

"Do you remember that day that I sailed in the regatta off Cape Cod, Mom, and you came to cheer me on? I think I was fourteen." Betsy waited for her mother to look up from her work. When she did, her mother's crystalline eyes brightened with recognition. Betsy continued. "I was so excited that you'd come to see me, and as I rounded the point by the lighthouse, I looked for you, thinking you'd be on your feet, clapping. But you were sitting on the beach, at the center of a circle of women, talking about something so important that you didn't even bother watching the race. I came in second! Maybe it wasn't first, but it was still good."

Her mother lowered her pen. "Betsy, honey, where is this coming from? Why am I the bad guy in this story?"

Betsy felt her stomach swirl like she was spinning on a terrible carnival ride. "Because everyone acts like Dad was never around. That he was absent, that he was so *complicated*. But Dad was here more than you were. He always paid attention. He was always clapping."

"Betsy! I was there for everything. Everything you did."

"You didn't come to my college graduation! That was a biggie, Mom. You didn't even come to that dance performance I did at the theater."

"Those are two events in an entire lifetime." Her mother rose, reaching her slender fingers out to squeeze Betsy's elbows. "Was I supposed to turn down a meeting with the president?"

"Yes, Mom. You were supposed to turn that down. I wanted you at my graduation."

"That's not fair, Betsy. Your father missed so much, and I missed one thing. In dedication to the movement."

"Two things," Betsy said, holding up her fingers in the peace sign. She ran out of the study, leaving her mother with her face contorted into a tight ball, and hid out in the hall bathroom, sitting on the lid of the toilet, willing herself to take a breath. She sniffled, squeezing her dry lips with her calloused fingertips rough from rigging boats, and she stared at the browning grout in the floor. The house would be considered a fixer-upper by real estate agents. She could see the listing already: *Charming summer cottage in need of some TLC. Great views!*

Her eye returned to the brown grout. It was disgusting; years of dirt built up. Her mind skipped to a different kind of brown that she hadn't uncovered in her underwear that week or the week before. Another swirl of nausea took hold of Betsy then, her spine tingling with a certain kind of panic.

No one brought up the tension or the conversation again after it ended that afternoon, the weight of their mother and father's complicated legacy making all three sisters retreat to the television that night. They squeezed onto the living room couch and watched *One Day at a Time*, *Alice*, and *The Jeffersons*. Her mother went to bed just before Betsy's favorite, *The Mary Tyler Moore Hour*. Betsy barely paid attention to what was going on in the show, her mind doing the mental math repeatedly. Her last period was early June, or was it end of May? She'd been so busy with her thesis paper to remember exactly, and she remembered having some spotting in June. Did it even count as a real period? Earlier she'd consulted the Steamship Authority calendar pinned to the pantry door, each month featuring a picture of the ferry crossing, and if her last period was a phantom one, then she would be several weeks late.

She could have chalked it up to stress, except for the strange swirling in her stomach she'd been feeling. She'd been eating crackers in bed some nights, which she hadn't thought odd until now; hadn't Aggie been hungry around the clock when she was pregnant? If Betsy was, in fact, pregnant, she had to be about nine to ten weeks. After her sister discovered she was having her second, Aggie had told Betsy that the doctor said the fetus was the size of a lima bean. Betsy swallowed down the sour taste of bile. Being pregnant would be an impossible turn. What the hell would she do?

"Calm down," Betsy whispered to herself, and Louisa turned to her in the glow of the television, a curious look passing over her face.

"Did you just say something?"

Betsy's lips tightened, then she smiled, not wanting to give away her nerves. "I was telling Mary to calm down. On the show."

Louisa turned her attention back to the television. A laugh track erupted, Aggie chuckling along with it.

Betsy recoiled at the inevitable. She was going to have to buy a pregnancy test. It wouldn't be the first time she'd taken one. Her mother had made her go on the Pill at sixteen, which had been one of the biggest arguments she'd ever heard her parents have. A screaming match in their Washington bedroom, her father saying that giving their youngest the Pill was like Virgie giving their daughter license to go out and bed a boy. He'd actually said "bed a boy," which had given teenaged Betsy and Aggie the giggles as they listened from the bottom of the rowhouse's steps. "Don't tell me you think your precious Betsy will wait until she's married. No woman does, and she shouldn't have to."

Her mother did that sometimes. Called her "your precious Betsy."

Still, after Betsy had lost her virginity to James on an ocean beach one August night, her period hadn't arrived that September. She'd panicked, taking the Metro to a doctor's office near Howard University—where she was the only white person in the lobby—and she'd gone in to pee in a cup, waiting for the results by phone: "Negative," the office said. The whole ordeal had been traumatic enough though that Betsy had been extra careful when she was with Andy. Which was why she was so confused sitting there watching *Mary Tyler Moore*. How could anything have happened?

I don't know anything yet, she reminded herself. She would pick up a test tomorrow after work, and she would put her mind at rest.

CHAPTER FOURTEEN

Betsy dove into the cold sea. She had five minutes before her morning meeting with campers, and she hoped that swimming would still her nerves. Even as she treaded water, though, her thoughts looped back to the worst-case scenario: *What if the test is positive?* After drying herself off and pulling on a pair of nylon shorts, Betsy got the kids out on the boats in the harbor and tried to lose herself in their endless curiosity. She was grateful when Wiley asked her to work with their most challenging students: three eleven-year-old girls who didn't feel comfortable on a sailboat. It was the perfect distraction. The girls were wary from the moment they boarded, and when Betsy asked for a volunteer to man the till, the children kept their hands in their laps.

"C'mon, girls. The worst thing that happens is that we capsize and go for a swim."

"I don't want to get wet," complained a girl with dark circles under her eyes, her shoulders freckly.

"We won't really fall over, right?" The towhead child had legs like string beans. She tugged on the buckles of her orange life vest.

Betsy angled her face to the wind, like she remembered her father doing when they would sail. "You need to be tougher, ladies. You think the boys are out there complaining about getting wet?" She pointed to a pair of campers in yellow life vests taking the wind at full speed, determination on the boys' faces as they bounded through the chop. "I want you to be so fearless that you believe you can sail this boat no matter how strong the wind is."

Betsy wanted to be so fearless that she could deal with whatever came next for her, too, and for a moment, the water gave her a sense of invincibility. Out here, she was always okay.

An hour later, the group rounded the curve of land by Edgartown light, and by the time Betsy returned the girls to the dock, she'd felt the children loosen up. While the string-bean girl was biting her lip, the other two had taken turns steering, one hollering "galley ho" when the boat had glided through gentle waves.

Back on land, Betsy unzipped her windbreaker and grabbed her purse from the small wooden locker in the yacht club's shed. The clouds had parted, and she walked out into the sunshine of Edgartown at three thirty in the afternoon. She planned to take a taxi to Oak Bluffs, where she'd be less likely to run into anyone she knew. How incredible that she could buy a pregnancy test in a store and take it in the privacy of her own bathroom! She walked up the main drag of Edgartown, deciding to check the grocery's small pharmacy section first. Her eyes traveled over the Pepto-Bismol and Excedrin bottles in the medicine aisle next to the yeast cream and maxi pads. Nothing. Instead, she bought a snack, hurrying outside to the crowded sidewalk only to find James on the curb, along with his dog. He wore the same Nike sneakers, a baseball cap with EDGARTOWN emblazoned across the top.

James offered a tentative smile. "I saw you at the register."

"Oh, hi," Betsy said. She bent down and fussed over the dog. "What a sweet girl." She smiled. Neither of them said anything else.

Betsy cleared her throat. She wasn't sure if he'd gotten her letter. "Okay, well, I'll see you around."

James pushed off the shingled grocery, falling in step with her. "I'll walk with you. Your house is on the way to the hardware store, kind of."

She watched Peanut Butter sniff at the lowest branches of an overgrown rhododendron. "I would like that."

They strolled along the manicured lawns of Summer Street, Betsy hyperaware of his presence. She waited for him to say something; he had chosen to walk with her, but he seemed comfortable with the silence. He'd been that way as a kid too. It was Betsy that chattered on. She tried to think of something to say.

"Do you remember Ellie?"

James eyed her curiously. "Our old sailing instructor, with the short red hair? Didn't we put a dead fish in her boat?"

She laughed, and Peanut Butter's enormous tail wagged, brushing against Betsy's legs. "Why were we so mean to her?"

"Ellie was a total blue blood, don't you remember? Her mother's name was Muffy."

The memory annoyed Betsy. "Yes. She always parked her parents' black Mercedes convertible with one wheel up on the curb. I wonder what happened to her."

He pointed at the manicured lawn of a captain's house with a bricked walkway and imposing front door. "She's probably 'figuring herself out' in one of those."

She and James had always thumbed their noses at the summer kids from Boston and New York, their families parking enormous yachts in the harbor and inviting locals to their lavish homes for parties because they thought it made them interesting. They went to a few of those gatherings, but they never felt at home with all those girls and their very big feelings snorting lines on a coffee table, the boys tossing footballs in the backyard while holding beers, everyone running to the beach for a midnight swim.

"You sound resentful." Betsy glanced at her watch. It was nearly four, and she needed to get to the pharmacy.

"You're different," he said. He leaned against a lamppost, watching her.

She adjusted the strap of her bathing suit. "Well, you're exactly the same."

"Yeah, well." He pushed his hands into the pockets of his baggy shorts.

A part of her worried she might have insulted him. "I mean, it's not a bad thing that you're the same. I always did like you." She smiled at him, and she was about to ask if he wanted to walk some more when her sisters turned the corner.

Louisa was coming down the sidewalk in bright red lipstick and heels. When she laid eyes on Betsy, her heart-shaped mouth pulled tight, and she glanced at Aggie, the two of them sharing a look. Betsy knew what that meant. She'd done something wrong.

"Did you forget about our appointment?" Aggie called down the sidewalk, her steps swift.

The sisters said a quick hello to James, inquiring how he was, while making clear they weren't all that interested in the answer. Betsy lifted her face out of her hands.

"I'm so sorry." Her mind had been so preoccupied with the pharmacy that she had forgotten their meeting at the Dukes County Savings Bank. "I'll just go like this."

Louisa looked at Betsy like she was holding in laughter. "You can't go to the bank in jogging shorts and a damp bathing suit."

"Of course I can. Don't be such a snob." Betsy turned to James. "Good luck with the house."

He smiled at her. "Good luck with your sisters."

"I'm going to need it."

Betsy trailed behind Louisa and Aggie as they walked off toward Main Street, Betsy wondering how on earth she was going to get to Oak Bluffs in time to buy the test. She also wondered if she and James would ever really be friends again, if he'd ever forget how cruel she'd been, dropping him from her life without an explanation.

The Dukes County Savings Bank was housed in a classic white clapboard house just off Main Street. Louisa opened the door, her heels announcing her serious intentions, and Betsy registered the confused look on the young teller's face. Most customers on the island likely came in wearing sandals and shorts, whereas Louisa stormed in like she'd bought the bank.

"Good afternoon. We're here to see Mr. Erwin," Louisa said.

The baby began to fuss, and Aggie picked him up out of the stroller as the teller disappeared into a nearby office. The man that emerged was shorter than Aggie by a head and wore freshly shined black loafers with tassels. Louisa held out her hand. "I'm Louisa Whiting. Thank you for seeing us today, Mr. Erwin."

"Please, call me Pat." He said hello to Betsy like he knew her. "Don't you teach my daughter Lilian at the yacht club?"

Betsy remembered his slick, oiled hair and thick black glasses from drop-off. "Yes! Hello! I have good news to report. I had Lilian steering the boat today. What a special girl you have."

He nodded, telling them that he had two Sunfish he kept on his dock, how he wanted his daughter to be comfortable on the water. They followed Mr. Erwin into his fluorescent-lit office, except for Aggie, who lagged behind and asked the teller, dressed in a pressed skirt suit, if Tabby could color at her feet. Minutes later, Aggie joined them in his office, holding the baby against her flowy chambray dress.

The sisters sat opposite Mr. Erwin's metal desk in wooden chairs that looked like they were bought at a local chowder house. Louisa got right to the point. "We would like to apply for a personal loan. Our mother is in financial trouble, and we need to help."

Betsy's thoughts flashed to a meeting she'd gone to with her mother on Capitol Hill several years ago, when Virgie had been advising college women about lobbying to end sex discrimination when renting a house or apartment. How they'd listened to her with rapt attention as she'd told them: "Don't demand. Don't be angry. Be nice and smile but be persuasive. Make it personal, make your cause about the mothers and sisters and girlfriends in these staffers' lives."

Mr. Erwin's elbows were on the desk, and he folded his stubby hands together. "Well, your father was a longtime member of our institution. If there's a way I can help, I will." His eyes trained on Betsy, which seemed to unnerve Louisa, but she played along.

"Why don't you explain everything to Mr. Erwin, Betts?"

The lights on his tan office phone blinked red, indicating a call coming through. Betsy tried not to race through their story in fear that he'd cut her off and pick it up. How her mother believed she needed to sell the house, but they wanted to take out a loan, the three of them applying together, to try to pay off the debts.

Louisa twirled the diamond stud in one ear. "We're coming to you in the exploratory phase."

He cracked his knuckles. "Do you know what you owe?"

"First, we'd like to know what we need, what documents we must gather, to apply for the loan." Aggie bounced the baby in her arms, shifting her weight from one huarache sandal to the other. Her blue eyeshadow made her light eyes pop.

The lights blinked on and off on the banker's phone. He folded his arms on the desk.

"Is it just the three of you applying?"

Mikey's gentle protests grew into a high-pitched howl. "Sh, sh, sh. Yes, the three of us."

He spoke over the baby's cries. "There will be no husbands on the loan."

Louisa turned to Aggie, her voice sharp. "Maybe he needs a diaper change?"

"I can change him," Betsy offered, her thoughts sliding away. *You have six hundred dollars in a sock in your top drawer. You can go to a clinic if you need to.*

Aggie popped a binky in the baby's mouth, nodding for Louisa to keep talking. "What documents do we need to apply?"

Mr. Erwin scribbled a list on a piece of notepaper. "W-2s. Any real estate holdings your family has, stocks."

"I don't believe our mom has much savings at all," Betsy said, her voice frantic. "I couldn't find anything in her records other than a joint bank account. There are two loans we're trying to pay back that total $150,000."

Mr. Erwin lowered his pen. "Well, I hope your mother has some savings."

Her mother had three hundred dollars in her account; Betsy had seen her checkbook.

Mr. Erwin stood abruptly from behind the desk. "Listen, girls. I'm afraid I can't help. If your father owes $150,000 and your mother is in the red and two of you don't have real jobs . . ."

"This is what I make." Louisa wrote a number on a notepad and turned it around for him to see, keeping it out of view of Aggie and Betsy. "My sisters have some savings. What do we need to do to get a loan for $150,000?"

He returned to his desk, sitting and clicking a silver pen a few times, then set it down. "I'm sorry, but this isn't going to work. A note shared by three sisters, two of whom don't even work real jobs—that is a red flag to us."

Betsy felt like she was disappearing into the scratchy fabric of the chair. "You'd at least consider our application, wouldn't you?"

"You're welcome to apply." Mr. Erwin pulled out his bottom drawer, licking his fingers and unsticking pages to slip into a packet thick with information about bank rates and requirements. "The law says anyone can apply. But the law can't measure the amount of risk, and this doesn't feel like a traditional setup. What if Louisa loses her job tomorrow? How will the two of you pay?"

They left his office, walking into the teller lobby with Tabby smiling at them. A sense of failure permeated all three of the sisters' moods as Betsy closed the screen door to the bank. They walked toward the harbor in silence, sitting on a rock with a plaque about the earliest settlers.

"Here's what I don't get. Mom and Dad told each other everything. He must have told her he was taking out these loans."

"That's the strange part, Betts. He didn't have to. Mom's name isn't even on the deed of the house, even though she is the one that inherited it. The deed is registered to Charles Whiting."

"Good God. Property is just one more way that women are disenfranchised in this country." Louisa got that self-righteous grimace on her face, like she was the only who could see the hypocrisy of the world. "It happened all the time when property transferred. Women couldn't own it on their own or it wasn't deemed acceptable for them to, so it was easiest to put real estate in their husband's name. You realize, right, that single women could only get a mortgage as of like four years ago."

"You're not the only one who read Mom's article." Aggie flicked her sister in the shoulder. Her mother had written a series of articles in the early seventies about the audacity of banks not to give single women credit cards or a mortgage; it had started a debate in Congress and likely helped turn public opinion to pass the Equal Credit Opportunity Act, a law that established a single woman's right to apply for credit.

Betsy's mind hadn't left her father. "But why wouldn't he tell her he was taking these loans? Was he in some kind of financial trouble himself?"

"Mom seemed to think it was more that he needed to keep up appearances of the life they'd had when he was in the Senate, and he planned to pay it back."

"That theory is just self-preservation on Mom's part." Louisa seemed confident of as much. "You can convince yourself of anything if it means you'll sleep better at night."

Still, the theory that her father likely planned to pay it back was in line with Betsy's thinking. Her father took some of the money out, planned to return it before anyone noticed, and then . . . Well, then he was gone. A small plane careening through the sky, nothing but a pile of ash when authorities discovered it in the New Jersey cranberry bogs.

"Can we get ice cream, Mama?" Tabby asked, spying a little boy and his brother licking at melting ice cream cones.

"Sure," she said, and as Tabby and Aggie joined the line outside the nearby sweet shop, Louisa turned to Betsy. Lines deepened across her forehead.

"I wanted to tell you first, because I know you're as upset as I am, but the house is in foreclosure. I found the notification in Mom's office yesterday."

"What?" The words hit Betsy like ice in a glass, sending a chill up her spine.

Louisa ran her hand up her slender arm, rubbing at it like it hurt. She pulled a folded-up piece of paper out of her purse, holding the page out to Betsy. "It says that we need to pay back the loan or vacate the house by the fifth of August, or they'll send the sheriff to evict us."

"Why wouldn't Mom tell us?" Betsy imagined their couch on the lawn. Her father's books in stacks on the steps. A policeman taking out armfuls of sheets and towels and tossing them outside.

"Jesus, Betsy," Louisa snapped. "You always ask the most obvious question."

"Can you relax? It was rhetorical." Because keeping the kicker of the story a secret was typical Virgie Whiting. She was direct with everyone except her own family.

That gave them only two weeks to save the house.

The day's tumult had settled into Betsy's nerves, particularly because she still didn't have a pregnancy test in hand. The last thing she wanted to do was watch Carol Burnett, which was what her sisters were doing. Instead, she carried a light sweater and a box of chocolates to the back patio. She wouldn't admit it out loud to anyone, but she'd picked a lounger facing the harbor, and the small spit of green beyond, so she could make out James's illuminated window.

She popped a chocolate filled with lush crème de menthe into her mouth, closing her eyes.

It was funny to think about the moment their childhood friendship grew into something more, but she remembered it clearly. They'd been skipping rocks in the curve of land near his house. He was doing that thing where he talked fast about something scientific, like why puffer fish blow up in self-defense to protect from predators. When he got into science facts, she would just wait for him to take a breath, swim a lap, finish tossing a stick as far into the water as he could, and finally *really talk*. That day, after he'd skipped probably a hundred rocks, he'd turned to Betsy and said, "Can I call you sometimes when you go back to Washington this year?"

"That's what you were so worried about saying?" Betsy remembered how she'd fallen backward on the floral sheet they'd opened on the beach in the sunshine, how she'd rolled onto her side with her head propped up on an elbow, her long brown hair falling around her face. "Yes, James Sunday, I, Betsy Whiting, would love to talk to you after the summer ends." His eyes had smiled back at her, and then he had switched on his beloved transistor radio and pretended to play air guitar.

Those phone calls *had* changed things between them, too, since suddenly James was in her life all year long, and the following summer, when she'd arrived on the island at age fifteen, he'd rowed up to the shore a few doors down to pick her up. He was three inches taller, his hair doing that thing where he let it flop about his face, but he couldn't come around the house. By then, her father had discouraged her from seeing him; sneaking phone calls after school had been easy when your parents didn't get home until seven o'clock every night.

That day, though, she'd sat down on the metal seat of his little boat after not seeing him for nine months, surprised when she felt his lips on hers. Fluttering her eyes open, Betsy saw that his were still closed, and she'd slowly closed hers again, realizing that it was finally happening. They were officially going to be a thing. After the kiss—a kiss that she had fantasized about but never had the guts to do herself—James had motored her to a small, secluded cove near a house without summer people yet and anchored them, the boat rocking gently as they lay on their backs and watched the clouds pass. It felt like they could remain that way for the rest of their lives.

And they might have, too, if time and distance and summers spent elsewhere hadn't driven them apart. And, of course, if James had answered the letter she wrote to him junior year, the one where she told him she wanted to be with him forever.

Her cheeks burned at the memory.

A firefly landed on her arm then, and she tilted her chin, watching its tiny abdomen light up gold. She carefully tried to slide her finger under it, raising the lightning bug to her face.

"I can't stop thinking about one very true thing," Betsy said aloud, staring down at the insect's glow, her eyes burning with overwhelm. "Every man I've ever loved has left me behind."

CHAPTER FIFTEEN

Virgie

1965

The first dinner party of the summer and it had been entirely forced upon her. Virgie pressed her fingertips to her temples, her face thick with foundation and blush. She lowered her hands back into the bouquet of flowers she had asked Louisa to clip from the garden, a bundle of deep pink roses, blue hydrangeas, and white dahlias, and she continued to arrange them in a large mason jar. She'd chosen to skip the gooseneck vase she'd use if she were hosting guests in Washington—it was the joy of a summer house to employ simple jars for everything from drinking iced tea to planting vegetable seeds.

Everything was more casual on the island, and she didn't want to change that, even if they were hosting someone Charlie deemed important.

Virgie checked the roman numerals on the kitchen clock. Her husband would arrive in an hour, their guests thirty minutes after that. She wasn't sure what to say to him when he arrived, perhaps only that she was pleased he was there. Keep things as simple between them as the style permeating her dining table. Informal. Pleasing. Without complication. It would be their first time together since she'd left for the island, and she felt anxious being in the same physical space as her husband. She didn't want a confrontation.

Or did she?

Earlier, before her afternoon had twisted into a tornado, Virgie had dragged out two rickety easels from the garage and set them up for Betsy and James, who wanted to paint watercolor pictures of the harbor. She had just delivered them cups of water and paintbrushes when the kitchen phone rang. It was Charlie's secretary from his offices on Capitol Hill. She'd announced in her sweet bouncy voice that the senator had asked her to deliver a message: he would arrive tonight in Cape Cod by airplane, and India and Russell Knight—possible donors—were coming for dinner.

"What time?" There were still breakfast dishes in the sink and laundry drying on a line outside. Louisa was having a sleepover with one of the Post girls, and Betsy and James had begged to stay up and catch fireflies.

"His plane will land at six thirty, ma'am. Guests will arrive at seven. Sorry, Mrs. Whiting, for the trouble, he asked me to set this up at the last minute."

"It's okay, dear. You are only doing your job." She'd been unable to hide the irritation in her voice. Hanging up, she immediately dialed Pamela Sunday to see if she could come and help cook. An hour later, Pamela arrived in a fraying pea-green housedress with orange flowers, stubbing out a cigarette on the front steps when Virgie answered the door. She agreed to prepare a crudités platter, reheat New England clam chowder Virgie would fetch from the local chowder house, and prepare steak Diane with green beans. This would give Virgie time to finish cleaning.

At six thirty, Virgie, wearing a lace sheath with daisies at the neckline, called her three daughters into the living room, sending James home; they'd been pouting about the change of plans all day, even if Betsy hadn't stopped talking about all of the things she couldn't wait to show her father. Already, Aggie was furious because she'd had to cancel plans to see a movie, and Louisa and her boy-crazy friend, Sylvie Post, would be here for the duration of the dinner party.

"You will need to stay upstairs until our guests leave. Louisa, you and Sylvie can have your room, and Aggie, you and Betsy should read or play a game in Betsy's bedroom. Don't come down unless you must, and if you do, please greet our guests politely."

"You already told us this, Mom." Louisa smoothed her pleated skirt. "Can we go now?"

"Remember, keep your voices down. These are important friends of your father's, and we don't want them to think we're a bunch of hooligans."

Aggie raised her hand, her face stone-cold. "I'm just curious, Mom. Why do we care so much what people think of us?"

Virgie inhaled an impatient breath, preparing to offer up her canned response to this question. Dad is a public servant. He's chosen by voters. For a voter to choose you, they must trust you, and trust starts with the home. If a man cannot run a household, then how can he run a country? Instead, she said: "Hush. Now go find something to do."

They were finished with the crudités platter, everyone already draining their first glass of wine, and Charlie hadn't arrived. Virgie had covered nearly every topic she could think of with India and Russell Knight, while slipping into the kitchen to check on Pamela, who was waiting to reheat the soup. The Knights were Washingtonians by way of London, India retaining her British accent, and thus far, they'd spoken about a recent trip they took to Acadia National Park in Maine. They discussed their young children, who were seven and nine, and the sleepaway camp they attended in the Adirondacks. Virgie knew that the couple recently rented a dairy farm in rural Chilmark, and Russell would travel back and forth in summer between the British Embassy in Washington, where he was the ambassador, and the island. That had been a surprise. An ambassador from England. It was only recently that more political types had started visiting the island, thanks to the Kennedys owning property nearby in Cape Cod, and still, it surprised Virgie how politically connected the summer population was beginning to feel.

Russell had a crown of dark hair parted to one side. He glanced at his watch. "Any update about the senator?"

Virgie breezed into the kitchen to get the bottle of wine, pretending that she didn't hear some kind of scuffle upstairs in one of the bedrooms. "Perhaps there was some air traffic," she said, smiling at the couple when she glided back in the living room. "Perhaps we could take a walk down to the dock and I'll show you Charlie's sailboat."

Everyone seemed relieved to leave the formality of the dining room. As the women's heels click-clacked down the slats, Virgie tried to keep up a lively commentary about various spots on the island they must visit. The couple explained they'd chosen the farm since India had grown up summering in the Cotswolds; she wanted her boys to be able to roam free in summer like she had. "Catch grasshoppers with their hands and such." India's hand went to her garnet earrings. "I'm not typically this fancy."

Virgie chuckled at the woman's long satin dress and strappy sandals. "Me neither. I despise wearing heels or anything with a zipper up the back in summer."

When Russell climbed onto the boat to look around, India turned to Virgie. A piece of her dark hair fell from her loose waves. "I love your Dear Virgie column," India said, sipping her wine. "The newspaper announced a replacement last week. Did they cancel you, or did you choose to walk away?"

"I'm just taking a break." It still hurt to say it.

"Oh, good, because I loved what you were doing in the column; your advice was so liberating. There's a hunger for that kind of writing these days. One of my friends recently applied for a job at a newspaper in Philadelphia and she was told the newsroom was no place for a woman. She did talk them into hiring her for the overnight shift, but don't you see? You're already *in the newsroom.*"

"I'm only giving relationship advice. Editors only let women cover fashion and gardening, maybe the odd feature on relationships."

India turned her back so her husband couldn't hear. "Your advice was empowering and rebellious. All the mums at my son's school were talking about the parent conference ideas." India paused. "You need to keep going."

If India had perceived that Virgie's column had been a subversive way to instill women with feminist ideology, then maybe it had been. Why was that a problem for Charlie? Isn't that what they'd stood for: helping the disenfranchised have a voice. "Thank you. I appreciate the support. Do you work?"

Virgie realized that she'd written India off as an ambassador's wife. It was rude and went against everything Virgie believed.

"Yes, I worked with a woman barrister with ties to Parliament. We lobbied for years on getting women access to the Pill in the UK, and we got it passed too. Well, for married women, but we still need all women to be able to buy it. I've had to pull back on my influence, since Russell was named ambassador this year. It's all too political, but I have a like-minded circle in Washington. We should gather a group of women on the island. As you know, there are a few rather influential people here, of both sexes."

"I would like that very much." Virgie thought she heard a car and looked up to see if it was Charlie, but it wasn't. "I wrote a Dear Virgie column devoted to the Pill, you know, whether a mother should talk to her eighteen-year-old daughter about it. Caused quite the stir."

"I saw that. See, you were onto something, something bigger than relationship advice. Because you weren't forming a commission or fighting for equal pay, like Betty Friedan, which is critical too. You were quietly making a difference by shifting public opinion. Your column was beginning to normalize conversations that no one is certain it's okay to talk about."

"I would like to shout more in that column." Virgie touched the bracelet on her wrist, a delicate gold chain with a tiny ruby charm; her father had bought it for her mother for her thirty-fifth birthday, but then she'd stopped going to her meetings and as a form of punishment, he'd given the bracelet to Virgie. She wore it as a reminder of her mother's longing to get better and her father's harsh judgments.

India looked at her with empathy, and for a moment, Virgie wondered if she could see the pain that sat like a well inside her own heart, so well-hidden she barely let it surface.

"We all would like to yell, and there are women in Washington yelling for us," India said, with a gentle nod of her head. "But that's not always the answer. Sometimes we get further with a whisper."

For a moment, Virgie fell still, the two of them nodding at the truth of her sentiment: a woman could holler, but not too loud or no one would listen. Perhaps every time Charlie had read her words, he'd felt as though she was hollering at him. How could she explain you could love a man fully and still feel angry with him for slighting you? An upside-down feeling overtook her; these last few weeks on the island she'd tricked herself into believing she was in control. But this dinner party, the sense that everything in her life needed to halt on account of Charlie, reminded her that she'd accomplished nothing. She could stand on the tallest mountain in the world and hold a sign reading I DEMAND TO BE TAKEN SERIOUSLY. The only thing that would matter was whether Charlie allowed her to stand there.

A light flashed in the upstairs bedroom, and a ruckus carried through the open windows, children laughing and jumping about on the floorboards. Forcing a smile, Virgie excused herself and raced inside to where Pamela stirred the soup. "Should I serve now?" The woman fiddled with the corner of her eyelet-trimmed apron with her other hand, glancing outside.

"No, not yet." Virgie kicked off her heels and took the crooked steps two at a time. She pushed open the door of Louisa's bedroom, but she and her friend Sylvia were quietly listening to records. In Betsy's bedroom, it was another story. Attempting to separate themselves from each other, her daughters hung sheets to isolate one half of the bedroom from the other. One of the sheets was balanced on a lamp, which had come crashing to the ground. James poked his head out from under the bed.

Her daughters avoided her gaze, and cursing under her breath, Virgie wished she could disappear. "James, you were supposed to go home."

"Betsy begged me to hide in the closet."

From outside, she heard Charlie's voice: "Lovely to see you, Mr. Ambassador."

"Don't move!" Virgie held up a finger like it was a pointed gun.

Relief flooded through her, and for a moment, she felt as though she might shed tears. Virgie rushed into the bathroom, reapplied her blush and Chanel lipstick, grinning to extinguish the possibility of emotion. It was time to play her part. Downstairs, she slid her feet into heels and motioned for Pamela to ready the steak Diane.

"Hello, darling." Virgie airily emerged from the screen door into the dusk of eight o'clock and leaned in to give her husband a kiss. She sensed his hand graze her back, and she stiffened, even as she portrayed herself breezily. "I've missed you."

He patted his hair to the side, much of it out place from the wind. "We had to land in Boston because of weather, and I didn't have a way of calling. I took the first ferry I could."

She smelled gin on his breath as she handed him a fresh cocktail with lime. Had he had a drink at the ferry terminal too? "Come, let's relax."

Virgie examined her husband then. It was a longtime joke that Washington was the Hollywood of ugly people: nerdy, bookish men who grew up to be powerful, few of them attractive like Charlie. His was the face of a politician you'd see in a film. A well of energy—sometimes he barely got five hours of sleep—but he was memorable to all who met him. She used to think she was drawn to him for those classic good looks, but they were a bonus. It was how Charlie looked at her, like he'd done just now, with tenderness and curiosity, how he treated her like he was lucky to be with her, not the other way around. It made it impossible to hate him.

The couples sat on opposite sides of the polished dining room table, Pamela serving soup with hands that trembled under the tureen. Charlie barely registered the woman, other than thanking her for his serving, acting as though a housekeeper always served him his dinner. The husbands immediately traded niceties about how much the ambassador was doing to improve the relationship of the two countries' defense teams. Within minutes, it was clear why the dinner was happening. The ambassador wanted Charlie to earmark money in an upcoming spending bill to revive the Skybolt missile program, canceled two years before due to waning interest in Cold War efforts.

The ambassador set down his soup spoon. "Obviously, this would be fruitful for other reasons too. I will certainly refer you to Dan Corning, who already agrees with you on trade relations. I'm sure you know how deep his pockets are. He said he might have more property on Nantucket for you."

"Ah, but my heart is on the Vineyard." Charlie grinned at Virgie, then dabbed his mouth with a napkin. Virgie wondered what property he was referring to.

Mr. Knight tapped a single finger on the gleaming tabletop. "I'm sure you realize that real estate is the cleanest way to move funds."

Virgie rose from her seat and entered the kitchen, hoping to avoid overhearing anything else. Every lunch or dinner she and Charlie had with people these days seemed to end in a request or a trade. Charlie called it the business of politics, but Virgie told him it was no different from taking bribes. "I wouldn't let lobbyists or their minions think they have a hold on you," she'd told him that spring.

He'd fumed, pacing at the foot of their bed. "Politics aren't as pure as you'd think. You want to get that childcare subsidy bill passed, right?"

As if she didn't know that politics were a messy muck of egos and power trades, and still, she'd wanted to believe that Charlie would function above it. "You haven't even introduced the childcare subsidy bill."

Later, she and Charlie would say good night to the Knights, and she would force him to look her in the eye. Would he go through with it and earmark money for Russell Knight's Skybolt program? Sadly, she wasn't certain he'd tell her the truth. He'd say no, but then she'd find out later at a women's luncheon when someone crassly mentioned the latest egregious (and deeply buried) earmark allotments. "To silly spending," Patti Johnson once toasted. Her husband was the speaker of the house. "It's really no different from me hiding how much I spent on the latest Chanel suit."

As Virgie helped Pamela add sprigs of fresh rosemary to each plate of steak Diane, the guests continued to talk. Inhaling deeply, her hands still trembling, Pamela accidentally dropped the entire bundle of parsley into the mashed potatoes. She fished it out, and Virgie looked up to find the woman's face balled up like a fist, her eyes sprouting wet in the corners. Virgie reached for a hand towel and tossed it to the woman, whispering, "What is it, Pamela?"

The woman dabbed her nose. "I'm sorry. I just . . . You make me realize what a failure I've been to my son." Pamela's frail center fell against the back of the cabinet like her stomach was in pain, but she kept talking. There were more tears. "All these important people in there discussing important things. You told me you're nothing but a mother, Virgie, but you have so much power in your voice you can't even hear it anymore. It's made me realize that I never even had a chance in life."

"A chance at what?" Virgie lifted two plates off the linoleum countertop, unable to connect the dots. What had triggered this much emotion in her?

She rubbed her nose. "A chance at doing something that matters."

"But you do matter. You matter to James, and you matter to me." Virgie's voice was patient, but she nodded to the doorway, making clear it was time to serve.

Pamela straightened the crisp eyelet apron. "Oh, Virgie. I had dreams too."

She paused before lifting the other two dinner plates, balancing them on her palms and recomposing her face. Together, they entered the dining room in a procession. No one would notice Pamela was crying because she was invisible, nothing but a housekeeper.

Virgie set down a plate in front of her husband, the ghostly echo of Pamela's words in her mind.

You have so much power in your voice you can't even hear it anymore. The question for Virgie was: What would she do with it?

CHAPTER SIXTEEN

The sound of the buoy bell wrestled her awake. Charlie wasn't in bed, and Virgie rose feeling uncertain about what the day would bring. Last night, she'd fallen into her pillows when the Knights left around ten, Pamela rousing a sleeping James and urging him outside to her rusted Buick while Charlie wrinkled his brow at the scene as he stood on the front porch smoking a cigar. She wasn't sure what time Louisa stayed up with her friend, but it must have been late since they were still asleep. Aggie and Betsy were gone from their rooms, their coverlets kicked to the bottom of their beds.

Virgie padded downstairs into the sunny kitchen, where she slumped into the banquette and stared out the window to the water. *Senatorial* was not at the dock. They'd gone sailing. Charlie must have woken them. A wonder that he got Aggie out of bed, since getting her up these last few weeks had grown so challenging that she'd been tempted to douse her with cold water.

Pamela's outburst the night before only solidified Virgie's feeling that if she did not empower her girls, they could end up feeling as hopeless as James's mother. They would be aimless and directionless and filled with a self-hatred that took over everything they did. They would be like Virgie's mother.

An hour later, Virgie watched the sailboat dock, her husband and the girls tying up the boat to the pilings. They entered the kitchen to steaming plates of pancakes drowning in syrup and butter. Charlie, with his hair tucked into an FBI cap, greeted her with a tentative smile, leaning in to kiss her on the cheek. "You look ravishing this morning," he said.

His comment had succeeded in softening the tension pulsing through her, since no one looked ravishing in the morning, especially not with last night's eye makeup caked on. "Oh, Charlie. Don't try to charm your way back into my good graces."

"Charm is all I have." He encouraged Virgie to sit down, she'd done enough. He would get the girls anything else they needed. He would clean the dishes.

Aggie ate her pancake with island honey, watching her parents with interest. "Are you in trouble, Dad?"

"Daddy is always in trouble with Mommy." Betsy thought she was being smart, and maybe she was, but Virgie made an impatient face at her anyway.

Virgie carried her coffee outside to the porch, the sun so bright she positioned her chair so it was fully in the shade of the striped awning. She knew Charlie would follow, and when he sat down, he commented on how busy the harbor seemed this summer.

"You seem rather busy this summer," she said pointedly.

"It's an election year, Virgie. It's always busy. I still can't believe you didn't tell me you were coming here—it hurt, you know." He pointed to the row of flowering potted plants on the patio, a mix of zinnias and geraniums. "I've been watering your houseplants. So far, everyone is doing okay."

Virgie smiled at him from behind her coffee cup; to him, even plants were people that needed tending. "Thank you. I didn't come here to get away from you. I wish you'd visit us more. The girls want the same."

Charlie tossed a few crumbs from his plate to a sparrow, the tiny bird pecking near his bare feet. "The other day I was in the Senate lunchroom with Byron and Jimmy, and Byron told a story about how his wife, you know Sara Edmonds, puts off her to-do list and gets nothing done in the house. I stuck up for her, Virgie. I said, 'A wife doesn't need to be managed.'"

Virgie knew what he was doing. "That's lovely, Charlie."

"I want us to go back to Washington together on Sunday. We can all fit on Senator Miner's plane."

A motorboat punctured the quiet, racing in the direction of Nantucket Sound. When Virgie didn't respond to his proposal, he changed the subject. "Betsy said she's been playing with that boy again. James?"

That anything other than his campaign was on his mind surprised her. Virgie fiddled with the ruby charm on her bracelet. "They play nicely together. That was his mother helping in the kitchen last night. They're really struggling, the kind of people you'd want to help if you met them."

"We don't need to give handouts to people to make up for their mistakes." Charlie raised both eyebrows with a question after she shot him an incredulous look.

"That was you once, remember? The person that needed kindness."

"It is your way to try to save people."

"And what is wrong with that?"

It was one thing she knew about her husband. He liked to think that he'd reinvented himself so completely that he'd never been that penniless orphan living without a family; that he'd never actually needed Virgie to prop him up. Sometimes she thought he believed he'd been born Senator Whiting of New York. Unless his darker moods took over. Then he was shadowed in doubt and depression; Virgie believed only she knew how much he overcompensated for a deeply held belief that he'd come from nothing and he was nothing, no matter how high his power climbed. It's why she tolerated his bad behavior. He could be explained.

He threaded his fingers together. "And what about Aggie? She said you've been letting her go to Oak Bluffs to some other kid's house. Another Black child?"

The couple had so much to hash out, and yet it was the girls' friendships that was consuming him. "I'm not sure which part bothers you?"

Sometimes he still spoke like a divinity student, even-keeled and believing, no matter what words came to the pulpit. "We don't even know *these people*, Virgie—there are plenty of other kids to play with." Charlie cuffed his sleeves up, leaning his strong forearms onto the table. "I know you love the island. I do, too, and I'm sure they're nice kids and no harm to their families, but I can't have any controversy in the papers."

"Controversy? Last I checked, most of your voters believed in Civil Rights, and it was you that helped pass the landmark legislation." Did he seriously believe that the girls should only befriend fellow white summer kids from Boston, New York, and Washington? Was it a question of money—or was it race?

"Northerners believe in equal rights, Virg, but they still don't want Blacks in their neighborhoods." Charlie's single dimple attempted to lighten the weight of his words. "It's a hot-button issue, and I don't need my girls photographed and testing people's tolerance."

"Charlie." Breathless, she waited for his shame. Instead, he wrung his hands, tanned and strong, the hands of a woodworker, not a senator.

"I've told you this before. You've got to move the public in baby steps."

She thought of India Knight's prescient words. "You need to whisper and not yell."

"Yes." He seemed pleased, sitting back against the Adirondack chair. "And this boy, with Betsy. She's developing into a young woman. We don't need another Louisa situation . . ."

Charlie might as well have slapped her cheek. “Don’t you ever bring that up so callously. That is Louisa’s story to tell.”

His Adam’s apple slid up and down. “Virgie.” He tried to sound tender. This was the voice Charlie used when he greeted a veteran at Walter Reed or a woman who lost her family in a fire. “These girls. We can’t let them run free because you think it builds strength. Your parents didn’t do that with you. You lived with rules.”

“Stifling rules.” Virgie sniffed. “I want them to be confident. I want them to learn to live on their own terms. Why does that make you so afraid?”

“Because everyone is watching us.” Charlie was resolute, his speech slowing to make clear she should listen closely. “I want to run for governor, maybe president. I must consider how we’re seen. How all of us are portrayed.”

Listening to him was like watching the harbor at low tide, the gunky shells and muddy sand creeping out from the pretty blue water. Charlie was a moderate Democrat, but he believed in the Equal Pay Act. He’d supported the Freedom Riders. He’d scoffed at separate water fountains for Blacks and whites. How would his daughters spending time with colored children reshape him in the public image?

“You’re losing sight of who you are,” Virgie whisper-yelled; she didn’t want the girls to hear. “When you pander to voters like this, they can sense it. What happened to True Charlie? The Charlie that speaks only the truth. Remember him?”

“I’m still true. You know that I am.” He smiled at the memory. It was a nickname given to him the year he gave the keynote speech at the Democratic National Convention; people still wore True Charlie buttons when they came to his political rallies. “But a man’s home is different from a man’s work, and times are different. There are video cameras following us now, not just reporters with steno pads. My personal life needs a water-tight seal. There can’t be anything, not a single thing, to distract from my policies.”

"They're having the time of their lives, Charlie. You tell me how their summer should be different."

"Sailing is good. Clamming. They can swim and attend the Ag Fair on each other's arms. Put them in modest one-pieces on the beach, be sure they're spending time with other educated young women their age."

"And what if they don't want that? What if they want to sail in a bikini?"

He rubbed the back of his neck, impatient. "They don't know what they want. They're kids. Girls."

The Ladies Tea, his daughters, her writings: it all needed to suit his needs. She stared off at Chappaquiddick, the way some houses were tucked into the tree line, hidden. "The tea is set for the eighteenth, and don't expect talk of campaign issues. I'm going to talk about our girls. I'm going to talk about what's important to women."

He studied her profile. "Everyone loves a good family story, assuming that's what you mean."

"Sure, dear. A family story." Virgie thought of the article she'd been working on. It was like a Fireside Chat for young women. It was her whisper, her battle cry. "I'll tell a very good family story."

After midnight, after the girls were asleep, Charlie came into bed, sliding his arm around her. She turned over to face him, her eyes rising to meet his in the moonlight. His voice, an apology. "Please come back to me, Virgie. We can disagree, but it doesn't mean you ever need to leave for good."

The buoy bell rocked with the waves. Virgie loped her arms around his neck. Sometimes she wondered what it would be like to be married to someone who had a mother to call, a brother to play golf with, a sister to anchor you to something more than your wife.

Her frustration from earlier remained fresh, and still, her heart grew tender. He was right; they could disagree and remain close. She kissed him, feeling the neediness in how he kissed her back. After a few moments, she pulled away, whispering: "I'm right here."

The following afternoon, Charlie gathered their daughters on the patio after he returned from a round of golf with a friend. His ferry left that evening after dinner, and she wondered if they would ever discuss the elephant in the room, how she wasn't returning to Washington with him. They'd gone about the rest of their day in the passive-aggressive manner of a happy couple subtly avoiding serious topics, talking casually about things like the striped bass derby, a shared craving for chowder at Nancy's, an island clam bar. On the patio, he stood in his bathing trunks and flip-flops, the girls sitting on the grass beside him, their knees pulled into their chests.

Virgie was too curious not to wander over and sit in a nearby Adirondack chair, close enough that she could hear what he was saying, but not so close that she couldn't pretend to read her book.

Charlie had the muscular legs of a soccer player, even if he hadn't played since his coed days. He pushed his wide hands into his shorts' pockets. "You see that buoy out there?" he said. A half mile, maybe less, out in the harbor was a red chiming one; the sound of it was the soundtrack to their island life. "You've seen me swim back and forth from that buoy many times. Well, your mother thinks I don't take you seriously because you are girls. So we'll prove her wrong. If I had boys, I would demand that they swim with me, so now I'm demanding the same thing of you."

Louisa glared at her mother, which made Virgie snap-shut the novel she'd been rereading, *The Awakening* by Kate Chopin; she planned to make each of her girls read this feminist classic.

"Don't blame me for your father's cockamamie plans," Virgie said. She knew what Charlie was doing in suggesting the endurance swim. This was his apology; he wouldn't say sorry, he'd show it, by proving to

Virgie that the girls could be free and strong and empowered without doing all the things he'd disavowed.

Well, two could play this game. "I'm in too," she said, pulling off her sundress to reveal a conservative navy-blue one-piece. She'd swum to the same buoy more than a hundred times in her lifetime, at least a dozen times with Charlie, who would insist she time him so he could beat his score.

"Good." Charlie's smile turned up; his eyes shining. He'd mistaken her acceptance as submission.

She steeled her voice. "Let's show him, girls, that we can be as hardheaded when it comes to getting what we want." No matter what he said, Virgie wouldn't enforce Charlie's paranoid rules about the children's friends or insist on a formality for their lives in case a reporter glimpsed them having fun, wearing a bikini, or playing with a colored child.

It was a long way out there, and she imagined Betsy struggling halfway. "I think Betsy should drag a buoy behind her, just in case," Virgie said.

Betsy stomped her bare foot on the grass. "It will slow me down. I can swim just as good as Louisa."

The sea would chill them to their bones this time of year. "This isn't about you and Louisa; this is about you being able to make it."

Charlie agreed about the buoy, and Betsy huffed into diving position at the end of the dock, a Styrofoam bullet strapped to her back. "We're not trying to get the best time," Charlie said, even though they were. "What's important, girls, is that you finish."

"I do not want to do this." Louisa had tucked her hair into a swimming cap.

Charlie smiled at her like she'd delivered a round of applause. "Oh, Louisa. You're our leader. We're all trying to keep up with you. Don't let us down."

"Besides, you're finally getting Daddy's attention." Aggie held her hands over her head in diving stance. "Enjoy it. I'm going to cream her, Dad."

Louisa turned her head away from them, but Virgie detected the slightest of smiles. Maybe things had finally thawed between her and Charlie; he had taken her to the soda fountain for a milkshake yesterday, even if Louisa's patience still ran thin with her father.

"That's the spirit," Virgie said, a competitive ferocity taking hold of her as well. "Let's pummel each other."

Charlie angled his body in the direction of the lighthouse. "Ready, Whiting girls. GO!"

There was the sound of five bodies splashing into the cool water, followed by the pull of their arms and the suction of their collective breathing. Virgie swam hard, stopping after a few minutes to check on Betsy, all her daughters hauling forward. Halfway to the buoy, Betsy yelled for help, and Louisa swam right by her, ignoring her like she was in an Olympic race with Aggie and Charlie.

"Mommy, the life preserver, it's heavy. Can I take it off?" Betsy treaded water, her lips blue and trembling.

Virgie treaded beside her; what was the point of competition if someone was going to get hurt? That was the part Charlie forgot sometimes. "I'll take the life vest. We'll swim together."

She and Betsy swam in sync, Virgie slowing her stride; it wasn't worth trying to win against Charlie now. Her youngest had more stamina than she would have thought, and still, minutes from the buoy, the other three shot past them on their way back. On an inhale, Louisa glimpsed Aggie ahead, and she kicked her feet with a vengeance.

Betsy panted, steadying her hand against the bottom of the buoy to rest. "Do you think Louisa could have swum this when she was ten?"

Virgie wiped the water off her face, wishing that Betsy would stop comparing herself to her older sisters. Virgie hoped she didn't spend a lifetime figuring out she was her own person. "Louisa can barely catch a ball with the boys in gym."

Betsy laughed, water specks like crystals on her eyelashes. Her chest was heaving. "I prefer to play with boys. Is that because I'm more athletic?"

"Maybe," Virgie found herself saying, although Betsy had taken four years of tennis and still couldn't serve properly. "Someday when you get older, you're going to see that playing with boys helped you navigate relationships with men. You will learn how to make things seem like their idea, even if it is entirely your own."

"So I'll be a good wife?"

"You'll be a good human." A fish nipped at Virgie's foot, an unsettling feeling that made Virgie want to get swimming again. "I know that you and James are good friends, but there's so much more to life than falling in love."

"I'm not in love with James!"

"Of course you're not, but it's okay if you secretly are. It's how Daddy and I had started out—close friends who fell in love."

Once again, mother and daughter swam in sync, slow and steady. As Virgie watched her daughter push through her fatigue, determined to finish, she was filled with so much hope for Betsy's future. She was pushing through the current, through the cold, through the discomfort.

Before Charlie left that evening, they ate dinner as a family, the water lapping a deep, vibrant blue. Hamburgers and corn on the cob. Crisp chardonnay.

Freshly showered, her husband came downstairs smelling of aftershave, his dark hair pushed back from his golden tan.

"What are you girls going to do this week?" he said, after asking Virgie where she got the corn; it was the sweetest they'd had yet this summer.

Virgie relaxed into her glass of wine, relieved that he'd made peace with her desire to remain on the island without him. Her mind glazed over with victory, and she lost track of the conversation, the girls piping in with upcoming plans of a lifeguarding demonstration and an art fair.

The citronella candle flickered, a stinging sweet smell puncturing the salt air.

Charlie leaned back in his chair, putting his hands behind his head. "It was so entertaining swimming with you girls today. You girls competed like Olympians." Charlie's smile was always so big and hearty, with the kind of shine that could feel like it was meant only for you.

They all giggled. Betsy ran inside and raced out with scissors, paper, and colored pencils, drawing gold and silver medals to cut out in an impromptu awards ceremony. Charlie played along, handing them out while crossing his eyes and talking like a goofy television announcer, calling Louisa "dogged but most ready to get out of the water"; Aggie, "speedy and determined to make waves"; and Betsy, "small, mighty," then he paused for dramatic impact like the comedian Bob Hope, "and diving into the case of why the race isn't fair. It's never fair."

After a round of goofy applause, Betsy falling into her father, holding her tummy with laughter, the girls yelled over one another, playfully appealing their designations. The children moved over to the grass, Aggie and Betsy doing cartwheels while competing to come up with the best swimming pun.

Virgie sensed Charlie staring at her. "This was fun," he said. "Way more fun than what I've been doing."

They clinked wineglasses in what felt like a celebration of the perfect summer night. Virgie's mind drifted to her article, the one she planned to ask Wiley to publish. How would her husband's adoration shift once he saw her words printed in a big city newspaper?

How much would he let her push—how much would he try to pull her back?

CHAPTER SEVENTEEN

Three days after Charlie left, Virgie finished typing "Flying Lessons" while Aggie and Betsy were at sailing, reading it over to check for errors. It needed a second set of eyes, and while she planned to ask India Knight to read it—she and the woman had talked on the phone yesterday about forming a women's political group on the island—Virgie wanted her eldest daughter to read it first. If the words resonated with Louisa, then the article would resonate with other young women. Virgie couldn't help but fantasize that her daughter would admire her for not being afraid to educate young women on the realities of their burgeoning selves. Because it wasn't enough to help women like Pamela Sunday by giving her a job; Virgie wanted to help as many women as possible see that it wasn't just their lives that mattered, but the ways in which they lived them. Each decision—to attend college or not, to quit a job or not, to persevere in a man's field or not, to have a child or not—added up to a belief system. It seemed too many women put the car in drive and accepted whatever they drove past. Herself included.

This morning, with puddles still lining the streets from last night's rain, Virgie decided she would surprise her eldest daughter at the bookshop with her article—and mint-flavored iced tea. A small treat she could enjoy on her twenty-minute break. Stirring in a lemon slice and sealing the mason jar with a wax cover and elastic, Virgie glanced in the mirror on her way out. Her hair was pulled back in a low ponytail too casual for Washington, her black clamdiggers and Keds giving her a youthful edge. The lace dress she wore the night they hosted the Knights had been put in a bag with other dresses she thought Pamela Sunday might like for church or a future job. One never knew what direction life would take you.

Stepping outside to the sun, Virgie inhaled the salt air.

A flashbulb popped in her face. She blinked twice, holding her hand up for a moment while trying to figure out who was taking her picture. As her eyes adjusted, she noted a young man facing her. He swam in a suit much too big for his narrow shoulders, and he wore glasses, round spectacles with wire rims.

"Mrs. Whiting, I'm Jay Clancy, a reporter with the *New York Sun*." He tucked the camera into a case, opening a crossbody satchel and pulling out a pen and notebook.

There was so much she could get angry about: that he'd surprised her at her front door, that she'd nearly spilled Louisa's iced tea. It was how his lip curled up as he said his title that got her most; he was arrogant. "Yes, sir. How are you?" She held out her hand to shake his, and he glanced at it, his eye going back to his notepad.

"I want to ask you a few questions, Mrs. Whiting."

She continued to hold out her hand, her tone turning stern at his inexperience. "Okay, young man, but you can shake my hand first." He raised his clammy fingers to hers, and she smiled. "You should have contacted my husband's press office if you wanted to talk. This is our private home, and I don't do interviews on the street."

"Your husband's office has been stonewalling us, so my editor sent me here."

"Well, you can tell your editor that you do not have permission to use the photograph you just took, and if you would like to schedule an interview with me, call my husband's office. At some point, his press secretary will call you back." She repositioned her purse on her shoulder. "Good luck, Jay Clancy."

At the corner of Field and Main, he caught up to her. "Are you aware that your husband has gone to Nantucket three times in the last few months?"

She stopped, turning her clipped face at him. "Why would that matter? He has dinners, fundraising events. He's always off somewhere doing the work of the nation, so why are *you* so interested?"

The man had hazel eyes with gold flecks, and he was having trouble looking at her. "We think he might be going there for something other than political business."

The *New York Sun*. That paper was one of Wiley's papers. Did he know that one of his cub reporters was standing here and harassing her? She retained her composure. No, her husband hadn't told her he was going to Nantucket—he hadn't even been to the Vineyard.

Virgie clicked open her purse and popped a breath mint. "Are you aware that Wiley Prescott is one of my closest friends?" She let the news settle into the reporter's sinking stature. "I am going to deliver this iced tea to my daughter, then I will return home and I will call Wiley. I'm going to ask him why he has a reporter following me down the road with so little respect for my privacy."

The reporter quickly nodded, apologizing, saliva pooling in the corners of his mouth. "I had no idea you were a friend of Wiley's. My editor doesn't know I'm here. I came on a hunch, and now . . ."

Virgie grimaced. "I will repeat myself once more. If you want an interview, you will need to call my husband's press secretary."

Somehow, she carried herself with composure all the way to the bookshop. *The nerve*, she thought. Is this what society had come to? No sense of privacy, an ambush at her home, all because he had a hunch. Her mind reeled. What on earth could that possibly mean, anyway?

The bookshop had always been one of the sweetest stores in the tiny village. Set in a house with a front porch, Island Books carried a variety of titles, from literature to nonfiction biographies. It was owned by a longtime family on the island, who passed it down like a treasured jewel. These days the middle-aged son, Gordon Pendleton, was running it with his wife, Sophia. Charlie and the husband were friends, which was how Louisa had gotten the job stocking shelves and working the cash register.

"Hello, Virgie." Sophia beamed, reaching over the counter to give her a hug. She glanced at the mason jar. "Is that for me?"

"There's enough to split." Virgie pretended it was her intention all along.

They made a few minutes of small talk about the shop and Louisa's role, how she'd hung colorful posters in the children's room and read for kids at their Tuesday story hour.

Virgie picked up the latest Flannery O'Connor off the shelf. "Is she here?"

Sophia waved to an incoming customer. "She left early today. Didn't she tell you?"

A child will break your heart again and again, Virgie thought, *and it's still within a mother's ability to think the best*. "She didn't."

"I believe she was meeting Aggie, maybe in Oak Bluffs?"

Virgie returned the novel back on the bookshelf. "Agatha is at sailing." She turned to go, realizing her girls were up to something.

She marched down the dock of the yacht club. The Opti boats drew lines in the sea, and she strained to see her daughter's head. Her eye found Betsy as she pulled her boat alongside James—the two of them side by side with orange life vests around their necks and laughing about something she couldn't hear from here. Waving her arms, Virgie hollered: "Betsy! Betsy!"

Betsy turned around, elated to see her mother on the dock. "What are you doing here?"

"Have you seen Agatha? I need to talk to her?"

"What?" Betsy hollered back. She and James drew back with hysterical laughter every time she heaved her voice over the sail.

"Aggie. Where is Agatha?"

Betsy shrugged. "Home? She said she wasn't feeling well."

Virgie pursed her lips, walking home at a clip, hoping that nosy reporter didn't have the gall to approach her again. Inside the house, she yelled for Louisa, then Aggie. The cuckoo clock in the kitchen ticked. Not here. In the garage, two bikes were missing. Nothing had seemed amiss these last few days, everyone falling back into a steady rhythm since Charlie left. She was thinking the worst because of the flashbulb, the reporter, the mention of her husband on Nantucket. She would have to bring it up to him. Her stomach flip-flopped.

Oak Bluffs. Maybe the girls had ridden to Aggie's friend's house? They could be meeting up with boys. They wouldn't take the ferry to the mainland, would they? She imagined reporting to Charlie that she'd lost two of her children, heat flushing up her neck. Snatching her keys, Virgie rushed into the station wagon.

The streets of Oak Bluffs traveled in unpredictable patterns, like someone had thrown a pile of sticks down and made roads of them. The bikes weren't outside Aggie's friend Junie's house with its freshly painted white porch. She drove up busy Circuit Avenue, creeping along so she could check the thin alleyways. Nothing.

I'm going to kill these girls, she thought, turning into a neighborhood of gingerbread cottages. There was a playground with a seesaw and swings. That's when she saw the bikes, parked against the chain-link fence lining the baseball dugout. She trained a watchful eye. A few women with kids at the playground. A trash truck emptying a garbage can. A dozen people on a makeshift basketball court. She watched the players a moment, and when a hulking boy jumped up to score, Virgie saw her. Lanky and tall and crouched in a defender stance, there was Aggie, her daughter's navy shorts riding up her slender thighs, sweat stains rounding in her armpits. She dribbled the ball, then spun away from a guard and passed to another boy. Her tennis shoes screeched as she yelled, "Here, Junie. I'm open."

Virgie hurried straight for the court, which was nothing more than packed dirt with hoops nailed to a tree at either end. Her daughter's teammates were all colored girls, and they were playing against colored boys. At least one of the young men towered over her daughter.

Virgie glanced sideways for the reporter. *Can you imagine if he shot a picture of this?* The wrath she would endure from her husband, who would taunt her for calling him paranoid. She saw red then. Virgie had trusted her daughters. She strode across the grass to the hoop, a white lady in white Keds, and grabbed Aggie by the ear, dragging her away from the game.

"Let go of me, Mom. LET GO." Aggie's pupils narrowed to slits, and she broke out of her mother's grip, her breathing ragged.

"You need to come home. Now." Virgie exited the court, waiting for her in the grass. She wasn't sure if she was angry because Aggie had snuck out, because she was playing basketball, or because Charlie had inserted himself into her head a little too much.

Louisa seemed to come from the bushes, carrying a lemonade that dripped down her hand; she was still wearing her Island Books pin on a scallop-sleeve sweater. "I told her not to join the tournament, but Aggie insisted, so I came to watch out for her. I wasn't sure if she'd be safe . . ."

Aggie headed to a free throw line they'd marked with a piece of yarn. "Why wouldn't I be safe? I'm playing with a bunch of Vineyard kids."

"You don't even know these kids!" Virgie followed her, very aware that the other teenagers were watching her. She imagined her daughter lying on the court after falling awkwardly and breaking an arm.

Aggie motioned to a friend to toss her the basketball. "You don't know these kids, but I do. I've been playing with them all summer."

Virgie gripped the metal fence links. "You've been sneaking out?" She couldn't help but look for the reporter.

"I didn't really lie. We went to Junie's house, then we'd come here." Aggie's hands went to her hips as the kids on the court began to whisper. She walked up to her mother, facing her, and Virgie realized how tall her daughter was; they were nearly the same height now. "You told me to go after my goal. You said that I can't let people stop me. All that stuff about how women want people to take us seriously, so here I am." Aggie bounced the ball. "Well, I demanded to be taken seriously, and now you're angry. So which is it, Mom? Should I listen to all those boys on the court who are telling me I shouldn't play because I'm a girl, or should I push back? Because it can't be both."

"I didn't mean for you to go do all the things we told you not to do." And still, her daughter's point was solid. She was doing exactly what Virgie had told her to.

"And why not? You told us to fight. Well, I'm fighting. I'm fighting to play a game I love."

Aggie wiped her nose with the back of her wrist. There was an image in Virgie's head suddenly. Aggie wearing her high heels in grade school, clacking around the house in a too-big tweed dress and pretending to be a hotel concierge. Asking Virgie if she wanted a pot of tea, approaching her sisters and announcing a concert pianist on the "back porch," meaning she would play "Row Your Boat" on the piano in the living room. It had made Virgie cringe because she didn't want Aggie to aspire to be at someone else's beck and call, and now this five-foot-eight woman was asserting herself. She was showing Virgie what being your own woman *looked* like. Rebellion was rarely convenient.

The game picked back up, one of Aggie's teammates eyeing Virgie as she trudged back to her car. Aggie caught the ball, her eye on the hoop. She shot a free throw. Time slowed as Virgie watched the ball careen straight into the basket, Aggie's teammates coming to her for high fives. It captivated Virgie, the way her daughter was dribbling the ball around the court, how she slammed her weight into one of the boys to pass the ball to her teammate. For a second, she couldn't take her eyes off Aggie: running up and down the center, fanning out to the edges, the studious focus in her eyes. Each time a teammate passed her the ball, she was ready to catch it, then dribbled it to the basket. All this time Virgie had been worried the boys would laugh her daughter off the court. But these boys passed to her. They took her seriously as a player.

It was so very surprising.

"She's right, Mom," Louisa said as she followed Virgie back to the car by the baseball dugout. "You did tell us to go after our goals."

Her frustration returned all at once. Virgie slammed her car door shut, keeping up her window, and instead of talking to Louisa, she yelled to the strawberry air freshener hanging from the rearview mirror. "That doesn't mean sneak off to some girl's house and lie to your mother."

Louisa was trying to get her mom to open the window, but she bounded out of the spot, peeling out. The worst part about seeing her daughter playing basketball was the realization that she was a really good player. Virgie had seen one boy grin into his hand at one of Aggie's shots, like he couldn't believe a girl could play like that.

It had been satisfying to see that, even Virgie had to admit. She turned on the radio to distract herself, then shut it off.

Charlie was wrong in saying Aggie couldn't spend time with colored children, but maybe Virgie had been wrong about forbidding her daughter to play basketball. The sport gave Agatha power, it gave her might, and maybe the only thing to fear about the sport was her daughter's pointed free throw.

She chuckled then, remembering the moment when Aggie had pushed right past a taller colored boy with the ball. The look of shock on his face.

Virgie carried in an armload of flowers from the garden, mostly fiery daylilies and delicate Chappaquiddick daisies that grew wild along the exterior walls of the house. It relaxed her to make small bouquets to place on bedroom bureaus and the kitchen table, and after her conversation with Charlie, and the scene that had played out with Aggie earlier, she wanted to stay busy. She'd caught Charlie on the phone at the imposing Russell Senate Office Building before he slipped off to attend a meeting of the Senate Budgetary Committee. He spoke quickly, his tone impatient and clipped, the voices of his staff carrying on in the background.

"I have no idea why this reporter wants to know why I was on Nantucket," Charlie said, saying something to his staff about finding him the Transportation files. "I did stop on the island on my way home last week—it was a planned meeting to see a donor with a house there. There's nothing foul to sniff out."

"Why wouldn't you tell me that?"

"Tell you what? That I was going to Nantucket?"

"Yes, Charlie." Her upper lip quivered as she filled a mason jar with water.

"It just didn't seem relevant. I'm always off to a dozen places."

"Well, that is what I told the reporter." She didn't like his answer. It was too vague. She gently set down the mason jar on the counter, afraid it might shatter. Perhaps she'd always felt it, a deep-seated fear that she didn't know her husband as much as she wanted to. That there were parts of him that were sealed off, even to her, like a honeycomb with empty tunnels. "If I hear from him again, I'll let you know."

Next week, she would hold the first meeting of the Edgartown Ladies of Social Concern, the "Tea" that she organized in Charlie's honor. She told him as much, but she didn't tell him that his name would be nowhere in the room. Only the suggestion of it. After a few more quick exchanges, he said, "I'm sorry, love, but the budget meeting is in five minutes and it's on the other side of the Capitol." He sounded so far away, and a part of her wished she could tell him about the stunning revelation she'd had about Aggie.

"Before I go, tell me something about the girls. Quick."

"This morning Betsy sang 'God Bless America' at the breakfast table." She smiled into the quiet as her husband laughed. "I love you," she said.

"I love you too," he said.

There were flowers in every room when Aggie came home that evening just before dinner. Her daughter didn't say a word when she dropped her canvas backpack on the table, and Virgie didn't either. The pesto was ready, and the spaghetti was boiling, but they'd waited for Aggie. She'd raced upstairs to take a shower, Betsy and James doing cartwheels on the lawn.

Virgie called through the screen. "James, I tried to invite your mother to come eat with us, but she's not picking up."

"I can go ask her, but can Betsy come with me?"

"Sure, I'll come." Betsy grinned. The two of them raced down to his small rowboat. Wiley had given him a small outboard motor, and James could get them across the harbor in half the time now. As he pulled the choke, Virgie yelled through the window, "If she can't come, ask if it's okay for you to eat with us."

Louisa was reading a romance that Virgie knew she should censor, but she was too overwhelmed with everything to try. Her daughter had spent a half an hour defending her decision to protect her sister's choice to play in the impromptu tournament until Virgie had scolded her, "Enough already! You did the right thing. Is that what you want to hear?"

She'd nodded. "In fact, yes."

The shower turned off, and minutes later, the stairs creaked from the other room. Virgie stiffened while tossing the salad. Aggie padded into the kitchen in a gingham sundress, walking straight to Virgie's back like an arrow finding a target. Wrapping her arms around her mother's narrow waist, Virgie felt her daughter's apology. Her whole body vibrated against her, and her daughter's tears wet her shirt.

"I'm so sorry, Mommy. I'm sorry for going to the courts and not telling you, and I'm sorry for yelling and not getting in the car."

Virgie exhaled and turned to face her daughter—Agatha was her easiest daughter because she was an open book; Louisa and Betsy held their emotions inside, and she had to spend hours interrogating them before they believed it safe to show their feelings. Aggie's mouth gaped, a mouse fearful of a lion. Neither one said a word until the timer for the garlic bread dinged. Virgie pressed a lock of her daughter's hair into a neat side part.

"It was wrong of you to lie to me," she said.

"I know." Aggie put her head in her hands. "I feel so dumb. I'm just so dumb." The phone began to ring, and something in Virgie told her it was Charlie. That he'd found out about the basketball game, that someone got a photograph with Aggie on a court filled with colored kids.

"You're not dumb, honey." She hugged her one last time, then said, "I'll tell you one thing: you knocked my socks off back there." She let her serious tone turn light. "You play some seriously good basketball."

When a child smiles, a mother can lose her bearings, changing from solid to liquid. Syrupy.

"You really think so?" Aggie said.

"Girls really can play ball. That's what I think. I shouldn't have stopped you—I was just so caught up in my own fears until I saw that they were unfounded." Virgie kissed the smooth side of her daughter's temple, the smell of Pert shampoo in her still-wet hair. The phone trilled again.

Sliding on an oven mitt, Aggie went to work, like she always did in the kitchen, helping her mother pull out the bread. Virgie raised the earpiece: "The Whiting residence."

It was Betsy's voice on the other end. Small, distant, panicked. "She's not moving, Mommy. I'm not sure if she's breathing, and James just keeps shaking her."

"Betsy? Are you okay?"

"I'm okay, but she's not. James's mom is not breathing."

"Call 911," Virgie instructed, as calmly as she could manage. "Call 911 right now, and I'll get on the ferry."

Louisa and Aggie jumped into the car alongside their mother, all three women holding their breath as the car raced down the narrow streets.

CHAPTER EIGHTEEN

Betsy

Edgartown
1978

Betsy parked her bike in the musty garage, the pregnancy test burning a hole in her messenger bag. From afar, she waved hello to her sisters, both engrossed in different novels on the back lawn while lounging in Adirondack chairs. Then she hurried up the steps and inside to the smell of cut roses and the sound of her mother's typing carrying through the house. That darn book. When Betsy mentioned the disparaging writings to her sisters last week, they'd shrugged it off. "It's probably a way of her grieving. It's like making sense of who you were with the person and who you are without them," Louisa said. Aggie nodded: "I think it's healthy."

The kitchen was clean of dishes. The living room vacuumed and everything in place. Betsy felt like she couldn't sit still, and yet she wouldn't take the test until later, once the chance of someone discovering what she was doing had passed. Betsy slipped up the crooked steps with her messenger bag, burying the bag behind the suitcases in the bedroom closet. She slumped on the bed, staring at the textbooks she'd lined up on the small desk. Rising, she grazed the titles with her fingertips and opened one: *Games People Play*. It wasn't a textbook, per se, but a pop psychology bestseller that she'd put off reading. With her elbows on the desk, she began to read, the pages turning quickly. The premise was that everyone needed "strokes" from others to feel good about themselves. Some got positive reinforcement from their fans, like an actor to applause, and some got good feelings from close family members. Betsy lowered the book into her lap and gazed out at the harbor still busy with boats and sailors. Is that why her family was always disappointing her? she thought. Were they the only ones she looked to for affirmation? Perhaps she should rewrite her term paper and finish graduate school, she thought then. Something about the possibility of a pregnancy making her ache for her status quo existence of a month before. She could use the sadness surrounding this beach house as the basis for a new thesis: "The Psychological Implications of Losing Home."

Dinner that night was a bit of a disaster, with Tabby wailing as Louisa lowered the lobsters into the giant pot of boiling water, while her mother melted butter in a small saucepan and tried to calm the child.

Betsy, who was slicing potatoes in half to boil, resorted to bribery, since red rings around Tabby's eyes had started to resemble a raccoon. "If you stop crying, I'll take you for ice cream after dinner?"

Aggie looked none too pleased, placing her daughter on her hip after placing the baby in the bouncy seat. "Please don't placate Tabby with sweets. That's dangerous as she gets older and thinks donuts will heal a broken heart."

"They do heal a broken heart," Betsy deadpanned. How many sweets had she'd eaten since Andy had left her? The day after, she'd consumed an entire box of chocolates.

Her mother stirred the butter. "Well, your midline won't appreciate that form of happiness, and no matter how much women complain that men still judge us by our midlines, they also still judge us by our midlines."

"That's hardly a feminist stance, Mom." Louisa wiped her hands on her apron, reaching for the salt to shake into the lobster water.

Her mother ran her hands down the front of her denim skirt. "Think of it this way: Who wants to see someone unattractive holding a protest sign? They let me go on the morning news show and speak my mind for one reason."

It was Aggie that piped in. "Because you're incredibly smart and interesting to listen to?"

"I wish that were the only reason." Her mother used an oven mitt to lift the lid off the lobsters, then placed it back down. "It's also because I'm not offensive to look at. Why do you think people liked Gloria Steinem more than they did Betty Friedan? It's because Gloria wasn't half bad to look at. Femininity is a form of power when it comes to magazines and television. An elegant woman can have a voice because men notice her and want to hear what she has to say."

"That's warped," Betsy said. "Maybe women want to hear what you have to say."

"Maybe." Her mother shrugged. "But men must allow it. We live in a man's world, girls, and we're not leaving it anytime soon, even if we have Jimmy Carter on our side. Jimmy Carter is not the savior of the feminists."

"That's a good cover story headline." Louisa smiled. "Can Jimmy Carter save the feminists?"

Her mother pulled a small notebook out of the drawer and scribbled it down in black marker. "That's quite good, Lou. I've been a bit out of ideas since Dad died. I only want to write about him."

Betsy shot her sisters a searing look, mouthing the words, *I told you so.*

That night, in the pitch-black of her bedroom, with everyone asleep and Louisa gently snoring in the bed beside her, Betsy pulled her messenger bag out of her closet. Carrying it downstairs to the green-tiled half bathroom, Betsy pulled out the Predictor test. Using a flashlight to see, afraid that turning on the light would alert someone she was inside, she carefully followed the instructions, peeing into a test tube and mixing it with a chemical to leave it in the provided container for two hours. She glanced at her watch. Twelve thirty. In the meantime, she'd continue reading for school, taking notes about this new idea she had for her term paper about the impact of a childhood home on development.

It was two thirty when Betsy put the Predictor's mirror on the top of the toilet, shining the beam onto the clear plastic cube. The instructions said that women who were pregnant should be able to see a small brown circle gathered at the bottom of the test tube, as reflected in the provided mirror. At first, since she was using a flashlight in the dark, Betsy couldn't see anything at all, not even the blue liquid. Then she shined the beam directly over the tube. A circle of light angled just right.

And there it was: a tiny brown halo floating in the blue dye.

CHAPTER NINETEEN

Virgie

Chappaquiddick
1965

The Chappy ferry parked at the tiny terminal on the other side of the harbor, Virgie adjusting her thighs as they stuck to the seats with humidity. She raced off the tiny ferry, the laughter of summer tourists punctuating her thoughts as she said a prayer to Louisa in the front seat. "Please don't let her be dead. Please tell me she didn't find Pamela dead."

Louisa licked her pallid lips, her eyes darting about the roadway.

For a second, Virgie couldn't remember where his house was, her mind whirring with worry. She blew by the driveway with the hand-painted sign reading, SUNDAY. Turning the car around with a screeching halt, Virgie pulled down the bumpy dirt driveway, wondering if the children had called an ambulance. Parking, she sprinted through the front door.

James had his body draped over his mother's, who was lying on the floor, while Betsy sat on the couch with a brown velour throw blanket around her shoulders, shivering, despite the eighty degrees. "Honey, go to the car," she said, instructing Louisa and Aggie to usher their baby sister outside.

A quick sweep of the room with her eyes. The house was still immaculate. The plastic remained on the sofa; the counters wiped clean. Two empty bottles of wine in the sink, a glass shattered on the floor near Pamela's fuzzy slippers. Virgie nudged the boy's small shoulder. "James, it's okay. Sit up, dear. Let me get a look at her."

The child didn't move, so Virgie reached under his arms and lifted him. His lips were inflamed, his nose goopy. "Stop," he roared. "Let me go!"

Virgie checked for a pulse. The woman's hands were warm and pink, the beds of her fingernails with color, a good sign. In her veiny wrist she felt the ticking of her heart.

"She's okay, James. She's okay."

Virgie felt her own eyes well up at the sight of the boy sitting up on his knees, yelling at his mother's unmoving form, a slight rise and fall in her marigold sweater, thinning at the seams. "I hate you!" he said.

"You don't mean that." But she remembered feeling similarly whenever her mother slipped into a drunken state, wishing her dead each time she woke up with a headache so powerful she'd keep the shades drawn the entire day. "James, she's not out of the woods yet. We must get her help. Did you and Betsy call 911?"

He held his mother's hand, nodding.

Why hadn't she called Pamela every morning this week? She knew how lonely she was, and she'd done nothing. Why hadn't she invited her over for tea?

Virgie peeled her eyes from the child. Outside, she found Betsy in the back seat in Louisa's arms. She kissed her youngest daughter's smooth forehead. "She's okay, Betts. She drank too much and passed out, but she's going to be okay."

Betsy sniffled into the blanket. "Do you promise?"

A siren blared, getting louder, tires racing along the dirt road. An officer jumped out of the squad car, and Virgie followed as he pushed open the front door. She told him the woman had drunk too much, and his face fell when he found the boy, sitting crisscross beside his mother, his face buried in his hands. The officer checked for a pulse, then pulled a small brown bottle out of his pocket and poured some into a cap, waving the smelling salts under her nose.

Pamela coughed and sat up with a start, coughing again and looking about the room like the lights were much too bright.

"Mommy!" James slammed his entire body into his mother, hugging her, and she pressed all one hundred pounds of herself against his small hands, steadying herself.

"Oh, honey," Pamela managed, her eyes blinking twice, trying to make sense of the police officer crouched by her kitchen table.

The officer stood, addressing Virgie. "She looks okay to me. Will you keep watch over her for a bit? If anything changes, call Doc Stewart."

Pamela began to cry into her son's unbrushed hair.

The officer left immediately, and Virgie returned outside to her daughters, leaning into the window where Louisa was sitting in the passenger seat. "She's conscious now but very sleepy. James is saying good night to her, and then he'll come with us when I take you girls' home. Aggie, can you serve the pasta? Betsy, you watch over James, and Louisa, you put Betsy and James to bed at nine. I need to stay with Pamela for a while."

Betsy began to cry. "Can we make her stop?"

"I'm sorry you had to see that." Virgie pulled her youngest daughter out of the car and into her arms, her long legs dangling by her side. "She needs to want to stop. No one can make her."

At the front door, James kicked at an uneven stone, then trudged toward them with his head low. He got in the back seat, his hands wringing at the corner of a small, tattered blanket. "She's going to be okay, James. That's good, right?" Betsy tried to sound upbeat, but he didn't answer.

After taking the ferry back to Edgartown and dropping the children at the cottage on South Water Street, Virgie just wanted to lose herself in a book and allow her thoughts to make sense of what happened. But she needed to save Pamela from herself. Steering the car back onto Chappy, Virgie parked out front of the Sunday house, inhaling the smell of the linden trees. *It's going to be okay*, she told herself. Lying on the couch and watching the television on silent, Pamela's eyes looked glazed over. Virgie covered her with a blanket and pressed a cool compress to her head. Then she cleaned up the broken glass, wiped out the sink, and hunted the house for bottles of wine, tossing them in the trash. It was dark when Pamela roused again, and she blinked her eyes open and closed.

"I'm so embarrassed." Pamela stared at the television. "You don't have to stay here, Virgie. I know you need to go home."

Virgie sat at the end of the sofa, the plastic cover crinkling under her. "I sent James and Betsy over on the boat to invite you to dinner tonight. They thought you were dead."

The woman grimaced. "Dear god. I'm so sorry."

"James is at my house and he's going to stay the night. I didn't want to leave until you were okay."

Her voice was hoarse, and Pamela played with the corners of the orange printed blanket. "You know when you stare at a piece of chocolate cake and you swear you're not going to eat it, and then you breeze into the kitchen and take just one bite, then another, and soon you've eaten an entire slice?"

Virgie didn't want to make a statement and disagree with her, so she nodded. "But you must try, Pamela. For James's sake. There are meetings."

She sniffled, lowering her chin in shame. "Sunday afternoons at the church."

"Yes."

"I've driven there and parked out front, but I never go in." Pamela frowned. "I didn't drink these last few weeks, not since you came to meet me. I needed that job, and I wanted to be good, for James and you."

"What changed?"

Pamela glanced at the counter where the two bottles of wine had been. "And then, when I served dinner to your important husband and that beautiful woman who was so smart, I started to feel useless. Like why was I even in this world when no one seemed to care that I was here?" Pamela pounded the blanket with her fists. "And I'm not trying to sound like a sour sport here, but . . ."

Virgie couldn't believe that inviting Pamela into her home and giving her a job had somehow made her feel worse. "But what?" Virgie said.

"But I wake up in this house that I grew up in and I think to myself: I'm never going to leave this house. I'm going to die in this house, and sometimes I don't see the point in living."

A jabbing sensation spread through Virgie's chest.

"It's always worth living," Virgie said. This woman needed serious help. If you were this unhappy, it wasn't enough to find a job or earn a degree or meet the right husband. You had to dig down deep inside yourself and figure out what the source of your unhappiness was. It was like a poison that would multiply inside you if you didn't stop it. Virgie scooted down the couch, so she was beside Pamela. She thought of Charlie's story about the woman at the Beech-Nut factory, how you could see a person's entire life in their eyes.

"Pamela, you have a reason to live. His name is James."

The woman raised her pale gray irises to Virgie's, her expression pained. Pamela smiled faintly at her. "You're right."

Virgie wouldn't kid herself into believing that solving Pamela's problems would be simple, but it was essential, women giving each other the support they needed to believe that everything would be okay. That they were in this terrible fight together. And so she would find this woman a therapist, an AA meeting, a new start.

Virgie walked to the sink, filled a glass of water, and handed it to Pamela. "I want you to be okay."

"I will be." Pamela's face was that of a woman used to convincing her loved ones that she would change.

Virgie's lids weighed a hundred tons as she drove back to Edgartown at midnight, rolling down her window to keep herself awake during the drive. When Virgie arrived home, she stepped into the living room, finding James sound asleep on the floor next to the sofa, clutching his baby blanket. Betsy was on the couch, tucked into her red sleeping bag, her arm reaching over the zipper, her fingers intertwined with the boy's below.

A simple comfort, holding hands.

Yet it frightened Virgie, how close the boy's body was to Betsy's, even if they were children still. She leaned over her sleeping daughter and nudged her gently. "You need to go up to your own bed."

Maybe Charlie was right. Maybe Betsy should steer clear of this boy, of his troubled family. Pamela felt like a problem that Virgie was stuck with now.

Her daughter rose from the couch, raising her arms up with eyes half-closed, like she wanted to be carried up the crooked staircase. Virgie lifted her, a warmth spreading in her heart. For now, she was still a child, and Virgie could protect her.

CHAPTER TWENTY

Betsy

1978

Betsy's mind couldn't focus on anything productive as she dragged herself out of her pale-yellow cotton sheets, brushed her teeth, and dressed in denim cutoffs. Over the last few days, the sisters had whispered updates about the possibility of saving the house as they passed each other in the kitchen; nothing concrete, just small missives, but they hadn't been able to find a solution yet. Without money, they were out of options.

I can't have this baby.

Betsy's mind jumped like a television changing channels. A lima bean was growing inside her, a complicated tangle of membranes tethering her to a future she hadn't planned for, let alone considered. She'd forgotten to make breakfast today, sleeping later than normal. On her way into the kitchen now, she bumped hard into the side of the navy overstuffed armchair, the perch where her father had worn an indent from reading in the nubby fabric seat. She imagined him sitting there with a newspaper stacked beside him, waggling his thick eyebrows over his tortoiseshell-style reading glasses: "You're on your own, kid," he'd say.

Don't you think I know that, Dad?

Betsy carried the large, wired laundry basket outside and down the cellar steps to the makeshift laundry room. It smelled dank with its partial dirt floor and windowless walls, but the washer and dryer worked fine. There was a laundry line in the backyard, but today's winds were gusty, too hazardous for the children to safely learn to sail. The yacht club had canceled lessons, so she'd be home all day.

You should be ashamed of yourself. This is all your fault. She envisioned her father storming off down the dock, refusing to look at her. Her mother would stick up for Betsy, saying that she was exercising her sexual freedom—until she realized it was her daughter she was talking about. Then her mother would curl into herself in her study chair, her heart turning to steel, glaring at Betsy: *How could you be so stupid?*

While waiting for the sheets to finish in the washer, Betsy brought a large box into the living room so she could begin to organize the bookshelf—a stack of her father's biographies aligned on the top shelf, her mother's row of pop culture titles in the middle one, everything from Erica Jong's *Fear of Flying* to *Valley of the Dolls* by Jacqueline Susann. A potential buyer didn't need to see all her parents' political opinions displayed, she'd decided, and a part of her agreed with her father's paranoia—what if someone snuck in a camera and snapped a photo of their personal belongings, their identities defined in a Smithsonian someday by that one photograph? Instead, Betsy dusted each book, wondering how the words between the covers had shaped her parents' thinking, before stacking several into the box. Then she went about wrapping family photographs into newsprint and tucking them in a second, smaller box.

Everyone had scattered after breakfast that morning. Her mother went up to the study to work on whatever nonsense she was writing, while Louisa and Aggie, desperate to get the kids out on a rainy day, took the children to a singalong at the public library. They returned home a few minutes ago, Aggie racing upstairs to get the baby down for a nap. Now Tabby worked her Play-Doh while singing a nursery rhyme at the dining room table.

"Hey, Betts?" Aggie called from the next room after coming downstairs. "You probably shouldn't pack up all the books. They look nice on the shelf."

From her spot on the faded Oriental rug, Betsy looked up from a stack of photos: her father holding a giant fish on a boat somewhere in Vineyard Sound; her mother, shading her eyes in a lounge chair and wearing a modest one-piece, with baby Aggie clapping on her lap, toddler Louisa digging a sandcastle beside her. It had been quiet since Louisa went back to Washington early this week; she was due to return on Friday, just after the house went on the market.

"I'm not, just some of the more progressive ones." Betsy adjusted the navy-blue bandana she'd tied around her head like a headband. Housework was like a salve. It kept her mind calm. "You know what I've been thinking? Mom used to make us read all those feminist books as teenagers, and I never felt like I could really express a true opinion. Maybe we should read them again now. Start a book club and talk about what we really think of them."

You could have the baby, you know.

Betsy shook the thought off, then waited for her sister's response.

"I think we should do the Ouija board again and ask about our futures."

"God no." Betsy rolled her eyes. Inside, a flash of panic about the lima bean. Imagine the Ouija board suggested that she was pregnant, and she had to explain over a midnight snack why she'd been carrying crackers into bed at night. "I have to go and get the sheets."

Aggie followed Betsy to the back door as she readied to brave the winds outside. "What's wrong with you, anyway? You haven't stopped cleaning the house for days. I mean, I appreciate you washing the spittle rags and towels, but it's starting to get weird."

Softly closing the screen behind her, Betsy forced a smile as a gust of wind blew her ponytail off her neck. "I get accused of not helping enough. Then I get accused of doing too much. I can't win in this house."

She felt her sister's eyes on her as she traveled down the concrete steps, the cool air of the cellar making her shiver. As she pulled the damp sheets out of the washer, she heard Aggie yell out to her: "I'm in for the book club."

The wind howled, blowing against the cellar door, and for a moment Betsy worried it would slam the metal door shut, sealing her into the darkness. But a square of light remained at the cellar stairs. The person she needed to talk to was Andy. He needed to know that there was a lima bean growing inside her, and a part of her wondered—her rib cage feeling tender at the very thought—if the news might nudge him in a different direction. On a walk in the Ramble of Central Park, he *had* told her that he wanted children.

Betsy finished stuffing the sheets in the dryer, adjusting the temperature to high heat, the drum of the dryer thrumming. Maybe he would see this surprising development as his one chance.

A second unexpected squall blew in from the Cape on Friday morning, this time with sideways rain and fog that made Betsy dig out a hooded spring jacket from the closet. She was free again, with sailing canceled a second day. Breakfast made, Betsy padded into the dining room and sat at the formal mahogany dining table with a piece of notebook paper in front of her. She twirled her pen once, and began to write. By noon, she had a finished version.

> *Mom, do you remember the summer you and I had a book club and we read all those rah-rah women books, like* The Yellow Wallpaper *and* A Room of One's Own*? What's funny to me now is that I realized in a psychology class last year that I wasn't honest with you about what I thought of those books. I was never honest with you about what I thought about anything, because I never felt there was room for anyone's opinion but yours. I kind of want to read those books*

again, all of us, and we can reexamine our ideas about womanhood. Because I've decided that what interests me most about you and Louisa and Aggie is not what we tell each other. It's the things we don't.

Setting the pen on top of the letter, Betsy went to the coat hooks in the kitchen and pulled on her windbreaker. She set out for the village, trudging along the cobblestones in the rain. She'd slept terribly the night before, waking up at three in the morning with a deep ache in her chest, deciding that today was the day she would tell Andy. She felt in her pocket for the roll of dimes she'd taken from the kitchen drawer, the sole of her sneaker finding grip on the slippery edges of the cobblestone sidewalk. Her body was damp with weather and nerves. There was a phone in the lobby of the Edgartown Town Hall, and she'd remembered as she'd pressed her cheek into her freshly washed pillowcase last night that it was one of those telephone booths with a door for privacy. Hurrying into the white clapboard building now, Betsy took a second to shake the rain off her jacket, closing her umbrella and gathering her wits. The silver booth stood in one corner of the red-carpeted lobby, and as she walked toward it, every soggy step took the energy of a hundred. Betsy tried to predict how the exchange would go, deciding that when Andy heard her voice, she'd know in an instant how he felt.

The folding door jammed as she tried to close the aluminum and glass panels, and she jimmied the handle to seal the booth shut, the smell of the musty New England Telephone phone book overtaking the stuffy air inside. Betsy heaved her hobo-style purse onto the aluminum shelf, pulling out her pocket-sized green address book. "Long distance, please," she told the operator. She relayed the phone number, and the woman instructed her to insert two dollars and ten cents. "Thank you," Betsy said, her body quivering as she stuffed the twenty-one dimes into the phone. She wouldn't have long, maybe a few minutes, before the operator returned to the line to tell her to insert additional dimes per minute.

She heard the click and pop of phone lines crossing. As she waited, she thought of her psychology professor, Dr. Birnbaum, with his yellow hair and rosacea-prone cheeks, telling the class, "People hurt themselves continually by believing in false hope, by believing these false narratives about people in their lives." It nearly made her hang up, but then she heard the perky voice of a Dartmouth College switchboard operator come on the line, and Betsy, clearing her throat, pressed her feet into the linoleum flooring of the three-by-three booth. She asked to be connected to Dr. Andy Pines in the Department of Psychology. Quiet static crackled along the lines, her mouth going dry as soon as a second phone trilled. She inserted three additional dimes.

Twisting at the metal phone cord, Betsy heard an elderly voice answer with a friendly greeting. "Dartmouth Psychology. May I help you?"

Betsy tasted the strawberry ChapStick on her lips, hesitating, and the woman barked into the receiver, "Hello?"

"Hi," Betsy said. She launched into a long-winded explanation of how she was an old friend of Dr. Andy Pines from Columbia, and did he have a moment to speak with her? There was the shuffle of papers, the thud of the mouthpiece being set down on a desk. Voices chatting in the background. Then, finally, footsteps.

"Hello?" The baritone of his voice, the friendly tone. Did Andy not have a phone in his office? She thought this conversation would be more private, but now she imagined him receiving the information while standing under the fluorescent lights of a department office, the ubiquitous filing cabinets and photocopy machine nearby, the rhythmic click of a stapler irritating him more than it needed to.

"Hello, Andy," she said, trying to sound friendly, worming her finger into the change dispenser. "It's me. Betsy."

Andy was the quiet type, a man that squinted when he listened closely, that pressed his thin lips closed as he hunted for a thoughtful response. This time, though, he responded like a game show host. "Betsy? Betsy from Columbia?"

She curled her toes in her swampy sneakers. *I'll give up sailing. I'll give up this island. This house of my family's. Just let this go all right.*

"Yes, it's Betsy from Columbia. I saw you a few weeks ago. In your office." *You failed me. In more ways than you know.*

"Ha, just checking to make sure," he said. It was his public voice, the voice he used when he stood at the front of the class and tried to win his students over with his sparkling personality. "I didn't expect to hear from you so soon."

So soon. The words were like an anchor tossed overboard, the heavy weight sinking to the sea floor, slamming with a thud in the sand.

Betsy wiped her nose with the back of her wrist and sucked in one solid breath while feeding the phone with two more dimes. "Yes, well, I just wanted to see how you were doing."

They made a few seconds of small talk about how beautiful the campus was, how he was working on a research project until classes began at the end of August. The rain picked up outside and the front door of the Town Hall opened. A middle-aged man in a cap entered and shook out an umbrella. Betsy turned her back to the stranger and pressed her forehead against the cool glass wall of the booth.

"I'm in the middle of something though, Betsy, so . . ."

"I'm pregnant."

The line went quiet. They would be forced to have an adult conversation, to work out the details. It would be the first in a series of phone calls as they figured out what to do.

Andy cleared his throat. "Sorry, but that's not possible."

The muscles in her abdomen contracted. Her mind recalled how he'd unbuttoned her wool dress in her bedroom on that first night, how he'd kissed up her back like he couldn't get enough of her. How they'd repeated the scene on several occasions. Yes, it was certainly possible.

The operator came on the line, reminding Betsy that every minute cost two dimes. She hurried in two more and hoped to God the operator wasn't listening. "There's been no one else, Andy."

I thought maybe I could move up to New Hampshire and we could get an apartment and have this baby together. A baby, not a lima bean. A baby.

His voice was so formal it was pressed flat, steamrolling right over her. "I'm sorry, but I can't be of much help. I don't have a student by that name."

She pressed a fist to her mouth, biting down hard on the fleshy part of her curved finger. Not only would he deny that he was involved, but he would also pretend that she'd meant nothing to him. The possibility garbled her voice, and her words oozed out of her like thick, muddy tar.

"There were no others. Not for years. It has only ever been you."

The mouthpiece was muffled suddenly, and she heard him say, "Just one more minute, Milly." Betsy put in two more dimes, realizing she didn't have many left now. He needed to get back on the line. Andy returned with his voice crystalline. "I'm sorry, but I don't have any information to help. For what you need, at least. I just arrived here, and I don't have a student by that name."

She continued to talk right over him. "I'm not calling you for any money if that's what you think. But I'm considering having this child, and it's yours, and I would like you to be a part of its life. This child cannot be alone in this world . . ."

The trill of a dial tone roared into her ear. "I thought we might have this baby together."

The last part she'd whispered as the line went dead, a piece of Betsy's heart felt like it had been lobbed off. Is that really what she wanted? To have this baby, all by herself. Perhaps it was. The realization made her dizzy, and for a moment she felt like she might pass out cold. She gripped the aluminum shelf of the booth and steadied her breathing. What had she eaten that morning? An egg, a cup of black coffee. Having a baby would give her purpose. She would be someone's mother, and just like every woman before her, she'd be forced to figure out the complicated balance of raising a tiny human while caring for yourself.

But then there was graduate school. Classes. She couldn't exactly waddle her way around campus.

A stranger knocked on the folding door, and Betsy jumped. A middle-aged man in a suit pointed to a sign posted on the wall outside: CALLS LIMITED TO 5 MINUTES, PLEASE. Betsy placed the black plastic earpiece back on the receiver and opened the telephone booth, pushing past the grumpy bearded man and running out of the Town Hall and into the pouring rain. She'd forgotten her umbrella, and she stepped in puddle after puddle as she made her way home. At the house, she rushed inside the front door, kicking it shut and ducking out of the rain. Betsy flicked on the living room light and tossed her workbag onto the coffee table. "Mom," she yelled. "Aggie?"

There was no answer. She checked the driveway, but the car wasn't there either. *Go figure*, she thought. She'd been waiting for one second alone in the living room all this week, and here it was at the very moment that she didn't want to be alone.

Betsy grabbed a jar of peanut butter and a spoon and slumped across the cool cotton sheet her mother had draped over the couch so her granddaughter didn't stain it with her sticky hands. She stared up at the medallion light fixture and the myriad jagged cracks in the ceiling. They would need to paint before they sold the house. Perhaps she should add it to her to-do list, which included *finding a goddamned place to live that doesn't involve staying with your mother the rest of your life.*

She curled into the chair, sobbing so hard while spooning peanut butter in her mouth that she didn't even notice, until it was too late, that Louisa had come in the house lugging a suitcase. Nor did Betsy notice straightaway that Louisa had been crying too; that her eyes had large red rings around them and she looked so exhausted that she might just collapse into a million little pieces right there on the living room rug.

Louisa raced up to the bedroom and slammed the door, while Betsy hurried into the upstairs bathroom. She plugged the bathtub drain and ran herself a warm bath, lowering herself into the bubbles and hot water while listening to the wind whip at the tree branches outside. She let herself cup her hand over her stomach.

It will be me and you, she told the baby. *We won't need anyone else at all, because I will take care of you and never make you choose between your parents.*

There was satisfaction in her decision, but an ocean of shame too. There was no good reason to have this baby other than the fact that she couldn't bring herself to go to a clinic, and still, the idea of a baby in her arms, looking up at her with those giant eyes and smiling, made Betsy's heart do a little flutter. It would be her secret until she was ready to share it with Louisa, Aggie, or her mother. The idea lifted a compressed feeling in her chest, but it returned immediately, the sight of her rounding belly popping into her head. Betsy could only hide a pregnancy for so long.

Lifting herself out of the warm water, Betsy wrapped herself in a fluffy brown towel and sat on the toilet seat. After dressing and brushing out her long straight hair, she discovered her sister was in their mother's study, rain pattering the windows and a single standing lamp illuminating the room. Louisa sat cross-legged on the floor with a series of folders around her.

"Are you okay, Louisa?" She stood in the doorway waiting for her sister to look at her, but Louisa kept her gaze trained on the files.

"I don't want to talk about it." The second hand on her mother's desk clock ticked five seconds, then twenty.

Betsy was about to leave the room when her sister turned, her face puffy and red, and said, "I'm in for the book club though. Mom and I think we should read *The Awakening* by Kate Chopin first."

There was no point in disagreeing. "Fine with me," Betsy said, handing her sister a box of Kleenex off their mother's desk.

Back in her bedroom, Betsy pulled her psychology book into her lap. She turned the pages, the theories slipping in and out of her jumbled thinking, and she remained there, hopeless and brooding and worrying about her sister, until night.

CHAPTER TWENTY-ONE

Virgie

1965

"This lip color would look grand on you." Virgie reached for her favorite Chanel lipstick in her handbag and handed it to Pamela. She'd already pulled the woman's hair out of her elastic and curled her wispy tendrils with the hot iron in the bathroom upstairs. "Try it."

Pamela leaned into the sunny hall mirror, puckering her pale lips while glancing at Virgie self-consciously with a half smile. "I can't think of the last time I put on makeup like this. It's typically a little blush, maybe one coat of mascara."

Virgie admired her handiwork. There wasn't much she could do about the woman's pineapple shift dress—the cut was all wrong for Pamela's slight frame—and still, she seemed to be standing a little straighter. "This may sound silly," Virgie said. She saw a pair of women walking up the back steps, motioning for Pamela to get to her post in the backyard. "But sometimes just getting dressed for the day gives you a sense of purpose."

"No one cares what I wear at the elementary school as long as I get their kids their forgotten lunches." Pamela carried a vase of daisies outside.

"Yes, well, this is different, and it's not about playing dress-up as much as it's about feeling you belong. We need to hear women's voices from across all spectrums, so I hope you'll speak up at today's meeting. Don't eat your salad like you have nothing to say. You have plenty of worthwhile thoughts, and I would like to hear them."

Pamela took her position behind the check-in table, a row of snow queen hydrangeas waving in the breeze behind her. "I don't deserve your kindness," she said, and to that, Virgie set a coconut square in her hand.

"You're as deserving of kindness as I am."

Pamela took a small bite, then grinned. "I used to make these for James. I need to start baking again." Virgie greeted the first few guests with overdramatic hugs, while Pamela cheerily raised her clipboard. "Welcome. Can I have your names?"

If anyone recognized the woman as an occasional waitress at the yacht club restaurant, then good, Virgie thought. Feminism wasn't only for the educated—it needed to find a place for all women, just like the National Association for the Advancement of Colored People made room for everyone of color. Well, as far as Virgie could tell.

At her mother's insistence, Louisa and her friend from Sidwell Friends School in Washington mingled with the younger guests, while Aggie and Betsy served hors d'oeuvres and white wine so they could hear the speakers as they worked. India Knight, the featured guest, talked from a borrowed podium about how essential it was for women to band together to put pressure on officials about issues of importance. Women listened and nibbled finger sandwiches as Mrs. Knight recounted the story about passing birth control legislation in England. She'd gone head-to-head on the five o'clock news with one of the elected officials against the measures, the gentleman with white shaggy eyebrows telling her, "A doctor gets to decide if a woman should get contraception." To which Mrs. Knight had responded with measure: "Is that what you'll tell your wife after she gets pregnant? That her doctor will decide what she does with her body?"

Aggie went from table to table refilling iced tea glasses, while Betsy tried to keep up with clearing the disposable plates.

"The Pill has been available in the United States for the last few years," Mrs. Knight said, "but not without work. If we want women to be treated fairly in the workplace, we need more than an act of Congress. We need oversight. We need justice. I urge you to lobby your senators and congressmen for a well-funded, and not just ceremonial, Women's Bureau in Washington."

Virgie had been to dozens of political gatherings over the years—she'd even organized many of them—but most had been about issues important to Charlie: the piloting of the food stamps program, which he'd recently helped pass with the support of then-President Kennedy, and increasing budgets for the Department of Education so it could bolster public schools in the neediest communities. Those things were important to Virgie, too, but her agenda was narrowing. Listening to India speak, Virgie could see that women had their own sets of priorities: equal rights in the workplace, access to good childcare, the freedom to decide what they did with their bodies. It was India who suggested they only invite women speakers to their luncheons moving forward. "If we're going to be a movement, we need to act like one."

Virgie liked that, a political group for women that would help them create a national voice for the priorities of their members. There had been talk of a national version forming in Washington, since smaller groups like Virgie's were sprouting up all over the nation, but nothing had coalesced.

There was a round of applause when India finished, and Virgie stepped behind the wooden podium, thirty pairs of eyes staring at her. *How wonderful it feels to be alive right now*, she thought, and she imagined marching into the senators' offices alongside these women and forcing them to listen.

"I want my girls to have a chance at happiness," she said, finding Pamela in the crowd clearing plates alongside Betsy. "And if I want my daughters to be happy, they need to count in their own lives, and if they need to count, then they need to count in Washington. We must stop letting public officials sideline our priorities. We must act."

A round of applause emanated, and Virgie beamed, her satin strapless dress reflective with sunlight. What would Charlie think if he heard her talking like this right now? Her essays would say more. She could write so much better than she could speak. Virgie cleared her throat. "And so, to the Edgartown Ladies of Social Concern, I say that we begin here today. Together."

It was after dessert that Virgie noticed that Wiley had slipped into the yard. On a lawn dotted with women in pastels, it was easy to spot his lanky frame and shorts. As he meandered through the crowd, women tried to stop him to say hello, and he'd nod politely, exchange a minute of small talk, then continue to Virgie.

"What brings you here?" Virgie reached out her hand to shake Wiley's like they were perfect strangers. "Would you like to be a member?"

Lines wrinkled his smooth forehead. "I would, in fact."

She'd been sitting on her finished article for over a week, but with Wiley here now, maybe she would fetch a copy to send home with him. They strolled over to the two Adirondack chairs positioned on the hill overlooking the harbor, and he sat, resting his forearms on the armrests. His foot was restless, rattling like an earthquake.

"What is it, Wiley?"

He fixed her with concentration. "I think one of the reporters at the paper came to see you last week, and I'm sorry. I've been holding them off, but he came on his own dime."

Her stomach flip-flopped. "I told him he should contact Charlie's press office."

"Yes, I know." Wiley pyramided his fingers. "I meant to come earlier and apologize, but the debate is growing in the newsroom."

Virgie realized that she was holding her breath and she exhaled, twiddling with the hem of her dress. "What debate?"

He hesitated, like he was standing on a diving board, trying to decide if he was going to jump. "It's Charlie. Has he talked to you about any possible bombs going off?"

She watched an osprey circling with a fish in its talons. "I asked Charlie about what the reporter said, and he told me it wasn't an issue."

The corners of his mouth tensed. "And you thought that was reasonable?"

"Yes, I thought that was reasonable. Why wouldn't it be?" Near the patio, Pamela cleared bottles of wine, and Virgie was pleased when she poured them out entirely before tossing them in the trash. Her voice was quiet then. "Is there something on Nantucket I should know about?"

"We don't know—but we think Charlie might have some kind of shell company on the island, that he's stowing money there."

"Charlie is not a thief."

Wiley leaned forward, balancing his elbows on his knees. "Maybe not, but I want you to know they're going to send a reporter to the island to investigate."

"What kind of shell company?"

He sighed. "Like I said, I'm not sure."

Had Charlie done something stupid? Taken money he wasn't supposed to and stashed it on the summer island?

But it didn't make sense. Nantucket wasn't Grand Cayman or Bermuda; you couldn't squirrel away illegal dollars there. It was a low-key summer island off the coast of Massachusetts.

"Why do you think he has any connection to the island?" That part she already knew from the reporter.

"Because he flew there three times this summer. We have no idea if we're going to find anything, and I really hope we don't, but I can't stop the paper if it's news. This November, Charlie's race is contested. There's going to be big coverage in New York."

Virgie pressed her lips together. "You realize I'm going to tell Charlie what you told me."

"Maybe I'm giving him a head start."

Her husband might have made a few wrong turns, but he certainly wasn't a thief. He wasn't *dishonest*. "Tell me the address, and I'll go to Nantucket tomorrow. Don't send a reporter, please. I'll go see for myself, and if there's a red flag . . ."

The way he leaned close and nodded sent a softness through her, like he'd run a finger slowly up her forearm. "I can tell you what we find. I can give you time to process it."

"No, please." Virgie had hung her entire life on Charlie Whiting. Losing her trust in him would be like losing her true north. "Give me the address."

"Of course," he said. She fetched a piece of scrap paper from the kitchen, and he scribbled down a street address. She felt like she'd been zipped in a corset when she looked at the address, reminding herself to take a breath.

12 Chapel Way, Nantucket.

CHAPTER TWENTY-TWO

Betsy

1978

The bad weather broke around midnight, and by morning, the sun rose on a water-logged island. The waters had calmed, the wind was light, and the sailing regatta was on. Betsy dressed and showered, her heart sore, her eyes burning from yesterday's tears. She whipped up some American cheese omelets and a platter of toast, trying to go on with her day like everything was normal. Aggie dozed on the couch while the baby napped on her chest and Tabby sat on the floor with a bowl of dry Frosted Flakes watching *Scooby-Doo*.

Aggie never complained about getting up alone with the kids every morning. She wasn't short with Tabby or Betsy, and she rarely asked for help. It had been on Betsy's mind since their talk on *Senatorial*: how different her sister's life was than it used to be. Not once had Betsy offered to take the baby for the afternoon; she shirked from changing a diaper. It was Aggie that warmed the bottles. It was Aggie that dressed Tabby and chopped bite-size apples and bathed the children each night. Even her mother had retreated to her study rather than spending time alone with her granddaughter and grandson. It's no wonder Aggie was unable to find thirty minutes to go jogging.

What would be left of Betsy if she decided to become a mother too?

The wood floors creaked underfoot as Betsy bent over the overstuffed couch and gently nudged her sister. Aggie's eyes shot open with surprise. She had the kind of thick lashes that appeared to be wearing mascara at all times, and her long nose and high cheekbones had grown sophisticated with age. But it was Aggie's temperament that Betsy envied. She was determined like their parents, but there was a serenity about how she went after what she wanted. A woman who checks on runners behind her in a race.

"Aggie, go jog or play tennis or something. I can watch them for an hour," Betsy whispered, careful not to wake the baby. Tabby pulled her blanket tighter around her shoulders, unable to peel her eyes away from the television.

Aggie ran her palm over the back of the baby's white onesie. "I didn't tell you that stuff on the boat the other day to get you to watch my kids."

Betsy scooched next to her on the couch. "I know, but I could use a little cuddle time with my nephew." She held out her open hands, motioning for Aggie to hand her the baby.

Her sister didn't seem convinced. She gently kissed the fuzz of the boy's head, pausing. "He might wake up and cry."

"So?" Betsy rolled her eyes and held her hands to urge her along.

"You're just saying what I want to hear," Aggie said.

"It doesn't mean I don't mean what I'm saying." Betsy lingered, insisting her sister get up. "I'll lean back at the same angle, and you can place him right on my chest. I'll let him sleep, and if he wakes up, I'll tell him how we used to sneak chocolate out of the pantry before bed."

"You wouldn't dare." Aggie allowed a smirk to spread across her face. She adjusted her position gently, lifting the baby's warm body and laying him down onto Betsy. Mikey lifted his tiny blond head and expressed his disapproval with a few raspy cries before settling into sleep. Betsy closed her eyes, too, listening as her sister rushed upstairs. Drawers opening and closing, a toothbrush scrubbing. Minutes later, Aggie was downstairs in track shorts with a stripe up the seam, tying her tennis shoes.

"I won't be long," Aggie whispered, pulling an elastic off her wrist and threading her blond curls into a high ponytail. "Shoot. I haven't even had water."

"I don't need to leave for an hour, so don't rush back," Betsy said. Aggie gave her a thumbs-up and popped a kiss on Tabby's tiny cheek. She planted one on Betsy's cheek too.

The back door latched shut, and Betsy felt her breath fall in sync with her nephew's. He had the sweetest little nose that reminded her of a button mushroom, chubby cheeks that fell slack with his lips open in sleep. His entire body rose and fell with his breath, and he smelled like the softest, cleanest pillowcase. Or maybe it was honey and milk, or the smell of soft powder warm in the afternoon sun.

Betsy imagined the baby inside her coming out with its own unique scent, how it would look up at her with wide eyes and a depth of curiosity. She could even see the child in later years waiting for the kindergarten bus and bouncing a basketball. He'd have muddy knees and wear collared shirts on holidays and the two of them would huddle over a school science project, making dioramas of the ocean floor. They would hold hands as she walked him to school, until he got too old and said he was too embarrassed, and she would take him to the beach and teach him how to sail. They would spend hours collecting shells and seeds and rocks and head to the library to look up the names of them in books.

This baby inside her, she decided then, was most certainly a boy. Betsy thought about shared vacations with Aggie's family, how the two boys could be brothers to each other. The fantasy ended quickly. Betsy would be the dreaded single mother, the biggest symbol of messing up in American pop culture. A scarlet letter of Betsy's own doing. For the rest of her life, she would be written off as reckless and misguided.

But some single moms could be happy, right? Betsy strained to imagine what her life would look like if she went through with the pregnancy, if she would have to tell people a fib about the child's father. It would be easy to say its father had died. That would get anyone to change the subject.

Her nephew slept as the rest of the household made its way downstairs, Louisa yawning as she sipped coffee and flipped through the newspaper. Her mother ambled by next, pouring Earl Grey tea that Betsy had brewed into her FEMALE mug.

"Wiley said you've returned to your status as star instructor." Her mother crossed her legs under her silk bathrobe in the striped armchair facing the couch.

Betsy gently squeezed the boy's small feet curled up on either side of her abdomen. "I kind of feel like a kid again, living here and teaching sailing."

"I don't want you to think this nonsense with the house will get in the way of your degree. I will find a way to pay for it. Okay?"

Her former lover told her he wanted nothing to do with this baby; Betsy was thinking of having it on her own. What did she have to lose in admitting to her mother her ambivalence toward graduate school? Last week, she'd committed to returning. Now she wasn't sure.

"I'm still trying to figure out if I should return to Columbia in the fall. I'm not sure I want to finish." Betsy braced herself for an earthquake, the collapse of the roof, the pain of being kicked in the chest.

A Chatty Cathy doll commercial interrupted the weight of what she'd said, and Tabby hugged Virgie's legs, grinning up at her grandma, before turning back to her show.

Her mother gave Betsy a strong decisive nod. "Okay."

There was no frown, no demand. It was almost disappointing. "You don't care if I finish my degree or not?"

Outside the living room windows, the hydrangea blooms pressed against the screen. "Oh, I care, honey, and I think it's a mistake, but I can't force you to continue. You're getting older, and that means, at some point, you're going to have to figure out what's going to make you happy. I wish you liked your program because you would be done with the tough part, figuring out what you want out of life. Not knowing means you're going to have to start over, and I don't envy that. It's hard work finding the thing that lights us up."

Betsy sank into her thoughts. She wasn't expecting the *approval* of her mother, and it confused her further. If she had this baby, Betsy would have no money, no job, no house, no direction. It was ludicrous, and yet why did she want it? Maybe because she was tired of waiting for a man to begin her life, maybe because she wanted to do things differently than she'd been prescribed. Career first, husband second, baby third. Still, she couldn't go back to Columbia and push a stroller around campus. Her professors barely took her seriously now. It was maddening. Andy would earn tenure at Dartmouth without anyone wondering how he would pull off being a father and a professor.

Betsy's thoughts churned. She needed someone to blame. "My classmates, they just make me feel so stupid. I have this paper, and I was told I had to do a complete rewrite."

Small lines around her mother's mouth deepened, her "thinking lines," she called them. "Do you know how many people have insulted my intellect, Betsy? Even your father was guilty of that, and he would call himself a feminist, at least in private. Don't let them win, Betts. You know that."

"I know." The baby was warm against her chest. "But I'm already flattened like a pancake. I'm not sure I have any fight in me. I'm not sure I ever did."

"Oh, honey, but you do." She started to offer examples of when Betsy had fought back as a kid, then stopped, inhaling deeply. "Listen, Betts, I'm happy you're enjoying sailing, and I know that you briefly reconnected with James, but going back in time, it won't fix things. It won't bring Dad back."

"I'm not trying to bring Dad back. Don't you think I know he's gone?" The baby startled at Betsy's rising voice.

Her mother crossed her arms, curling into herself. "You don't talk to us, Betsy. You don't tell us what's going on in here." Pressing her hand against breastbone, her mother's voice wavered. "You aren't processing. You're avoiding, and I'm worried that if you keep avoiding—"

"Stop telling me everything I'm doing wrong, Mom. Why don't you tell us about what you're writing up there all day long?" Betsy rose from the couch, pacing in front of the television while holding the baby, motioning for Louisa to come inside. "How you're typing up horrible things about Dad, and for what, some article?"

Internally, Betsy scolded herself for engaging in this fight. *Go silent*, she told herself. Louisa leaned against the doorjamb.

"I'm writing our story, journaling."

"For what publisher?"

Her mother didn't move. "Betsy, writing is how I process the world around me, and for now, what I'm doing is none of your business. You shouldn't have been in my drawers."

The baby started to cry, and Betsy lowered her voice. "Now look at what you've done. You woke up the baby." She bounded past Louisa into the kitchen. "You know, sometimes you make me never want to come home."

"All I was saying is that you can't go backward, and now you're flipping out." The concern in her mother's eyes made Betsy feel like she might throw up.

"I'm not going backward; I came here because you asked me for help!"

"But you brought everything you own? You moved back here like you were coming for good, even your winter coat and Stevie Nicks records. I don't understand what that means."

"It means that the one person who should always be looking out for me is worried that I'm going to inconvenience her."

"That is not true." It was quiet for a while. Her mother followed her out the back door in bare feet. "I know we're not perfect, Betsy. I know I'm not perfect, but with Dad gone, we're all you've got."

"Gee, thanks for the reminder. Let's talk one more time about how much we mean to each other when no one in this house seems to like each other!"

Betsy stormed down the lawn, still cradling her nephew. She paced the dock beside *Senatorial*, wishing her father were there. That was when he would have come outside to talk to her, to offer a balanced voice and urge her to come inside. Sliding one of his strong arms around her shoulders, he would have said something like, "Your mother needs to feel like she's in control. You and me, we don't like as many rules."

Betsy trudged through the muddy grass to the front of the house, where she would wait on the porch for Aggie to get home. Then she'd go to the yacht club and race those boats as deep into the harbor as she could.

Fresh flowers in every room. Open windows. Beds made with hospital corners.

The house was in the best shape they could manage, and after a few days on the market, the first real estate showing of the Whiting cottage was set to happen that Sunday afternoon. Then there were two more the following morning. If they didn't sell right away, their father's enormous debt would follow Virgie back to Washington. The house was listed for $175,000, a bit higher than similar ones, thanks to its pretty views and dockage along Edgartown Harbor, but after commissions and taxes, her mother wouldn't entirely be in the clear. Sally Channing said she'd report back about the showings and share any feedback they received about the house, particularly if it had to do with the presentation of their belongings.

Louisa had already dropped off the application for the loan at the Dukes County Savings Bank. Mr. Erwin called for her pay stubs and also to inquire if Aggie's husband would cosign the loan. When Louisa had replied no, she asked if they should expect a denial. Mr. Erwin hedged. "Not yet, I have an idea. I'll be in touch."

That night, she and her eldest sister had whispered in the dark long after their mother's light switched off. "Are you going to tell me why you were crying the other day?" Betsy asked.

Louisa sounded distant, even if her bed was a few feet away. "Work stuff. My boss promoted one of my colleagues."

"Why don't you go back, then? We can finish up here, and you can come back during Labor Day."

Louisa flopped onto her back, sighing. "I can't, Betts. Mom needs me here."

"It's such a Whiting trait, isn't it? To assume the world won't march on without you. I've been feeling the same." It grew quiet between them after that, Betsy thinking that Louisa was right. All three sisters needed to remain until they figured out, once and for all, what would happen with the house. "I'm glad you're staying," Betsy admitted. For a second, she worried she was being too sappy, until Louisa rolled onto her side and whispered: "Thank you."

On her lunch break the next day, Betsy called a midwife up island that was known as "the baby lady." She was also the person you turned to when you were in trouble, and Betsy decided she would confide in the woman and ask about her options. She wasn't committing either way until she had that conversation.

Somehow Betsy had managed to avoid being alone with her mother the last few days. Theirs was a disagreement hitched to invisible threads that Betsy knew had been fraying their connective edges since she was a teenager. As always, her mother worried that Betsy wouldn't find her way, that she didn't work hard enough at anything, that she gave up too easily and didn't have clear goals. All it took was one pinched look from her mother that said, *What is going on with you?* and Betsy would feel her insides twist. Because there she was disappointing her mother all over again, disappointing her sisters too.

"We'll talk about *The Awakening* on Sunday, a week from today," Betsy told her mother and sisters that morning. "Does everyone have a copy?"

Aggie said she'd take one out of the library later, and whoever finished first would pass it on to Louisa, the speed reader of the family.

And there it was, a discussion about a book that had everything (and nothing) to do with their lives. They would commence the second annual feminist summer book club, something they hadn't done since she was a teenager.

With her mother out to dinner with Wiley and Aggie at a barbecue with a shared acquaintance, Betsy found herself standing in the kitchen alone eating a bowl of cereal for dinner. Cleaning out the house these last few weeks had uncovered photographs that no one had looked at in years, and they'd tacked several to the front of the old Frigidaire: a photo of her mother in the hospital, a long-limbed newborn Aggie cradled in her arms. Her father rounding the sparkling point of Vineyard Haven with Edward Kennedy on *Senatorial*, her mother in a hot-pink caftan and big white glasses holding up a cocktail to whoever was taking the picture. Looking at them always made her parents feel like strangers, Betsy thought. She didn't know them as individuals. She only knew them as her own.

Someone had stowed pictures in an old soup tureen in the dining room hutch, which was where Betsy had found the photo she stared at now. Her, Louisa, and Aggie posed in bathing suits on the back lawn, the picture snapped by her father just after he'd forced them to swim to the buoy and back the summer Betsy was ten. Her mother had shorter hair then, her arm around Betsy's narrow shoulders, the two of them pressed together like it was the easiest thing in the world to be close. They felt like such a different family then, their paths seemingly aligned and destined to run alongside each other like rivers that would inevitably converge. They were girls whose parents expected them to act like ladies but fight like the toughest boys on the playground, and still, they'd had a softer side, where the sisters would sometimes snuggle together on the couch, reading under one blanket or taking turns making each other's beds. The most magical days, Betsy thought, were the ones where her older sisters would invite her to tag along with them for ice cream cones in town or boy watching at the State Beach jetty. While Betsy knew that they bickered like crazy even back then, she also remembered thinking that she and her sisters would grow up to be best friends.

She thought of a conversation she'd had the day before with Wiley. After sailing, she'd gone to punch her time clock in the sailing shed on the beach, mentioning to him that she couldn't believe James didn't consider this place home anymore, but that she was relieved he'd gotten off the island. Wiley had placed a gentle hand on her shoulder, something her own father would have done. "You don't move on from the past, Betts. You take it with you."

His words had settled into her thinking overnight, and she was beginning to see the wisdom. She liked the idea that memories, whether soft or sharp, shaped us like the ocean shaped the contours of the beach. Distancing herself from her mom and sisters wouldn't make for smoother sand along the shore; it would simply stir up the bottom, the emotions between them growing even murkier.

Betsy rinsed out her bowl in the sink. Soon someone very lucky would buy this sweet little cottage by the sea, and she and her sisters would be forced to carry the boxes in the attic into a moving van. It felt like a bad breakup, the kind that sends you to your bed feeling sorry for yourself, and Betsy wondered if you grieved a house like you did a person, if she was finally moving toward acceptance.

With *The Awakening* tucked under her arm, Betsy climbed the stairs with a glass of chocolate milk. Passing her mother's study, though, she heard a sniffle, then a hiccup. She tiptoed into the doorframe, then poked her head in. Louisa had her back turned, and Betsy stared at the back of her smooth, glossy hair.

"We've done enough, Lou. We can take a break now." Betsy sat on the edge of the sofa; this time, she wouldn't leave until her sister told her what was wrong.

"I just . . ." Louisa's voice took a dive, and as soon as Betsy heard the quiver, she sat on the rug beside her sister.

"Is it your boss again?"

Louisa shook her head. "Seeing Daddy's handwriting while going through his papers." She cleared her throat. "I'm tossing anything irrelevant. Empty notebooks, anything too personal. I really need to get it done before more strange people trample through the house."

"Can I help?" Betsy said, and Louisa nodded, moving around some of the files on the carpet to make room.

They worked in comfortable quiet, Betsy following Louisa's instructions: pull files from the bottom drawer of the wooden filing cabinet onto her lap and riffle through the papers. Anything related to his job as senator went into the cardboard box, while everything else, unless deemed important, could be tossed. The first file Betsy opened was labeled: CORRESPONDENCE WITH THE WAR OFFICE. Inside, there were several typed notes about a POW in Vietnam, a plea from her father to arrange for the release of the young man. She held it up to Louisa. "This letter, do you know if Dad ever helped him?"

Louisa scanned it. "Oh yes, you should put that correspondence aside. He told me once that he counted saving this POW as one of his greatest victories. We all went to a ceremony honoring this man—you probably don't remember, maybe you were too young to care—I remember Dad squeezing Mom's hand and saying, 'This is why we do this.'"

"He always had everyone's best intentions at heart, even when it didn't seem like he did." Why did she always feel like she was convincing Louisa?

"Sure." Louisa buried her face in another file.

The next file was labeled NIXON. Betsy flipped through handwritten notes about a phone call her father had had with the disgraced president. "Honestly, I don't think I know the half of what he's done. I mean, the good or even the bad."

Louisa stacked a few typed pages and stapled them. "Passing the equal rights act for Blacks is by far the most important part of his legacy. At the last minute, eight Republican senators said they wouldn't support it because they feared they would lose their elections back home if they voted to help Blacks. Dad went and sat with each of them, one-on-one, sometimes for hours. All but one of those senators changed their mind. I asked him once what he said to turn them."

Betsy opened a large manilla envelope, this one without any label at all. Inside there was a single white letter. "Oh? What did he say?"

"A typical Charlie-ism," Louisa said. "He told me he begged them to vote with their hearts, not with their constituents, which is not at all the real story. The truth is more complicated. I think he promised to use his star wattage to campaign on their behalf in their home states whenever they needed him to, so they could serve as evidence that Republicans and Democrats could work across the aisle. Remember how often Dad was in the south those last several years?"

Betsy felt like her father was always off doing something important. It was her mother who was home, even if she often had her office door shut and her typewriter humming, relying on Louisa to bring Betsy to her ballet class. "You know, we spend so much time thinking about Dad, but don't you wonder about Mom sometimes? Whose legacy is greater?"

Louisa tossed a yellow lined notebook she'd been flipping through into the trash pile. "What do you mean?"

"Well, Dad was elected and he voted important legislature through. Mom's writing appeared in major magazines. Dear Virgie was syndicated. In the end, who do you think had the bigger reach?"

"I'm not sure, actually." Louisa lay down on her side, pushing herself up on one elbow and pulling a stack of notebooks closer to her. "I always thought having two parents do so much should have made us feel irrelevant, like there was nothing we could do that would rival them. Maybe it was the opposite. They made us want to rival them."

Sunset cast the room in gold. "We had no choice. If I got a B on a paper, Mom would flip."

Louisa groaned. "Or those endless extra essays she'd make us write when we did something she disapproved of. Remember when we had to all write about the importance of kindness to your sisters, and then she critiqued the papers in the living room and gave us grades? Those arguments prepared me for law school."

It was funny to think that. "I think they thought competing against each other would make us better." Her parents competed too. Her father once threw a fit because her mother had been invited on *The Today Show* to talk about an article she'd published in *Vogue*: "The Tragic Consequences of Women Without Bank Accounts." Betsy hadn't been older than fifteen, but she remembered her mother yelling back at Betsy's father, "Are you upset that I went on national television to talk about women getting their own credit? Or are you upset that they didn't ask you to come on TV?"

"I find marriages such a mystery," Louisa continued. "The partners at my firm, for instance. They seem so happily married at a company cocktail party, and then later, one of the men will make a pass at you."

"That's disappointing." As she watched her sister, Betsy felt like there was a precipice in front of her. A realization about her mother and father becoming clear.

"Louisa, do you think that Mom and Dad made us believe that we had to win to be loved?" The idea of it stirred a sadness in Betsy, how

Louisa's and Aggie's accomplishments were highlighted at family dinners, whereas Betsy's sailing was treated as charming, not impressive. How irritated her mother had been when Betsy quit the debate team. If Betsy had simply stuck with one thing—if she'd become passionate about the Model UN or if she'd been the leading scorer on a tennis team, then Betsy would have drowned in her mother's attention.

But to be average? Average grades and average drive and dreams. That is what had worked against Betsy.

Louisa thumbed through newspaper clippings about her father. "Win what? It's not like you and I were athletes."

"Win at everything. Getting in a top college, having the most confidence at our sweet sixteen parties, winning at life." Betsy leaned into her flattened palms. "I've always felt if I'm not reaching as high as you and Aggie, then I'm not worth noticing."

"You think Mom and Dad taught us to compete with one another to earn their affections?"

"Mom even said it herself, that her favorite child changes based on the day." Betsy sat up onto her knees. "For us to get their attention, we had to be doing something extraordinary. Which is why you wound up at law school and you're determined to make partner. It's likely why Aggie ran the marathon at such a young age."

"And you?" Louisa's eyes bore into her, waiting.

Betsy's expression fell. "It's probably why I feel so bad every time I muck things up. Because I still have no idea what I want."

Louisa put down the pages, sighing. "No, Betsy. It's not that no one thinks you're worthy, it's that you haven't found something that makes *you* feel worthy yourself."

Betsy was lying on her back and staring up at the ceiling. "That's actually very insightful, Louisa."

"You typically never let me finish my sentences." Louisa pressed her lips together with validation. "Are you sure you want to quit your degree program?"

"I think I'm a good listener, but the work, getting there, it's like swimming upstream."

"What made you want to go in the first place?"

"A conversation with Mom. She told me I was easy to talk to and that I should be a psychologist."

"Huh." Louisa handed her two thick files labeled Bills and Ideas. "Can you look through these too?" Betsy sat up and turned over the white envelope she'd been holding all along, surprised to see BETSY written in capital letters on the smooth face with black Magic Marker. It had come from the blank hanging file.

"Are you going to finally tell me what's going on at work?" she asked Louisa.

Louisa talked right over her. "Don't change the subject. We were talking about you."

It was her father's handwriting on the envelope. He always wrote the first letter of Betsy's name with a flourish, like he was adorning a place setting at a fancy wedding. She lifted the seal and could see that inside was a handwritten letter. As she fished it out, eager to see when he'd written it and why, she wondered if he'd had an intuition that his plane might unexpectedly crash, like it had just after taking off from Teterboro. Perhaps he'd always worried that he'd walk out the door one morning and never return. He *had* always been superstitious.

Betsy opened the folds of the stationery. She sped through the words at a clip, her face turning white. Then she read it a second time, more slowly, and this time she called for Louisa to look. Her sister crawled over on her hands and knees, swiping it from Betsy's hands.

When Louisa finished reading, she let the paper drift out of her hands and onto the woven carpet. The heft of the letter moved with the weight of a feather.

Louisa sunk back onto her heels. She was trembling. "Why on earth did he write this to you?"

Betsy honestly didn't know. It was dated four years ago. She read it once more.

To my Betsy girl,

I am uncertain if you'll ever see this letter, which makes it an oddity to write, but if you are reading it, then it's likely you're cleaning out my papers. It's hard to imagine there will be a time when I won't be on this earth, but I suppose, like everyone, my time will come. You are nineteen as I write this, and we've just returned from depositing you at college for your sophomore year. The entire drive home from Barnard to Washington, I carried something on my mind that I need to expunge.

In 1965, I was gifted a piece of land on Nantucket, a few acres in Madaket, that is in my name. For reasons that I am not free to explain, both politically and personally, I have kept this property to myself. I could not make anyone aware of this transfer for a myriad of reasons, so I will rely on your discretion in handling this information.

12 Chapel Way, Nantucket.

I love you always and forever,

Dad

CHAPTER TWENTY-THREE

Virgie

Nantucket
1965

Maybe they'd sail to Nantucket this century. The car ferry in Woods Hole was full, so Virgie sat in the standby line watching walk-on passengers lugging suitcases onto the boat. There were three cars ahead of Virgie's, and a new ferry was docking.

Betsy and James were in the back seat reading a *Spider-Man* comic. One of the sailing instructors had given them a stack of comic books the day before and they'd been huddled over the *Superman* and *Spider-Man* stories since. It was risky bringing Betsy, but Virgie couldn't leave her home all day. Aggie and Louisa would go to a friend's house in the afternoon, but she didn't trust Pamela to watch the children, especially when she was prisoner to the ferry schedule.

The tender waved them on the boat, and Virgie parked. They shuffled up to the sundeck for the two-hour trip, the departure horn sounding. Virgie pressed her lips into a tight line. She checked the tiny gold face of her wristwatch; it was after twelve. She didn't have much of an appetite, but she'd need to feed the kids. "Would anyone like a cup of clam chowder?" she asked the children. They followed her to the canteen, still reading the comic.

It's probably something innocent, she told herself, handing the children each a packet of oyster crackers and creamy soup. She crossed her legs and watched them eat. *A huge misunderstanding.*

Virgie stopped at a small gift shop just after driving off the ferry to ask for directions, but they sent her to the tourist office down the road where a nice young man used a red marker to hand draw a map showing her the way to Chapel Way in an area called Madaket. When she got back in the car, she tucked a few strays into her French twist, the children in a tickle fight, whooping it up in the back seat.

"Quiet down, children. I need to focus." She smacked the passenger seat harder than she needed to, and they fell silent, returning to their comic.

"What a lovely bookshop." Virgie pointed to a brick shop housing rows of novels in the windows. "If the day goes well, maybe we can stop there on the way home." They were driving rural roads out of the town soon after, making their way through acres of open land and grassy moors, and while it took some turning around and backtracking, after twenty minutes or so, Virgie steered the car into a small grid of houses. She located an unpaved single lane road labeled CHAPEL WAY.

How strange that the address led to a house.

A small, shingled saltbox-style house. Virgie had imagined something sinister, like a big empty warehouse with the windows drawn black with shades. She pulled in beside the Ford truck and parked in the drive, shushing the children in the back seat. There were two bikes on the side porch next to a charming swing. A little girl was in the backyard on a playset, and behind it, a calm inlet with a boat rocking lazily in the blue.

"Can we go play?" Betsy asked. The child waved to them, and Virgie had the eerie sense that she'd seen the girl before; she was lanky and knobby-kneed, wearing an adorable bathing suit with a strawberry printed on the front.

"First, let's see who else is home," Virgie said, feeling a bit hopeful that maybe she wouldn't discover anything damning. On the door was a shiny brass knocker in the shape of a sailboat. She knocked it twice. She could hear a television inside, studio applause and phony laughter coming through an open window.

Footsteps. Virgie adjusted her skirt suit, retucking her blouse and sucking on her teeth to remove any errant lipstick, poised to smile as the front door opened.

A tall, elegant woman answered the door holding a small Igloo cooler. She was Virgie's age and wearing a red one-piece bathing suit with a fashionable matching headscarf. She took a small step back, dropping the plastic cooler by her foot, then rushing forward to pick it up and returning to stand.

"I can't believe it," the woman said. She pulled off the headscarf, crumpling it in hand, almost like a person couldn't know her wearing it.

The ground under Virgie felt a little less steady.

It was Melody. Her old best friend from Washington. Melody, with that pretty dark reddish hair that fell blunt to her shoulders. Melody, who had abruptly moved to Boston. How terrible Melody had been about answering Virgie's letters, sending one back for every four Virgie had written. At some point, Virgie had stopped writing. But it had bothered her; for a time, Melody was her closest friend.

Virgie snuck a glance into the hall behind her. Was there someone else inside? A husband that would turn off the television and come to the door?

Melody's smile looked pasted-on. "Virgie, oh my goodness, Virgie Whiting. What are you doing here?"

Virgie wasn't sure she was happy to see her, waiting a moment for her brain to catch up with her eyes. "I'm not sure."

The little girl ran into the front yard, alighting at the sight of the other kids, and the three children ran off to squeeze into the porch swing. The rusted chain link creaked as they rocked.

It had to be the child Virgie nearly hit with the car at South Beach earlier this summer. She wouldn't forget that little girl's face. Fear had burned it into memory. And she'd thought her familiar then, too; she'd looked like her old friend Melody Fleming.

Virgie peeled her gaze away from the girl. Melody still had that pasted-on smile.

"Gosh, I'm being rude," Melody said. "Come inside." The woman looked to the car to see if someone else was inside, swallowing before turning to go in.

Virgie felt for the back of her French twist, like she wasn't sure her hair was still in place. "I don't mean to impose like this. I have a personal policy to call before I show up at someone's house, but I didn't know. I didn't know it was going to be you."

Her friend seemed to relax then. "Of course, no, please. Come in."

Virgie became hyperaware of her every step in the narrow hall as she followed Melody to the kitchen. Her eyes swept around the adjoining sunny living room, and then the dining room with its mahogany turn-foot table and dated chandelier.

"I'm so sorry; we are meeting some friends at the beach. Jetties in town, you might have seen it as you arrived on the ferry. It's calmer. The water out here will sweep you away. A few little girls from Vera's camp, since camp was canceled, and I just had no idea you were going to come. I wish I did because I would have had tea on or a platter of sandwiches ready." Melody pivoted at the sink; she'd been talking so fast she needed to catch her breath. She reached for two glasses. "It would have been nice to have lunch and a proper visit. Well, we have some time now."

"I won't be here long," Virgie reassured her. "I'm just trying to understand . . . do you live here?"

Melody squeezed her lips with her fist, then released them. "I'm so sorry. I'm so very sorry. I really am. I tried to." She turned her face away from Virgie, and Virgie thought it sweet that she still had her freckles, even as a grown woman. "I didn't know how to tell you."

"Tell me what?" Virgie said, or maybe she'd only thought she said it. Now she followed her friend, carrying two glasses and a bottle of soda, into her living room, where she shut off the blaring television. There was an upright piano, a scatter of picture frames on top, wide-open views of the reedy inlet. Virgie wondered if she was dreaming—she had the strange sensation of floating—and she guessed she might wake up in her bed in the Vineyard, remarking to the girls at breakfast that she had the strangest vision. She ran her hand along the nubby fabric of the couch as she sat, pinching her outer thigh; both felt real.

This house with the weathered cedar shingles. The refrigerator covered in a child's artwork. This living room with the big windows overlooking a gnarled oak tree with a tire swing. It was all somehow connected to Charlie.

"I'm really sorry I didn't tell you," Melody said, her voice shaky and speeding. "I just thought it would be best to leave DC, and the mystery was less hurtful than the truth."

There were others, there were always others, Virgie thought in her head. A painful sensation socked her in the chest, and she worried she might be having a heart attack or a stroke, and she worked hard to slow her breath. *You are fine. You will survive. You need to understand.*

Illegal dealings, maybe a criminal enterprise. That is what Wiley led her to believe she might find. But Melody?

The woman crossed her long, freckled legs, her toenails painted a coral color Virgie never would select for herself. "I've barely seen Charlie. Honest to God, but he has dropped by once or twice. I guess I've wanted him to see Vera, even if Vera has no idea who he is."

Melody trembled as she poured Virgie a glass of ginger ale. It had always been Melody's favorite drink. Outside, Virgie watched James, Betsy, and another child taking turns climbing the rubber tire. The girl sprinted inside, her face balled up with anguish. "They're hogging the swing," she said, and Melody leaned into her ear, whispering something.

It was then that Virgie gripped the edge of the sofa. She'd been uncomfortably seated on the sunken couch in this sunny living room with its wide-planked solid wood floors. She leaned closer to the girl so she might see her with more clarity. And there they were: Charlie's eyes.

There was screaming in Virgie's ear, her own voice.

She did not sip her ginger ale as Melody talked at a clip, and it was then that she imagined the year she was pregnant with Betsy. How often she'd dragged the children on the campaign trail as her stomach rounded to a ball. How Charlie had won his Senate seat, how he'd waved and smiled and told her he couldn't have done it without her. How she'd pushed Betsy into the world that year, and Charlie had cradled his baby girl in his arms under the fluorescent lights of the hospital and said he was the happiest man on earth.

"How old is your daughter?" Virgie interrupted the woman, her pulse skittering, her body feeling like it might propel itself through the window.

Melody folded her hands in her lap, then tapped one finger on the table. "She's ten."

Betsy's age.

"It's why you left. It's why I never heard from you again. Did Charlie buy you this house?"

The answer was no; he invited her to live there. Charlie never gave her money. "I promise you. He only loves you. I've been doing him a favor, depositing the checks he mails here. I'm doing it because he showed me generosity."

"Vera is Charlie's? You and Charlie were . . . ?"

Melody let her face fall into her hands, and Virgie felt a wave of nausea. "You and Charlie? When? I don't understand."

Melody's cheeks were wet and red, maybe they had been all along, and she seemed to be pleading with Virgie. "It was only once, and while I want to say that I had no part in it, I did. I loved him, differently than you, but we were always together in those days. We were always up late writing speeches, talking on opposite sides of his desk, and one night, it just happened. We both felt terrible, and as soon as it started, it ended, and I left town because I couldn't do that to you. And then . . . This house came up and he offered it to me."

This house.

To think Melody had been so close by, living in Nantucket! All she could think about for a moment was how Charlie would console her in those months after Melody left, counseling her to let go of the friendship, since her friend didn't return her letters. He'd called the friendship "one-sided."

But it had been Charlie's fault. He'd carried on a relationship with her best friend. He'd had a child with her in the same year that she and Charlie had Betsy. Two girls, the same age, the same father, living on two different New England summer islands. The cruelest thought entered her mind, a bedrock of jealousy loosening itself from deep down inside: Guilt is what drove him to spend so much extra time with Betsy over the years. When he looked at her, he must have seen his mistake. He must have always tried to make up for it.

Virgie had to remind herself to breathe. "I might have thought Charlie capable of something like this, but you? You came to my house for dinner on Sundays. The two of you sat at my dining room table together. The blind trust I put in you. In both of you."

Melody kept saying the same thing: "I'm sorry. I'm so very sorry."

The words slipped through the air. Virgie wasn't even listening anymore. "I knew you were desperate for a husband. But I never thought you'd try to steal mine."

Virgie heard the woman blubbering behind her. "Please, Virgie. You need to know that I tried to protect you. I've prayed every night that you and I never had to have this conversation."

Virgie and the children were back in the car then, driving the wide-open roads of this island that was shaped like a splatter of ink on a page. Virgie kept turning down the wrong streets, driving sandy dirt roads that dead-ended at the ocean. The kids were hyper in the back seat, begging for ice cream. A whiff of perfume on Charlie's collar, a matchbook from a hotel in his jacket pocket. But it had been okay, hadn't it? She knew two other Senate wives who had suffered similarly, and during one luncheon where they'd had more than one mimosa, they'd admitted that they thought it was normal. *That men just needed that*... Virgie blocked any indiscretions out of her mind. True Charlie. That was her husband, and he would stand by her until the end of time. She would stand by him.

But the myth of Charlie Whiting was a story that could no longer be told.

Virgie saw a pay phone in front of a store selling postcards. She dialed the operator and called Charlie's office collect, his secretary accepting the charges. "Charlie is at lunch and will be back in about fifty minutes," she said. "Do you want me to have him call you?"

A passing car blasted the song "Ticket to Ride" by the Beatles, the sound overtaking her ears. Virgie slammed down the earpiece. His grin when he laughed. His navy suits. A whiskey on the rocks, and a waitress who giggled after writing down his order.

Virgie found a park bench near a small pebbly beach at the edge of town. There was a woman sitting on the seawall with a small toy poodle. Virgie dangled her legs over the side, the wet nose of the dog rubbing against her fingertips. A shudder carried through her, her eyes growing wet.

"Are you okay, miss?" The woman handed her a tissue, waiting for Virgie to take it.

"My husband has a secret second family."

What did it matter if she told a stranger? What did it matter if she outed True Charlie?

She took off down the street in a daze. Had two minutes passed, or two hours? A church made of cedar shingles. A statue of St. Mary out front. Mary, who was God's mother, not his equal, but his birther. Opening the mahogany doors, its panels made of stained glass crosses, Virgie found the confessional at the back of the pews.

Perhaps there was no one as true as she'd thought Charlie. She stepped inside the small dark confessional, closing the black silk curtain and thinking it sounded like the one on her shower. She waited for the voice of the priest to emerge.

"I welcome you, my child."

Her voice sounded so quiet she could barely hear herself, but she didn't know how to yell without yelling so loud that her voice cracked the statues. "Forgive me, Father, but my husband has sinned. He has done something unforgivable, and I don't think I can recover from it."

The face of the girl in the strawberry bathing suit. Her eyes like Charlie's, her skinny legs like Betsy's.

The shadowy voice sounded like God itself. "Forgiveness comes to anyone who seeks it, and he deserves to earn back your forgiveness. Everyone we love deserves forgiveness."

It was nonsense. A priest was just another man in a special suit. Virgie ripped open the curtain, her voice clear. She banged on the confessional. "That's bullshit. Don't try to protect him."

In the bright sun, Virgie tripped on a cobblestone. There was the bookshop, a hardware store. She circled the Athenaeum. The gift shop with the postcards. She called Charlie's office collect once more, his secretary answering again, and when she said he still hadn't returned from lunch, Virgie yelled: "Tell him to go to hell."

When she came across the statue of St. Mary once more, she collapsed on the church steps. The sun was low in the sky. She needed to get the children off Nantucket, but first, she would need to stop crying.

CHAPTER TWENTY-FOUR

Betsy

1978

Betsy opened all the windows in the living room to encourage the soft summer breeze inside. The three sisters were reading on the couch, with Aggie's children long asleep upstairs. Each sister would glance up every so often at their mother, who was showing unrelenting stamina with *The Awakening*. They needed to tell Aggie about the letter.

"I can't wait to discuss this with you girls." Their mother was wearing her cutoff denim shorts, her wavy hair pulled into a loose bun. "Water is such a symbol for Edna. It's like the more she swims, the more she realizes how boxed in she feels."

"Well, she's free in the water," Betsy said. She was nearly done with the book too. "Then she feels the vise tighten once more because she's a mother, a wife. Identities that make her feel conflicted."

"But she loves her children. Sometimes she seems uncertain why she made these choices, like someone forced her hand."

They all wanted to force their mother to go to bed so they could talk about this mysterious plot of land on Nantucket. Finally, around ten, their mother dog-eared the novel, announced she was exhausted, and climbed up the crooked steps. Now they were huddled together at the far end of the sofa, whispering. Louisa had a lined notebook on her lap. "So, Mr. Edwin called from the bank today and said we've been approved for a loan for $15,000. It's something, and I will sign for it, but it's certainly not enough to save the house."

"He did tell Louisa that he would call the mortgage company though and ask for an extension on our foreclosure date." Betsy broke in, trying to get to the point. She smiled. "Because there's been a development, Ag, something with potential."

They caught Aggie up on the letter. As she listened, she twiddled the baby's pacifier.

"Louisa and I think that maybe we can sell the land on Nantucket, since we don't really care about it," Betsy said, feeling lighter than she had in weeks. "That money could pay off the rest of the debt on the house here."

"We may even be able to use the land as collateral to convince Mr. Edwin that the bank should approve us for additional cash." Louisa talked quickly, a growing confidence in her words. "We just need the deed from the records office. I have no idea if the lot is buildable or how much it's worth, but Nantucket is just as expensive as here, if not more, so it must be worth something."

Aggie ticked her head back and forth, listening closely. She reread the letter once more, folding it back into thirds and sliding it into the envelope. "But why doesn't Mom know about this? It feels rather clandestine of him to hide property all this time and then write Betsy some mysterious letter he was never certain she'd receive. It's making me feel worried somehow, like we're buying a carton of eggs only to open them and find rotten ones inside."

Tourists ambled down the street, the critique of a rubbery steak dinner drifting through the window. Betsy pulled her knees into her chest. "But what other option do we have at this point? We might as well investigate, and you said yourself that trying to save the house is worth a shot. Let's go to Nantucket tomorrow."

With the letter addressed to Betsy, she felt like the leader, suddenly taller, stronger, and smarter.

Aggie's eyes widened. "Don't you have work tomorrow?"

"I'll call in. We must, don't you think, Louisa? We need to go see the land and retrieve the deed from the records office."

She exhaled when Louisa nodded.

That sparked a new discussion. How would they explain their absence to their mother? They quickly agreed that they would blame their excursion on the senior partner at Louisa's law firm. He was visiting his house on the nearby island, and he'd called Louisa and invited her for a last-minute luncheon. She didn't want to go alone, so she'd begged Betsy to come with her. Oh, and they needed to borrow their mother's car.

Aggie fiddled with her wedding ring. "Mom's never going to believe that Louisa begged you to come. If she did, it would only make you want to say no."

Betsy chewed the inside of her cheek. "You're right. I'll say that I begged Louisa to go because I've always wanted to see Nantucket."

Louisa nodded. "Then I'll say that I *reluctantly* agreed to let you come so I didn't have to stay in a hotel on my own, and I can act all annoyed about it."

Aggie agreed she should stay behind with the kids, since it would be too challenging to travel with them. Plus, she could keep their mother busy so she wouldn't suspect that they were up to anything.

Aggie picked a fuzz off Louisa's pajama top. "Don't you need to go back to Washington again, Lou?"

Louisa swallowed a large gulp of air. "Something happened," she said.

"Hold on," Betsy said. She went into the kitchen to get a bowl of potato chips, and she ate them by the handful, offering her sisters the bowl. Her appointment with the midwife was tomorrow. She would need to cancel it.

"I didn't want to worry you both, but the partners took me off the case." Louisa couldn't look at them, her gaze on the hem of her pajama bottoms. "I've done almost all the work. I researched the law. I wrote the arguments, but they go to court. Maybe it's punishment for taking so much time away. Maybe they would have done it anyway. But they won't let me argue, saying it will distract the justices from the case." A vein jumped in her alabaster temple. "My boss told me when I get back from vacation, I'll be assisting Timothy Schumacher, but Schumacher treats his female associates like secretaries. It's a complete demotion. I told my boss that if he put me there, then I quit."

The tension in the room tightened, stretching like rubber. "So you quit?" Aggie said. "I hope you weren't that hotheaded."

Louisa inhaled sharply, exhaled, her voice steady. "I nearly did. I told him I wasn't rushing back. Honestly, my boss might fire me first, but I'm so humiliated I'm not sure I can ever go back into the office."

"You're not a secretary!" Aggie narrowed her eyes.

"I'm going to put in my resignation. I must." She turned to Betsy. "That's why I came back early, and it's why I'm still here. I'm a bit turned inside out too."

"Do you think *Michael* had something to do with your move?" It had been Betsy's first thought. Her sister's boyfriend was working on the opposing side. Perhaps he'd called his buddy at Louisa's firm and made a "helpful suggestion" about shifting around a distracting employee.

Aggie's eyes landed on Louisa, who paced the living room. "Who is Michael?"

"This man I met, and yes, I've heard that there are questions about our relationship. Apparently, it wasn't the secret I thought it was."

Betsy was certain her sister would hate that, too, going back to a job where everyone knew the details of her love life. "If he loved you, he would take himself off the case." Betsy crunched on the chips, wishing she had onion dip. "He wouldn't expect you to step away. If he truly loved you, he wouldn't allow this to happen."

Louisa stuffed the chips into her mouth too. "Why do women always say that? The entire women's movement has been built on the idea that men hurt women all the time. A man can love you, but it doesn't mean he wants you to be his equal. Can't you see that?"

Betsy thought back to her conversation with her sister earlier in her mother's study, just before she'd discovered the letter. Maybe her father was threatened by a wife who saw herself as his equal. Maybe her father had always needed to feel one step ahead.

It was troubling that her father had addressed this letter to Betsy, that it wasn't written for her mother. But he had always made Betsy feel like they had an alliance, and it felt dangerous to name the dynamics in a family.

Rising from the couch, Betsy lifted the model sailboat off the mantel that she and her father had built when she was little. They had spent hours gluing the pieces in place, but she had the sudden urge to dismantle it. Then she realized that it had only looked perfect from far away. Now that she held it close, Betsy could see the spots where the glue had dried. There was a piece of the bottom peeling backward with time.

Look too closely, and suddenly, all you can see are the flaws.

Their mother refused them the use of her station wagon, but she did drop Betsy and Louisa off at the ferry terminal in Vineyard Haven at ten the following morning. Here, they would catch the passenger ferry, docking in the tiny village of Woods Hole and taxiing forty-five minutes to star-studded Hyannis, thanks to the Kennedys. There, they'd board a second ferry to Nantucket.

A well of possibilities had blossomed inside Betsy's mind since she'd found her father's letter the day before, and she was chattier than she'd been in days, even with that little dark cloud following her.

"What an ordeal," Louisa complained of the crowds, as she and Betsy pushed through the throngs of tourists. Each sister carried a small overnight bag slung over one shoulder, although they had no idea where they even planned to sleep that night, since neither had ever been to Nantucket. The two islands were close in distance but worlds apart; you were either a Nantucketer or a Vineyarder, never both, and the Whitings had pledged their allegiance long ago.

Louisa grimaced when she tripped over a teenage boy who abruptly stopped on the busy sidewalk to tie his shoe. "We're really going to need a car. Nantucket isn't small and taxis are expensive."

"We'll be fine." Betsy blew at the bangs sticking to her forehead. "Nantucket is half the size of the Vineyard. Besides, the records office will likely be right in town. We can walk."

They found seats topside at a picnic table, Betsy shuffling off to the café. She returned holding a chocolate milk, a buttered roll, and a bag of Lay's chips. "The salt is just perfect," she moaned, gobbling down the chips.

"That's disgusting." Louisa stroked her throat, her fingers finding her gold locket and gently tugging.

"You're just jealous because you don't let yourself eat *anything*."

The ferry pushed off from the dock, the water a clear aquamarine with seagulls gliding overhead. Betsy guzzled the carton of chocolate milk. In the distance, she did a double take at a familiar face, a man wearing Nikes, a faded red T-shirt, and a baseball hat. A dog trotted beside him.

James spotted her from the start, waving.

She felt butterflies, squeezing her abdomen to force away the fluttering.

"Hi, James." She'd tried to "run" into him the day before, swinging past the hardware store in case he was inside.

"Hey, how are you?" He sat at the picnic table beside them. "I'm running errands off island."

"Ah."

"Hi, Louisa."

"Nice to see you," she said.

James sat at the next table, unwrapping the plastic from his Danish, using a small plastic knife to cut it into quarters. He'd never said anything about the letter Betsy wrote. "You look great," he told Louisa.

"Thank you," she said. Peanut Butter nudged Louisa's hand. Seeing as much, James said, "I can move. I don't want Peanut Butter to bother you."

Betsy was about to say, *That's probably a good idea.* How would she talk to him for forty-five minutes now that she barely knew this adult version of James?

But then Louisa spoke up first and told James to stay. "We love dogs, don't we, Betsy?"

"Sure." Betsy faked a smile.

Another colony of seagulls flew overhead. There was always a stray bird that followed the boat to the mainland. James offered Betsy a piece of the Danish he'd sliced on a napkin, and she popped it in her mouth. "It's from this bakery in Vineyard Haven."

"You always did love your sweets," she said. "Thank you."

Betsy folded her hands on the tabletop and pretended to be engrossed with the scenery. Her mind drifted to Wiley's words. *The past follows us wherever we go.* The past seemed to follow her all over the island.

A leashed Labrador meandered past, Peanut Butter going in for a friendly sniff. "Where are you two off to?" The conversation skimmed the surface so expertly they could have been strangers on a Manhattan bus.

They were going to visit Louisa's colleagues at a luncheon on Nantucket, she said.

As if on cue, Louisa placed her book down on the table. "Except our mother is a true model of kindness and wouldn't let us use her car, so we have to take a taxi to Hyannis." Louisa stood, adjusting her shorts where they had ridden up, and she announced she was going to the restroom. Betsy nearly reached for her hand and yanked her sister back down.

The ferry was busy even on a Monday, families ending their vacations staring mournfully out at the passing cliffs. Betsy distracted herself by watching a young girl sitting on her father's lap, giggling as he bounced her on his knee; a memory of her father doing something similar making her smile. Then she remembered she was sitting beside James, all awkward and trying to act normal, when it was her father that had driven them apart.

Her lips parted with a nervous smile. "How is the . . ."

James started as well, "I wrote you back . . . ," and they both paused, neither one wanting to say anything then. Lifting her gaze from the floor, she said, "Sorry, you go first."

The ferry sounded two powerful horn blasts, and they craned their heads to see why. A powerboat had crossed in front of the larger boat's path, a dire warning to move out of its way.

She turned her hands over in her lap as James called Peanut Butter back, gently petting the dog's head. "I was just saying that I wrote you back."

She felt the color drain from her face, thinking about what he might have written, since his expression was hazy. "I really am sorry we didn't call or write after your mother died."

A group of children ran by, chanting another child's name. "Your mother came to her funeral. Do you know that?"

She felt his eyes on her, a pang of surprise reverberating down to her fingertips. Her mother had sworn off James and his family the same year that her father had encouraged Betsy to distance herself from him. When had her mother been able to sneak off to attend services for James's mother? "At some point, I think she thought of you as one of her own children."

James had a deeper voice now, more serious. "Maybe because she couldn't ever get me to go home."

A schooner sailed by with three masts, and the conversation lightened when he asked about *Senatorial.* They got up from their seats and walked to one side of the ferry, both resting their forearms on the railing and staring off across the water. *This was progress*, she thought.

He told her a story then.

"When I was in college at Berkeley, your mother was speaking on campus at Zellerbach Hall. I saw it in the campus paper, so I went." Afterward he waited in line to talk to her. When Virgie saw him, she'd beamed and given him an enormous bear hug. Then she'd said she was so proud that he'd gotten off the island.

James stared straight ahead, a corner smile lifting, then slipping away. She turned her body to one side, facing him. *Her mother had seen him at Berkeley?*

"Your mom was impressed that I wanted more than the hand that I was dealt, she'd said." James tapped the railing with his fingers.

"Sounds like something she'd say, and it's pretty rude too." Her mother could be so direct. Too direct sometimes.

"Nah," he said.

She looked away, her eyes landing on Louisa, who was pushing open the ferry door and striding along the deck with her hair freshly brushed, big sunglasses on her face, and lip gloss applied.

"I had gone about as far away as I could get from this island, thanks to Wiley's help. Your mother, she'd write me letters sometimes, encouraging me." Now he turned to face Betsy, her rosebud skirt blowing behind her legs with the wind. "Betsy, you may have moved on from my life, but you shouldn't feel bad about it. Your mother remained with me all along."

Betsy folded her arms tight around her chest despite the warm sun. "My mother wrote you letters? Why are you telling me this? You realize that you're making me hate her more than I already do."

"You don't hate your mother," he said. He began to tap his foot. "And I don't know why I'm telling you. Maybe because your letter was so apologetic that it was almost insulting, like you thought I was still sulking about things between us. I needed you to know that I'm not."

"I don't think that." She dropped the fabric pleat of her skirt, gripping the railing in front of her. "You've made clear you've moved on, and as you said, I have too. I have a boyfriend; he's a professor at Dartmouth."

A muscle in his cheek twitched. "I'm happy for you," he said.

"I'm happy for you too." She pushed the subject of her mother away, wrinkling her nose at him. Why did she love that he was wearing the wrong kind of socks? "Don't you know that everyone is pulling their socks up these days?"

He stared down at his feet, the beginning of a grin. "What have I done without you correcting my fashion missteps all these years?"

"It's a very good question," she said.

Louisa joined them moments later, announcing they could see the Cape in close range. "Where on earth is the taxi line when you arrive at the terminal? I've never even paid attention."

The thoughts swirled: her mother writing James letters, his visit with her mother at Berkeley, how her mother had attended his mother's funeral. Betsy snapped at her sister: "It's not going to be that hard to get a taxi, Louisa!" She marched back to the table to gather her belongings. Her gosh-darn stomach was growling.

Louisa had come to gather her bags, too, while James brought his wrappers to the nearby trash can. When he returned to the table, Louisa projected her voice beyond Betsy when she said, "It would be great if we knew someone going that way and could get a ride." Louisa made a show of getting up on tiptoe and looking around the ferry goers.

Betsy's voice couldn't be any sterner. They would not take up his time. "We are *fine* with a taxi."

There was some finagling of Peanut Butter's leash around the table leg, James holding the navy cord. "I can drive the two of you to Hyannis if you need me to. There must be a hardware store there."

"It's okay. We're fine." Betsy made a face at her sister, who smiled primly. She'd always disliked when her sisters took advantage of James's kindness. When they were younger, Louisa had convinced James to paint all their toes, and he'd done it, even though Betsy told him he should charge them.

"We wouldn't want to put you out, James," said Louisa, fully intending to put him out. "I know it's been years, but it would be really great if we could hitch a ride."

Early in summer when they were sixteen, Betsy had snuck out of her house to meet James at the lifeguard stand at South Beach. They climbed the ladder and sat side by side on the simple white wooden bench, and as the moon rose over the ocean, they got lost in each other, kissing and kissing some more. They continued to see each other in secret that summer. She'd borrow one of the small sailboats from the yacht club and use the wind to silently weave her way through the darkened harbor to pick him up on his lawn. They would lie together rocking in the boat, staring up at the stars and talking. On some mornings, she would take the passenger ferry with her bike to Chappy, and they'd meet each other at the end of a woodsy path that opened to a private stretch of sand. They would bring cameras and shoot fiddler crabs on the beach, Betsy complaining how the girls at school thought her dull for caring too much about books, how debutante balls were insanely boring, whatever fight she had with her mother. She and James had existed in an alternate plane: Meeting for old movies in a dark theater and finding one another in a quiet row. Talking in between teaching classes as instructors at the yacht club. Watching television on Friday nights at his house, while she told her parents she was with her girlfriends in Oak Bluffs.

"It's not a big deal if you want me to take you to Hyannis." James was talking to Betsy, not Louisa. "My car is at the front of the ferry lot, so we'll be the first ones off the boat anyway."

They followed him to a burgundy-and-white Toyota Land Cruiser. James popped the trunk, holding his arms out to lift their duffels inside.

"What a neat truck," Louisa said as she handed him her overnight bag and sat in the passenger seat.

Betsy put her bag in the car herself. She begrudgingly climbed inside. "I'm sorry about this," she said.

His good nature showed in his face. "Hey, it's an excuse to catch up, right?" He pointed at his socks, which he'd pulled up as she'd suggested. She pretended to be relieved.

"Well, at least now I can be seen in public with you."

The ferry docked in Cape Cod, the cars filing off. As they pulled the Land Cruiser into the terminal, James switched on the radio, tuning the dial through the static until a mainland station grew clear, playing "Summer Nights" from *Grease.*

"You know, if the only thing you're doing today is buying a lawnmower"—Louisa rolled down the passenger window—"maybe you'd be willing to come with us to Nantucket?"

The wind blew her sister's blond hair off her face, and Betsy willed Louisa to look at her in the back seat so she could pretend to slice her neck with an invisible blade. Instead, Louisa said without flinching, "We could really use a car over there, and I know my mother would be so happy that we weren't getting a ride from a stranger."

CHAPTER TWENTY-FIVE

When James stepped out of the Land Cruiser to buy a round-trip car ferry pass for Nantucket, Betsy dug her fingers into the upholstery seam. "He shouldn't be here with us, Louisa. We could have found our way around. You're so quick to take advantage of people, and we can't even tell him what we're doing."

"Oh, what does it matter if James knows what we're doing? Dad left behind a property on Nantucket. So what?" Louisa didn't seem to be fazed by anything Betsy was saying, which made Betsy even more upset. "He offered to help, and we need the help. Why are you so against him coming along?"

"He didn't offer. You made him." Betsy's voice dove into the deep end. "And I don't want him here."

"Why not?" Louisa watched from afar as James stepped up to the ticket window. "All you wanted was to spend time with him as a kid, so you'll get to spend time with him now."

"If you don't remember, we haven't spoken in several years." Plus, being with him was bringing up all these memories and nostalgic feelings, which was growing an anxious pit in her stomach. "And where is James going to sleep? Does he even know we're spending the night?"

Louisa made a "duh" snort. "He can go home today without us. At least we'll be able to get around." Her sister didn't realize that James never said no to anyone, and it didn't take a psychologist to see it was because he'd received so much help from Betsy's family when he was young. "Anyway, I barely know James anymore. Do you know how much anguish you're causing me, forcing him into our day?"

"You get anguished at the sight of clouds," Louisa shot back.

From here, Betsy could see James opening his wallet. She hit her forehead against the back of the driver's seat. "Cripe, Louisa. He shouldn't be paying."

"Why? He's not broke." Louisa spanked the leather dashboard. "He's a professor now. Anyway, we'll pay him back. Now listen to me. We need a car, and he's an old family friend, so shut up and let's be grateful we ran into him. James driving us around Nantucket is not a *real* problem. A *real* problem is being demoted at work. *Okay?*"

"Maybe it's not a problem for you." Betsy leaned back against her seat and crossed her arms, still fuming.

Traffic crept through the cobblestone streets of Nantucket, a series of cars winding through the town on roads so narrow it was hard to fit pedestrians and automobiles at once. Men with well-fed bellies and expensive Italian loafers maneuvered along the streets next to wives whose accessories sparkled around their elegant necks and delicate wrists. A series of low-slung buildings charmed with cedar shingles and crisp white trim. Clam bars and lobster shacks, surf shops and boutiques, dotted the main drag.

"These people are fancy," Betsy declared with curiosity, spying a leggy woman in high-heeled sandals attempting to unstick her heel from the cobblestones. She and Louisa had played chess on the endless two-hour ferry ride over, and she'd trounced her sister, James taking her on after. The victory had improved her mood.

"Well, people have more money here," Louisa said, the car slipping past a mother and her two daughters in matching pink-and-green floral dresses. Peanut Butter stuck his head out the window, barking at a small yappy dog on the sidewalk.

There wasn't an AAA map of the Cape and islands in the glove box, so Betsy and Louisa decided to scrap the plan that included requesting a copy of the deed at the land records office in town. Instead, they asked James if he would drive them straight to the "luncheon." Then they could get a sense of their father's mysterious property.

"I see a tourist office," Betsy said. A cedar-shingled cottage announced as much with a sign over the door, pink roses growing in a tangle up an arbor shading the front gate. "Let's stop and get directions."

Inside, two teenage girls with nearly identical pin-straight auburn hair sat behind a counter, stacks of brochures organized in individual plastic stalls. Betsy asked if they knew how to get to Chapel Way, and the two of them bantered about whether Betsy should go east away from town to access it or west, neither seeming to know where it was at all.

"Let me ask our father," one of the girls said. Minutes later, a red-haired man in a bow tie and short sleeves emerged from a back room.

"What's the number on Chapel Way?" he said. "It's pretty far out, in Madaket."

"Twelve."

He seemed surprised and studied Betsy over his wire-rimmed glasses. "You're going to see Melody Fleming?"

"The land I'm looking for doesn't have a house."

The freckled man eyed her suspiciously. "Twelve Chapel Way is Melody's house. I deliver milk from the dairy there."

Maybe there was a house on her father's land? Betsy didn't want to get into details. "Ah yes. Melody. So how do I get there?"

A few minutes later, Betsy stepped into the sunshine holding two pages of directions, thinking about a line in her father's letter that had been niggling at her since she'd found it. *For reasons that I am not free to explain, both politically and personally, I have kept this property to myself.*

She opened the back door of the Land Cruiser, Louisa sighing, "What took you so long?"

"Apparently, the house is far."

James revved the engine and Louisa whipped around and said, "Thank goodness we have this ride."

He peeled out with a boyish smile, a puff of exhaust stinking up the back seat, and Betsy made sure he saw her roll her eyes.

It was easy enough to make their way out of the main part of town, the road tracing lines through grass pastures once used for grazing animals and interspersed with rambling, shingled beach houses. When they drove by a curvy blue inlet, situated along a marshy stretch of country road, Louisa turned to James.

"We need to come clean about something. There's no colleague's house. We're going to look at some land that my father owns, and we lied to you because we haven't told our mother about any of it. I hope you're not upset with us."

"I suppose I'm only offering you a ride." James pretended to lock his lips with a key. "Why doesn't your mother know about the land?"

The oldies radio station grew staticky. "We're not sure yet. We found a letter from Dad telling Betsy about the property."

"You might be fixing up your house, James, but we're losing our house." Betsy stretched her hand out the window, wondering if she'd ever again feel as carefree as she had as a child. "It looks like my sisters and I are leaving the Vineyard for good."

He glanced back into the rearview mirror.

The pastoral scenery reminded Betsy of driving up-island on the Vineyard to Chilmark, with its fields of milky Queen Anne's lace, wild-growing daisies, shimmery blue coves and crystalline ponds, and houses built on hills overlooking the wide expanses. As they drove, the sisters told James everything they knew, trying to piece together the puzzle out loud.

"Families are so wild," James said, clicking on his blinker and turning onto a road with a row of antique houses. Louisa said he needed to go straight, and he turned around. "When my mother died, I found myself on a similar paper trail. She had an estranged aunt that she'd hidden away from me. She was dead by the time I found out about her—the aunt, that is. I wondered why my mother didn't want me to know her."

The truck bounced over a pothole. Betsy grabbed for the handhold. "There are secrets in every family. You just hope they're not ones that will hurt anyone when they surface."

Last night in bed, Louisa had written in her legal pad until two in the morning, angling the notebook so that Betsy couldn't see it from her vantage point. Betsy *had* seen it this morning though, when her sister was in the shower: it was a numbered list of the ways she planned to fight the law firm; how she could sue under the Equal Rights Act if it was ratified again next month.

The ocean was always near in Nantucket, but now it was so close that you could hear the roar of the waves. A series of smaller roads drew a grid fingering out from the main road to the beach. James turned the car, following the quiet road to Madaket Beach, a small parking lot half-full of cars, with a roaring ocean crashing along the shoreline. "We must have missed the turn," he said. "Let me turn around."

They backtracked for a few minutes until they found F Street, and then Chapel Way. Betsy ruffled Peanut Butter's ears, trying to relax. She'd woken up convinced that confirming the ownership of this land would transform her family's fortunes, but the gentleman at the tourist info office had said there was a woman in the house. Melody Fleming. The woman in her mother's wedding album. She'd always loved that photo of Melody and her mother, young and glamorous and genuinely happy.

For reasons personal and political . . .

"Maybe we should turn back." Betsy didn't want a confrontation with a person named Melody. What would they do if there was in fact a woman on the land? "Dad may have meant to discard that letter. Maybe we're not even supposed to be here."

Louisa turned around in the front seat. "You're not even making sense. You said it yourself: this land is the best news we've had since he died."

A murder of crows was perched along a telephone wire. A bad omen. Betsy looked away from the birds and swallowed hard.

James slowed down the Land Cruiser at number twelve, and even though it wasn't marked, he pulled the truck into the driveway. Pebbles and dirt stretched in a straight line through neatly trimmed grass, ending at a small saltbox-style house with a tiny side porch and swing. A Ford truck with a dented metal bumper was parked in the driveway. Behind the house sat a serene harbor with several boats moored to sphere-shaped buoys.

"This can't be right." Louisa motioned for James to turn the car around. "Someone lives here."

The number on the door said twelve. "It's definitely the right house," James said.

Louisa craned her neck to look at the property, her eye landing on a large window with potted plants hanging in it. "Is someone renting it?"

Betsy cataloged the rusted pink bike leaning up against the shed, the well-tended vegetable garden with mesh strung up. "Maybe we're about to meet our long-lost aunt."

All three of them remained glued to their seats in the idling truck, while Peanut Butter panted out the window. Betsy debated getting out at all. Having a person here, even if it was her father's property, was complicated.

"Let's go to the records office." Louisa's voice had an edge to it. "There must be some mistake. Maybe Dad wrote twelve, but it's eight or ten."

James turned off the radio, then the ignition. He didn't say anything, turning in his seat to see what Betsy would say, the springs under his seat squeaking.

Betsy was usually the one who gave in the easiest, the one who chickened out on a dare, but this time, with James watching her and with her eldest sister ready to flee, she decided to be brave. "Well, we came all this way."

"I'd rather return with the deed in hand. Then we have a case." Louisa always relied on logic when she was most uncertain. Betsy agreed, but the car was in the driveway. They needed to see if anyone was home.

"You made poor James drive us here, and I'm not turning back until we see if this is Dad's house." Betsy caressed Peanut Butter's snout for courage, told James she'd be right back, then pushed open her car door and marched up the brick path. She raised her fist to rap on the door and paused, sensing that Louisa hadn't followed. Closing her eyes, Betsy willed her sister to come. One, two. She was truly afraid.

Betsy tipped her head to the shingled colonial, a momentary sense of satisfaction crossing over her. Something about the house, the handsome molding over the front door, the brass knocker in the shape of a sailboat, felt familiar. She heard footsteps approaching.

Please, please, please, Betsy thought. *Please let this house be ours.*

A memory of her mother in high heels standing at this front door. A pale blue suit. Her hair pinned in a French twist. She and James poking at each other on the grass; Betsy doing a handstand. Her mother shushing them.

She turned back to glance at James in the car. He was gazing up at the house, squinting. There was a knowingness when he and Betsy locked eyes.

"Louisa, I think I've been here with . . ."

But Betsy didn't have time to say more.

CHAPTER TWENTY-SIX

Virgie

1965

"You've been sleeping since yesterday." Pamela sat on the edge of the bed in Virgie's Martha's Vineyard bedroom, holding a cool compress to her head like Virgie was sick with fever. She sat up in her blue bouclé jacket; why hadn't she changed out of her stiff skirt suit? She felt okay, no aches or sore throat. Then the reality came to her. Melody's face, the girl with the strawberry bathing suit, the house on Nantucket—why did Charlie have anything to do with a house on Nantucket?—and Virgie felt the weight of an iron anchor press against her chest.

"When you didn't get out of bed this morning," Pamela said, a kerchief tied around her head like she'd been doing housework, "Betsy came to get me."

Virgie couldn't remember getting home from Nantucket, parking the car, climbing into her bed. It scared her. "Has Charlie phoned?"

"Twice," she said. "I told him you weren't feeling well, and Louisa would call him tonight with an update."

The ugly details of what she'd discovered on Nantucket wasn't something she could share with her daughters. As angry as she was with Charlie, she wouldn't take him away from her girls. Virgie turned on the shower, letting the bathroom grow cloudy with steam. Lathering her hair, her mind went to the reporter who stopped her last week. The photo he'd snapped. If the news of this other woman made its way into the world, the morality police would close in. There was only so much decency you could expect from a newspaper, even the *Sun*, who would call it something obnoxious like "Mr. Whiting's Love Nest."

The humiliation she would suffer as his wife, forced to smile despite the gossip rags, holding his hand at a campaign rally. Unless she refused.

Unless she filed for divorce. She certainly had the grounds.

With her damp hair brushed straight, Virgie padded down the crooked stairs. Pamela was in the kitchen preparing a fresh bouquet of hydrangeas and daylilies. It was two p.m. and sailing let out at three. Then the girls would waltz in with smiles and happy stories. Virgie needed to pull herself together. There was a bologna sandwich waiting on a plate, and Pamela fetched her a glass of ice water. Virgie stood at the window and nibbled the sandwich, staring out at the weeping willow. Pamela appeared next to her.

"Thank you for being here," Virgie said, forcing herself to eat and drink despite the bowling ball spinning in her stomach.

"You don't have to tell me what's wrong, Virgie. By the look of you, I know it's bad. But you asked me what would make me happy recently, and I think I know what it is." She wrapped her fingers around the back of the chair. "It's faith. I need to have more faith in what's possible and what seems impossible too."

"Faith and trust and pixie dust." Virgie smiled weakly.

She was repeating the quote from *Peter Pan* that she'd said to her girls often when they were younger. The words had rung true all these years because it had made her think that everyone needed to believe in the unknown. It always made her think of Charlie too. His faith that he could be elected, that his background as an orphan would be his greatest strength. Everywhere he went, a little pixie dust followed. To her, Charlie was magic.

"Maybe some pixie dust, sure." Pamela smiled wanly, then she pulled Kate Chopin's *The Awakening* out of her apron. "I finished it." A few pages were dog-eared. "It's such a sad story, and some of the racy scenes made me blush, but I think I see why you like it."

It touched Virgie that Pamela had read it; she didn't think she'd bother. "I just wanted you to know that a woman is not alone in her feelings. Anyone can feel empty inside, even the women you met here who seemed to have everything with their baubles and beautiful houses."

Pamela adjusted the folds of her skirt. "I think I can stop drinking, and I think you can get over whatever happened in Nantucket."

Virgie fell silent. She imagined going to a divorce attorney. Carrying a stack of papers over for Charlie to sign, his grimace when he realized what she was asking for. A darker thought emerged too. Charlie in their bedroom with the shades drawn, the depths to which she'd seen him despair when he'd fallen into his nervous condition. It had happened only once, but the doctors had said extreme stress may cause it to resurface. As much as Virgie hated him right now, as much as he'd hurt her, she knew what a divorce would do to him. For once, it had nothing to do with the campaign. He would be losing the only family he ever had.

Well, he should have thought about that before he had a love child with your best friend.

Virgie moved outside to the porch, pulling a soft throw over her on the wicker sofa, despite the day's warmth. It was true. She should be coming up with a plan to pack up her things in Washington. Maybe she and the girls could move to the island full-time, but she knew it wasn't what she wanted. It would make the *most* sense for Virgie to rent another apartment in the District with at least two bedrooms—they could squeeze in—but she didn't exactly have a job to pay for it. The fighting, the confrontations that would ensue, a shared custody plan where she and Charlie avoided each other on the days they exchanged the girls.

The idea left her feeling like she'd been zipped into a corset. She exhaled, folding her hands in her lap, watching Pamela as she joined her outside. "I just don't know how to fix it this time."

The wicker sofa squeaked under Pamela's weight. "No, Virgie. Don't say that. You told me that I must keep getting up. I must keep trying. You must too."

It felt so natural to slide her arm around Pamela's shoulders, to feel her drop her head against Virgie's upper arm. Weeks ago, she had looked at Pamela and thought her circumstances quite different from her own, but they weren't really. They were two women saddled with the greatest responsibility of all: taking care of those that they loved while trying to take care of themselves.

"I will try, I promise," Virgie said. She had always said she wouldn't leave Charlie because he needed her, but maybe it was vice versa. Maybe she wasn't as strong as she thought. She considered what her life would look like without Charlie. She was always telling her girls that they didn't need to be married, that they could do anything on their own. But maybe she was selling them a falsehood. Because it was so much harder to do everything on your own. Look at how challenging this summer had been.

Her head felt wobbly then. Did she want a divorce or didn't she? *Of course you don't want a divorce*, she heard herself say. She wasn't ready to leave Charlie. They had met for a reason in 1947—they had given each other strength and security and possibility—and cosmically, she believed, they were not finished with each other yet, even if she wasn't sure how she'd ever forgive him.

"Do you remember the part in *The Awakening* when Edna learns to swim?" Virgie had always been drawn to the scene. It was in the first third of the book, a turning point for Edna's character, because learning to swim gave her certain freedoms to move through her life (and the sea) without fear of being swept away.

Pamela went inside and fetched the novel, opening it to the appropriate page. "Yes, here," she said. After her life-affirming solo swim,

Edna lies in the hammock, her husband beckoning her into the bedroom: "She wondered if her husband had ever spoken to her like that before, and if she had submitted to his command. Of course she had; she remembered that she had. But she could not realize why or how she should have yielded, feeling as she then did."

The Awakening had given Virgie strength when she'd read it as a college student—whispering ideas to her about marriage that her parents had never displayed—and the book had given her a boost when she'd read it last year, just before she wrote her first Dear Virgie column. Books didn't just transport you to faraway places, Virgie believed. They could sharpen your identity and remind you who you aspired to be.

She was hungry then, suddenly famished, and she went inside to get her sandwich, Pamela on her heels. "Well, Pamela, maybe that's what you and I need to do. Figure out how to swim." Pamela nodded along, but Virgie could tell by the way she stared down at the book cover that she was confused. "What I mean is, you'll need to relearn how to live, and I will need to learn . . . " Here, Virgie paused. She squeezed her eyes shut, feeling the rays of sun warming her face. "I will need to relearn what it means to be Charlie's wife."

It was too much to explain to Pamela, but Virgie knew she was right. To overcome, she couldn't give in to sadness; she needed to swim against the tide. She would keep her principles and she'd be a good mother. She would be strong, stronger than she believed herself to be as a senator's wife, and she would stand on her own, cutting down those branches that had grown into Charlie's. She would *trust* that she could emerge from this mess in one piece, she would write her way out of it so her daughters learned what strength really looked like.

With her eyes still shut, Virgie imagined herself standing under a meteor shower, each spark sending a bolt of bravery through her bones.

She opened her eyes wide to the bright blue harbor outside. The answer was in front of her all along. All this time she'd defined herself as Charlie's wife, Charlie's friend, Charlie's biggest supporter, and when she grew angry with him this summer, she'd fought back by being everything he didn't want.

But that had failed too. Virgie had to dig down deeper, she had to look in the mirror, and she had to say to herself: *What is important to* you, *Virgie Whiting?*

She knew the answer. It was so simple, and it had been right in front of her all along. It was control. She wanted to be in control of herself, of her girls, of her future.

CHAPTER TWENTY-SEVEN

Betsy

Nantucket
1978

There was an upright wooden piano in the living room overlooking the inlet, a scatter of picture frames arranged without pattern on top. The loveliness of the space's decoration, with its mix of colors and patterns and wide-plank floors taunted her. Whose home was this? Betsy and her sister sat straight on the velvet green sofa, though Betsy felt as though she was riding on a train with an uncertain destination.

"What a lovely view," Louisa said, gazing out the windows.

"Every once in a while, we get lucky and see a seal," the woman said. She handed Louisa a hulking pair of binoculars. "You're welcome to take a look."

"That's okay," Louisa said, handing them back to this woman. This perfect stranger who seemed to know who they were as soon as she'd cautiously opened her door. After introducing herself as Melody Fleming, the three of them shook hands. She invited them in for iced tea while James waited in the car.

"Aren't you Mom's friend from the wedding album?" Louisa looked as confused as Betsy felt, and she dreaded, without any knowing at all, how these dots would connect. She noticed that Melody didn't wear a wedding ring.

"I am an old friend of both of your parents," the woman said, carrying a pitcher into the living room along with three glasses on a serving tray. She poured each of them a drink.

So far no one had touched theirs.

Louisa cleared her throat. "We're here because we have reason to believe that this land is our father's, Charlie Whiting's, and we need to understand if you're here as part of a legal contract." She might as well have been wearing power heels and the tailored suit she wore at the firm.

"Okay." Melody wore no makeup, not even blush, and her reddish brown hair was pulled into an elegant bun, like she was on her way to dance class. She spoke slowly and deliberately. "You seem like you have many questions, and I'm happy to answer all of them."

Betsy glanced at Louisa to see where she wanted to begin, but her sister seemed to be cataloging the features of the woman's face: the dark outlines of her almond-shaped eyes, her long slender nose, and the way it all came together with a kind of brilliance. Sensing she was being studied, Melody self-consciously adjusted her denim skirt, then drummed her fingers together. She looked from one sister to the other, waiting.

"It *was* you," Louisa whispered as though she were the only one in the room. Then, louder, "Dad denied it, but I always knew I was right."

"Knew what?" There was a prickling in Betsy's scalp as she waited for Louisa to answer her. Outside the window, Betsy spied a gnarled oak tree in one corner of the yard. There was a familiar curve of hedges underneath, and she stood from her place on the couch, drawing closer to the oversized picture window. Turning to face the statuesque woman, Betsy said, "I've been here before, haven't I? There was a tire swing on that branch."

The woman opened her mouth to say something, then closed it.

"Have I been here?" Betsy returned to sit beside Louisa, the formal sofa pushing against her like it wanted her to leave.

"Yes, you were here once." Melody didn't seem to know what to do with her hands, but they finally settled in her lap, her palm clutching the other hand's fingers. "Vera was about ten then, and I think she took you outside to play so your mother and I could talk."

Betsy remembered swinging on the rubber tire with James, the child named Vera running in the back door and crying that they were hogging the swing. Betsy's mother had marched outside in her pale blue jacket and skirt and scolded them for being unkind, her face angry and impatient. She'd sighed, told them that if they behaved themselves, she would get them ice cream in town. Why had James come at all? She remembered more then, a flood of scenes surfacing at once.

"My mother was so upset that afternoon when we left here." Betsy felt her throat constricting at the memory. "She'd promised to get us ice cream, and when we parked in town, she hit the bumper of another car, denting it, and some man with big thick black glasses started yelling at her, calling her a stupid woman, and she screamed back, *I am stupid, I am a very, very stupid woman and I hate myself for it.* James and I were so embarrassed we hid in the back seat of the car. Then she disappeared for hours. We hunted the shops and taverns for her, and I was crying, and James kept telling me it would be okay, but then we finally found her. She was back in the car, fully composed, and asking us if we were ready to get off this godforsaken island."

Melody stacked a set of coasters on the coffee table, small round circles made of glass with paintings of the beach set inside. Once she'd made a small tower with them, she took the tower apart one by one and made another stack. "That day may have been the hardest of my entire life."

Louisa seemed to be calculating something, counting her fingers. When she spoke, her speech was exacting, precise, full of accusation. "I won the debate in April of my sophomore year, and that's when I went to his office to tell him. That was the summer he barely visited the Vineyard, the summer I thought he and Mom were getting divorced."

The saliva in Betsy's mouth thickened to paste, her voice soft and trembling. "How do you know our father?"

Melody pushed the coasters away and tucked her palms under her thighs on the burgundy chaise opposite them. "I knew you would come back here someday." She cleared her throat, offering Betsy a sympathetic look. "Your parents and I, as I said, we were friends. Old friends from Washington." The woman's face contorted into an ugly knot, like she might cry. "I made a mistake being with your father, and there was a part of me that believed I would take the secret of my baby to the grave. That your mother would never know. I said a prayer for her the day she found out, that she would be okay."

For the last few minutes, Louisa had been lost in a stupor of puzzle pieces she was snapping and unsnapping in her head, but now, she sat up with attention, her gaze narrowing to a sharp point. "You said a prayer for my mother? Did you say a prayer for my mother when you bent over the desk in my father's office?"

Betsy furrowed her eyebrows. "Louisa!"

"Thank you for gifting me the worst possible image of my father, you stupid bimbo." Louisa inhaled a deep breath.

The memory remained sharp. That day she'd skipped a celebratory outing with friends to go to the Hill and tell her father that she'd won the debate. His secretary was gone for the day, but she could hear voices from inside his office. "I was a kid, so I didn't knock, bounding inside to tell him my good news. I saw her and dad stretched out across his desk, and when I came in, he jumped away like she was on fire, his eyes locking with mine. That's when I saw her, adjusting her dress while holding her hand out, like she wanted to shake my hand. I took off running."

Betsy tried to picture it. The wide hallways and dim lighting of the Senate offices, her sister racing past the American flags outside. "Did Dad catch up to you? What did he say?"

Louisa paused, remembering. "He came into my bedroom that night, saying that he was sorry. He hugged me and swore it wasn't anything 'bad.' He said a crazy constituent had tried to kiss him, and he'd been trying to get her off him when I walked in. I knew it wasn't true, though, or he would have told Mom. Instead, it became this twisted secret that neither of us acknowledged ever again."

Melody blanched, nibbling on her pale lower lip. "I think you're describing the one and only time I visited Charlie in his office. When my daughter was in grade school, I went to Washington with her, and after, I sent her down the hall with the rest of her field trip and I hung back to see him. It had been years since we'd spoken. I don't know what you think you saw, some kissing, but Charlie was my one great love, and we were hugging, and I was telling him how challenging it had been, being a single mother, and then . . ."

If Louisa heard her, she continued her story as if she hadn't. "I hated my father after that, and so many days I hated myself for expecting anything at all from him, for thinking he'd care about my accomplishments. Gosh, how I wish I never opened that door."

"What?" Betsy stammered, trying to unsee it herself. "But Dad always looked at Mom with so much adoration. What he wouldn't do to please her." It left her with an uncomfortable thought. Was it possible that no one really knew anyone in this life? That we simply projected onto individuals the versions of them that we wanted, rather than ever seeing who they really were. All those years, when Louisa's relationship with her father was frosty, she wasn't being difficult; she was angry at her father for cheating on her mother. Her father had known that all along, and instead of admitting as much, he accused Louisa of being moody and disrespectful.

"You're probably wondering why I didn't tell anyone." Louisa had a wounded expression. "It was simple. I was afraid Mom and Dad would split up."

"I'm terribly sorry." Melody had inched closer to the sisters, so she was beside Betsy.

Louisa was in the final points of her argument, the moment on TV when the lawyer drove a stake through the defendant's heart. "You're sorry. What kind of person does that to her best friend? You were her maid of honor."

"Your father came on to me in the office. He offered me this house to live in after I had Vera. He came to the island periodically to visit us. These were *his* choices."

Betsy tapped her foot, hating the fact that this woman was right. "Why would he continue to visit you? Did Vera think of him as her father?"

It was hard to explain, she said. Melody let her eyes rest on a photo of her grown daughter in front of the Eiffel Tower. "Charlie and I agreed it would be too complicated for Vera to know who he was, unless he was going to act like her father. Instead, I told her he was a friend from college, and when he'd visit, she'd call him 'Uncle Charlie.' He wanted to know Vera, and rather than writing Charlie out of my life, like I should have, I let him show up sometimes. He'd sit at the kitchen table sipping tea and talking about how he felt like an imposter in Washington, which always surprised me. I'd always hoped that maybe a part of him still loved me, even if years of therapy taught me that I was delusional."

"You should have told my mother; she should have known who my father really was."

Melody's eyes turned down. "I think she knew who he really was."

Her mother had shown up here when Betsy was ten, not having any idea how many secrets lie under the floorboards—and now so had Betsy. Her entire childhood felt like a book with all its pages ripped out, nothing left but an empty spine.

Betsy could feel the corners of her eyes pooling.

Feelings of her own betrayal with Andy bubbled up inside her. Is that what her mother had done? Had she hidden her pain from her daughters and pretended that everything was fine when her core throbbed with sadness? And why had Virgie stayed with him?

"Did you ever tell Vera? Does she know who her father is?" Betsy wiped at the corners of her eyes. She needed to know if this young woman knew she had three half sisters.

"She does. I told her after his plane went down."

It was then that Melody told them the story.

Virgie Whiting had been Melody's closest friend in Washington. They'd met at Barnard when they were freshmen and they'd connected from the start, both ambitious, modern, and committed to their futures. When the two of them moved to the Capitol—Virgie when Charlie was elected and Melody when she got a job as a press person for a New York congressman—they'd get together for lunch and gripe about how dull and gray Washington was compared to colorful Manhattan. How they longed for pastrami at Barney Greengrass or cosmos at the Rainbow Room. Still, they each had a knack for politics.

"Your mother was always trying to set me up on dates." Melody hadn't smiled since she started talking, but she did now, with distance. "She'd hunt cocktail parties for handsome single men and force us into conversation."

Melody ran into Charlie one afternoon in the hallway of the Russell Senate Office Building, and he'd seemed flustered in his navy woolen suit. His press secretary had walked out on him, there was a big setback on the budgetary legislation, and his overworked legislative assistants were answering the phones. Virgie would come with the children toddling about and try to help, but Charlie asked Melody if she would do him a favor: call in sick to her job and work for his congressional office for the day. She leaned forward, her eyes watery and glimmering. "I'd barely been there twenty minutes when he offered me the job of press secretary, with a modest increase in salary."

It was a big promotion, since she would be the only woman press secretary in Congress that year. At first, Virgie would visit her and Charlie at lunch, sometimes bringing baby Louisa and eating ham sandwiches at the formal desks of the offices smelling of paper and old curtains. Then Charlie began working through lunch and sometimes dinner, and Melody would type up press releases or take journalists' phone calls late into the night. One dusky evening, she and Charlie were working on a speech that he needed to give the next day, when he kissed her out of the blue. "I was flattered—I looked up to your father just like most of his staff did, and if I'm being honest, I had developed feelings for him."

One thing led to another, Melody said, pushing up her sleeves as she tried to rush through this part. "Soon after, I realized I was pregnant," she said. From there, the outcome was rather textbook: one of them wanted the child (her), the other didn't (him), and both agreed that if Virgie found out about the two of them it would destroy her—and it would threaten Charlie's political career. To protect her friend, whom she'd hurt in ways she hated herself for, Melody moved to Boston for a year, then home to Nantucket to be closer to her brother, a fisherman, and her parents, who owned the movie house in town.

Virgie wrote her letters, but Melody didn't answer them, trying to distance herself from her old friend.

Melody wrapped her bare arms around herself. "I'd always wanted children, and I'd been so jealous of your mother, who already had two. I named my daughter Vera because it means 'faith,' and I'd never been so scared in my life."

There was a loud thump, and Betsy thought it was her head doing a flip-flop, until she realized that Louisa had chucked one of the coasters from the coffee table, the glass thudding against the wall. Betsy grabbed the remaining coasters off the table and traveled to the piano, where she gripped the glossy top. There was a row of photographs of Vera at various stages: a newborn with eyes pressed shut and bundled tight, a toddler in pigtails and saddle shoes on a tricycle. Nothing about the child's face felt familiar until she morphed into her double digits. Then there were her father's eyes, his nose, and smile. Betsy swallowed hard.

"But why did he keep coming back?"

Melody hesitated. "I suppose I offered something different from what your mother did—I'd like to think it was a softness—and great men need that kind of comfort. Maybe he needed it more than most."

Betsy's anger shot out of her like an arrow, ricocheting and hitting her dead center in the chest. This woman! Talking about her father like this.

"I'm a bit in shock." Betsy tried to still the tremble in her voice, breathing in, then out. "But can you help me understand how you ended up with this house?"

"He didn't want to be a part of her life, but when Vera was little, he showed up on the island, finding me at my parents' house. He said he had this empty cottage here on the water and told me I could stay here as long as I didn't tell anyone about Vera. He added the parcel next door in sixty-five. I didn't hear from him very often after that, even after I saw him in Washington, until recently."

"You think we're going to take pity on you?" Louisa slammed her hand onto the coffee table, making Betsy flinch once more. "You destroyed my relationship with my father."

"I'm sorry, but I'm not at fault for whatever your father did and didn't do."

The gall of this woman, a peasantlike pointedness in the features that Betsy had mischaracterized as austere. Betsy was afraid that Louisa might slap Melody, and she grabbed her sister's clenched hand and yanked her up. Betsy's voice dropped like a bomb.

"We fully expect you to leave the premises in three days' time. Please take all your belongings. You are living here illegally, and we plan to sell. As far as we're concerned, this is Whiting property, and the Whiting family is here to reclaim it."

Betsy felt Louisa squeeze her hand, and it made her feel closer to her sister than perhaps she ever had in her life. Louisa couldn't find the words, but Betsy had.

Melody folded her hands in her lap. "I've kept this secret for years. This is my home."

A single mother. A child without a father. Sleepless nights walking a house with nothing but ghosts. She felt a sharp pain in her chest. This was what her life would look like if she had the baby, only no one was giving Betsy a house to raise the child in. Even as a complete and utter jerk, her father had displayed more empathy than Andy had. She gave him that.

The sisters hurried to the front door, whipping it open and following the path to James's truck. He put down his book, his friendly smile vanishing in an instant. Betsy wanted to fall into his embrace, to feel the calming strokes of his hand against her cheek. Instead, she pressed backward into the back seat, feeling like she couldn't breathe. When James asked if she was okay, she turned her head to look out the window and didn't say a word.

"You look like her, Betsy," Melody called out from the slate walkway. "My daughter, Vera."

Louisa wiped at her wet cheeks as the engine roared to life over the sound of crashing waves. Betsy must have bit down hard on her lip, because she tasted metal. All she wanted to do was go home.

James drove them straight to Madaket Beach and parked in the sandy lot. He didn't ask any questions. From the back seat, Betsy stared at the back of Louisa's head, still and fixed. It made her sick that this little girl grew up feeling rejected by her father, and it made her sick to think that her father had known the child. Betsy wished he was alive just so she could pound on her father's chest with her fists and call him what he was: selfish, a hypocrite and a liar.

"I wish I never found that stupid letter," Betsy said. She pushed out of the back seat and broke into a sprint, her throat feeling like it was closing in on her, and she ran harder, working for air. She was halfway to the ocean when she heard James calling her name. She spun on her feet, screaming back at him: "Leave me alone. All I want is for you to go away."

Out of breath, his chest heaving, she expected all six feet of his frame to shrivel. Instead, he edged closer. "Since my mother died, I've been all by myself, Betsy, and it's terrible, and you—you have all these people. All these people who want to be close to you, and you don't even see it."

"You don't know anything about me anymore." She marched down the beach, the pads of her feet slamming hard into the soft sand. She cupped her hand against her belly. "Nobody does."

He walked hard to keep up with her. "You know why you're going to be a good psychologist? Because you spend so much time trying to fix the people around you, but you never fix yourself."

Her bangs blew into her mouth as she pivoted to face him. "My family is falling apart, and my father isn't who he said he was. The perfect little Whiting family is a gosh darn mess, and you can rest easy that you're not part of it. We're the most screwed-up family in the entire world, and you're right, I have no idea how to fix it."

He kicked at the sand, the soft grains tickling her ankles. "Maybe you don't have to fix it, Betsy. Maybe you just have to learn to live with the truth."

Betsy collapsed onto her knees in the sand. "Since when are you a therapist?"

"Since I spent many years in therapy." He looked off down the beach, then swept his eye up to her. "If you keep everything in, you'll become like my mother. Angry and resentful and broken. We need people in our lives, Betsy, and if my mother taught me anything, it's that everybody needs a lot of somebodies to be okay."

Melody had moved back to Nantucket to be near her brother and parents when she got pregnant. It couldn't have been easy, even if Charlie visited sometimes, but her family had given her the help she so badly needed. She'd found her somebodies.

"Can we go now?" Betsy said to him, and he nodded. They trudged back to the car in the warm sand. Halfway to the car, James stopped her.

"That night your father caught us at the Agricultural Fair, there was something I didn't tell you."

Betsy didn't think she had the energy to do this right now. "What didn't you tell me? Not that it matters, since my father forbid me that night from continuing to date you."

"No, Betts. Stop thinking it was you. It wasn't you," he said, pushing his palms into his back pockets.

"Well, it was me who ran away that night, begging you to take the boat out in the storm, with those waves; it was dumb. I blame myself for all of it."

They took a few more heavy steps, and James stopped again, stooping to pick up a perfect scallop shell. He handed it to her. "We're lucky the coast guard picked us up on a routine patrol. I remember being soaked to the bone. It's the only time in my life I thought I might drown."

Betsy shivered at the memory. "Do you know my mother slept in bed with me that night? She followed me around for weeks, and they forbid me to see you, as you probably figured out. I couldn't talk to you or write you. Maybe Wiley told you, but I stayed in Washington and worked in my father's office the summer after."

He pressed his lips together. "It was hard. I missed you, but . . ."

Betsy's face grew wet. Years of doing everything her father wanted so he'd love her best; how much he'd taken away from her and how she'd pretended that she was okay with it. How much she hated him now. "I listened to him and didn't contact you, and I lost you because

I was following a man who was such a hypocrite, who didn't even love me the way he said he did."

"No, Betsy. He did, and he was a good person, at least to me. Whatever he did that has you this upset, whatever is happening here, I want you to know that he came to my house the day after the storm. He told me I was a good kid, that I had a bright future, and he would make a call for me when the time came. To a college, any college I asked him to, but I would have to agree to stop contacting you."

She wiped her eyes with the back of her wrist. "I thought I was the one who put distance between us. Wait a second. My dad is why you got into Berkeley?"

James reached for her hand, then dropped his fingers to his side. "I've been so ashamed that I agreed to it, and yet, he already made clear I'd never see you again. I tried to write you, I did. But . . ." He sighed, glancing at the cloudless sky, then back at her.

"No, James. You did the right thing. I've only ever wanted what was best for you, and you needed him to make that call for you. It changed your life."

"Wiley helped me apply the following year, and he called your dad and reminded him to make the phone call to the dean. Berkeley was the only school I got into, you know. Wiley helped me pay the bills, and he's helped me so much since, but your father, he was generous. He wanted what he thought was best for you, and he did what he could for me."

"God, I hate him," Betsy said, shaking her head. "But I am grateful he helped you. I'm so very grateful he had the right mind to do that."

When they got back to the car, Betsy and her sister locked eyes as she climbed into the back seat.

"Are you okay?" Louisa asked. She had the look of a feral cat, mangy and lost.

"Not really." Betsy lay down on the back seat, Peanut Butter licking her forehead. "But we might as well find a place to stay the night."

CHAPTER TWENTY-EIGHT

Virgie

1965

The very first person that Virgie called after discovering the connection between Charlie and Melody Fleming was India Knight. Though she hadn't known the British expatriate very long, Virgie trusted her. They went for a brisk walk to Fuller Street Beach the following morning, and Virgie admitted everything that happened with Charlie. She told India about the reporter, the threat to Charlie's campaign, and what she feared this meant for her marriage.

They sat on the splintered bench at the beach, an open view of the lighthouse. India turned to her. "Of course I'll help. What do you need?"

Virgie peppered her with questions, but one counted most. She remembered the dinner party with the Knights, when India's husband had dangled "additional property on Nantucket" as an incentive for him to earmark funds for the missile program. "Can you find out if your husband had anything to do with giving Charlie this house on Nantucket?"

India knew that Russell had friends with homes on Nantucket, but she didn't think he'd purchased one for Charlie. "If it's a shell company that bought it, it will be hard for me to track." She also seemed wary of looking too closely into her husband's business dealings.

"India, if you can't find out about the house, can you try to get Russell to tell you why Charlie went there three times this summer? If it wasn't to see this woman, which she swears is the truth, then why was he there?"

They decided to walk along the water, trying to puzzle it out. "It has to be a coincidence," India said. "Nothing else makes sense unless that woman is lying through her teeth and she and Charlie have been carrying on all along."

Virgie grimaced. She could always smell another woman on Charlie, but she'd never gotten a whiff of the same one twice.

Louisa took the week off from the bookshop. Virgie had asked her to help her get everyone packed for a surprise trip to see their father in Washington. It was the end of July, and she wouldn't wait for Charlie to get up to the island. It was hard enough waiting until tomorrow, since this wasn't a conversation that they could have over the phone. Charlie had called her again this morning, and she'd made pleasant small talk with him, even as she gritted her teeth thinking about him all those years ago, knowing that she and Melody were pregnant at the same time.

But no, she needed to remain calm. An emotional woman was a powerless one. Virgie would bide her time. If she acted too rash, she would lose the upper hand.

They would be on the seven a.m. ferry the following morning, and it would take eight hours to drive from Woods Hole to Washington. First, there was one more person Virgie needed to talk to.

A rainstorm earlier in the week had caused seaweed to wash ashore the small sandy beach where the yacht club stowed the sailboats. The air was briny when she located Wiley fixing a sail near the work shed. He painstakingly pushed the needle through the thick fabric.

"How was Nantucket?" he asked. They made small talk about the ferry, how different the islands were, how very much the same. Virgie sat down in the sand in her long sundress, letting her bare feet splay out.

"I need a favor," she said.

Wiley lowered the sail, sat next to her. "Are you okay?"

She buried her hands under the sand so he couldn't see her gripping it. "There is nothing untoward happening on Nantucket, at least not from an election standpoint." India had called her last night, saying that her husband admitted easily that Charlie was going to earmark money for the Skybolt program; it wasn't a secret. Her friend whispered into the phone: "He obviously doesn't know why I'm asking, but we talked about how wonderful the two of you are, and he did say that he'd seen Charlie twice, once in Washington, and once in Nantucket, where they met with a potential investor."

That was the nugget that the reporters would want: a backdoor deal playing out on an exclusive New England summer island. The rest was for the tabloids. Virgie didn't want to destroy Charlie, and she wouldn't lead Wiley to that shady detail, but she would lead her journalist friend away from 12 Chapel Way.

"What did you find at the address I gave you?"

Virgie liked Wiley. She'd always liked him; perhaps that was why her husband hated him so much. She cleared her throat.

"Wiley, I need to talk to you as a friend." When he nodded, a gentle expression crossed his face, one of concern. "One of my closest friends in DC lives in the house at 12 Chapel Way. I didn't realize that she and Charlie had some kind of *friendship*," and when she said this, she rubbed up and down her calves, watching the gentle lap of the water.

Wiley leaned forward, his tone disappointed, maybe even surprised. "A friendship?"

"Yes." She forced herself to look at him so he wouldn't doubt the veracity. "You must trust me that the only story on the island is one for the tabloids. Please don't let them ruin us."

"Virgie, you shouldn't accept that from him."

She put a hand on his arm. "I'm not accepting it." Her sack purse was on her lap, and she reached in and pulled out three Dear Virgie columns. Her story "Flying Lessons" was there too. "I'm hoping you can help me get my column back."

He took the typed pages. "That will be easy. Readers loved you."

Virgie nodded, pleased. "But I want to talk to you about writing a more serious column too. I don't want to just solve the dilemmas of housewives; I want to reinvent the housewife."

This caused him to waggle his eyebrows. "Charlie's going to hate it."

Virgie shrugged. "Good."

CHAPTER TWENTY-NINE

Betsy

1978

Near the docks in Nantucket town, they found a small motel built on stilts. Louisa signed for two rooms, since James decided to stay, the sisters carrying their overnight bags to a row of white-painted doors, small navy anchors painted at the centers. James settled into the room adjacent to them. After jimmying the skeleton key in the lock, Louisa pushed open the door to the smell of musty Captain's furniture.

"Ugh, there's sand on the floor." Louisa frowned at the indoor/outdoor carpets. They dropped their bags on a wicker chair near the door. "The sheets better be clean."

Betsy wasn't sure if it mattered whether there were fresh linens on the bed—she'd still feel this crushing disappointment in her chest. She lay back on the stiff bed, placing a pillow on her face, wishing she could be alone and yet too afraid to be. They needed to call Aggie, but first, she and Louisa needed to talk about what they were going to do about Melody.

Louisa disappeared into the bathroom and took a hot shower. The spray of water came fast and hard, while Betsy's thoughts tumbled to her mother. The summer when she was ten and her father rarely came to visit and sent a police officer to check on them. How she'd always believed her father wholeheartedly when he said he had meetings on the Hill, that he couldn't get away from work—she'd never had reason to doubt him. Her mother knew about Melody, though, and about Vera, and she hadn't left him. Now every memory Betsy had of her parents felt like a lie.

Betsy lifted the pillow off her face, staring at the water stain on the ceiling. All these years, she'd thought she had two sisters, but she had three. Three! She, Aggie, and Louisa had been cheated of any relationship with this half sister named Vera, and she couldn't help but wonder what Vera was like. If she and Vera, as the youngest, would have been bonded by their age, or if they would have competed harder for Louisa's and Aggie's affections. Had her mother thought it best to keep this child away from her girls? Or had it been a decision to protect her father's political career?

Betsy felt the hairs on her arm stand up as she thought of another possibility—that there could have been other women, other affairs.

Louisa emerged from the shower with her hair wrapped in a towel and sat at the corner of the scratchy bedspread in her pajamas. They watched a rerun of *The Price Is Right* on the television without sound.

A row of grocery products were rolled onto the stage, the contestants asked to predict the price of each item. When the first contestant was called on, Betsy said, "I'm sorry, Louisa. I had no idea that you'd been saddled with that knowledge all this time. Why didn't you tell me or Aggie?"

Louisa shook her hair out of the towel, brushing it straight. "I didn't want you to know. I didn't want anyone to know." Louisa began to cry, and Betsy rolled on her side to face her. She continued. "But what was the point of torturing myself when Mom knew all along? I had no idea she knew. It's shocking that she kept so much of it to herself and stayed with him. I still don't understand why she did."

"Because it would have crushed her if we thought of her as a woman who chose to stand by her cheating husband. It doesn't compute with who she is." Their eyes struck like a match, a knowingness in the explanation. "With Dad's little mistake hidden over on Nantucket, maybe she just pretended it never happened." Betsy pulled at the loose threads in the bedspread. She knew something about what a woman would do to keep a secret. "Anyway, I owe you an apology."

"You don't need to apologize."

But she did. Louisa had always seemed so perfect, neatly sewn up. She thought her mother and father were, too, and that was why Betsy's failures had always felt so big. None of them was perfect though—far from it—and it was loosening something inside her. A sense that she could fail and still be worth loving. A sense that she could be honest in this scrappy little room.

"Mom and Dad were always fawning over every little thing you did, and I was so envious that I never stopped to consider whether you were happy or okay. That wasn't fair."

Louisa's Harvard Law T-shirt had faded, the heather-gray fabric soft and worn-in. "Oh, Betsy. I am nowhere near perfect. There are things in my past that I'm so ashamed of that I cannot say them out loud."

"That's why I'm apologizing. Because I never took the time to get to know you. It's as though you froze in time in our teenage years, and we've been playing out the same storylines ever since." Betsy sat up, tucked her legs under her. "But I do want to know you better. I do want to be closer to you."

Betsy felt like a grown-up saying that. For years, she'd resented her sister and how close she was to their mother. Now their intimacy seemed like a lifeline for Louisa. The day she'd walked in on her father with another woman was the day she'd lost him, and in keeping the secret, she'd allowed Betsy to have him for the next decade.

Louisa smiled. "Being home these last few weeks has drawn us closer, don't you think? Being in this nightmare with the house, with Dad, it's the beginning of something new."

"I hope so." Betsy bit the inside of her cheek. She took a deep breath; what she wanted to say next would be particularly hard to admit. For years, it was the only power she'd had over her sister. "You know how you always used to say that I was Dad's favorite?"

Louisa picked at a scab from a mosquito bite on her arm. "You *were* Dad's favorite."

It was a falsehood that would be painful to dispense, but she needed to, for her sister's sake. "I was only his favorite because you pushed him away. I was his second choice, and I'm not saying that to make you feel better. I mean, I am, but I'm also saying it because it always bothered me. You were Mom's favorite, and deep down, I knew you were Dad's, too, and that left me feeling so alone. I think it's why I was always so angry at you."

Louisa reached across the blank space between them, what had minutes ago felt like an ocean. She took Betsy's hand with care. "Betsy, we don't love people the same way every single day, and maybe that's the part no one told you. There are moments when I feel so connected to Mom, and some days I'd rather jump off a building than be in the same room with her. There were times when I couldn't get enough of you, and times when I avoided you. But I do love you. I love you so much that I felt incredibly empty inside when you pushed me away last year, like I was walking around without an arm or something. A sister's love is an enduring one. Even if we have a bad year, I'll never give up on you."

Betsy felt a single tear slip into her mouth. "But I annoy you. I annoy you and you hate me, and I'm so lame."

It was the first time that they'd laughed since they got off the ferry this morning, and Louisa seemed genuinely happy to be having the conversation. "I annoy you too. I drive you crazy."

Betsy nodded, then nodded again. "You really do drive me crazy."

Maybe Betsy would begin the work of getting closer to Louisa right now, just by sitting beside her and listening, sharing the complications they'd been sheltering in their hearts.

A buoy bell chimed out in the harbor, and Betsy grew homesick for the house on Martha's Vineyard. They'd only been gone a day. How would they leave for a lifetime? Betsy wiped her nose with the back of her wrist. She grew serious then.

Gazing straight into her sister's light blue eyes, she said, "I'm pregnant."

Betsy waited for her sister to release her hand. To scoff. To scold her for being such an utter disaster. Instead, Louisa squeezed her hand harder back and grinned. "I know. Aggie and I both know. I've been listening to you eat crackers in bed! We've just been waiting for you to tell us."

Before night fell, they began discussing a general plan for what they might do about the Nantucket house. Both sisters put on their pajamas early, the need to relax from the day's events feeling paramount. There was a small round table in one corner of the room, and Betsy sat in one of the chairs, her knees pulled up to her chest.

"If Melody lived there for the last fifteen or so years, how can we just kick her off the property?" Nothing about this conversation felt good to Betsy, and still, there was no skirting the issue. There was a woman living in the house that they wanted to sell.

Louisa bit her cuticles. "It does feel a bit heartless. And yet . . . Daddy presented the house in the letter as an investment you should know about, which feels like he intended to reclaim it at a certain point. Melody might have conveniently left those details out."

They hadn't pressed Melody on the conditions of their agreement. "What if she paid us rent? Would it be enough to float the loans on the Vineyard house?"

Louisa jotted down the numbers, doing quick long division. "Unfortunately, no."

"Well, maybe there's a way we can sell the house but not leave her high and dry. Maybe she wants to buy the house from us."

Louisa drew spirals on the notepad, starting big and getting smaller and smaller. "Doubtful, but I suppose we need to talk to Melody again. Then again, do we? It's our house, Betsy. It doesn't matter what she thinks—she's not our problem. The house is in Dad's name. It's ours."

They agreed to table the conversation and stop into a real estate office in the morning to ask an agent about their rights versus a tenant's.

Betsy's stomach growled, and she asked Louisa if she'd mind if they invited James over. They'd dragged him to the island with them. They should include him in their plans.

Minutes later, he knocked on the door three times, employing the secret code they used as kids. The three of them ordered mushroom pizza and squeezed into the small room to watch *The Love Boat*, then *Fantasy Island.* James perched on a wooden chair near the beds, his feet up on the motel room's pine dresser.

"Do you think Julie has a thing for Captain Stubing?" James asked, flashing his brows and looking amused. They were all engrossed in an episode about a tennis pro meeting up with his ex-flame, and Louisa shushed them. Betsy spoke quietly.

"Absolutely not. Julie has a crush on Gopher. See how she lights up every time she sees him." Betsy pushed herself up on bent elbow. "Besides, gross. Captain Stubing could be her father."

"Shush!" Louisa tossed one of the flattened bed pillows at her, which made Betsy toss one of the grimy throw pillows back. James reached for the pancake-thin pillow and tossed it at Betsy. He fit right into their family, almost like he'd never left.

That night, after James returned to his room and they turned off the light, Louisa propped herself up on one elbow in the springy queen bed. "If you don't want to have this baby, Betts, I just want you to know something."

"Okay," Betsy said.

"I had a procedure when I was fifteen, to get rid of something, really early on. Remember all that stuff with Brandon Millerton?"

Betsy had always wondered about that time, what really happened. "Did Mom and Dad know?"

"Dad drove us. Mom came inside. I don't think Dad ever saw me the same way." She flopped backward onto her pillow. "Anyway, I always felt so ashamed by it, and I don't want you to feel that way, in case you decide to do it. It's your right."

"Why didn't you ever tell me? Does Aggie know?" Betsy kicked the bedspread off; even with a cool breeze coming in through the window, the room felt stagnant.

Louisa scoffed. "It's not something you advertise, and no, Aggie doesn't know. But listen, I can take you to get help, if you need me."

Betsy's voice squeaked out. "I want this baby."

"I know, I'm just reminding you."

In the morning, James left a note on their door saying he was going for a ride to a lighthouse; he'd be back by ten. The sisters had a quick breakfast and waited for the Realtor's office to open around the corner. Sitting opposite an agent named Peter Collins, whose work attire seemed suited for a sunset sail—cherry-red shorts, leather boat shoes, and a short-sleeve collared shirt—he confirmed they could indeed sell the Nantucket house, even if they had a tenant. "As long as there's no lease holding you to a certain rental date, this individual would be forced to vacate." Peter picked up his pen, ready to make a note on a yellow legal pad. "Do you want to give me the address and I can give you an idea of the home's worth?"

"Not yet," Louisa said. She took his card. "But we'll be in touch."

While they waited for James at the ferry dock, Betsy watched Louisa walk over to a pay phone with her Chanel purse on her shoulder, loading the booth with coins. She talked animatedly for a few minutes, then returned to Betsy's side in the scorching sun, their overnight bags at their feet. "What was that about?" Betsy asked.

"I called the firm and told them I'll be back in a few days to begin my new position." She pretended to be gleeful, then rolled her eyes.

"You could hold out," Betsy said. "There have to be other law firms, better people."

Louisa crossed her arms over her tank sweater. "Maybe, but it could also be worse. I'll pay my dues with the old man and I'll transcribe his stupid notes, and I'll work so hard, I'll run circles around him. Next summer, I'll request to assist a different lawyer."

It was too depressing to consider, that you could work as hard as Louisa had and still be relegated to menial office work. "What made you change your mind?"

"Love. I realized that Mom and Dad stopped putting each other first, choosing their careers, and I've never done that, put Michael first. I want to try."

"Good for you." Betsy watched the ferry as it docked, workers tossing ropes to the tall wooden pilings. "But you're not giving up on your career, are you?"

Louisa's purple pleated shorts were as prim as her smile. "Goodness no. But maybe Mom is wrong. Maybe I can get married and still make partner. Maybe a woman can have it all *and* be happy."

Betsy liked that idea. In two years' time, it would be a new decade: the 1980s, and the lives of women would change once more. Her mother was already saying that more women were joining the workforce than at any point in history. They would have to find a way to be there for their kids in ways that Betsy's own mother had failed to be there for them. Fathers would have to learn to step up. Women would need to rely on their families again.

Betsy would need to rely on her family again.

James drove them onto the ferry at ten, all of them walking upstairs to the open sundecks of the boat. As the ferry pushed off from the dock, James mentioned that he'd been offered a tenured position at New York University.

"I may stay on the East Coast after all," he said, petting Peanut Butter's head. "It's a good job, and it would allow me to spend summers here again. I forgot how much I loved this island."

Betsy smiled. "When you love something, you should never let it go," she said, kissing Peanut Butter on the top of his soft furry head.

It was three in the afternoon when they got back to Martha's Vineyard, the sun dappling the roadway, the tall swaying oaks welcoming them home as they pulled up onto South Water Street. On the lawn was Sally Channing's real estate sign, gently rocking in the breeze.

James put the Land Cruiser in park, and he stiffened when Louisa leaned across the front seat to give him a hug. "Thank you for your help," she said. "You're a Whiting in spirit."

They all got out of the car then, standing at the open car trunk. Louisa yanked out her bag and said, "Seriously, James, I'm forever grateful for what you did for us."

"Anytime," he said. He gazed up at the green shutters of the house; they hadn't changed since they were kids, small cutouts of seashells cut into the upper panels. "Gosh, I hope your family doesn't sell. This house was a constant for me, just knowing you all were here . . . It got me through some dark times."

Louisa hoisted her quilted weekend bag on her shoulder. "Well, those days are behind you now, and besides, we're not going anywhere. Right, Betsy?"

Betsy leaned against the car, the corners of her mouth turning up. "Right."

A couple of kids pedaled by, squeaking their horns for fun. Louisa disappeared inside.

"Thanks for calming me down yesterday," Betsy said, embarrassed by her outburst on the beach. "You know I don't think you're some kind of leech, right?"

He kicked at the rubber tire with his Nike sneakers, his hair curling up from the ferry winds. "I *am* kind of a leech. I mean, not now, but before." When he looked up, he smiled. He presented like he was shy, but he wasn't. He was gentle. "Anyway, we all lose it sometimes. I certainly did after my mother died."

She wanted to hug him, but she felt funny; her embrace would feel different from the sisterly one Louisa had given him.

Betsy lifted her backpack, tucking her long brown hair behind one ear. "Well, it was nice seeing you, and like Louisa said, thanks for helping us out."

He smiled. "I know you're on the island for a little longer, but before you leave, can we take out my old boat?"

A tingling surged inside her chest, a million little beats pulsing through its center. "The little rowboat?"

"We'd still fit." He rose up on his heels, grinning. "We can bring it over to the cove, float around and talk about life."

Betsy chuckled. "You sound like one of those stoners with a guitar."

He laughed. "I can bring a guitar if you'd like."

Betsy had the sense that she was suspended above them, watching two friends become close once more. Theirs would be the truest kind of friendship, where they talked on the phone and visited each other sometimes. If he took the NYU job, he'd get to see the baby after it was born. He could be Uncle James.

It was a decision Betsy had made all over again that morning on the ferry back to the Vineyard. In the end, just like Louisa, Betsy would choose love. It was hard to explain, even to herself, why she loved this little lima bean that was growing inside her, but she did. She would be a woman who chose to do things on her own, even if she was the last person in her family that anyone ever expected to have those kind of guts.

Betsy hugged James, and he hugged her back. He was right. She would need a lot of somebodies to make it in this life, but she also wanted him to be one of hers. He'd been her best friend for so many years, and she'd been wrong to write him out of her life, simply because it was too complicated to keep him in it.

"Can we take out *Senatorial* too?" Betsy said. "You never did get to sail on her."

She wished her father could see James now, how he believed in himself, how he had been determined to be better than his mother.

A dimple formed in James's left cheek. "Okay, but the rowboat first."

She shook her head, even though she loved the idea of it. "We're going to sink that thing. We're grown-ups now."

"But we can still act like kids sometimes, right?"

"We can," she said.

At that moment, James kissed her. Just once, soft on the lips. He met her stunned expression with confidence, his face inches from hers. "I don't want to just run into you sometimes, Betts. I want to see you. On purpose."

It no longer felt like there was a hard layer around her heart. "I waited for you outside the hardware store the other day, but you never came." She hid her face, then found the courage to lift her eyes to his. Perhaps, all this time, Betsy had been looking for the wrong things—degrees and achievements and men who thought her sexy rather than smart. She wondered then if Andy had simply been a placeholder until she found her way back to James. If she was finally where she was meant to be.

"Look out your window tonight," he said, his head motioning to her house. His hand opened and closed, and she knew what he meant. He would say good night.

Betsy stepped away from him, walking up the steps to the front door, feeling his eyes on her as she moved. He had never stopped being hers.

There was another conversation waiting inside for her, and this one would be even harder. Betsy waved goodbye as James slid into the driver's seat, revving the engine just once so she'd turn back and smile one more time. Then she went to open the imposing front door, inhaling a breath so deep she imagined filling the baby's lungs inside her.

CHAPTER THIRTY

Virgie

1965

The drive to Washington wasn't as bad as she remembered, all of them somehow more prepared for the monotony of the New Jersey Turnpike. While Louisa and Aggie were excited to return home and see their friends for a few days, Betsy had cried as she hugged James goodbye. Pamela had helped her pack the trunk with suitcases, and when Virgie tried to pay her—for all her work helping that week—the woman refused. "It makes me feel happy to think that I've helped you too," Pamela said, tucking the money back into Virgie's palm.

Virgie slipped the money into James's shorts pocket, just before they drove away.

They weren't leaving for the summer, so it wasn't necessary to pack up the kitchen cabinets or wipe down the cloudy refrigerator shelves, but their return was open-ended. After her showdown with Charlie, she wasn't sure when she'd have the energy to drive back up to Cape Cod to catch the ferry, and she certainly couldn't expect the girls to do that long drive too soon after returning.

Around four that afternoon, they pulled up to their small red rowhouse on P Street in Kalorama. It was swampy hot, and inside, the living room smelled of cologne. Cigar smoke. A few dishes were still in the sink. *Charlie.* Living alone as a bachelor. Would she ever be able to look at her husband again and think him true? How had she been so blind to his relationship with Melody? Then again, she'd been home with toddlers, trying to cook dinner while keeping them away from electric sockets.

The girls were tired from the drive, but Virgie felt energized, knowing that Charlie was in the same city. She settled them into the house, then hurried back into the car. Charlie was five miles away at the Capitol. She needed to see him immediately.

Parking on a leafy street near the Russell Senate Office Building, Virgie walked with a sense of purpose down the sidewalk until she reached the grand rotunda of the beaux art Senate office building, eighteen Corinthian columns surrounding her in the lobby. Men strode by in suits, ignoring her as she hurried to the elevator bank. *A woman belongs here just as much as a man does*, she reminded herself.

When the elevator doors opened, she heard the lonely click-clack of her heels through the quiet hallway; most staff went home to their states or took vacation about now. In his office, his secretary, in her twenties with cat-eye glasses, stood when Virgie entered; even if they hadn't met, the young woman knew who she was.

"Mrs. Whiting. Nice to meet you." The girl's white blouse was starched, tucked astutely into a trim burgundy pencil skirt. "The senator will be so happy you're here." She moved to let Charlie know of his guest, but Virgie ignored her, pushing right through the dark heavy wooden door, blustering into the chamber as though she was walking into a room of standing applause.

Charlie was at his desk, his frame hunched over a stack of bound pages. A bill, no doubt. He lowered his fountain pen and grinned; it hurt to see him smile like that. Truly happy to see her. "What are you doing here?" He seemed astonished.

"The girls and I decided to come home for a bit."

"I'm so glad." He was in front of her now in his navy-blue tailored suit, his hair freshly cut as it always was, and he leaned in to kiss her. She turned her head, leaving him to stare at her cheek, and then she moved past him and sat with purpose in the royal-blue office chair opposite the one at his desk.

"Welcome home," he said, irritation in his voice. *Good*, she thought. *Let him suffer.*

"Yes, well, it's not a happy visit, I'm afraid." Virgie kept her posture prim, legs turned to one side, her hands folded in her lap.

He clasped his hands together in prayer. "But I have such big news."

This much she hadn't anticipated, and her curiosity got the better of her. "Oh?"

"Oh, my love. My dear Virgie. I didn't see this coming, but Rockefeller is polling poorly in New York, and there's a good chance that he won't win the governorship next year. I have some backers that want me to jump into the race. People believe it's the perfect springboard." This was the point when Charlie was used to Virgie cheering him on; when she remained silent, forming her thoughts, he said, "We all know governors have a much better chance at winning the presidency than senators. I'll be in a better position, and I can make an enormous difference in New York."

It would never be enough though. For him, the goalpost was always changing. She and the girls were always following.

Her voice sailed through the room like a dagger.

"Well, you'll never win," she said.

Maybe it was cruel, but she didn't care. It was true. He'd always said he had to work three times as hard as the other men to get elected, but had he? She proceeded with her thinking slowly, making sure that Charlie had time to hear every word that she was saying. "That reporter who knocked on our door. He returned, and he said if I really wanted to know you, I needed to visit 12 Chapel Way. On Nantucket."

A truth, and a lie. At this, Charlie felt his chest pocket for his pack of cigarettes. Pall Malls. He swore the brand tasted of a beach bonfire, and he lit one, leaning back in his chair and taking a long, slow inhale. His face sat expressionless, unreadable even, and she wasn't certain what he was thinking. The clock ticked on his desk, a small square clock, and outside his office, she could hear his secretary on the telephone, "Good afternoon, Senator Whiting's office." Virgie thought she knew Charlie so well, but she'd never seen him so utterly frozen.

"I asked Wiley to kill the story, and he will, at least in the short term, but I think you'll have to pay him some favor for it. As you know, nothing is free in this town. Not even money from fat cats on Nantucket."

Charlie let his cigarette burn in the ashtray, the fiery tip turning to ash bit by bit. "This has nothing to do with my chances at governor."

It stung, how easily he could toss away her feelings, to protect what he wanted. He hadn't always been that way. Politics had done it to him. The need to win. The city hardened the softest of men.

"But a divorce will ruin your chances." Virgie shot again, a dagger hitting him square in the chest. "No man can make it through a divorce and a campaign, not even you." Her eyes fell onto her hands in her lap. It was easy to be brave when you were accusing someone of wrongdoing, but this was terrible of her. She was threatening him. As much as she believed it was in her right, it didn't feel moral.

Charlie came around to the side of the desk where she sat in her dotted blouse and summer skirt. He crouched down so he was on his knees looking up at her, like a puppy heeling for a bigger dog. "You are right. I made a big mistake, Virgie, and I only ask that you listen to my side of things. I tried to do the honorable thing."

"I don't think anything you did was honorable." She moved away from him as gently as she could, standing to pace the royal-blue carpets. "Where did that house on Nantucket come from?"

"It isn't just my name on the deed. It's yours too." There were voices in the hallway, and it made Charlie stand up from the rug, brushing off the pinstripe sleeves of his jacket. He seemed frustrated that she hadn't given in to his apology; was that how easy it had been for him before?

"That doesn't make it okay," she said. Now it was business between them, details that needed clarifying.

He sighed, sitting against the edge of his desk, his pants leg rising and revealing argyle socks. He tracked her walking. "I was lonely back then. You were always with the children, and I was always here working. One night I had too much to drink at the Willard, and I came back here to work on a speech with Melody. The way she used to look at me, it was different from how you did after a day with the children. The kids, they took up all our time, and there really wasn't any time for you and me."

"I really don't think . . . " She crossed her arms, poised to tell him not to blame the children for his misgivings.

"Just listen to me, Virgie. I swear there's a lesson here."

"You and your empty lessons. Why would I believe anything you say?"

His hands gripped the edge of the desk, and she realized then: he was trying to remain steady. "You know that I wanted those girls every bit as much as you did. But you must admit that they changed things between us, and while it's not a reason for a man's eye to wander, I just want you to know that I was lonely. From the moment it happened though, I regretted it, and Melody came to me ten weeks later. She was so happy, telling me I didn't need to have anything to do with the pregnancy, but she would return to Boston and distance herself from you. All I could do was offer her money to get rid of it. I was so scared you'd discover it. That you'd leave me."

"I'm sure she was thrilled to be a single mother, to raise her child without a father."

"Melody promised to remain quiet." He held his face still. "You remember how much she wanted a family, and she knew I couldn't give her that. That I had a family of my own. After she had the child, she sent a photo of her to my office, one of those small squares, and it brought on so much guilt. I decided I would give them the house to live in, and every month I sent a fifty-dollar bill in an envelope." He took a step toward Virgie then, holding his hand out and cupping the smooth of her cheek. "I am so sorry. But it was one night ten years ago. It wasn't love. It's not like what you and I have. We are different. You know that, right?"

She turned into his palm, a momentary comfort in his touch, while knowing nothing he would say would ease the sting of what he'd done. "But Charlie, all you ever said is that you didn't have enough money for the campaign. We've lived so modestly—my uncle's house is the only thing we have that's extra. Where did the money for the Nantucket house come from?"

He turned around and got a piece of paper, writing on it. Virgie froze, wondering what it would say, why he was writing at all. Moments later, he handed her a page of scribbles and she read it: *I don't know who's listening . . . the house was a gift. It was a gift from a man who needed help, and I helped him, and what's done is done. Please forgive me.*

They locked eyes. It wasn't enough of an answer, and perhaps it would take many more discussions to get to the truth, but she did know one thing—Charlie's truths might have started to blur, but hers would not.

"Lucky for you, I do not want a divorce." She lifted her bag off the chair where she'd been sitting. There wasn't much longer that she could stand here and pretend to be this in control. Charlie sat down at his desk, his hands folded atop his papers, and listened carefully.

"Next week, my column will begin appearing regularly again in the *Herald*, and I will no longer edit what I say for your voters. I will be me, and I will tell readers what I think. Not what you think I should think."

He stubbed out the cigarette. "I was wrong in taking that from you."

Neither one of them said anything for a moment, the ticking of the clock, the keys of a typewriter. He tried again. "I was wrong in hurting you in all the ways that I did."

A flame in her heart ignited. She pressed her lips inward, feeling the entirety of her young life in a single breath.

"If you want to have a chance at loving me, you need to remember that you're not the only one whose voice matters. Your girls matter. They matter more than a United State Senator's does because they are ours, and I will spend my life teaching them what real power looks like, what good can come of true power, when a woman has the courage to use her voice."

She whirled out of his office, afraid to hear his response. Virgie listened to the clip-clop of her heels through the wide marble hallways, the flags of Nebraska and Pennsylvania blurring in her sight line, feeling as though she'd won a marathon.

As she left his office, she heard the young woman at the front desk call out to her.

"You're amazing, Mrs. Whiting. I love your Dear Virgie column. Please keep writing it. You inspire so many of us."

The elevator doors opened. She descended to the lobby, her pulse nicking her clavicle, a smile overtaking her face. It was time to swim.

CHAPTER THIRTY-ONE

Betsy

1978

Betsy had completely forgotten. Tonight was their first meeting of the feminist summer book club since they'd been forced to postpone it a day. Her mother had put out pigs in a blanket and cheese puffs on the back patio, a tray of fresh-cut veggies and onion dip. Betsy carried her dog-eared copy of *The Awakening* outside under her arm, her hair wet and smelling of Pert, her silver hoops still in her ears from the morning in Nantucket. To mark the occasion of their first meeting, Aggie had brought throw pillows from the couch to the wrought iron chairs, resting them against each chairback so they could be comfy during the discussion.

Her mother dipped a pretzel in onion dip, waving happily at Betsy as she padded outside and sat beside her. Her mother's blue maxi dress fell to her ankles, the spaghetti straps showing tan lines on her back. She wondered how her father could have cheated on this beautiful woman, how her intelligence, their long history together, hadn't kept him faithful.

Her mother scooped more dip, finished chewing. "I would like to welcome you . . ."

"Mom?" The book club had been Betsy's idea, and she wanted to start the meeting. She knotted her wet hair up with a plastic clip. "Can I begin?"

Her mother waved her on. "Of course. Go ahead, Betsy."

Betsy pressed her palms on the iron table. "I would like to welcome you to the first meeting of the Feminist Summer Book Club." She smiled, holding up the small paperback copy of *The Awakening*. "But first, before we get into the book, I have a very big announcement." She paused once more. "Mom, we don't have to sell the house."

Betsy waited for her mother's applause, the sound of a laugh track with everyone hooting. When it didn't come, she continued.

"We know about the house on Nantucket, Mom." Betsy pulled her father's letter out of her denim shorts pocket and handed it to her mother, giving her a moment to read it. Virgie shifted in her seat, then crossed her legs.

Her mother put down the letter. "Yesterday, while you were in Nantucket, my editor at Doubleday said he would give me an enormous sum for the book that I'm writing."

Betsy felt her temples begin to pulse. "When I asked you, you said you were journaling, that it wouldn't turn into anything."

Her mother handed her back the letter. "Because I wasn't sure what I was writing, but then it started to become something special on the page. I sent eighty pages to my editor, and he wants it. He wants it fast before everyone's memory of Daddy fades." Her mother swept her gaze at Louisa, then Aggie, then Betsy, where she lingered. "I won't have the entire sum up front, but I talked to the bank, and they will give me a six-month extension on the house if I pay them a quarter of what we owe. I was going to tell you tonight."

Louisa gave her mother a sideways glance. "But isn't that your entire advance? You'll need money to buy groceries, pay your electric bills."

"It will get us through," her mother said. *How?* Betsy wanted to ask. *You'll be short anyway.* But this was her mother: She always believed everything would work out all right in the end. Maybe Betsy needed to absorb some of that blind optimism.

"So what is the book about?" Aggie asked. She'd been on the phone with her husband an hour before, whisper-yelling into the phone in the kitchen: *I shouldn't have to ask permission, Henry.*

No one had touched the hors d'oeuvres. Their mother shooed a fly buzzing around the dip.

"It's a memoir, but I will write nothing about the Nantucket business and nothing that will embarrass you, if that's what you're worried about. This is my story to tell, girls, and I have an important one about my years with your father in Washington and on this island. Even as I've been writing it, I've realized how much of your father and me didn't make sense. Yet we were just right. I need to do this to make things right between us."

Louisa stood, tossing her napkin over the cheese plate. "Can we cover this stuff? The bugs are landing." She paced the patio.

"Sit down, Louisa. You're all out of sorts." Her mother fiddled with the top button on her dress bodice, one of three pearl inlay circles that glistened in the fading sunlight.

Louisa did as she was told, squeezing her arm with her opposing hand. "Dad had a child with that woman. I saw the house on Nantucket. I'm pretty sure he loved her."

Betsy watched her mother closely, how her features sharpened, then loosened, like she wanted to yell but found a calmer voice. Her mother would treat this as one more unfairness she'd need to explain to the girls about the world. "That discovery years ago, that conversation with Melody. It was a pain I never thought I'd come back from. But girls, I had the three of you, and mothers can't just stop doing their job because we have a bad day or even a bad year." She used her finger to draw a snaking line along the tabletop, staring down at it as she spoke. "Charlie and me, our marriage was a long road that was riddled with potholes. I didn't have a job, other than raising you all and supporting your father's career ambitions. There weren't as many options for me then as there are now, and also, I did still love your father in my own funny way. Enough that I decided to stick with him, so I didn't split the family up." She sighed. "Couples stay together either because they're afraid to be alone, or because they love one another, no matter the mistakes or how gray the hair or wrinkled the skin. I knew I had to make a choice about your father when I discovered Melody, and while I didn't condone it, I did use it to my advantage."

"That doesn't even make sense." Betsy frowned.

"Let her talk," Aggie said.

Her mother's eyes were so blue they were like robins' eggs. She held up the novel *The Awakening*. The cover depicted a woman in her nightgown, white and ethereal, ghostly, and floating. "It may not seem like the right moment to talk about the book, but I'd like to."

Betsy looked off to the water; her mother had once again hijacked the conversation. Still, she tuned in to what her mother was saying.

"I relate to the main character, Edna, so much. She marries Mr. Pontellier without understanding how much of herself she'll have to give up. I did the same, but once I discovered your father's secret life on Nantucket, his other secrets too, I had no reason to hold back in my work, even if my early essays made him uncomfortable. But this news about Melody changed everything. I had no reason to placate him anymore, and I did as I wanted. I decided to be strong for all three of you instead."

"That summer when I was fifteen, the summer we went flying with Wiley," Louisa started. "Was that when you found out about Melody?"

Betsy remembered how her mother had stayed in bed for two days when they returned from Nantucket, how Betsy had begged her to play Parcheesi or Scrabble, go get an ice cream. But her mother hadn't budged from under her cool sheets.

Virgie seemed surprised that Louisa guessed correctly. "After I stood in Melody's kitchen, after all I'd done for your father, I swore I would mother you girls by being everything I'd been afraid to be. I would write uncensored and without apology. So I wrote about families and marriage and the economy and the workplace, all from a woman's point of view. Dad hated it. Boy, did he hate it, but what could he do? He was devastated that I knew about Melody, and I had it over him for the rest of our lives."

Betsy felt the melancholy of grief settle into her bones. "So you bribed him?"

"Bribe is a nasty word," her mother said kindly, twiddling with her long hair. "I used the information to urge him onto my side."

As Betsy memorized her mother's delicate silhouette, she could see that she'd gotten her mother wrong all these years. As a teenager, Betsy had thought her mother self-absorbed; her father had suggested as much through various complaints about the inconvenience of his wife's career. Her writings were too revealing, too personal, too provocative.

But Betsy wasn't sure that was true anymore. It was her mother's articles—both essays and reportage—that had given her the armor to survive her husband's disappointments, his preoccupation with serving in the Senate, and of course, his nasty mistake. Writing wasn't just a distraction for her mother. It had been her power, and Virgie had changed the way women thought about their place in the home and at work by talking about all the issues no one wanted to talk about. It was Virgie's own mistakes that had informed much of her parenting too. Writing about inequality had helped her level the playing field in her own household.

Betsy flipped through *The Awakening*, scanning some of the lines she'd underlined lightly in pencil. She looked up, her mother staring at her from across the table, curious. "Edna's 'awakening' came from expressing her sexuality with that man at the resort, but your awakening, Mom, was finding your voice. So many women watched you gain self-ownership as you wrote yourself into their hearts and minds. Your words gave them courage to take charge of their own lives as they watched you take charge of yours."

"Yes, honey, I think that's right."

From upstairs, the baby cried, but Aggie remained in her seat, transfixed. "Not only that, you gave us a model for building our own sense of self. That's why I became a marathoner. I called Henry this week and told him I'm putting my name in for the New York City race in October."

Louisa raised an eyebrow. "What did he say?"

"He said, 'Good for you, honey. Who will watch the baby when you train?'" Aggie buried her face in her hands, like he didn't get it. "I told him I'd hire a babysitter, and he said he supposed that was okay."

Betsy took in the image of her sisters, her mother, and herself, the four of them like shiny pearls packed together on a newly strung necklace. Maybe this was when they returned to each other for good. For the first time in Betsy's entire adult life, she thought: *I want to read every book with my sisters and mother, and I want to hear everything they have to say about what it means to come into yourself, to live on your own terms, to raise your hand and say I am here, and I matter.*

Her mother wanted the best for her. This reminded Betsy of all the subjects this conversation had taken them away from. It felt like there were cotton balls lodged in her throat when she said, "Can we stop talking about the book for a second?" Her stomach grumbled; she reached under the napkin for a cracker. "We own this house in Nantucket, and if we sell it, we can pay off the other half of the loan Dad took out and secure the Vineyard house for good."

"You can't kick that woman out. Charge her rent." Her mother drank down the last third of her wine. "It's her home. I didn't like what your father did, but I do empathize with his decision to help her."

Betsy stuffed another Triscuit in her mouth. "We had a feeling you'd say that."

Louisa opened a small notebook she'd carried to the table earlier, the notepad containing a diagram they drew of the land on the ferry that morning. "That's why we have an alternate plan. Betsy and I went to Nantucket's town records office, and we looked at the boundary survey. The house, while modest, sits on three acres of land." They could subdivide the lot into three, one-acre parcels, and sell two of them for a sum large enough to pay off half of the loans their father had taken out on the summer house. Then Melody could stay on her third of the property in the house and pay them a market rent. It was a fair plan; one they felt their mother couldn't argue with.

Virgie threaded her fingers on the table, her nostrils flaring, the latter a telltale sign that she was uncomfortable. "Fine," she said. "But I want no part of it. I will not speak to her."

"It's okay. We'll do all the talking." A surge of joy rushed into Betsy, and she and her sisters took turns wrapping their arms around each other, the reality that the house would remain in their family sending a carousel of happy emotions through them. With or without their mother's memoir, the house was theirs for good.

Their mother rose and joined in the revelry, picking up her granddaughter and hoisting her on her hip. "But I'm still writing my book, girls. I will let you read it before it goes to print, but I need you girls to understand that my story is not your story. You could write a different version of the same exact events, and they would still be true."

CHAPTER THIRTY-TWO

With her mother typing steadily in her study the following morning, Betsy trudged up the crooked stairs and knocked on the door. Louisa and Aggie had taken the kids to the playground so Betsy could talk to her mother on her own.

"Good luck," Aggie whispered before they left, kissing Betsy on the cheek. "Emphasize all the good. Mom likes to know that there's a way out."

At Betsy's knock, her mother called out, "Come in."

Let's hope this isn't the biggest regret of my life, she told herself.

Betsy's appointment with the midwife was tomorrow. Was it naïve to think that her mother might come with her? Just because she'd decided to have the baby didn't mean she wasn't scared.

Her mother sat behind a typewriter at her desk, her glasses falling down her nose.

"Hi, Mom. Can we go for a walk?"

Her mother typed a few more words, then said. "Five minutes?"

Betsy waited on the porch, her hands clammy and warm. She decided in the midnight hours, while nibbling on saltines in the dark, that she would tell her mother the entire story from beginning to end. How she hadn't been looking for a boyfriend at all. How she was trying to do well in school, but life had thrown her a curveball.

The front door clicked open, and Virgie emerged in her huarache sandals, flowing skirt, and straw hat. Betsy nearly blurted out her news, but just as quickly lost her nerve. Instead, she smiled, the corners of her mouth trembling. Walking down South Water Street, mother and daughter remained quiet, her mother sensing that this wasn't her conversation to begin. They strolled to Lighthouse Beach, kicking off their sandals and moving toward the water, sitting side by side on the sand.

Her mother watched two children digging sandcastles down the beach. Betsy needed to begin. Her body grew hot and her mind sputtered in stress. "I'm going to go back to Columbia this fall. I want to finish. I decided that I truly want to be a psychologist."

There was pride in her mother's look. "I'm happy to hear that. And I'm sorry for what I said about you trying to go back in time. I'm so proud of you, Betts. My precious little Betsy."

Betsy flinched, the words bringing a wave of sour memories. "Do you remember when you would tell Dad about something you didn't like that I was doing, and you'd say to him, 'your precious Betsy.' It always felt so awful, like a part of you hated me."

This took her mother by surprise, and she jostled Betsy in a playful manner. "Hated you? I've never hated you."

Her mother leaned her head back, letting the sun blanket her face as she closed her eyes. When she opened them, she leaned closer to Betsy, her voice steady. "But I have been thinking of our family a lot lately, writing this memoir, and there is something I want to say. I'm sorry if I splintered this family with my work. That I made you girls feel like you needed to take a side: me versus Dad. All these years I thought I was only doing good for you girls, but there was an unintended outcome. I alienated you. Your father and I were just . . ."

It was easy for Betsy to fill in the blank. "Complicated."

Her mother smiled. "To say the least. But I shouldn't have let that come between me and you. You know that I couldn't imagine my life without you, even when you drive me so batty I could scream. I could never let you go."

"Mom?" Betsy knew she sounded scared.

Her mother was still smiling. "Yes?"

"I'm having a baby." Betsy made fists in the sand, letting the words lodge into her mother's brain. "I know it's not what you expected from me, and it's certainly not what I expected of me. But here's what I know: I don't want to fly airplanes or go to the moon. I don't want to argue before the Supreme Court like Louisa or run marathons like Aggie. I want to help people with their problems, and I want to be a mom and I want to come back to this small little island and teach my boy how to hunt for minnows and sail a boat and dig for clams in Sengekontacket Pond. Maybe having a small life isn't good enough for you, and maybe it will be a big mistake for me, but it's all I want right now."

There were shells by Betsy's toes, small slipper shells with smooth backs and pretty fronts, and she stared at them because she was terrified to look up. Her eyes were damp, and she was upset at how badly she needed her mother to say something. Anything.

When Betsy felt her mother's slender arm slide around her back, she lifted her gaze. Her mother angled toward her, pushing Betsy's bangs to one side of her face.

"I want to tell you a story, Betsy. Is that okay?" Her mother waited for her to nod, then she closed her eyes. "Once upon a time there was a young woman who met a handsome young man in midtown Manhattan. They fell deeply in love, spending every moment together, even as they nursed their own dreams. When the young woman found out she was pregnant, she worried about telling the young man. The young man had taken her hand and kissed her; this was a child that he wanted and that she wanted, and so they quickly married to hide the error. It was a marriage steeped in love and understanding, and when a second child came soon after the first, this one also a girl, the husband and wife cheered. They wanted this family, and it was the third baby they had wanted most, even though it had been hardest to get pregnant. So, when the young woman finally did, she discovered the child was a girl and she said a silent prayer. Because she'd always wanted three girls."

Betsy looked up at her mother, confusion knitting her brows. "You and Dad got pregnant with Louisa before you were married?"

"It was terribly scary at first, but it happened, yes. But you were the most wanted children in the world, and because of that, I know what it means to want a child, even in a predicament like yours. Because if your father hadn't wanted Louisa, I would have found a way to have you and Aggie and Louisa anyway, no matter what that looked like."

It was difficult to understand. Betsy was always being pushed to be something extraordinary, and the message she received from her mother, through innuendo and example, was that being a mother was secondary. It was a career that came first. You didn't start with a baby. Without a husband. But maybe what her mother was saying is that it didn't matter what order you did things, if you did them with intention.

"So you're not mad at me?" Betsy needed to know how her mother felt. One hundred percent honesty.

Her mother tilted her chin down, kissing the side of Betsy's temple. "Oh, baby girl. If I've learned anything in this life, it's that women need choices. If this is your choice, then I will respect it. I'm glad you're going back to school. You're going to need to make a living. This isn't going to be easy."

"Yes." Betsy's mind wandered to her term paper. She would finish as much as she could by the end of the summer. The baby would come sometime next winter. That would leave her pregnant during the first semester, with an infant during the second. "I know it doesn't make sense, but I have so much faith inside me about this baby, like I can shape this child into something special."

"Someone told me as much when I was younger, that we all need faith that things could be better to feel strong."

"All this time, I thought you would think I'm a failure if I didn't do what you and Dad wanted," Betsy said, wiping at the goop under her nose.

Virgie twirled at a piece of Betsy's long brown hair. "Maybe you misunderstood me." Her mother pressed her body into her, their sides touching with the same ease and comfort that they had when Betsy was young. "Feminism isn't *only* about swimming upriver to do a man's job. It's not *only* about electing a woman president or Supreme Court justice or CEO of a major corporation. Feminism is about having the freedom to chart your own path, whatever that may be. It means that if you want to have this baby, then you can have it. No one will fault you."

Betsy wished she could turn back the clock on summer, that she and her mother could have had these conversations from the start. The last few weeks seemed like wasted opportunities.

Her mother smiled, her voice turning somber. "Your decision, it's going to make your life harder. You are choosing the most challenging path."

Betsy felt like a soldier getting ready for battle. "I know." But maybe she didn't. Maybe this baby would ruin her.

Then her mother's face lit up. "But a child is the single most worthwhile thing you'll do, and I can say that because I've done it three times, and each one of you has brought me closer to who I was meant to be. It's hard to explain with your children, but even when you long for the days before you had them, you'd never be able to return to that state of mind. Because you and your sisters are within me now."

It was then that her mother removed her arm from Betsy's shoulder and slipped it on her daughter's belly.

"I may want to come live in the Vineyard house someday, set up a therapy practice here in Edgartown. I want to help all kinds of women, just in a different way than you did."

"Oh, Betsy. I love that idea. You are welcome here. For good."

Betsy was smiling broadly even as she wiped her eyes with the back of her wrist, a release of at least ten years' worth of disappointment she'd stored inside her body. "I will need your help with this baby though. Will you help me?"

"We will all help you."

Her mother pressed her cheek to Betsy's, the fleshy part of their skin sticking from the crying. Betsy wanted to say: How? Will you come live in New York so I can finish school? Will you help me pay for a babysitter while I'm finishing? These details mattered. Betsy might be able to do it on her own, but being home this summer had shown her she didn't want to.

"I will work and go to school, but will you babysit sometimes?"

Her mother's reaction was knee-jerk, like she'd been waiting to be called into action her entire life. She said she'd pack her typewriter and revise her book between Betsy's classes. "I can stay in New York for a few months and help you get on your feet, of course. But you need to be sure that you want this. I can't undo it after it's done."

Betsy swallowed. "It is what I want."

Her mother gave her an impish grin. "And if I come to New York to help, will you please forgive me for missing your graduation?"

"I would say we'd be even." Betsy released one last great big exhale.

She would write that paper and she would return to Columbia. She would have this baby, and she would graduate. Then she would return to Martha's Vineyard in time for summer, and she'd stay as the leaves fell and the snow blanketed the harbor. She'd rent a small office space in Edgartown, hang a sign on the door that read: BETSY WHITING, WOMEN'S THERAPIST.

I can do this, she told herself. Betsy drew a line around the lighthouse in the sky, a glow warming her at the thought of watching the lighthouse's bright fiery light in all seasons.

She smiled. No one could say otherwise then. Just like her oldest friend, Betsy would be an islander.

THE END

ACKNOWLEDGMENTS

The idea for this book came to me while I was on vacation in Martha's Vineyard. I was walking around historic Edgartown and ogling all the old houses when I began to think about my husband and I first discovering the island twenty years before. I was a fledgling reporter in Washington, DC, working for *Washingtonian* magazine, my husband having just finished his advanced degree, and we were trying to figure out where to go away that August. Many of our Washington colleagues would talk about this magical place called Martha's Vineyard so we decided to give the island a try. (I'd grown up visiting nearby Block Island, so a New England summer island was very appealing to me.)

On that first visit we stayed in a small bed and breakfast in lively Oak Bluffs with our new puppy, Sadie, who we kept busy with long walks in between biking and languorous stretches reading on the beach. The island immediately felt like home, and we vowed to come back as many summers as we could. It wasn't just the unspoiled beaches, historic villages, and cobblestone streets; we loved the island for its interesting mix of locals, politicos, creatives, and do-gooders. In the coming years, we'd run into Children's Defense Fund legend Marian

Wright Edelman on the beach. We'd wave to Larry David passing the Chilmark General Store in his wood-paneled Wagoneer. I'd come face-to-face with Malia Obama. We'd see Seth Meyers pass us on the street. The island was glamorous, but it always managed to be low-key.

Our Last Vineyard Summer came to me two years ago while renting a house on Summer Street in Edgartown. I'd started to think about the now-famous Washington, DC/Martha's Vineyard connection, and I began to imagine that the owners of our rental house were an old political family from DC. I thought about three young daughters and an iconic feminist mother, someone akin to Gloria Steinem. After staring at the oversized antique map in the rental house's living room, I read aloud the cartographer's name: Charles Whiting.

With that name, the story clicked into place. I could envision the Whiting sisters and their legendary parents, Senator Charlie Whiting and his ambitious wife, Virgie.

I tell you this only to say that books are odd little creatures that often begin in a writer's mind when she's free to daydream—and I'm always daydreaming on the Vineyard. If I hadn't met my dear husband John in Math 110 at the University of Maryland in 1995, and if we hadn't visited this island twenty-something years ago together and nearly every summer since, I would have never had the idea for my first novel, *Summer Darlings,* and I wouldn't have dreamt up *Our Last Vineyard Summer*. The Vineyard is a source of endless inspiration for me—and I often do my best plotting and character development just sitting on the beach scribbling down notes. Like my character Virgie Whiting, who thanks her waterfront study in her book, I need to thank the island, my husband, and my two kids. They bring me the best times when we're visiting this beloved summer place.

Many, many thanks to my editor, Hannah Braaten. There's nothing better for an author than receiving a well-thought-out and insightful editorial letter, and I always look forward to Hannah's. I'm so grateful for her tender eye on my novels, and I appreciate her humor, sharp insight, and her ability to raise the stakes, improve the plot and the quality of the writing in both of my books. Sarah Schlick, thank you for keeping me on track and for your careful reads of my drafts; you always come with insight and a kind smile. Jen Bergstrom, I wouldn't be a novelist if you didn't greenlight my stories these last several years, so thank you, thank you! Jessica Roth, you are an integral part of this winning Gallery team that I've been gifted with. I'm so thankful for the time you put into championing my books.

Immense thanks to Kathleen Carter, who may be the hardest-working publicist in the business! Thank you for tirelessly toiling for these last two books—and for shouting about my books to anyone who will listen.

This novel wouldn't have been written if my lovely and smart agent, Rebecca Scherer, didn't read early drafts and urge me on. She's always in my corner, and I have so much gratitude for all that she does for me and my work! Another thanks to the entire JRA team, including Meg Ruley and Andrea Cirillo, and all the other whippersnapper agents who always lend a helpful critique to book titles and covers and everything in between.

Infinite gratitude to all the independent bookstore owners who have invited me into their stores for a signing or a talk, and to all the others who stock my books on their shelves. I get so happy when I walk into an indie bookshop and find my book on the table! Also, there have been so many bookstagrammers who have championed my work—Beyond the Pages Book Club has blown me away!!—and I'm immensely grateful. Authors need you, so please keep up the good work! And to all my readers: You are why I write. Your letters, kind reviews, and impassioned questions always help me see things in my writing that I didn't before.

So much thanks to my Sarah Lawrence writing group, my Tuesday writing pal, Laura Bower, and my buddies Samantha Woodruff and Jackie Friedland, whose work I admire and who are always quick to hop on a call and talk out ideas. To Lynda Cohen Loigman, thank you for being such a great author friend and fellow Vineyarder, and thank you for to my June 4th author crew—Annabel, Susie, Jane, and Julie; why can't we all put out a book on the same day again this summer? Also, I need to give a special shout-out to Sara Farnsworth and Kelsa Debrabant, who went on book tour with me to keep me company (and well-fed). To Nancy Fann-Im, your insight and critical comments always help me transform rough drafts into finished novels.

Finally, this book is about family. In my own family there are complicated relationships and just as many ups and downs, but in the end, I feel lucky that we all still love each other. I'm grateful for each one of you. Special thanks to my little sister, Chelsea, who always believes in me, even when I'm having trouble believing in myself. And to my husband, Harper, and Emi, we are the happiest little family I know. That's what my Aunt June often says, and it's true. xo

Our Last Vineyard Summer

BROOKE LEA FOSTER

INTRODUCTION

"A radiant, sun-flushed summer novel packed with beaches, sisters, and secrets."

—Nancy Thayer, *New York Times* bestselling author

Martha's Vineyard, 1978: After suffering through her first year of graduate school at Columbia following her senator father's death, Betsy Whiting is hoping to spend the summer with her boyfriend . . .and hopefully end the summer as his fiancée. Instead, her mother—a longtime feminist and leader in the women's movement—calls Betsy and her sisters back home to Martha's Vineyard, announcing that they need to sell their beloved summer house to pay off their father's debts.

When Betsy arrives on the island a week later, she must reckon with her strained familial relationships, a long-ago forbidden romance, and the complicated legacy of her parents, who divided the family even as they did good for the world. Following a dual timeline between 1965 and 1978, and filled with the vibrant, sunlit nostalgia of the cherished New England vacation setting, *Our Last Vineyard Summer* poignantly captures two generations of women navigating love, loss, and womanhood while trying to find the courage to stand up for what they believe in—and the strength to decide if the home they once loved is worth saving.

Perfect for book clubs interested in discussing mothers and daughters, the complex relationships of sisters, long-ago summer romance, the impact of birth order in a family, and the pull of our childhood homes.

TOPICS AND QUESTIONS FOR DISCUSSION

1. Many of us have places in our lives that we return to because they help us connect to our authentic selves. Why do you think Betsy connects so closely to Martha's Vineyard? Share your own special place with fellow book club members and discuss why this place figured so prominently in your life. Do you still return to it?

2. In a disagreement with her mother, Betsy brings up moments when she felt that her mother wasn't there for her. Did Betsy hold her parents to the same standard? Are daughters harder on their mothers than they are on their fathers? How was your relationship with your mother different or similar to the one Betsy has with Virgie?

3. Betsy feels frustrated that her mother sometimes put her career before her family. Is it a fair criticism? How have you struggled

with any of your choices as a mother—or with your mother's choices that impacted you growing up? If you're a parent, how did becoming one change your view of your own mother?

4. If you were to consider the three Whiting sisters—Louisa, Aggie, and Betsy—which one of them do you relate to the most and why?

5. Psychologists have long believed that birth order can play a role in a child's development as they age into adulthood. How did their place in the family impact each sister's identity? Do you think Betsy would have been a different person if she were born first? Think about your own siblings. How might you have been different if you swapped birth years with one of your siblings?

6. Sisters often have complex relationships—they love each other fiercely, but they may compete for their parents' attention or categorize each other as the "smart" one or the "pretty" one. How has the baggage of their parents influenced the three Whiting sisters? How did it impact your own identity in your family?

7. Virgie is always trying to empower her girls with her feminist principles. Do you think she ever manages to balance her desire to be a great mother with her dreams of creating lasting political change for women? How do her viewpoints impact her grown daughters in ways that are both positive and negative?

8. Selling a house can bring forth a complex wave of emotions. In this story, the sisters uncover family secrets as they begin to pack up the beach house. Why do our childhood homes carry so much significance in our lives? Would you have tried to find a way to save the house like the sisters do or do you believe it was time to let go?

9. The author has said that her own family had secrets and that uncovering them was unsettling, but also freeing. Have you discovered any secrets about your family you'd be willing to share? How did it influence how you saw yourself and the people you love?

10. When Betsy runs into her old boyfriend, James, she's brought back to her childhood palling around with him on the island. How did her relationship with James shape her, both good and bad? Would you have listened to your father if he forbade you to see a boy at that age—why or why not?

11. Why do you think Virgie and Charlie's marriage is under strain? Why didn't he turn out to the be the man she thought he was?

12. Charlie Whiting passes away before the book begins, but he looms large in the story. How did each of the Whiting women's relationship with him color their view of their themselves and their family? How does that perspective change and evolve as the book progresses?

13. Forgiveness is an important theme in this novel. Have you ever been briefly estranged from one of your siblings or family members? Discuss what happened and the conversation that ultimately led to healing.

14. What do you envision happens next for Betsy and her longtime best friend, James? What about Virgie and Wiley? Do either pair have a chance at serious long-term love?

www.ingramcontent.com/pod-product-compliance
Lightning Source LLC
Chambersburg PA
CBHW010519200726
48244CB00001B/1